The
Barsoom Expedition

Charles P. Howerton

The contents of this work, including, but not limited to, the accuracy of events, people, and places depicted; opinions expressed; permission to use previously published materials included; and any advice given or actions advocated are solely the responsibility of the author, who assumes all liability for said work and indemnifies the publisher against any claims stemming from publication of the work.

All Rights Reserved
Copyright © 2023 by Charles P. Howerton

No part of this book may be reproduced or transmitted, downloaded, distributed, reverse engineered, or stored in or introduced into any information storage and retrieval system, in any form or by any means, including photocopying and recording, whether electronic or mechanical, now known or hereinafter invented without permission in writing from the publisher.

Dorrance Publishing Co
585 Alpha Drive
Suite 103
Pittsburgh, PA 15238
Visit our website at www.dorrancebookstore.com

ISBN: 979-8-88925-061-6
eISBN: 979-8-88925-561-1

PROLOGUE

The clock above the door read exactly 12:00 when the Chairman entered the conference room through the door from his private office and took his place at the head of the table. Looking down the table he saw only ten of the other eleven members present.

"Where is Number 5?" he asked.

"She said she would be a few minutes late, sir, due to poor weather at her home airfield," his assistant replied, paused for a moment listening to his headset and then continued. "Just a moment, sir, security reports she just arrived and is in the building."

Just as he was about to suggest the rest partake of the refreshments whilst they waited, Number 5 entered the room through the far door, nodded towards the Chairman, said, "Sorry, sir" and took her seat.

The Chairman nodded his recognition to her, picked up his gavel, and tapped on the sound block. "The meeting will come to order," he announced and eleven faces turned towards him in rapt attention.

"I am pleased to announce that Captain Slovanovitch notified me this morning that the launch of the command and crew module was successful and they were in geosynchronous orbit with the other three modules and the shuttle. As planned, over the next twelve hours the shuttle, acting as a tug, will assist in uniting the two auxiliary fuel modules and the cargo and supply module with the command and crew module, after which the shuttle pilot will dock the shuttle, and our Mars ship will be complete. So far all systems have checked out perfectly, the crew is ready to proceed, and after all the modules have been joined, we will be ready for departure for Mars just before sunrise tomorrow morning."

The entire operation will be telecast and displayed on the screen behind me. From this point on and until the ship is complete and ready for departure, the meeting will be informal. Those of you who wish to watch are welcome to stay and partake of the refreshments, the rest may retire to your rooms. Lunch and dinner will be served here in the conference room at appropriate times, and you will be notified fifteen minutes prior to the meal service. You should all return to the conference room for the departure. Following departure, we will begin to discuss phase two of our endeavor." He then picked up a microphone and said, "You may proceed Captain Slovanovitch."

"Thank you, sir. Proceeding as directed," Captain Slovanovitch replied.

Several of the members left the table to partake of the refreshments. None of the members left the room. They all watched the evolution as the elements were joined to complete the ship and make it ready for departure from Earth orbit.

At 0642, Captain Slovanovitch announced, "Ready for departure, sir."

"Proceed, Captain, and good fortune to you and your crew," the Chairman said as the rest of the committee applauded.

As soon as the ship was no longer visible on the screen, the Chairman once again called the meeting to order. "Now, ladies and gentlemen, may we have the reports of the committees? He nodded to Number 2 to start the proceedings.

"Ladies and gentlemen Number 8 and I have compiled a comprehensive list of all rocket and spaceship crews past and present and have begun the process of discouraging potential crew from accepting a position with the International Consortium for the Exploration of Space, ICExS program. We began with the most experienced commanders, pilots, and crew members, and have made very good progress so far."

"What has it cost us, Number 2?" Number 5 asked.

"Surprisingly little, relatively speaking," Number 2 replied. "About a year's pay for the most experienced and somewhat less for those of lesser experience. In some cases, the implied threat of harm to families was sufficient, and for others, the threat of revealing things they would not like made public worked. All but a few have been allowed to remain in their current positions. The few have found employment on a less risky profession. We are continuing on with the list we compiled and expect to finish long before ICExS begins its planned training program. Number 8 do you have anything to add?"

"Just that it's an unpleasant job destroying people's lives and careers," Number 8 replied. "I think I would rather be on a different committee."

"I think that can be arranged, Number 8," the Chairman said in a monotone as he beckoned for his assistant to join him. A short conversation with the assistant ensued after which the assistant went to Number 8, spoke briefly to her and they left the conference room together.

"Would any of you like to invite Number 8 to join your committee, or would any of you like to exchange committees with Number 8?" he asked the assembly. He waited a few moments for a reply and received none as most of the other committee members avoided making eye contact with him. "I thought not," he continued. "I think we now have a vacancy for a new member on that committee. If any of you have anyone to nominate, we can discuss that later." Again, the remaining members avoided eye contact as they made it look as if they were studying their reports. "Number 2, can you proceed with the subornation without someone to replace Number 8?"

"Yes, sir. I believe I can continue without assistance since at this time only low-level individuals are being contacted. "However, if our ICExS contact reveals higher level candidates, I may need to call for assistance," Number 2 replied.

"Good, Number 2. Do you have anything more to add to your report?"

"No, sir."

"Now, Number 3, how are you and Number 9 proceeding with discouraging the scientists and academics from seeking a spot on the science team?" The Chairman asked.

"Well, sir, the number of scientists and academics is almost astronomical so we have sought assistance elsewhere. We have contacted a certain functionary in the Vatican. That was Number 9's idea, so I am going to have him explain what he did and how it is going to work." Then she nodded to Number 9.

Number 9 who had obviously prepared for this event stood and began his report. "Sir, and ladies and gentlemen, my family has had a long and active relationship with the Vatican Office of **Keepers of the Faith**. A cousin of mine is the director of that department. We contacted him and sought his suggestions of how we could effectively block some scientists and academics from participating in the ICExS planned expedition to Mars. He came up with a plan that all but guarantees reluctant participation by the scientists. With your approval, he is going to sponsor a multiethnic conference in which he will convince the participants to use their influence in the academic world to discourage scientists and academics."

"How is he planning to do that without outside interference, Number 9?"

"All of the participants in the conference will be senior prelates in their individual faiths. He is going to explain to them why the exploration of outer space and especially Mars is in conflict with the almost universal religious doctrine that the Earth was created solely for human beings to live and prosper and that anywhere else in the universe and especially Mars was in conflict with that doctrine. They will be given the lists of the institutions they are to affect. Then he will plant the idea that they should go back to their enclaves and through their direct or indirect influence with academic institutions and religious or publicly funded organizations suggest that funding for research projects in the area of exploration of space beyond what has happened so far would not only be sacrilegious but in the interest of preserving the doctrines of faith would result in the elimination of funding and the cancellation of positions." When he finished his rather lengthy report, the room erupted in applause.

"So, you are saying that for only the investment in this conference we might eliminate most of the competition for positions on the team of scientists and academics? Is that correct?" the Chairman asked.

"Yes, sir, that is exactly what my cousin has proposed. However, in some instances, it will be necessary to provide financial inducements as well."

"What are the expected costs for this conference or religious retreat?"

"Not as much as you might expect. He is planning on utilizing a remote monastery as the facility. The monastery has the facility to house and feed all the planned participants for a relatively minor investment in the infrastructure for the facility itself. We should plan on making the investment in advance of the conference so the friars or monks are assured that we are serious. The only other thing is perhaps funding or supplementing the travel expenses of the participants and making available the appropriate financial inducements."

"That seems like a rather large investment to me," the Chairman said.

"That is how it looks on the surface, but considering there will be upwards of five hundred or more participants from over 150 denominations and faiths and that we will not have to contact each individual with various other threats, the price is cheap."

"If it works," the Chairman observed.

"Oh, I believe it will work, sir. My cousin is quite persuasive and he has a team of other priests and religious functionaries who will be suborned, to use your expression, and find it difficult and disastrous to their careers in the Vatican if they do not go along with the plan."

"What is in it for your cousin, Number 9?" Number 7 asked.

"He wants to look forward to a very comfortable retirement in a villa in a few years," Number 9 replied.

"I'm sure we can arrange that," the Chairman said. "Promise that to him with an annual stipend at least ten times his present salary and a very comfortable villa as well."

"Thank you, sir, I will do that."

"When are you expecting the conference or retreat should occur?"

"In about four months, that will still be two months before the ICExS ship will depart."

"What? Wait a minute, Number 9," Number 3 said. "If it takes us more than eight months to get to Mars, how does that fit into the timetable? Shouldn't we plan to have the conference almost immediately?"

"Are you up-to-date on the ICExS program?" asked Number 9.

"No, I'm sorry, I'm an investor in our program, not a scientist and do not really understand how these things work," Number 3 said.

"Our ship is chemically powered and will be coasting almost all the way to Mars. The ICExS ship is atomic powered and will go under power all the way at incredible speeds so they can do it in about 6 weeks, I think. One of our projects is to find ways to delay the departure of the ICExS ship so Captain Slovanovitch's ship will arrive earlier than the ICExS ship and this gives us control over Mars." The Chairman said. "Haven't you read the project report Number 3?"

"Yes, I read it, but I must confess that most of it was opaque to me," Number 3 replied. "So why don't we have an atomic powered ship too?"

"Because they have to be built in orbit. Atomic power's saving grace is that it can start slowly and over a relatively short period of time gradually build up to an enormous speed."

"So why didn't we build our ship in orbit too?"

"Because if we had done that, the whole world would know what we were doing and we did not want that to happen for a variety of reasons. Suffice it to say that things are the way they are for good reasons and we have to stick to our plan, Number 3," Number 1 said with a smile on his face. "You stick to the financial side of things and let our scientists and engineers stick to theirs. Right?"

"Yes, sir, that is right," Number 3 replied.

"Now, Number 4, what is happening in the sabotage phase of our program?" The Chairman asked.

"Almost from the beginning, we have had people in place who are doing the job ICExS hired them to do. They report in regularly describing what they have done and what they think needs to be done. It's important to note that they have taken it upon themselves to cause minor disruptions beyond what we have asked them of them. Over the past several months, we have managed to send a number of additional agents provocateurs up along with groups of newer mechanics and construction workers. We have sent many parts to devices that can be used to destroy things both big and small. It has been difficult to send explosives, but our agents have been trained in how to create explosives from common materials. Number 12, would you please explain what you and your agents have been doing?"

"Of course, Number 4," she replied. "My area is to create agents from the existing complement of workers through inducements of one sort or another. To do this, we have some of our agents trained for this purpose, thus they can go out to the Moon with nothing more than what is in their heads. We have authorized them to do whatever is necessary to cause disruptions of one sort or another. To facilitate this, we have set up a radio station not too far from the facility that we use to provide assistance where necessary. The assistance can be financial to their friends and relatives here on Earth and answers to questions they have on what are the most critical areas to disrupt and how to disrupt them without revealing what or how.

"They identify areas where they think they can do some harm but not be detected. For example, they may cause machinery to lock up because the oil was not properly applied to the bearings and things like that. Things that just might happen anyway but can be hastened through subtle activities by our team. Most of our team members do not know one another so they cannot give anything away or provide names of others to the authorities in case they are discovered."

"Excellent, Number 12, keep up the good work," Number 1 said. "Now, what about the distribution of resources when we get to Mars ourselves, Number 6?"

"That, sir, is becoming more difficult every day. The various rovers and technical devices that have been landed on Mars prior to this have uncovered or more appropriately discovered a large number of physical resources that are spread all over the planet. There are underground lakes that contain water, which is possibly saline but which could be mined much like oil wells are used by pumping heat down a shaft and melting the water that is then pumped up to the surface and desalinated if necessary. Water ice has also been discovered at both poles, which can be melted and used. Of course, this will require the infrastructure necessary to pump the water to where it is needed.

"We are still working on how to divide up the land areas into sections that will be fair and equitable. At the moment we are thinking that both poles should be held in common down to the 80th parallel. This represents a fairly large area but one that is of virtually no use to any one person versus another. This might also provide a reservoir for the water that is pumped out of the underground aquifers. So it can be shared fairly.

"This leaves the rest of the land mass, which can be divided up into four major parts. The area 10 degrees above and below the equator should probably be held in common and act more or less as the capital. The areas between the 80th parallel and the 10th parallel to be divided into 60-degree partial gores that are more or less equal in area, six above and six below the equator. We're thinking that the best way to do this is to have the six partial gores below the equator offset 30 degrees from those above the equator, thus providing overlap as needed.

"There are many other possible ways to divide up the property, but this seems to us to be the simplest and fairest. Selection of the individual properties can be drawn by lottery. We know that some of you are planning to use your property in one way and some in a somewhat different way. For example, farming versus mining where some areas are more amenable to one use versus another.

"How does this proposed plan seem to you, and if it needs revision, how should that be done?" Number 6 asked the assembly.

"Very well done, Number 6 and 7. Rather than have a discussion of your proposal at this time, may I suggest that we conduct the discussion electronically and have each alternative stated in detail and posted where all can see and vote for or against each one independently; then after an adequate amount of time has passed where there are no more suggestions, the results be published for decision at the next meeting." The Chairman said. "I might also add that your recommendations do not allow for the fact that Number 5 is no longer with us, leaving one area unassigned. Should we seek another member or simply leave it alone or empty and designate the least desirable area parcel as held in common? That can be part of the electronic discussion before our next meeting in a month.

"Is there anything else that we need to consider at this moment?" The Chairman asked as he polled the assembly with his eyes. Then, receiving no indication of further discussion, he announced, "We are adjourned until next month and we will only be meeting then if there is something to be discussed that cannot be done electronically. Concur?" Receiving no opposing indication from any of the members, he nodded and returned to his office.

PART ONE

CHAPTER ONE

Commander Ian McMichael was holding the usual morning get together of his supply unit where the discussion ranged from women to sports to politics to women when his intercom alert tone sounded.

"McMichael here," he said, pressing the key.

"Commander, the admiral has asked that you report to him at your earliest convenience," the admiral's yeoman announced.

"On my way, Yeoman," Ian replied, snapping off the intercom key, then turning to the rapidly decreasing group around his desk. "Sorry, chaps, the old man seems to want me yesterday."

Lt. Commander Claude Easterbrooke, Ian's deputy, raised an inquisitive eyebrow and asked, "What have you done now, Ian?"

"I have no idea, but I had better get moving. I can't remember the last time I got an 'earliest convenience' order. I think it was perhaps when I was a Sub Lieutenant on a submarine over twenty years ago."

Ian reached for his uniform blouse, checked that his tie was straight and his hair combed and hurried down the hallway towards the admiral's office. Before he could reach the yeoman's desk, the yeoman said, "Go right in, Commander."

Ian knocked once and as he waited for the invitation to enter, he read the sign on the door:

Adm. Clancy W. Einright
Commander In Chief
Western Reaches Submarine Fleet
Royal Australian Navy

"Enter," a voice announced from within.

Ian entered the admiral's office and snapped to attention saluting as might be expected from an 'earliest convenience' call from his commanding officer. Then using strict Navy protocol reported, "Commander Ian McMichael reporting to the Admiral as requested, sir."

Admiral Einright returned the salute without rising from his chair and said, "Sorry, Ian, new yeoman, eager and all that. Have a seat."

With that greeting, Ian knew he was not in any difficulty. "What's happening, Admiral?" he asked.

"Do you still have your go-bag packed, Ian?" the admiral asked.

"Yes, sir. Where am I going?"

"According to the packet, Zürich, Switzerland. The rest of the orders are sealed, Your Eyes Only."

"Switzerland, Admiral?" Ian asked.

"That's what the envelope says. It's all very hush-hush. I sent an inquiry back to HQ immediately and received only a 'Most Secret' in reply. Now you know as much as I do, except they must want you badly because, according to the outer envelope, you leave in two hours and they apparently provided a First Class seat all the way to New York. The ticket will be waiting at the airport."

"Since when has Switzerland had a Navy, Admiral?" Ian mused aloud.

"I know they have a Coast Guard of sorts to patrol their borders on Lake Geneva. Maybe they're planning to either build a submarine or defend against one." Ian laughed then continued. "Wait, why New York if I'm going to Zürich?"

"Who knows why anyone does anything these days? As a guess, I suspect there are security issues. Anyway, I suggest you change out of your uniform into mufti. In fact, I suggest you leave your uniform here, no point in advertising your connection with the Navy any more than is absolutely necessary. Oh, and you're traveling as John Michaelson. Everything you need is in the kit."

"Thank you, sir," Ian replied, then added, "I rode in with Claude since it's an indefinite assignment."

"Of course," the admiral interrupted, then pressed his intercom key and said, "Yeoman, would you order a car for Commander McMichael?"

"It's waiting at the rear entrance, Admiral," the yeoman replied.

"Thank you, Yeoman," Admiral Einright said, then raised his eyebrows and smiled at Ian. "As I said before, eager."

The admiral stood and extended his hand. "Good luck, Ian, and send us a postcard from time to time to let us know where you are and what you're doing… that is, if you can."

Ian shook the offered hand and, with a somewhat less-perfect salute, turned and left the admiral's office. Before he was able to thank the yeoman, the intercom interrupted.

"Yeoman, bring your pad and come in, please," the admiral called.

"Good luck, sir, your plane leaves in three hours," the yeoman said as he hurried into the admiral's office.

"Thanks, Yeoman," Ian replied to the yeoman's back, then hurried back to his own office.

It took less than ten minutes for Ian to change into his civilian clothes in the locker room and prepare to depart for the Perth Airport. He took a minute to read the sealed orders. The packet included a well-used passport with many endorsements in the name of John Michaelson and orders that he was to travel under that name. His destination was Zürich where he was to report to an organization known only as ICExS.

Claude was waiting in Ian's office when he returned from the locker room. "What's it all about, Ian?"

"Sorry, Claude, I can't tell you, mostly because I don't know myself," Ian replied. "Here are the keys to the office. I suspect the Ad—"

Ian's reply was cut short by the intercom. He keyed down the reply button. "McMichael here."

"Hello, sir, are you still there?" the yeoman asked.

"Just about to leave, Yeoman. What do you want?"

"Would you please send Commander Easterbrooke to the admiral's office, sir."

Claude reached across the desk and pressed the reply key. "On my way, Yeoman." He held out his hand. "Cheerio, Ian." And left for the admiral's office.

Ian started for the door, then returned to his desk to pick up his favorite traveling novel, *Ramage's Trial*, and hurried towards the rear entrance for his ride to the airport. He was surprised to find the driver had not brought a Navy car but rather an ordinary sedan.

He recognized the driver who was dressed in civilian work clothes and waiting with front and back passenger doors open. He reached for Ian's bag and tossed it unceremoniously into the back seat slamming the door as he did so. "The admiral's yeoman said your trip was hush-hush and suggested I bring my own car, sir. If you will ride up front with me and retrieve your kit yourself when we get to the airport, I'm just a guy taking his pal to the airport, sir."

"Thank you, Seaman," Ian said as he slid into the passenger seat.

"That's First Class now, Commander," the driver said with pride.

"Oh, sorry, Jack. I didn't know you had struck for First Class, my congratulations."

"No worries, sir. It just went through."

Ian and the driver chatted pleasantly on the way to the airport. When they arrived, as suggested, Ian fetched his own kit from the back seat and walked around to the front and shook hands with the driver who resisted the urge to salute. "Many thanks, Jack, I appreciate the ride."

"Have a nice trip," the driver paused, and overcame his training as well and quietly added, "Take care, Ian," before he drove off.

Ian entered the airport concourse and looked around for the ticket agent so he could check in. "Good morning, I'm John Michaelson. I believe you're holding a ticket for me," Ian said to the ticket agent.

"Yes, sir, right here," the ticket agent said. "You're in seat 3D. That will be a window seat on the shady side of the plane."

Ian glanced at his ticket package and saw that his tickets, under the name John Michaelson had been purchased through a travel agent in the United States. His itinerary, Perth to Tel Aviv to Zürich to London to New York with a short stay in London was common enough for a casual traveler from Australia.

The ticket agent continued, "I would offer to check your bag, sir, but you have a rather tight connection at both Tel Aviv and Zürich, so I recommend you give your bag to the cabin attendant when you board the plane. They have a cupboard near the door for situations like yours. To make sure that security doesn't hold you up, attach this baggage marker to your bag and they will pass you right through. Have a nice flight, Mr. Michaelson. Oh, sir, see that nice-looking woman over there with the koala? She is your seatmate."

Ian looked where the agent was pointing and saw an attractive woman who he guessed was in her thirties. She was trim, with a well-proportioned figure, dark red hair, and the soft golden complexion that indicated a true redhead. She was holding a tame koala that was a key feature of the Perth Airport terminal tourist attractions. Admiring her from a distance, he looked forward to talking with her on the plane.

After passing through what was euphemistically known as a security check, Ian wandered towards the departure gate where the clerk directed him to the departure lounge reserved for First Class passengers.

Rachael Purlman was making chitchat with a vendor whose main attraction was a well-trained and friendly koala. The animal was curled up in her arms like a baby, and she was petting it while holding a conversation with the vendor and following the actions of Ian McMichael, as well as scanning the people in the terminal, looking for anyone who evinced more than a casual interest in Ian.

It took several minutes before she tagged a watcher. It was not the same person who had followed her from Zürich to Perth. It was someone she had not seen before but who was obviously watching her and ignoring Ian.

On the flight to Perth, she had deliberately bored her seatmate to tears with a detailed travelogue of Jerusalem. She also made it clear that she was just a tourist looking forward to visiting Perth and her adoptive cousins who had a villa down the coast from Perth.

She had managed to throw her original follower off the trail as she "touristed" her way around Perth and the surrounding countryside and then down the coast to visit her adopted cousins. It was a certainty that another watcher had been put at the airport to record and report her departure. The new watcher was clearly more interested in her and what she was doing than in anyone else. She continued looking for others and decided that, if anyone was looking for McMichael either he or she was very good or they did not know about or recognize him as a person of interest to ICExS. She hoped for the latter and dreaded the possibility of the former. At this point, there was little she could do except play out her part on the way back to Zürich. She had booked exactly the same seat on the return flight to further avoid suspicion.

Sitting in the First Class lounge, Rachael leafed absently through her magazine while casually observing Ian as he read his book. She reviewed what little she knew about him. He was forty-two years old, widowed, no living children, and no siblings or other close relatives. He was a career officer in the Royal Australian Navy Submarine Service. That was all she had been told, the rest came from her observations. Even though he was not wearing a uniform, his high and tight haircut marked him as military. It was a certain giveaway as were his off-duty clothes, especially his three shades of brown houndstooth tweed jacket with leather patches at the elbows.

He was not what she would call a very handsome man, but neither was he plain. He was around 175 centimeters tall with a trim physique that bespoke regular exercise and careful eating. Then she realized, in appearance, aside from his haircut, he looked quite the ordinary tourist. Not someone who would stand out in a crowd, which could be why ICExS was interested in him.

Her orders were to engage him in casual conversation on the flight from Perth to Tel Aviv, the same sort of seatmate boring she had used on the flight from Zürich to Perth. At an appropriate moment, she was to identify her connection with ICExS and tell him to "miss" the connecting flight from Zürich to London, necessitating an overnight stay in Zürich at a specific hotel. The message would be short and easily inserted into the conversation.

Rachael waited for Ian to board so she could board last to see if anyone was trailing him. The watcher she had seen on the concourse did not board the plane, but she took it as a given that the word had been passed to someone, if not in Perth, then to take up surveillance when the plane landed in Tel Aviv. Since she was not continuing on to Zürich, she hoped that whoever was assigned to track her movements in Tel Aviv would follow her and ignore McMichael.

The door to the plane was closed immediately after she boarded, there were no last-minute passengers. She exchanged pleasantries with the cabin attendants and then took her seat next to Ian. Ian was looking out the window when she took her seat and he continued to do so until the First Class cabin attendant asked, "Excuse me, sir, would you like something to drink?"

"Foster's if you have it, please," Ian replied.

"Departing Australia, we always have lots of Foster's aboard, sir," she replied pleasantly. She opened and handed him a can of Foster's beer and a glass.

Rachael requested and received a glass of white wine. This gave Rachael the opening she needed to start a conversation with Ian.

"Do you really like Foster's?" she asked.

Ian seemed to be distracted and took a moment before he replied, "It's the Australian national drink. Have you tried it?"

"Once, but I prefer the European beers. They have more body," Rachael replied, then added, "Hi, I'm Rachael Purlman, sir."

"John Michaelson," Ian responded, offering his hand.

They chatted pleasantly for a few minutes before Rachael asked, "Where are you bound, John? Are you stopping in Tel Aviv?"

"New York eventually after a stop in London," he replied. "I have a connection in Tel Aviv, and you?"

"Oh, just to Tel Aviv. I'm on holiday. I plan to spend a few days with my parents in Jerusalem before I have to go back to work. I've never been to Australia before. It's quite beautiful. After wandering around for a week, I went to visit cousins down the coast south of Perth. I spent a very relaxing week with them," Rachael responded, deliberately overexplaining. "It's too bad you're not stopping in Tel Aviv. You really should. There's a bus from there to Jerusalem."

Then before he could answer, she launched into her travelogue about the wonders of the Holy Land and made it as boring as possible. After twenty minutes, she could see that his eyes were glazing over while he pretended to be attentive.

"You should be a travel guide, Rachael. You make it sound so interesting. I'm on holiday too. Visiting friends and family in London and in New York. Maybe, I can stop in Israel for a few days on my return trip," Ian said, finishing his beer. Then to preclude further discourse he said, "It has been a long day, if you don't mind, I think I'll take a nap before they feed us."

"Oh, certainly, John," she replied, feigning slight displeasure at not being able to finish her travelogue. "Go ahead, enjoy your nap."

"Excuse me, miss, I couldn't help overhearing what you were telling the gentleman about Jerusalem," the woman across the aisle from Rachel said as she patted Rachel on the arm. "Could you tell me something about it too?"

Rachel turned to look at the woman. She wore a very expensive business suit with the Star of David with diamonds on the points pinned above the pocket. "Certainly, ma'am. What would you like to know?"

"Everything, it's my first trip to the Holy Land."

Rachael spent the next half an hour regaling the beauty and historical sites to be seen in Israel.

Ian sighed quietly in relief, reclined his seat and closed his eyes. He was surprised when the cabin attendant woke him up to take his meal order. He glanced at Rachael, and it was apparent that she was totally engrossed reading an electronic book on her tablet computer. Within what seemed to be seconds, the cabin attendant returned with their meals. He decided to try a more casual conversation as they ate.

"What do you do, Rachael, when you're not on holiday. I mean, are you a travel agent?"

"No," she laughed. "I'm a shuttle pilot. And you?"

"Really, do you like it?" he asked, ignoring her question.

"I do. I was an interceptor pilot in the Israeli Air Force after university. But, then along came the automated defense systems with robot planes and such and there wasn't much need for a whole cadre of fighter pilots. So I left the Air Force and became a shuttle pilot. It was that or becoming a physician's assistant in some clinic treating people for colds, boils on their bottoms, and other less-pleasant problems. Once you've experienced the thrill of high-performance flying, everything else is pretty boring."

"Interesting. What did you study at university?"

"I was a premed student. My father, adopted father actually, wanted me to become a physician like him because I seemed to have an aptitude for it. I was in the military training corps while in university. The Air Force offered me a way out, so I took it. I qualified for flight school and spent six years flying interceptors before they were outmoded. The Air Force offered to retrain me, so I went back to school to get a physician's assistant certificate. I had no desire to become a doctor, but felt the PA Certificate might be useful someday. With my premed experience and what I had learned from my father, it was easy for me to complete the program."

"Then, thankfully, along came the expanded space program with a need for shuttle pilots and I signed up. I've been doing that ever since."

"Fascinating," Ian commented. "Me, I've been an officer in the Australian Navy since I left school."

"Where did you go to university, John?"

"I was fortunate to be selected for an exchange program with the United States military. I went to the US Naval Academy at Annapolis to learn the basics and eventually all the latest wonders the US Navy was developing and using."

"Did you have any particular area of interest?" she asked.

"Submarines mainly. Of course, I had to go through the whole program from aircraft carriers to patrol boats, but I decided that submarines were what interested me most, that besides a certain American girl who became my wife when I graduated. After a short stint aboard a nuclear submarine with the US Navy, I returned to Australia. There weren't very many submarines available, but I managed to serve on a few and eventually ended up commanding one for three cruises. Then I had to give up the ship, so to speak so that those junior to me could have a go. Now, I command a desk and a grand bunch of chaps in supply at the RAN Sub base in Perth. When you're a career officer, you go where they tell you and you do what is needed until you're superannuated and retire. I have five years before I'll be put out to pasture, so to speak."

"So, you are married, any children?"

"Widowed, actually. My wife and daughter were killed in an auto accident several years ago on the way taking our daughter to her first year at university." Ian took a hanky from his pocket to blot his eyes when he finished.

"I'm so sorry," Rachael said. "Those are difficult memories to live with."

"I'm mostly over it, but sometimes it overflows," he explained, then followed with "Well, back to Lord Ramage and the Napoleonic wars." Ian showed her the cover of his novel.

Rachael nodded and returned to reading her e-book. She waited almost an hour before she began laughing aloud, apparently at what she had been reading.

"Would you like to read something really funny?" she asked, offering her tablet to Ian.

"Surely," he said, accepting the tablet. "Sometimes, Dudley Pope can be a bit wordy even if you are a fan."

"Begin here," Rachael said, indicating the humorous passage.

When she removed her finger, the screen changed and Ian read:

I am an ICExS agent, Commander McMichael. When you get to Zürich, deplane as close to last as you can. You are to miss your connection in Zürich. Go to the loo or something, but do not go on to London. Act disappointed, even angry. There will be no other flight until tomorrow. Take a taxi to the Hilton House where you are to register under your assumed name, John Michaelson. Tomorrow morning, depart the hotel by the front entrance at 0900 exactly. The driver of a tourist autobus parked there will offer to give you a tour of Zürich. Take the tour. He has been instructed to deliver you to the ICExS building at 1000 following the tour. After that, the need for extreme secrecy will no longer be necessary as you will most certainly be observed as you enter the building.

Ian read the message quickly and then laughed and said, "That is very funny."

Rachael removed her finger from the tablet screen, and the message disappeared to be replaced by the text of her e-book, which Ian quickly scanned and did find to be humorous.

When the plane landed in Tel Aviv, Rachael loitered in the area of the gate waiting to collect her checked carryon baggage and her watcher. She quickly spotted the watcher, a short, older man wearing a baseball cap. She had seen him before when she was in Israel. Her intent was to draw him into following her as she left the airport rather than possibly spotting and following Ian as he moved from the arrival gate to the departure gate for the flight to Zürich. She stalled over her baggage apparently searching for something while watching to observe if anyone suspicious was looking for Ian or boarded his plane from Tel Aviv to Zürich. Once the Zürich flight departed, she left to catch a bus to Jerusalem with her faithful watcher in tow. What she disliked most was he made no effort to conceal his activities; it was almost arrogant.

CHAPTER TWO

Missing the connection from Zürich to London was not as difficult as Ian had anticipated, thanks to a gate change for the departing flight. Ian picked up his kit from the arrival gate attendant and searched for a restroom. He saw a restroom sign that pointed in a direction away from the new departure gate. He wasted ten minutes in the restroom with his kit spread out on the floor at the sink farthest from the door, shaving, combing his hair, adjusting his tie and wasting time. He was alone in the restroom, so there was no one to observe his clumsy performance for which he was grateful. When the final announcement for his flight to London was called Ian "accidentally" dumped his kit on the floor and by the time he was able to repackage it, he was sure he had missed the plane to London.

Ian ran to the departure gate waving his ticket, arriving winded and, finding the plane had left the gate, gave a very convincing act of a disgruntled First Class passenger frustrated at being left behind.

"When is the next flight to London, Miss, er Hammelschlager?" he asked the gate attendant after checking her name tag.

"I'm sorry, Mr. Michaelson our next flight to London is not until tomorrow, and First Class is all booked for that flight," she replied. "May I make a hotel reservation for you, sir?"

"Yes, if you please. Thank you," Ian replied. "A friend told me that the Hilton House was a good place to stay."

"Just a moment, sir, while I see what is available." She worked on her terminal for a few moments, then giving her best customer relations smile said, "All done, sir. That's strange. It seems they were expecting you. There's a free limousine service to the major hotels outside the baggage area. They're expecting you too, sir."

"If there is any change, please ring me up," Ian said, then, giving his best Colonel Blimp imitation, Ian hrrrumphed and walked away, mumbling aloud about the unacceptable service.

As directed, Ian took the airport limousine service to the Hilton House. When he arrived at the Hilton House, he was prepared to go through his act again with the hotel clerk. "Good evening, I am Mr. John Michaelson."

"Good evening, Mr. Michaelson, we have been expecting you," the desk clerk replied. "May I see your passport, please?" The clerk checked the passport, then continued, "You are already registered, sir. Here is your keycard. Our porter will show you to your room."

As he followed the porter to his room, Ian thought things were a little strange but then everything from the admiral's office to the present moment had been strange.

. . .

The next morning, Ian checked out of his room and went to breakfast in the hotel restaurant. He selected a table near a window where he could watch the area in front of the hotel. Just before 0900, a tourist autobus pulled up outside the entrance. He watched a well-dressed couple try to engage it, and who were obviously angry when they were turned away.

Ian paid his check and went out to the tourist bus and rapped on the door.

"Mr. Michaelson?" the driver asked.

"Yes, I'm Michaelson," Ian replied as he entered the autobus.

The Barsoom Expedition

For the next hour, Ian was given a very rapid tour of Zürich's high points while he casually chatted with the driver. It was raining when they finally arrived in front of a building that was not particularly impressive. It was a typical modern office building constructed of stainless steel and glass. Above the entrance, there were large black letters in relief that simply said ICExS.

A crowd of demonstrators was milling about carrying signs and placards and chanting slogans in various languages. The rain fogged the windows, making it difficult to see clearly, so Ian was not able to read any of the signs.

"Here we are, sir, at the I-Sex-s building as it is known here," the driver announced with a chuckle.

"What is the fare?" Ian asked.

"It was prepaid, thank you, sir," the driver replied.

Ian paid a generous gratuity nonetheless over the protests of the driver and exited the autobus. He was immediately assaulted by the demonstrators as he began to walk up towards the entrance. He made every effort to pass through the demonstrators politely but was jostled about sometimes rather forcefully as they waved their placards and shouted their slogans. When he reached for the door handle a man wearing Arab garb and wielding a sign hit Ian on the head and cursed him in what sounded like Arabic.

The noise ceased abruptly when the door closed behind him as he entered the building. "Good morning, sir, how may I be of service?" the receptionist greeted him with professional grace then continued, "Sorry about the protestors, sir. I saw one bash you on the head, have you been hurt?" Before he could answer, she repeated her greeting equally rapidly in French and then German.

"Good morning, miss. No, thanks to my hat, I am not hurt but thank you for asking." Then deciding to drop the charade he continued, "I am Commander Ian McMichael. I believe I am expected."

"Yes, sir. The director has been expecting you," she replied. "Would you like to leave your coat and bag with me? I'll keep them safe," the receptionist offered as she dialed a number and said, "Hello, Cynthia, Commander McMichael is here." Then to Ian, "If you will have a seat, sir, someone will be here to guide you to the director's office directly."

Ian handed his coat and kit across the reception desk, straightened his tie, shot his cuffs, and stood at ease waiting for the guide. A few minutes later, an older woman wearing a tweed professional business suit entered the lobby. She held out her hand in greeting. "Good morning, Commander, my name is Cynthia Burroughs, I am the director's executive assistant. Follow me if you please," she said, then added as she led the way to the lifts, "The director's office is on the third floor." When they exited the lift, she led the way through the usual labyrinth of hallways and cubicles common to modern office buildings.

Ian followed Cynthia to the office of the director. She knocked once, opened the door, and announced, "Commander McMichael is here, Director." At some signal from within, she stepped aside allowing Ian to enter. There were three men in the room, all were standing when Ian entered. The oldest of the three, a short, perfectly groomed gentleman with white curly hair crossed the room towards Ian smiling warmly and extending his hand in greeting.

"Welcome, Commander, I am David Palmquist, the Executive Director of the International Consortium for the Exploration of Space, ICExS for short. I see you made it through the reception committee outside. The receptionist reported that you had been assaulted by one of the protestors. Have you been injured?"

"No, Director, I was wearing my hat and it was only a glancing blow with the flat of the sign."

"Good! I'm sorry you had to go through that. They have been there for several months now. They never seem to tire. But, I am being rude. Let me introduce you to Dr. Walter Cartwright of His Britannic Majesty's Royal Academy of Science and Herr Hans-Joseph Schmidt, Managing Director of IAG Farben." Hands were shaken all around in the European custom. Cynthia offered coffee and Ian accepted to the surprise of the others.

"Four years at the US Naval Academy where the coffee flowed freely and drinking tea was frowned upon gave me the coffee habit," Ian explained.

Then it began.

"Do you know why you're here, Commander?" the director asked.

"No, sir, I haven't the foggiest idea. All I know is that my commanding officer gave me a ticket with a strange itinerary and sealed orders to come to Zürich and wished me good luck," Ian replied.

"What do you know about space exploration, Commander?"

"Just what I read in the newspapers, various scientific journals, and what is reported on the telly."

"Have you heard of the Barsoom Project?" The capitals were evident in the way the director said the name.

"Not much, in fact not much at all," Ian replied. "It has something to do with Mars, right?"

"Yes, that is correct," the director interjected. "We had hoped you might have heard more than that, but we appreciate your candor."

"The Barsoom Project is a planned scientific expedition to Mars in search of life and possible life support systems with the ultimate goal of possible colonization," Dr. Cartwright explained.

"Barsoom, sir?" Ian asked. "Yes, I believe I know that much from reading *Scientific World*. But why Barsoom?"

"We named it that in honor of the name given Mars by the fictional inhabitants in the John Carter novels written by Edgar Rice Burroughs more than a century ago," the director replied.

"Thank you, sir. I've never read any of Mr. Burroughs's novels. My taste lies more in eighteenth- and nineteenth-century English Navy novels than in science fiction. In any event, what has that to do with me? I was told I was coming here to be a consultant of some sort."

"That is correct, Commander. We are nearing launch and need the assistance of someone who has commanded a complex vessel designed to operate in an alien environment with a minimal crew. You were nominated by several sources including your superiors in the Royal Australian Navy, and vetted by ICExS Security as a person capable of preparing the crew for the voyage," the director explained.

"Me?" Ian asked in disbelief. "I'm an ex-submarine commander, sir. I know next to nothing about spaceships."

"What is the difference between a submarine and a spaceship, Commander?" Herr Schmidt asked rhetorically then answered himself. "A submarine is a closed ship with a hull designed to submerge in the alien environment of the sea and keep the water out, yah? A spaceship is a closed ship designed for travel in the alien environment of outer space where the purpose of the hull is to keep the air in and the vacuum of space out. Do you follow me, Commander?"

"Yes, sir, I suppose so," Ian replied slowly while pondering Herr Schmidt's reply. Then he added. "But, again, what has that to do with me?" As he waited for an answer, he wondered why all three men were present but felt it might not be proper to ask at this juncture.

"In simplest terms, Commander, you have a great deal of experience serving on and commanding nuclear vessels, including those with international crews and passengers. Furthermore, you've also commanded scientific expeditions with teams of international scientists. You come highly recommended both by the international scientific community and by the naval establishment.

"In simplest terms," Dr. Cartwright explained, "the *Barsoom Explorer* is a nuclear-powered vessel. It is designed in much the same way as nuclear submarines and demands the same degree of dedication and expertise. If I understand correctly, the crew of a nuclear submarine must all be completely familiar with the operation and purpose of every pipe, valve, control, wire, and every other piece of equipment on the ship. Further, as it was explained to me, each crew member is required to prepare a personal diary in which he or she details all that has been learned about the operation of the submarine. We need someone who has done all that and who knows how to teach the rest of the crew how to do it and enforce it."

For the next two hours, the three men grilled Ian about his career in the Navy, about his personal life, about his beliefs, and about his goals. At the end of that time, Ian felt satisfied with the answers he had given.

"Do you have any more questions for us, Commander?"

"What about the nuclear power system? I told you I've been trained in vessels that were nuclear powered, but I am hardly a qualified engineer when it comes to running one and or teaching others how to do so," he offered.

The Barsoom Expedition

"The nuclear power plant was designed and installed by a very talented Russian nuclear engineer. I believe you know him, Alexi Gargorin? We believe that he was the Chief Engineer on some of the scientific expeditions you commanded."

"Alexi Petrovich?" Ian asked without thinking using the Russian patronymic surname in surprise. "I certainly do know him. He was actually on two of my commands and he also acted as an advisor on one of my ships when we were testing a new nuclear propulsion system. He's a great engineer and a personal friend."

"He is in the conference room down the hall. Why don't you go and spend some time discussing the project with him before you decide whether to help us."

Cynthia led the way to the conference room and opened the door. When Ian entered, Alexi Petrovich Gargorin was smoking a pipe and staring out the window at the demonstrators in front of the building. He was a man of medium height and built like a wrestler. His beard, like his hair, was trimmed and grizzled. He wore a blue blazer, a white turtle-necked jersey, and gray slacks.

Without turning, Alexi asked, "Well, Digger, did they convince you?"

"Not yet. I'm keen to hear what you have to say, Alexi Petrovich. How are you, you great Russian bear?"

"I am as good as can be for someone who spent the last year and a half on the far side of the moon!"

"The far side of the moon?" Ian asked. "What the hell were you doing on the far side of the moon?"

"That's where the *Barsoom Explorer* is being built. It is in orbit above the far side of the Moon at the L2 LaGrange point. It is being built there because it cannot be seen from Earth. There are far too many prying eyes that want to see what's going on and to see if they can somehow impede the progress or destroy the ship."

"Fascinating," Ian exclaimed. "How are they getting the materials there to build the ship without the people on Earth being able to observe what is going on?"

"ICExS has a complete manufacturing plant on the Moon. We are using the minerals and other resources that are available in the Moon's crust to construct the ship. We have a series of shuttles that ferry supplies and equipment up from the surface of the Moon to the ship."

"How big is this ship?"

"Ian, she is 155 meters long from nose to tail. The command deck, living quarters, storage, the garden, and other spaces are in the nose structure which is 35 meters in diameter and 35 meters long. They are much more roomy compared to submarines, but then almost everything is fairly roomy compared to submarines. In the middle is the reaction mass tank, which is 95 meters long and 60 meters in diameter with a tunnel through it connecting the nose to the tail. We are going to use water as reaction mass. The reactors are aft and the reactor deck is again 35 meters in diameter but only 15 meters long. At the extreme tail are the rocket exhausts and other equipment that add up to another 10 meters.

"The Reactors are capable of producing gigawatts of power. The ship will be propelled by water or more properly by steam that is super-heated to a plasma and squeezed magnetically so the exhaust product exits the nozzles at a significant percentage of the speed of light."

"Water? You are going to use water to drive a rocket ship?" Ian was incredulous.

"Of course. It is readily available and very cheap. Would it surprise you to know that Hydrogen and Oxygen have been the principal components of rocket fuel for years and when they combust the product is water, very hot water. Ours will be infinitely hotter."

"Available, cheap? Where do you find water on the Moon?" Ian asked astounded, then continued. "How do you get it out to the ship?"

"Surface to ship shuttles, of course, to answer your last question first. As for being available and cheap, a significant percentage of the minerals on the surface of the moon contain water in one form or another. In addition, we have found several huge reservoirs of water below the surface of the Moon, some are filled with ice and some are actually filled with liquid water."

"You're serious, aren't you? I have a million other questions and hardly know where to begin. Have you tested this rocket engine?"

"We have and it performs flawlessly," Alexi replied with a smile. "Ian, you will love it. It is quiet. It's efficient. And, it is unbelievably powerful. Ian, all you have to do is say yes and we will have you on the far side of the moon by next week."

The whole concept fascinated Ian. While he was still an active naval officer, he was in what would be considered an "end of a career" job. He was, by training, a line officer, not a staff officer. All the command positions above him were filled and none of the occupants seemed ready to retire. So he was relegated to a staff job with an occasional command for a month or two with reservists not always on submarines. He thought for a few minutes about what he might be leaving behind. He was a recent widower due to an automobile crash that killed his wife and his only child. His parents were deceased and he had no siblings. So aside from a few friends, who were mostly military, there was no one who would really miss him if he spent some time on the moon consulting on operational procedures and such. He would have to square it with Command, but then they sent him here, so they must have some knowledge of what it is all about. He doubted there would be any problems having himself seconded to the Barsoom Project.

Ian walked over to the window, looked out at the protestors, turned to Alexi and asked, "What is that business in front of the building all about?"

"That is a very long story, my friend," Alexi said. "Take a seat. I have been delegated to tell it to you, and you really need to hear it and what it implies before you completely commit yourself.

"Six months ago, Fr. Paolo Sabatino, director of the Keepers of the Faith from the Office of the Protector of the Faith in the Vatican secretly called a meeting of the senior officiates of every faith and sect with a creation dogma. The meeting was held at the Abbey of the Eternal Faith in the Carpathian Mountains in Moravia. There were almost 400 attendees altogether. They included members of nearly every Christian denomination, a Jewish delegation from Israel and delegates from every one of the major Islamic sects as well as a few others not as well known. Father Sabatino began by broadly implying that he was representing the Holy See with the blessing of the Holy Father himself.

CHAPTER THREE

The Abbey of the Eternal Faith, Moravia:
"Good morning, ladies and gentlemen, I am Fr. Paolo Sabatino. I am from the Office of the Protector of the Faith in the Vatican and I am the director of the Keepers of the Faith. I bring you greetings from the Holy Father," Father Sabatino said to the assembled delegates. As he said this, his secretary and assistant, Fr. Julio Domingo, standing beside him looked down in astonishment at Father Sabatino wondering whether he had heard correctly.

Father Sabatino dismissed him with a gesture. Then he said under his breath, "Not now, Julio, later." Father Sabatino continued, "I trust you all had a good sleep, good morning prayers, and a good breaking of the fast." He waited until the murmurs quieted. Then continued, "I expect you have all done this already but take a moment and look around you at all the people in this room. There are representatives here from every major faith, many branches of the faiths and a great many others who represent believers throughout the world. You have been called here because our beliefs are being threatened."

Again he waited for quiet. "Yes, you have all heard me correctly. The foundations of our beliefs are at risk. God created the Earth for man and all mankind. Those of you who are of the Judeo-Christian faiths and the followers of Mohammad have all read the ancient words of Moses from the Old Testament in which he describes the creation of the universe, all that is in it and gives it to mankind to rule. Those of you who are of other faiths all have similar scriptures that you believe and follow." He said this slowly so that the interpreters for those who did not speak English could translate his words.

"Now, the foundations of our faiths are being put to the question." He deliberately said it using the terms that had been used by the Inquisitors in the Inquisition. "I say this not because we wish to recall a shameful and desperate time in the Catholic Church. That was a time when a great many people did not know what to believe and as a consequence were led into various forms of disbelief. The Inquisition was intended to lead them back to the faith. Similar events have occurred in many of the other faiths of the world, but we are not here to discuss that.

"We are here because an effort is being made by the scientists of the world to establish that there is or has been life on another planet. If they are able to prove they have discovered life on another planet, whether it is true or not is irrelevant. Any such claims are sacrilegious by any definition you choose. The International Consortium for the Exploration of Space is mounting a mission to Mars with the purpose of proving life may have originated there. They are basing the need for this exploratory mission on what are claimed to be fossils of single-celled organisms found in some meteorites that were discovered in Antarctica. It is claimed that the meteorites originated on Mars. There is no proof of this, of course.

"Nevertheless a great deal of money has been raised to fund a mission to Mars. Right now a ship is in the final stages of assembly on the far side of the moon, where it is not visible from Earth. This ship is designed to make the trip to Mars carrying between twelve and twenty people. Half of these people will be scientists whose job it is to analyze the surface of Mars to determine whether it ever contained life. The scientists chosen for this trip have all espoused the findings of those who analyzed the meteorites. From this, we assume they intend to search for any signs that there had ever been life on Mars and gather support for those claims.

"Whether or not those claims are valid is not in question. What is in question is how the followers of our faiths will be swayed in their beliefs that God created the universe to be the dominion of Man. Any such information must never be allowed to be returned to Earth. The scientists are all avowed heretics. Some of them attend and belong to various faiths, but they do not necessarily believe what is being taught or they would not be going on this mission. I ask you what the effect would be if by chance life is found on Mars?" Father Sabatino concluded.

For the rest of the day, the delegates discussed among their own and other delegations the possible effects of what Father Sabatino described. The discussions varied from whispered to shouted as various individuals tried to impress their opinion on others.

Father Sabatino sat quietly in the front of the Great Hall with his secretary, Father Domingo. Father Domingo was greatly troubled by some of what Father Sabatino had said. He asked, "Father, when did the Holy Father send his blessings?"

Father Sabatino looked with disapproval at his secretary. Then replied, "We are here, are we not? We came from the Vatican, did we not? We come from the office of the Keeper of the Faith, do we not? Then it must be assumed that we come with the blessings of His Holiness, should it not?"

"But—" Father Domingo began.

"Silence, we are here as representatives of the Holy See. That is all you need to know. As you can see, there are others from various enclaves of the Catholic Church present here as well. There are times when it is necessary to do things in the interest of God regardless of what they are and how they are done. Now let us mingle and sample the reactions of those who are here. There will be no further discussion. Do you understand that?" Father Sabatino said.

Father Domingo opened and shut his mouth several times as if he intended to speak. "Do you understand that?" Father Sabatino asked a second time. Father Domingo avoided looking directly at his superior and finally nodded his assent. "Follow me," Father Sabatino ordered.

The two men wandered among the delegates and went from delegation to delegation being very careful not to show favoritism to any of the delegations. Father Sabatino sensed after an hour or so of listening in on various discussions and arguments that there was general agreement with what he was proposing. There were those who seemed to be wavering but none of the them threatened the success of the meeting. What most of the delegations did not know was that Father Sabatino was adept or conversant in nearly all modern languages including many of those from the Orient and the Middle East. He was able to actually eavesdrop on many of the discussions without the delegates being aware that he could hear and understand what was said.

The delegates from the Orient, for the most part, did not seem to care one way or the other about the issue. Their creation stories were not consistent with those of the Western religions. The delegations from the Middle East, with the exception of those from Israel, were in a great furor over the possibilities described by Father Sabatino and for a change, there seemed to be agreement among the various sects represented. The Israelis who were augmented by rabbis from various parts of the world were predictably unable to reach an agreement with the ultra-orthodox opposing the reformed.

When they broke for lunch, Father Sabatino made a call on his cell phone. "Things seem to be developing nicely. The only problems so far have been with the Jews." He listened for a moment then said, "How did you know that?" Again he listened. "You have spies here among the delegates? Why?" Some explanation was given after which Father Sabatino ended the call with, "I will keep you informed even though that would seem to be unnecessary."

Father Domingo heard much of the one-sided conversation. When Father Sabatino hung up, he asked, "Was the church unhappy with what we have been doing?"

"No, but there are spies here that are watching the proceedings and reporting what is happening."

"From the Holy See?" Father Domingo asked.

Father Sabatino frowned at Father Domingo and said, "Perhaps. But there may be others as well."

"Why?"

"Drop it. I am in control and that should be sufficient."

Father Domingo tried not to show that he was concerned. He nodded to his superior and walked away.

The discussions went on through lunch and into the late afternoon. Several delegates approached Father Sabatino with clarifying questions. He answered them with essentially the same words that he had used to address the assembly with appropriate variations depending on the belief system of those asking.

For the next two days, the tone of these discussions ebbed and flowed from one position to another. But Father Sabatino found as he wandered among them, the trend was in support of opposing the mission to Mars.

At noon on both days, his cell phone vibrated in his pocket. When this happened, he excused himself from whatever he was doing and went outside, away from prying ears to take the call.

On the afternoon of the third day, Father Sabatino polled the delegations. In varying degrees, they all supported taking some action to prevent the trip to Mars.

One delegate from an English-speaking country asserted that there had been many scientific and exploratory robots sent to Mars and that none had ever found any proof of life there. He then suggested that any trip undertaken with the intent of finding life on Mars was, as he put it, "a colossal waste of money." He further suggested that the money being used to fund such a mission would be far better spent feeding people throughout the world who were in dire need. Not exactly the response Father Sabatino desired, but many of those present, especially from the Western religions agreed with the sentiment.

Near the end of the afternoon, the chief Rabbi of the Israeli and Jewish delegation took the floor. "We have discussed the many facets of information that the proposed mission might satisfy. We number a great many scientists among our citizens in Israel and elsewhere throughout the world. We can see no reason why the finding of life on Mars would be any threat to the Jewish faith. As you have said, God created the universe and gave mankind dominion over it. Why wouldn't that dominion include Mars? We, therefore, find no problem with allowing the mission to go forward as planned."

When the Rabbi had finished, there were some quiet discussions around the room and it appeared that his statement may have swayed some of the others to some extent. Father Sabatino allowed no time for the doubt created by the Rabbi to take root and destroy the consensus of the delegates.

"Ladies and gentlemen," Father Sabatino began, "we seem to have found common ground amongst ourselves of a need to defend our faiths. The defense of faiths is not as complex as it might seem on the surface. All we need to do is persuade our scientists to refuse to participate. We have a list of those who are being considered for selection. They come from all over the world. We will supply each delegation with a list of scientists over which they might be able to exercise some control. It is our intention to use whatever means is necessary to prevent a scientific expedition to Mars."

"Thank you for your participation and may you all have a safe trip back to your country and your congregations. Again, I thank you," Father Sabatino said, ending the conference.

His cell phone vibrated almost immediately. Again, he went outside to take the call. Father Domingo followed him at a distance trying to hear what was said. All he was able to hear was, "…the only problem is with the Jews and Rabbis. You will have to deal with them. I will take care of the rest." After which Father Sabatino ended the call.

As the delegates and delegations were departing, Father Sabatino went and spoke with several other Catholic clerics who were stationed around the room. As he gave each cleric what were obviously orders. They immediately left the Great Hall presumably to carry out those orders.

On the trip back to Rome, Father Domingo tried several times to speak with Father Sabatino and was repeatedly cut off. When they arrived in Rome, Father Sabatino escorted Father Domingo to his chambers and instructed him to pray about his doubts. The next morning the news spread through the Vatican almost instantly: "Father Julio Domingo from the Office of the Keepers of the Faith was found dead in his chambers of an apparent overdose of sleeping pills. He had committed the unforgivable sin, just not the one usually cited."

That same day, the international news on religion reported that the chief Rabbi of Israel and five of his associates were killed in an automobile accident when the automobile they were in missed a turn and crashed down a mountainside. An international day of mourning was observed. The selection of a new Chief Rabbi was to take place at an emergency meeting of the Rabbinical Council in Jerusalem. The new Chief Rabbi made it clear that he was opposed to any waste of money searching for life elsewhere in the solar system or universe.

Olathe Kansas, The Church of the One God:
A promising biochemist was asked to meet with the minister of his church. The minister suggested that it would not be in the interest of either the church or the biochemist if he were to accept an invitation to participate in the mission to Mars. The biochemist agreed and declined the invitation.

Medina, Saudi Arabia, The Mosque of Allah the Compassionate:
A world renowned geologist who specialized in desert environments was intercepted as he was leaving after his morning devotions and asked to speak to the Imam. The Imam suggested that it would not be in the interest of either Islam or the future of the geologist if he was to accept the offer to go to Mars. He declined and was immediately promoted to chair of his department at the university.

The University Of Dusseldorf, Germany Department of Planetary Sciences:
It was strongly suggested to the principal planetary scientist that the university would view dimly his actions if he were to accept an invitation to go to Mars because it would interfere with his research and teaching duties. He declined the offer for unspecified personal reasons.

And so it went all over the world wherever scientists worked or studied who might possibly be selected for the mission to Mars. Nearly everyone declined. The two exceptions found the funding for their research and support withdrawn for unspecified reasons. They quickly fell into line and decided not to go on the mission to Mars.

Alexi continued. "It would seem that most of the major religions and even more of the minor religions and sects are opposed to us going to Mars to find life. It is their avowed position that God created Earth alone for the home of mankind. There are zealots of every kind you can imagine out there who are doing everything they can to stop this.

"We have found that it all originates with an Eastern European Cartel that wants to be the ones who colonize Mars so they can claim it for themselves and set up an oligarchy as some sort of feudal system. The Cartel instigated the religious backlash through the Catholic Church in Rome.

"We have a complete record of the meeting that was provided by an attendee who recorded the entire proceedings. His commentary indicates there was some dissension between Father Sabatino and his assistant almost from the beginning when he announced he had the blessing of the Holy Father. We have since found that he did not have any authorization to either conduct the meeting or to represent the Holy See.

"Father Sabatino began with an exhortation to the attendees that God created only Earth for the home of mankind and that any effort to colonize Mars was sacrilegious and would be an affront to God. He went on for some time in that vein and then turned the meeting open to questions and comments. As an aside, it is helpful to know that Father Sabatino spoke eight languages including Hebrew and several other Middle Eastern dialects. The meeting continued for two days at the end of which Father Sabatino called for a poll of the delegations. Every delegation with the exception of the Rabbinical Counsel from Israel agreed to support the ban.

"After the meeting was adjourned, the Rabbinical Council was driving back to Brno to catch a flight home. On the way, they met with a horrible accident missing a turn on a narrow mountain road. All the Rabbis were killed."

"That should give you some idea of what the opposition is prepared to do to prevent the Mars mission."

Ian looked at Alexi in disbelief. He had never been a religious person himself but he had no problems with what others might believe. But to think there might be people who were willing to destroy and even kill to prevent the possible discovery of life on another planet was beyond his comprehension. He said, "Oh, my G—" then realized how inappropriate or perhaps appropriate such an expression might be in this situation.

"That's not all. Somehow the Cartel has been able to bribe some of the workers at Farside Base to perform acts of sabotage. Even some of the workers who worked on building the ship have tried to sabotage the project. We have discovered many attempts, some very amateurish and some quite professional. So far we think we have found them all, but I would not bet on it."

"I have a different question for you, Alexi," Ian said. "How did ICExS come to select me as a possible commander for the ship?"

"The short version is, I nominated you," Alexi replied. "We have interviewed every one we could think of who had command experience in space programs. Every one of them turned us down. We found out as we went along that the Cartel had gotten to them first and threatened them and their families if they accepted the captaincy. Then we looked for anyone who had commanded a scientific expedition with the same result. The director called a closed meeting and asked us to think outside the box to find someone qualified, but to only tell him who they were. I remembered the Antarctic expedition you commanded as the captain of the *Ageas*. You had responsibility for the military crew and for the international science team. I also knew you had no special attachments that could be threatened. I told the director who went through channels presumably seeking a consultant. He knew someone in the Australian Office of Naval Operations, and made the call. Whoever he spoke to was willing to go along with the consultant charade and send you up, and here you are."

"One more question before we go back to the director's office," Ian said. "Why didn't you take the job. You were an orphan and a commander in the Russian Navy and apparently, you thoroughly understand rockets?"

"Simple, Ian. I am an engineer and although my rank is commander, I have no command experience outside of reactor teams. I, we, wanted a true commander. I have worked with you before, I know you know how to command, so to me you were the obvious candidate. Now, what are you going to say to the director?"

"I accept, of course."

"Good, now let's go tell him."

CHAPTER FOUR

Ian and Alexi returned to the director's office and were admitted immediately. The three men again stood to greet them. "Well, Commander, have you decided or would you like to have a few days to think it over?" It took a moment before Ian noticed that each of the men wore a large signet ring, which he did not remember from his earlier meeting with them.

"I have decided, sir. I would very much like to be on the Barsoom Project team. From what Alexi tells me, it should be a very interesting job."

"Very good, Commander," the director said, then continued. "From this moment you are promoted to captain. We are not much for uniforms, but you may add a fourth stripe to your Navy uniform sleeve. The promotion will be recognized by the RAN as soon as we wire them your acceptance. From what we have seen of your service record, you are fit and should not require a great deal of conditioning. However, you will have to take a ride or two on what is affectionately called 'The Vomit Comet,' the plane we use to acquaint new people with the feeling of weightlessness. If you are prone to motion sickness, which we seriously doubt, this will help you to overcome it. When will you be available to go up to the moon?"

"I have nothing important on my schedule, so I can leave whenever it is convenient for you," Ian replied.

"Right! We will schedule you for a fast week of training and send you up on the next shuttle to the International Space Station," the director said. "We look forward to working with you. My assistant will arrange your schedule and let you know when and where."

"Fine, gentlemen. I checked out of the Hilton House and will need new hotel arrangements," Ian said. He felt great relief at having made the decision, one which he knew was the right one for him.

Ian stepped out into Cynthia's area where she handed him a manila folder. "I have booked you at the Zürich Hilton, Captain. You will be in a suite on the 15th floor which can only be reached by a keyed elevator, so you will not have to worry about being harassed again." Then she indicated a uniformed man who was standing by her desk. "This security guard will lead you to our basement garage where one of our cars will take you to the hotel. Oh, sir, excuse me, but where is your baggage?"

"I travel light. Everything I need is in the bag I left with the receptionist. In the military, we often get orders to go somewhere in a hurry, so we all keep a 'go bag' packed and ready."

"Very good, Captain. If you would please follow the guard," she said, turning away, then turned back and added, "Commander Gargorin is also staying in the suite until the two of you depart. He will be joining you shortly."

Ian was halfway to the garage when he realized that the secretary had called him Captain. *How did she know?* The guard placed Ian's coat and bag on the front seat, then opened the rear door for him and ushered him into the car. The trip to the hotel was smooth and uneventful. The guard stopped at the rear entrance to the hotel where Ian was met by another guard who took his bag, led him to the elevator, and gave him the key to the suite.

When the guard left them, he said, "Take care, Captain. We recommend you stay in the hotel, order room service, and eat in the suite. The bar is fully stocked so feel free to partake, you prefer gin, I understand. There are several excellent gins in the cabinet."

As the elevator door closed, Ian noticed the same signet ring on the lift operator's finger. The guard saw him looking at the lift operators ring and said,

"Yours is being made as we speak and will be ready in the morning. Good night, Captain."

Again he was addressed as captain. Ian began to wonder if everyone in town knew he was to be the captain of the Barsoom Expedition, and what was it with the signet rings. He started to ask Alexi when Alexi said, "They know you are captain because you are here. As for the rings, everyone who has been vetted by ICExS security and is a member of the organization has a matching ring that was made explicitly for them."

The suite was beautifully appointed like no other he had ever seen. Alexi broke the silence, "You get the bedroom to the right, I am in the other one. Go freshen up and I will meet you back here in fifteen minutes." Fifteen minutes later the two men sat in easy chairs, each with a drink in hand and began to catch up on what they had been doing since last they were together.

Several hours later, there was a knock on the door of the suite. Alexi went to the door where he was handed a typed schedule for the next ten days. They quickly went over it, then set it aside to spend the rest of the evening catching up, well lubricated with excellent gin and vodka.

The next morning, they left the hotel in an ICExS limo and were taken to a private airstrip. The limo drove into a hangar and stopped next to an unmarked Lear Jet that was identical to two others in the hangar. Ian and Alexi exited the limo and boarded the plane. There were no other passengers. The three identical planes left the airport virtually at the same time just moments apart. Alexi explained, "It's for security. We have had various incidents with the protestors and take great care to insure privacy and security in everything we do. Once we are well away, the other two planes will return to the airport."

Ian tried to look out the window as they were preparing to take off but it was covered by a curtain. He began to slide the curtain covering the window when Alexi said, "Don't try to see out, Ian. The windows are covered with black curtains to keep us from seeing out and anyone outside from seeing in."

Before they had even reached cruising altitude, a cabin attendant offered them breakfast. When she returned with the trays, she said, "Here is your breakfast, Captain." On the tray was a signet ring.

Alexi was watching Ian as he picked up the ring. "Put it on, Captain. You are now one of the chosen. From now on wherever we are when we are with the organization wear the ring. If you see someone without one, avoid him or her at all cost." Then he added, "You will notice that your ring has four stars in recognition that you are the captain."

While Ian and Alexi flew to the training facility, Director Palmquist called a meeting of all the members of the ICExS Board of Directors in the conference room.

"Ladies and gentlemen we have a problem. Someone leaked our list of potential scientists for the Mars mission. Every scientist we have approached has refused to go for one reason or another. These are men and women who it was thought would give everything they had for such an opportunity. We now know why that happened. In every case, the individual or the individual's family were threatened in some manner by either religious authorities or by operatives of an organization that wishes to kill the mission. We believe we know who leaked the list."

The director pressed a button on his communications console and two uniformed ICExS security officers entered the room. All eyes turned to see who or what was interrupting the meeting. At a nod from the director, the woman nearest the door was helped to her feet, handcuffed, and led from the room. As she was being taken away, she protested her innocence. Another of the attendees watched this and commented, "I would've guessed it was her." At a sign from the director, the security guards came back into the room and placed the speaker in handcuffs and removed him as well.

After the doors were closed the meeting resumed. The director said, "A new list has been drawn up that is known to only three people in the world. The people on that list are all competent scientists and excellent in their fields. They were not our first choices, but they are never to know that. To prevent another occurrence similar to that which we just experienced, the individuals on that list will not be contacted until the last possible minute before they are told of their selection and are asked to go. Not everyone will be contacted at the same time. They will be notified immediately before they are needed. There are multiple alternatives for each position in the event someone declines. If they accept, they will leave where they are at that moment under the protection of our security personnel and be escorted directly to the training facility.

"The leaks must not be allowed to happen again. The same procedures will be followed in the selection of the crew. We can take no further chances with the success of the mission. We are aware, however, that things being what they are, some of our selectees may have been contacted in advance and threatened or worse yet, recruited as agents to sabotage or otherwise ensure the failure of the mission. Over thirty individuals at Farside Base have been caught planning or doing various acts of sabotage to the ship or our facilities."

As the director finished his comments, the door opened again and his assistant entered the room and placed before him a tray on which there were two broken ICExS rings. The director put the pieces of the two broken rings into a small envelope, which he placed in the safe behind his desk. Then he said, "I sincerely hope that I never have to do that again. The director of Farside Base has a whole cupful of broken rings in his safe." With that, he adjourned the meeting.

CHAPTER FIVE

"There, my friend, is our ride to the International Space Station," Alexi said, pointing to the shuttlecraft on the launchpad.

"How bad is it going to be?" Ian asked, half dreading the answer.

"The first three minutes are a bitch. More noise than you thought existed, and an elephant sitting on your chest during the takeoff. Once the shuttle separates from the launch vehicle and continues on its own engine, it is not nearly as noisy nor is the acceleration as bad," Alexi explained as they were putting on their space suits for the shuttle.

Thirty minutes later as they rode the elevator from the ground up to the boarding ramp for the shuttle, Ian looked around at the immense space facility. There were five more launch pads that he could see. Three of them had vehicles being prepared for launch. He had been told that there was a launch every two weeks and it took more than a month to refit a vehicle for the relaunch. When the elevator reached the top and the doors opened, Ian could see a small crowd of people all in space suits waiting to board the shuttle. He made a rough count and including himself and Alexi there were twenty people altogether.

"I never realized the shuttle could carry this many people," Ian exclaimed.

"Da, it's almost like taking a bus to the library anymore," Alexi replied.

A woman, who was not wearing a space suit, stood to one side holding a clipboard. Soon after Ian and Alexi arrived, she began to call numbers and names and direct those who were called across the ramp to the shuttle. Ian and Alexi were numbers 13 and 14 and they joined the queue on the ramp. The queue moved forward at about the same rate as it would for boarding an aircraft. They walked down a ramp and entered the shuttle. There another woman, this one wearing a space suit without a helmet, directed them to seats 13 and 14 which were across the aisle from each other. "If she gives the speech about fastening your seat belts and noticing where the drop-down oxygen mask is—" Ian began.

"Oh, she will and a whole lot more besides," Alexi replied with a grin. "We have to put on our helmets, which will be passed out in a few moments. She will check that our oxygen is turned on correctly, firmly fasten our seat belts for us, and make sure the seat is locked in position. She doesn't do the bit about raising your tray table to the up and locked position only because there are no tray tables."

When the cabin attendant finished her spiel, she passed out helmets and connected each oxygen line to the supply in the armrest, and tested for a positive oxygen flow.

Once all the passengers had been checked, the entry door was shut. The attendant took her place at the rear of the shuttle, and the vehicle began to rotate into a vertical position

A moment later, the pilot, also a woman, announced, "Liftoff in five."

Five minutes later the entire vehicle began to shake like a pickup truck driving across the outback, and the noise was deafening. After a few very long moments, the engine settled down. Then Ian felt the launchpad locks release and the shuttle began to rise. Initially, the acceleration wasn't too bad but as time went on and the fuel was consumed, the pressure from the acceleration gradually grew greater and greater while the noise remained essentially the same.

A click and the helmet speaker preceded another announcement from the pilot, "Booster separation in ten seconds."

Ten seconds later the shuttle jarred as the booster was released. The shuttle engine continued to burn, but the acceleration and noise dropped off considerably. A few minutes later the pilot announced, "Shuttle engine cut off in ten."

This time no duration was specified, Ian assumed that it was to be ten seconds. Ten seconds later, Ian felt a brief surge of reverse acceleration as the seat cushions thrust him forward against the restraining straps when the engine cut off and they were suddenly weightless. Unlike his sessions in the Vomit Comet, he was not able to drift freely and do didos and flips.

Again, a click in the helmet speaker preceded an announcement by the cabin attendant, "Ladies and gentlemen please remain in your seats with the restraining straps buckled until the shuttle docks with the space station."

Ian and Alexi looked at each other and both broke out laughing. Travel will never change no matter how you go.

After a little more than twenty minutes of drifting weightlessly, another announcement from the pilot warned them that there would be brief surges as the steering engines matched the shuttle to the space station's velocity. There was a clunk like a train coupling and moments later, the airlock at the front of the cabin opened. Then the cabin attendant floated forward through the cabin to the front. She unbuckled the first two passengers who immediately drifted off their seats in the weightless environment. The first passenger was obviously disoriented and needed to be guided by the cabin attendant through the airlock to someone outside the shuttle. The second passenger was obviously experienced in space travel and managed to steer himself through the airlock into the space station unassisted. Two by two the passengers were taken from their seats and passed into the space station.

Alexi had more experience with weightlessness and guided Ian through the airlock. Ian could see the other passengers being passed along the corridor to an elevator where an awaiting attendant helped them strap in. The shuttle dock was at the hub of the huge wheel that was the International Space Station. When all the passengers were strapped in, the elevator operator announced, "Ladies and gentlemen, you are in an elevator in what will be the standing position when we reach the rim of the station. We will ride the elevator up a spoke from the hub to the rim of the wheel. The wheel rotates at a speed that maintains a one 'G' environment at the rim. When you arrive, you will be in a standing position relative to the apparent floor so as I unstrap you, you can just walk off the elevator into the arrival area. There you will remove your space suits and assistance is available for those who might need it."

"Well my friend, how did you like the ride?" Alexi asked.

"It wasn't as bad as I expected, but I wouldn't want to do it every day," Ian replied.

"It will be two days before the next shuttle goes from here to the lunar station. So why don't we do what you Aussies call a 'walkabout' and look the place over. I don't know about you, but I could do with a drink after that ride, and I know a good bar about 20° anti-rotation. Come on." Alexi led the way along the corridor that seemed to curve up as they walked. He noticed Ian's concern and said, "Everybody has that reaction the first time they realize they are walking on the inside of the outer surface of the rim of a huge wheel."

Two days later, they returned to the dressing rooms at what they now thought of as the bottom of the elevator and put on their space suits over their jumpsuits. There were only six other people on the elevator as it rose towards the hub and they were all men. The other six men all appeared to be experienced space travelers as they all swam down the corridor to the waiting lunar shuttle. There were far fewer helpers between the elevator and the shuttle airlock, so Alexi guided Ian from the elevator to the shuttle.

"Like they told you during orientation, this leg of the trip takes about eight hours and the best thing to do is sleep if you can," Alexi said then added, "As soon as we disconnect from the space station and the cabin is pressurized you will be able to remove your helmet, which should make the ride more comfortable. There will not be any ridiculous announcements on this trip like there were on the way up. The establishment assumes we know what we're doing, but they are not always correct."

Seven hours and forty-five minutes later, the pilot directed the passengers to put on their space suit helmets as a safety precaution for the docking procedure. Fifteen minutes after that, there was a bump and a clank as the shuttle attached itself to the docking mechanism in the hub of the Lunar Space Station. Once again they left the shuttle and took an elevator from the hub to the rim of the Lunar Space station. The Lunar Space Station was much smaller than the International Space Station and only rotated at a speed that maintained the one-sixth gravity of the lunar surface.

"Watch your feet, my friend," Alexi said. "You will find yourself bouncing along the corridor if you are not careful. The first time you bang your head on the overhead, you'll wish you hadn't. Just shuffle or take small steps until you get the hang of it. I checked the schedule as we disembarked and the shuttle from here to Farside Base leaves in about four hours. They will announce it about fifteen minutes in advance. They're not nearly as formal here as they were on the International Space Station."

Ian shuffled along the rim corridor and after a few minutes tried taking tentative steps.

The first step was too much and Alexi had to grab him and pull him back to the floor.

"Gently, my friend, gently. It's not as easy here as it will be on the surface. All of the structures on and under the surface have 12-foot ceilings to keep people, especially newcomers, from banging their heads. For the moment, just keep on shuffling and gradually increase the length of your stride, but don't lift your knees too high."

Ian practiced and after a few minutes, he began to get the hang of it. He found that everything he did had to be done in slow motion so that the inertia of his leg movements did not cause him to lose his footing. "Is there a bar in this place, Alexi?"

"Not much of one. There are several bars down at Farside Base that range from what I would call rough to comfortable. So just keep practicing your walk and by the time we've gone around the station a couple of times it will be time to suit up for the trip to the surface," Alexi informed.

They walked three times around the Circum-Lunar Space Station before the announcement for the shuttle to Farside Base was made over the public address system. Ian and Alexi returned to the dressing station and redressed in their space suits. This time, however, there was an attendant in the assembly area with a backpack containing an oxygen tank to be put onto the backs of their space suits.

Ian gave Alexi a quizzical look as if to ask *"what's this all about?"*

"Like I said, things are a lot less formal here than they are on Earth and at the International Space Station. When the shuttle lands, you are going to have to walk from the landing pad to a rollagon. The rollagon will take us to Farside Base where we will have to walk from the rollagon to an airlock in order to enter the base," Alexi said.

"Well, that was easy," Ian said an hour later as they were removing their space suits in the dressing room of Farside Base.

Before he could do anything else, an attractive young woman approached them and said, "Greetings, Captain and Commander. The director suggests that you have something to eat and then go to bed. He will see you in the morning. Your rooms are ready; here are the keys."

"Thank you, Susan. Tell the director we will see him in the morning," Alexi said to the woman.

"Dinner and bed? It's only two o'clock in the afternoon," Ian said.

"You are still on the launch facility clock. All of the moon bases keep Greenwich mean time. As far as the people here are concerned it is ten o'clock at night. So let's go put our stuff in our rooms and find something to eat and maybe a drink and then go to bed. What do you say?" Alexi asked.

"Righto," Ian replied.

• • •

The next morning, Ian and Alexi reported to the director's office as requested. The sign on the door said, "Helmut Stassenfelder, Director, ICExS Farside Base. Susan, the same woman who greeted them at the dressing room greeted them, "What would you like in your coffee, gentlemen?"

Then she showed them into the director's office where they were greeted by the director of Farside Base, "Welcome aboard, Captain, and welcome back,

Commander. I trust your trip was not too arduous." Then he said to Ian as he shook his hand, "Call me 'Chris Craft,' everybody else does. It's an honorary title that dates back to the original Apollo program when the program director was actually named Chris Craft. Besides that, it's a lot easier to say and spell than Stassenfelder. We are much less formal here at Farside Base than back on Earth, of course, it is abused by some, so do not be offended if someone addresses you as Ian, just smile and wave. If there is anything you need or anything I can do to make things simpler or easier for you, feel free to let me or Susan, my right-hand girl, know."

"Thank you, sir," Ian replied. "At this point, I wouldn't know what to ask for. Alexi has been keeping me from stumbling over my feet and I have really appreciated his help. When do we get to go up to the ship? I'm eager to get started."

"There is a shuttle standing by to take you up whenever you're ready to go. Now, are you sure you're ready to go? If you wish to spend a few days here on the surface to become accustomed to the reduced gravity that's okay with me. Look around. Check out the facility. Think of it as a sort of remote submarine base. As the captain, there will be a shuttle up or down available to you at any time. The same goes for Alexi," the director said.

"Actually, sir, the sooner I start becoming accustomed to weightlessness the sooner we'll be able to get on with the job. So I would like to go up as soon as possible. Alexi and I will get started on The Book so I can get on board with the system. I assume there is no problem communicating with the base, or is there one considering the security issues?"

Alexi interjected, "I have not had time to brief Ian on all the aspects of how we do things around here in the interest of security."

"Okay, Captain, in order to prevent eavesdropping, we use a tight beamed laser for secure communications between The *Explorer* and my office. Any other communicating can be done over the radio. The construction crews use radio and even though we're on the far side of the moon, it can be overheard. We know that anything the construction crew does is recorded in several places and forwarded God only knows where. The laser traffic is encrypted and the encryption code changes daily. We will upload the daily encryption code directly into a password and encrypted file on your tablet computer.

"As I'm sure you can understand I cannot stress too strongly the importance of secrecy in everything you and your eventual crew will be doing. Zürich is doing its best to vet the crew and the scientists. That is easier with the crew because they are all technically trained and security can check them out very thoroughly. The scientists are a different matter. We are making a great effort to learn everything we can about them before we choose the rest of the science team. But someone leaked the names of all the original scientific contenders. Our security team on Earth is doing its best to see who was talking to them and if possible what they are talking about. If all of this seems to be a bit Machiavellian, Captain, it is because we have almost 500 billion dollars invested in the project and we need to protect it from those who would destroy it and us in the name of religion. There is not much more I can tell you except that you're in very good hands with Alexi. Again, let me know if there is anything I can do."

"You said the rest of the scientists, Director. What did you mean?" Ian asked. "Alexi never mentioned there would be anyone else on the ship while we inspected it."

"It slipped my mind. Dr. Jamilah Burns came up while Commander Gargorin was down on Earth. Dr. Burns is a specialist in dry climate agriculture. She will attempt to grow vegetation on Mars. At the moment, she is planting our garden on deck three of the *Explorer*."

"Garden?"

"The garden will provide fresh vegetables and greens for the galley and it will also be a test to see if it can filter out the carbon dioxide and convert it to oxygen efficiently. I doubt Dr. Burns will be in the way. She is totally immersed in her project to grow vegetables in a weightless environment."

"Thank you, sir. I'll look forward to meeting her. I would like to have Alexi show me around the base and the factory today. Then we can shuttle up to the ship tomorrow after lunch," Ian replied.

"Good. Watch out for anything out of the ordinary because there are undoubtedly those here who could claim a reward for putting you out of action."

As they left the director's office, Ian wondered what he had gotten himself into and what he might expect from this point on. He knew that Alexi would cover his back and he would do the same for Alexi. He was accustomed to commanding a submarine where the crew were all committed to doing the job. He never needed to worry about any danger from a member of the crew or from anyone in the shipyard. Clearly, this was going to be a whole new kettle of fish.

The tour of the facility took several hours during which Ian and Alexi observed hundreds of workers going about their business. He noticed several who seemed to be watching them as much as they were watching the other workers.

Alexi looked where Ian was looking and said, "Relax, Ian, those men in the jumpsuits with the yellow stripe on their arms are security people who are constantly on the lookout for problems."

In the interest of anonymity, Ian and Alexi were wearing plain blue jumpsuits with no insignia other than the shoulder patch of ICExS, which was in evidence on all the other jumpsuits in view. He had no doubts, considering the capabilities and resources of the opposition that all of those who wanted to know already knew who he was. It did not help any that he was in the company of Alexi who he was sure was very well known by now.

The size of the underground facility was immense. As they drove about on a golf-cart- like vehicle, Alexi kept up a running commentary. "You have no idea just how big this place is. It is larger than the largest cave system on Earth. Through those doors is a steel plant. The doors keep the noise down for the rest of the facility. There is an aluminum refinery, a glass plant, and equipment from rolling mills to casting foundries that produce virtually everything that is needed for the project."

Alexi had already told him that the hull of the ship was made of an aluminum alloy that was stronger than steel and considerably lighter. All of the interior furnishings were cast from various kinds of plastic, which were made by processing oil from underground petroleum reservoirs that were discovered during the initial development of the facility. Ian was amazed to learn that there was virtually nothing that could not be produced from resources available on the moon.

"Come with me, my friend, I want you to especially see a forest being grown here."

"A forest?"

"Yes, one thing we could not make is anything made from wood. So, an unused factory chamber was converted for growth of plants of every kind. This includes food plants, plants to convert the CO_2 in the air to oxygen, flowers for decoration, and some fast-growing trees which will eventually be used for creating wood products."

"That is amazing," Ian observed after visiting the arboretum, as it was called. "Is that much like what Dr. Burns is doing on the ship?"

"Yes," Alexi replied, "except for the trees, and it would not surprise me to find that she has a couple of them too."

"I am overwhelmed," Ian said. "But let's go out to the ship. I'm eager to get started."

"Tomorrow after lunch," Alexi said. "All the shuttles are busy today; I checked. Of course, you can probably override the schedule if you are really eager to go."

"No, no, I'm hungry. Let's go find something to eat."

. . .

At 1400GMT the next day, Ian and Alexi donned their space suits, walked out to the rollagon parking area, and went for a ride to the shuttle launch facility. The rollagon driver greeted Alexi with a wave, "Hi, Commander, welcome back." Then to Ian, "And you must be Captain McMichael. Pleased to meet you, sir. I'm Mike O'Conner late of His Majesty's Royal Marines. Take a seat and we'll roll out to the launch area in a minute. We're waiting on your pilot. Ah. Here she comes. Hi, Rachael, did you have a good time on your holiday?"

"I did, Mike, thanks," the pilot replied as she climbed onto the rollagon.

"I know that voice, how were things in Jerusalem, Rachael?" Ian asked.

"My family was happy to see me, sir. How was your ride to Zürich?" Rachael asked.

"Not as interesting as the ride from Perth to Tel Aviv," Ian replied.

Rachael laughed.

"What are you two talking about?" Alexi asked.

During the ride to the launch facility, Ian and Rachael described the flight in hilarious detail. Even the driver was laughing.

"This is the end of the line, folks," Mike announced when they arrived at the shuttle launch facility.

Ian was baffled when he saw no rocket or rocket launch pad. "Where's our ride?" he asked Alexi.

"Through those doors," Alexi replied as he pointed to a pair of huge doors set into the side of the cliff. "Come along, I'll show you," he said as he led the way to a "people door" airlock set into the leftmost larger door.

Rachel went ahead to open the outer airlock door and led them through into the launch facility. Once they were inside she said, "Excuse me, gentlemen, I have to go do my preflight and check the manifest."

When they entered the launch facility, Ian found himself in an immense cave cut into the mountain. Inside, the cave was larger than most of the factory space and much longer. His eyes were immediately drawn to a large brightly painted cylinder lying on its side and sitting on a pair of rails that pointed off into the distance. At the far end of the cave was another pair of huge doors that were closed at the moment. Alexi led the way to a group of people who were standing on a platform beside the cylinder.

"It almost looks like a railroad station in a large city," Ian observed. "Is that our coach?" he asked as he pointed to the canister.

"Da, it is," replied Alexi who then gave the description of the operation of the shuttle facility. "About sixty years ago a science fiction writer named Robert Heinlein described a mechanism for launching vehicles from the surface of the moon. The escape velocity for the moon is not very great and there is no air to provide drag to be overcome. What you are looking at is a giant rail gun. When we are ready to go, the shuttle pilot will activate electromagnets that levitate the canister above the rails. The launch operator will then seal the launch tube and pump all the air out. Then he will open the doors at the far end of the cave. With a salute and a wave of the hand from the pilot, he will activate the rail gun mechanism.

"We'll be shot electromagnetically down the rail up the ramp at the far end and into a trajectory that will carry us out to the ship. The initial acceleration is pretty intense, but it's very brief. After that we'll coast until we get close to the ship and nearly stop relative to it. At that point, the pilot will maneuver the capsule and dock us at one of the two airlocks on the ship."

"Don't let it worry you, my friend. Everybody who works on or in the ship gets to it exactly the same way and so far there've been no problems."

Alexi led the way to the shuttle and to a smaller individual in an obviously specially tailored space suit. By this time Ian was no longer surprised to find that the pilot was a woman. Alexi explained, "Almost all of our shuttle pilots are either women or men the size of jockeys. It reduces the weight or mass for the launch, and they all have excellent reflexes." Then he switched to a more general radio frequency and introduced Ian to the pilot. "Captain, may I introduce you to Miriam Steinmetz. She will be our pilot today."

"It's a pleasure to meet you, Captain," Miriam said. "If you would like to look things over before we go, be my guest. Because, relative to Farside Base and the launch facility, the position of the *Explorer* is almost stationary. So, we don't need to worry about the launch window. May I show you around?"

"Would you please," Ian replied with a smile. "What happened to Rachael?"

"Rachael is my sister and she's flying the other shuttle today out to Circum-Lunar Space Station."

Miriam and the launch manager gave Ian a complete tour of the launch facility or at least to the business end of it. When they were finished, Ian was asked to step onto a scale.

"Every time we launch, we have to compute the mass of everything and everybody in the vehicle. The launch manager will use that data to determine the amount of power required to propel us down the rail gun at the proper speed to get out to the ship. This launch facility is also used to launch shuttles into lunar orbit to match up with the Circum-Lunar Space Station. They just change the rails at the exit end much like switching the points in a rail yard on Earth."

"Rachael's shuttle is that red one over there. She'll launch after we exit. Are you ready, sir?" Miriam asked.

"Lead the way, Madam," Ian said, sweeping with his hand towards the canister and bowing from the waist as best he could while wearing a space suit.

"Thank you, sir, follow me!" Miriam said in the spirit of Ian's formality. She led the way to the capsule. "We do the launch with all aboard standing up with their backs against a padded shelf, or bunk, if you prefer. Of course, we have restraining straps to keep you from rattling around inside the capsule once we're in freefall."

Miriam and the two men entered the capsule. She strapped Ian and Alexi to the padded shelves and made sure that everything was tight. Several crates (or more properly containers) were loaded next and strapped firmly to the deck. Miriam took her place on the pilot's pad and asked, "Is everyone ready?"

She waited a few seconds to see if there would be any replies then flipped a switch on the instrument panel. The capsule lifted up from the rails levitating on its magnetic field. She waved and saluted the launch manager through the window much the same way a pilot on an aircraft carrier does prior to being catapulted into flight.

Ian could see through the windows in the front of the capsule. The doors at the far end of the launch facility opened. The canister began moving slowly at first. Then with increasing acceleration until it felt like about two gravities. Within seconds they exited the far end of the launch facility and went up a steep ramp that gradually became close to vertical. When they left the ramp, the acceleration ceased.

Ian waited a few moments as he thought about how things worked and then asked, "At this speed won't we just go on past the ship?" He knew he had put his foot in it when he heard Miriam chuckle.

"That is the most common question we are asked, Captain," she replied. "We're in the gravitational well of the moon. We're actually decelerating right now as the moon's mass tries to pull us back to the surface. Our exit speed is computed to about three decimal places so that by the time we reach the ship we will be almost at a dead stop relative to it and about 100 meters away. Small maneuvering thrusters are about all we require to take us over to the ship and mate up with the airlock."

"Sorry, it's been a long time since I took elementary physics and I guess I missed that one altogether. If you could see me I'm sure you would notice that my face is quite red with embarrassment," Ian replied and then continued, "I'm sure my next question is equally sophomoric, but I have to ask, what keeps us and the ship, etc. from falling back to the moon's surface?"

"Not to worry, Captain. You are neither the first nor will you be the last to ask that question either. Many scientists have asked the same question. The ship is in a neutral gravity field known as the L2 LaGrange point. It's an area in space where the gravity of the Earth and the moon exactly cancel out. The ship orbits slowly around that point. We will too when we get there. After I drop you off and unload, I will fire some small retro thrusters, which will drop me out of the L2 point and put me back into the gravity field of the moon and accelerate me into a descending spiral back to the surface of the moon. I will fire the retro thrusters again to land, which should leave me within walking distance of the launch facility."

"Amazing."

During this interchange, Alexi was quietly chuckling to himself. "Don't worry, my friend, I walked into exactly the same trap."

"See that bright star, Captain?" Miriam asked. "That is the ship, the *Barsoom Explorer*. It doesn't look like much from here but as we get closer you'll be able to see the whole thing. What is really amazing is that every piece of that ship, every nut, bolt, girder, hull plate, and everything else was brought up here exactly the same way. There is a larger launch facility near where we took off that provides for the heavy lifting. It's capable of launching massive loads up to the ship. They go up with only a pilot aboard. I've lost track of the number of trips I've made, but I never cease to be amazed."

As she spoke, the star that was the ship got brighter and bigger until it really looked like a ship. Their approach speed dropped gradually until they were barely moving relative to the *Explorer*. The closer they were the more of the structure became visible. It was not at all what he expected a spaceship to look like. He had seen pictures when they were in training, but they were small and lacked detail. What he saw now he saw with a clarity that defied description. He was expecting to see something more like a naval ship, but this was mostly a web of girders holding three separate parts of the ship together. Now, he understood the drawings that he had seen and that had been described during the training session. One end was the control and living pod. The middle was a rugby-ball-shaped tank that would hold the reaction mass. At the other end were the two reactors and the rocket nozzles that would provide the thrust to propel them to Mars.

The ship continued to grow in size until only the front could be seen as the Moon's gravity slowed the canister. By the time they were near the ship, they were barely moving.

"All right, gentlemen, I am now going to fire the steering thrusters and maneuver us over to the ship. I tell you this so you won't be surprised at the noise they make. They're attached to the hull of our capsule. You will feel them firing through your feet," Miriam alerted them.

The steering thrusters were not actually very noisy, but some vibration could be felt inside the capsule through contact with the capsule's hull. It took Miriam nearly five minutes to maneuver the capsule's airlock to mate with the airlock of the ship. There was a jolt as the magnetic docking locks engaged. Miriam unstrapped and pushed herself weightlessly to the capsule's airlock. She checked to insure everything was properly engaged before opening the capsule's airlock door. She did the same thing at the *Explorer*'s airlock. She then opened it as well and air filled the capsule. Then Ian and Alexi were unstrapped and guided through the airlocks into the interior of the *Explorer*.

This was the first time Ian actually understood the feeling of being weightless in freefall. He floated into a large room that was clearly the ship's storage deck. There were numerous cartons and containers clipped to the walls and deck. He felt rather helpless as he drifted slowly towards the overhead. He saw handgrips and reached out his hand to grasp one. He nearly missed it. When he extended his arm quickly toward the handhold, his body began to rotate in the opposite direction. Once he was stabilized, he turned to push off back towards the airlock when he heard Alexi shout.

"Ian, don't! Until you get the hang of moving around in a large weightless environment you have to go very slowly. Every motion has to be as gentle as possible. If you had pushed off as you were preparing to, you would've shot across the room and hit the wall on the other side. It is not as easy as it seems. After we get everything stowed, you can practice," Alexi instructed.

"Watch out, gentlemen," Marion said as she steered a bulky container through the airlocks into the storage area and guided it slowly to rest at an anchor point on the bulkhead. "Captain, it would probably be best if you just continued to hang on to that hand grip until we're finished. I have several more containers to transfer. Commander, if you can help, I would appreciate it. Then you can button everything up and I will be on my way back to the surface. But, as before, I won't leave until you have pumped the air out of the capsule as a safety precaution."

Alexi helped Miriam maneuver the other containers from the capsule into the storage area where they were secured. He did it with an expertise that showed he had learned how to maneuver in a weightless environment while working in the ship. When all the containers were properly locked down, Miriam waved to Ian and returned to her capsule. Alexi closed the *Explorer*'s airlock and secured it. After checking to ensure that the pressure was steady, he told Miriam to unlock, and after she did, he checked again to make sure the pressure was steady before releasing her to return to the surface.

Alexi removed his helmet and attached it to a clip near the airlock, launched himself toward Ian and helped him remove his helmet. "Hang on to me," he said. Then, taking a firm grip on Ian he pushed off gently and launched them toward some lockers near the area of the airlock where space suits were stored. After removing his own space suit Alexi helped Ian remove his.

Alexi said, "Captain, I know you're anxious to tour the ship, but until you become accustomed to maneuvering in a weightless environment I think it best if you just worked at that. Ask me how I know that," Alexi said with a smile.

"Where's the scientist, Dr. Burns, isn't it?" Ian asked.

"You will meet her shortly. She's in the next deck up or forward through that hatch over there in the middle of the upper deck. Her hatch is sealed now so the air inside stays inside when the storage deck is in a vacuum. The only way we can get to the command and living decks is through her garden."

Meeting Dr. Burns was a very pleasant surprise. She was working on the hydroponic water and fertilizer system when they entered the "Farm" deck. She was upside down relative to Ian and Alexi, so all they could see was her legs.

"Dr. Burns, could you come out of there please to meet the captain?" Alexi said.

There was a definite clunk as she backed out of where she was, it was followed by some polite cursing in Spanish. When she came into view, she pulled herself hand over hand along the hydroponic tanks and stopped right side up in front of the two men. "Good morning? I'm sorry, Captain. Is it morning? I lose track of time in here. I've been alone except for Ferd for days maybe even weeks."

"I suppose it could be difficult to keep track when you're all alone, Dr. Burns," Ian said. "Who's Ferd?"

"Ferd is my pet ferret, Captain, and please call me Jammy, everyone else does. I take him with me everywhere. I asked if it would be okay before I brought him up to the ship and there were no objections, but I was warned that he might not take to weightlessness and could get ill. Is it okay, sir?"

"I don't see why not. I gather he did not get ill," Ian said. "I see his cage, where is he?"

"Oh, he's around somewhere. He loves weightlessness and acts like a flying squirrel in here. He likes people… or most people. I put him in his cage at night to keep him out of trouble. I'll call him. It's time for him to eat anyway. Ferd!" she said followed by a high-pitched clicking sound. "*Click, click,* dinnertime."

As soon as she called, Ferd hopped up and perched on a planter on the far side of the room. Then he launched himself towards Jammy and flew across the room squirming in midair to turn himself around to land in her arms.

"Ferd, meet the captain," Jammy said.

"Pleased to meet you," Ian said as he reached over to scratch the ferret on the head. A treatment that the ferret obviously enjoyed based on the low sounds he made as Ian scratched him. Ferd made a short jump from Jammy to Ian and, perching on his arm, looked him in the eye. After a long moment, Ferd rubbed his head on Ian's cheek.

"You have been approved, Captain," Dr. Burns said as she retrieved Ferd and put him in his cage.

"Thanks, Jammy. Later, after I get settled, could you show me around your farm and explain how things work? I've heard of hydroponics farms, but have never seen one in operation. You have the tanks everywhere on the deck, the walls, and the overhead."

After dinner, Jammy showed Ian how the farm worked. She showed him the plants and identified them for him. Ian was concerned about the hydroponic fluid getting out of the beds when they were weightless.

"That's not a problem, Captain," Jammy explained. "The medium in which the plants are growing is only moistened and it was specially fabricated for the 'farm' so that it would not leak no matter what position it was in. The tanks are suspended in their racks. Each tank has its own lights, so it does not matter much what position they're in. The tanks are suspended in the frames so that when the ship was under acceleration the tanks would swing to an upright position relative to the aft deck." Then she briefly explained how the controls worked.

"That's it, Captain. We have a little more than half an acre of tanks. It's not enough to feed everyone, but it's enough to provide fresh vegetables, especially greens on a regular basis and the occasional flower for the dinner table," Jammy concluded.

"Thank you, Dr. Burns. You have an amazing operation here," Ian said. "I would like to learn more about it later."

"You are welcome any time, Captain."

CHAPTER SIX

Two days later, Ian felt confident that he could navigate inside the ship without banging into things too often. He had learned to swim through the air, twist his body around, and to anticipate the reaction whenever he moved one of his limbs too quickly. He had been through the entire command and crew module, visited every room, every accommodation, the command deck, the dining room also known as the Common Room, and the sleeping quarters. The storage deck and the hydroponic farm were fairly easy because there were handholds everywhere. He had yet to investigate the cooking equipment and the electronics equipment.

When he awoke on the third day, it was to the smell of bacon and coffee. He was still learning how to eat from a covered tray so the food wouldn't wander away. He could drink from what he thought of as a squeezable baby cup with a trigger that opened the spout. Because the ship was in a gravity-free condition all eating and drinking had to be done under cover and under pressure. The coffee maker forced water through a small combination of a coffee grounds container with a filter into the cup. To drink the coffee or any other liquid for that matter you had to put the spout of the cup in your mouth, press a valve button on the opposite side of the cup and suck the liquid into your mouth slowly—especially slowly for hot coffee.

If you failed to do it in exactly that order, the liquid in the cup could come spouting out into the air. If the liquid got loose, it was a mess to clean up because you had to chase down every drop and blot it out of the air with a towel. He was learning that eating and drinking in a freefall, weightless environment was a pain in the neck. He had learned how to deal with the intricacies of using the head on a submarine. The head on the *Explorer*, which was called a "fresher" for some damned reason, was nearly impossible to use without making a mess. This had all been covered in the training program. But listening to a lecture and watching a movie and later applying what was taught were definitely two drastically different things.

Ian swam from the captain's cabin into the common area following the good aromas. A few moments later Alexi came into the common area from the fresher. "Good morning, Captain. Did you sleep well, sir?" Alexi asked with a grin.

"Fairly well, thanks," Ian responded grumpily. "Waking up tangled in a net and trying to get out of bed by finding the seam with hook and loop fasteners is a nightmare. I hope I never have to do it in a big hurry."

"In another week or so you'll wonder how you ever slept without it. Did you wake up with a backache or a stiff neck?" Alexi asked.

"No, no other aches or pains except for the ones that I've received while bouncing around the inside of this tin can. The only real problem I have with the net is it makes my preferred sleep position nearly impossible. Like everything else, I'll get used to it eventually and as you suggest I'll wonder how I ever got along without it. Anyway, thanks for fixing breakfast. Let's eat," Ian replied. Followed by, "Where's Jammy?"

"She's a farmer and they get up early to tend the farm. She ate over an hour ago."

When they had finished eating, Alexi took his Book from the book rack and handed Ian an empty one. "Let's get to it. What do you say?" Alexi asked. "Do you want to start with the reactor or the navigation deck?"

"We haven't been back in the reactor area. Do you think I'm ready to make the trip without breaking anything important on either me or the ship?" Ian asked. Alexi nodded assent.

"Okay, let's start at the back and work towards the front because that's where the action is."

"Follow me," Alexi said. He led the way through the maze of the farm where they waved at Jammy. In the center of the farm, there was an open area with a hatch leading to the storage compartment. Another hatch in the aft deck of the storage area led to a tunnel that ran from the storage area, through the reaction mass tanks aft to the reactor room.

Alexi turned on the lights in the tunnel and said, "Notice, Captain, there are handholds every few feet and all around the tunnel. All you have to do to get to the reactors rooms is pull yourself hand over hand through the tunnel."

It was actually an exhilarating experience similar to swimming but requiring a lot less effort. The tunnel was 75 meters long and 5 meters in diameter. As they traveled down the tunnel Ian noticed several hatches in the sides of the tunnel. "This is fine when we're in freefall, but what do you do when we're under power? It's a long way down to there and if you missed your grip, falling even under low G over 225 feet from the storage area to the reactor deck would kill you, wouldn't it?"

"Yes, it would undoubtedly kill anyone who fell," Alexi replied, then, "Look over there, Captain." Alexi pointed to a square object apparently attached to the tunnel wall. "That is a seat attached to a rail and a cable that runs from here up to the storage area. When we are under acceleration, travel from here up to the storage area is via a one-person elevator. Note also that there are six of these cabinets. The lifts operate in pairs like a ski lift. When one goes up or forward its partner comes down or aft. The lights on the cabinet indicate the state of each seat.

"Green means the seat is here, ready to go to the other end of the tunnel. Red means the seat is parked at the other end of the tunnel and yellow means it is in transit. There are always three seats available at each end or in transit. The speed can be regulated with an override in the event of an emergency. It is not perfect, but it will work."

"What are all those hatches in the tunnel walls?" Ian asked.

"Some of those hatches lead to other storage areas and others provide access to the reaction mass tank. We will investigate those as we work our way forward from the reactor room," Alexi replied. "I had the same questions the first time I came out to the ship. I didn't come up to the ship until it was time to install the reactors, so I didn't have a chance to see how it was built and where things were.

"Of course, I got the same outside view you did when I came up on the shuttle, but as you know, things look much different from the inside than they do from the outside. From the outside, the big rugby-ball-shaped thing is our reaction mass tank or rather tanks, there are four bladders inside the external tank walls. The tunnel goes through the center of the tank. Each of the four reaction mass bladders will hold approximately one million cubic feet of water which works out to about 62.5 million pounds of water per bladder give or take a million or two. That will give us enough reaction mass to go from here to Mars and back with a comfortable reserve."

"I knew it was big from the orientation lectures but had no idea how big at least not in the terms as you explain it. I remember them saying something about it in training, translating that into a huge volume, I just never thought about it," Ian explained, then asked, "How do you keep the water from either freezing or boiling?"

"We continuously circulate heated nitrogen inside the tank when necessary. When we can, we heat the nitrogen using sunlight. Once we are underway, we will heat it using the reactor. Now, this," Alexi continued, pointing to the hatch in the center of the tunnel aft bulkhead, "leads to the reactors. Just a minute while I do a safety check to see if the radiation levels are okay. They have been every time I've checked it, but it's a very good habit to get into to, checking for radiation before you enter a reactor room," Alexi explained as he checked. "The fission reactor is a design that is fail-safe. There is no chance of a runaway reaction. It is much safer than anything we had on the submarines. This one shuts down automatically if there should be a problem. The fusion reactor that actually runs the propulsion system only works when the fission reactor is running."

With that, Alexi opened the hatch and led the way into the reactor rooms.

Ian's immediate reaction was, they did not look like any of the reactors on the nuclear submarines he had commanded. The reactor room was open, four spiral staircases mounted against the outer walls led from the fission reactor on the upper deck to the fusion reactor on the lower deck. The reactors were big but lacked many of the external controls that he was familiar with.

"Get your Book, and follow me. We are going to trace every pipe valve and wire in this room. To be safe, I came back here last night while you were sleeping to check and make sure there was nothing to be concerned about," Alexi said.

They spent the next six hours crawling all over the reactor room and documenting everything that could be seen or felt. Ian noted every item in his Book along with an explanation of what it was, how it was used, what it was connected to, and where it was with respect to everything else. He knew this was the first of many times he would have to do the same thing before he could find everything in the dark with alarm bells ringing, as was necessary on a submarine. When they finished, they returned to the common area to have a late lunch and discuss what Ian had seen.

"It all looks so simple compared to the submarine power plants," Ian said.

"It has to be," Alexi said. "It has to operate automatically under some very difficult conditions. We have our own computer systems in the power area so we do not have to rely on communication with the Command Deck. Also, we don't have space on the *Explorer* for a large power crew. There will only be me and my assistant to run the whole thing."

. . .

For the next two weeks, Ian spent every waking moment crawling around inside the ship. Alexi told him that eventually they would be required to put on space suits and venture outside as well. While they were searching, they failed to find anything that had the appearance of a possible sabotage attempt. Alexi showed him several disarmed devices that were left in position in hopes that they would eventually be able to catch any saboteurs.

"I've not shown you all of the sabotage devices that we have found in and on the ship yet. Those that we were unable to disarm or were concerned about were removed and destroyed outside the ship or shot off to do their thing somewhere in the cosmos. On the next pass for the Book, we will open up every electronics cabinet, every equipment cabinet, every removable inspection plate, and everything else that is sealed closed. This should take us a month at least. We do this both for the Book and to look for any problems," Alexi said. "Miriam is due up today, how would you like to take a ride down to the surface and relax a little?"

"I wondered what happened to her. It's been over two weeks and we haven't seen her or anyone else," Ian said.

"You are sleeping better in that net hammock than you think you are. Miriam has been up here three times in the last two weeks ferrying reaction mass for the water tanks. She comes during our sleep cycle so she won't bother us. Today, she's just bringing supplies and stopping in to see how we're doing. So, I ask again, would you like to ride down to the surface to cut up a little or whatever before we start the next round?" Alexi asked.

"Sure, why not? It sounds like a good idea. I could use a drink besides that, maybe I can have coffee that I can drink out of a real cup instead of sucking on a nipple. When is she due? Should we invite Jammy?" Ian asked.

"In about three hours," Alexi said. "Don't bother getting cleaned up. We'll do that down at Farside Base in a real honest-to-goodness shower with lots of hot water and soap and not have to worry about soapy water drifting out into another room. That alone is worth the trip," Alexi observed, smiling. "I did ask Jammy, but she decided to stay on the ship and tend her garden."

Three hours later Ian heard and felt a clunk as Miriam's capsule locked on to the airlock. Alexi went to cycle the airlock so that Miriam could enter without releasing any air. "Good afternoon, gentlemen, your friendly bus driver is here with supplies and is offering you a ride back to good old Luna Firma. Cocktail hour starts in about two hours. We don't have much besides vodka simply because it's the easiest to distill from the materials on hand. It doesn't pay to have a bottle of scotch shipped up from Earth. Even cheap stuff would cost several hundred dollars for a pint bottle. But before we leave would you mind suiting up and scavenging the air in the ship, and helping me unload some supplies?" Miriam asked.

Both men donned their space suits, buttoned up, hung their oxygen packs on their backs, and checked to make sure everything was working correctly. Alexi initiated the scavenging program that pumped all the air in the cargo compartment back into storage tanks.

"I picked this stuff up hot off the truck. We didn't get a chance to clear it before I took off. We better do that as we unload it," Miriam said.

There were four cargo containers to be moved from the capsule into the ship and stowed. As each one was brought into the cargo area, it was thoroughly checked outside and then a fiber-optic camera was inserted through a small port between the hinges to look at the inside. The first two were perfect, no problems. They were stored and locked down. When Miriam pushed the third container through the airlock into the ship, Alexi reacted immediately. He checked all over the outside, inspected the seals, and checked the container number against the number on the manifest. That is what caught his attention.

He had checked the manifest before they started to unload and automatically noticed the shipping numbers of the containers. The third container had a shipping number, which did not quite match the manifest. Two digits in the shipping number had been transposed, which was not an uncommon problem. But that was enough to catch his attention. When he took the container from Miriam and started to move it, he immediately knew that something was wrong.

"This container isn't balanced correctly," Alexi explained to Ian and Miriam. "The cargo guys always balance everything so that they can be stowed in any order without any concern for inertial imbalance while handling in freefall."

"The guys on the truck loaded these for us. It was the same guys who always do it and we had no reason to believe there would be anything wrong," Miriam said. "What do you want to do with it?"

Miriam and Alexi went over the container inch by inch looking for any problems. It appeared to be exactly what it was supposed to be.

Alexi asked, "What was the mass of this container as stated on the manifest?"

Miriam checked the manifest and said, "Five hundred kilos, like all the rest."

"Did that seem a little out of balance when you moved it?" Alexi asked.

"I didn't notice it, but you may be right," Miriam replied.

"I'll scope the inside and see what I can see," Alexi said as he began to insert the scope into the access hole. He stopped immediately. "I can see a very thin wire or thread across the inspection hole so I am not going to go all the way inside with the scope. What do you suggest? He asked Miriam.

"I think we'd better dump it, Captain," Miriam replied. "It's the only safe thing to do."

"I agree," Ian said. "There might be a timer as well as a mechanical trigger. The sooner we get rid of it the better. And, if we shove 500 kilos of peanut butter out into the cosmos I doubt that anyone will blame us for being overly cautious. Can we just push it out of *Explorer*'s airlock after you move the shuttle?"

"We could," Miriam replied. "But I doubt we can give it enough of a shove to have it go very far away from the ship. We really need to get it outside the effect of the LaGrange point, build up enough speed to send it on its way on a vector away from the ship to be safe, and to do that we need the shuttle. Let's unload the fourth one, check it, and get it stowed. Then we'll reload this one into the capsule, and once we're several hundred kilometers away from the *Explorer* we'll open the capsule airlock and shove it out. Does that sound reasonable?"

"All but the part about hauling it back out there," Alexi interjected. "I'm not too keen on putting it back in the shuttle and riding with it. What do you think, Captain?"

"I don't like it any more than you do, but I don't see any alternative. So, let's get it reloaded and get out of here."

Miriam computed and filed a new approach program that would allow them to deviate from the standard approach pattern and advised Security of the possibility of an explosion. Then explained, "I will fire the retros briefly which will give us enough velocity and distance away from the ship to be safe after about ten minutes. Ready, gentlemen?"

"Ready," Ian and Alexi announced in chorus.

Ten minutes later, they opened the airlock and gave the container a strong push away from the capsule and the ship. They did not wait to see what might happen. They closed and latched the airlock, then strapped in.

"Ready, Miriam?" Ian asked.

"Ready, Captain," Miriam replied. Then fired the retros to return them to the surface. "This approach," she explained, "is going to require a long slow orbit of the moon as we spiral down into a normal pattern approach after which we can begin our final descent."

Mike the rollagon driver greeted them at the landing area. "Good afternoon, ladies and gentlemen. Would you like a ride to the main facility?"

"Hi, Mike," Ian replied, then added jokingly, "A ride would be most appreciated. After three weeks of drifting around inside the ship, it's great just to be able to walk even in lunar gravity."

"Captain, Security just radioed that they observed an explosion near where we dumped the container," Miriam announced.

"Have they found the driver and his helper so we can find out why they did it?" Ian asked.

Miriam spoke briefly to the Security office and then said, "Yes, sir, they found them. They were dumped outside an airlock, both dead."

"Thanks, Miriam." Ian said.

"Miriam, would you like to join us for refreshments and dinner?" Alexi asked.

"I would be delighted, gentlemen. Would it be okay to include Rachael, if she's available, to make it a foursome?"

"Absolutely, bring her along," Alexi replied after receiving a nod from Ian. "Why don't you meet us at the Bon Ton Bar and Grill in, say, two hours so we have time to get cleaned up and presentable."

When Miriam and Rachael arrived at the Bon Ton, Ian rose to greet them. "Hello, Rachael, it has been a while since we saw you last."

"You just saw her less than a month ago on the rollagon, Captain."

"Yes, I did, but did I tell you that Rachael escorted me from Perth to Tel Aviv?" Ian asked.

"No." Alexi turned to Rachael with a raised eyebrow.

"ICExS wanted to make sure the captain would not be exposed at the airport or on the plane. My job was to act as a spotter and to distract anyone who might be interested in him, I did not see anyone who looked interested in the captain. I had to maintain my persona as a tourist even though we are sure that the Cartel knows who I am. So I bored him with a travelog of Jerusalem. Later, as I was pretending to read a book, I passed on the instructions on what he was supposed to do when he arrived in Zürich. Meanwhile, I deplaned in Tel Aviv and led my spotter on a merry chase to Jerusalem."

They chatted over drinks consisting of vodka and carbonated water with a twist of lemon rind for flavor. Then Ian asked, "Are you two ladies related? Wait, didn't Miriam say that you were sisters? I notice a certain similarity in your accents."

Rachael answered, "We are adoptive sisters, Captain. Our parents were all doctors working at the same hospital. They were best friends and so were we. The parents all went on holiday to the beaches. We were six years old, so they left us with another couple who were also doctors at the same hospital. One evening while they were having dinner, a Hamas suicide bomber blew himself up in front of the café killing our parents and a lot of other diners.

"The couple we stayed with were close friends to both our parents. They had no children of their own so they adopted and raised us essentially as sisters."

"How fascinating and, of course, kind of them," Ian said.

· · ·

The next morning, Ian and Alexi both slightly hungover reported to Chris Craft's office to make their reports and be brought up-to-date on the status of the project. Security had already advised the director of the sabotage attempt and of finding the bodies of the two drivers.

"How did you discover the bomb?" the director asked.

Alexi reached across the desk to pick up a tablet and pencil. He wrote on the tablet, 'is your office bugged?'

The director took the pad from Alexi, and wrote "it was checked two days ago." Alexi nodded, and asked, "Director, have you had breakfast yet?"

"Yes, but I could do with a coffee and doughnut. I know just the place."

The three men left the director's office. He led them on a winding trek through the facility until they arrived at a small coffee bar in the foundry. The noise level in the foundry was fairly high, so they could talk safely there without risk of being overheard.

Again the director asked, "How did you discover the bomb?"

"There were a couple of things that were off," Alexi began. "When we were moving the container from the shuttle to the *Explorer* it felt slightly out of balance, which was unusual. When you have moved as many containers as I have in a weightless environment, you can actually tell when one is a little off. The guys that pack the containers are very careful to make sure the containers are balanced. Then, I asked Miriam to check the manifest against the shipping number on the container and we found that two digits had been transposed between the manifest and the container. Once we found that, I recalled Miriam mentioning that the shipment was delivered late to the launch facility, which happens occasionally for a variety of reasons. She also told us that the driver offered to check the container numbers against the manifest while his helper loaded the containers into the capsule so she could do her preflight checklist. No one suspected any trouble."

The director shook his head in amazement. "Every time something like this happens we have to rewrite the procedures to prevent a recurrence. Security has already taken steps to ensure all deliveries will be opened, weighed, balanced and inspected when they are packed, when they are loaded onto the truck and again when they are unloaded onto the loading dock. Only after Security is sure there are no discrepancies with the containers will they be sealed and loaded into the capsule for the trip up to the *Explorer*. It will add a complication to the process, a necessary one. The capsule pilots have been thoroughly vetted and we are absolutely certain they would never be part of the problem, agreed?"

Ian and Alexi both nodded agreement.

"With that settled, we need to change the subject to a discussion of the people who are being considered for selection for both crew and as the scientific team for the *Explorer*. The biggest problem is finding people with the right combinations of skills and ability in order to minimize the number of personnel required for efficient operation of the ship.

"Selection of the scientific team is highly politicized with all of the countries that have contributed to the project, demanding that one of their scientists be included on the team. This is not too surprising, but it does create a major problem considering the total complement is only going to be twelve people."

"Why twelve?" Ian asked. "There are accommodations for twenty."

"We simply can't pack in enough supplies for more than twelve," the director replied. "Six are required at a minimum to operate the ship which leaves only six slots for scientists. Of course, the contributing countries want to politicize the crew selection as well but ICExS was not about to let that happen. The crew has to be selected to fill the need with as few bodies as possible.

"I did not tell you before, but the names of the scientists being considered were leaked by two members of the board. Within days everyone on the list had been contacted directly or indirectly by one or more religious organizations or Cartel operatives. Families were threatened, or their employers, mostly colleges, universities, or research organizations were encouraged, shall we say, under penalty of losing grants, or funding for their research. Some were even encouraged to take the position and once aboard or underway to disable the ship or somehow sabotage the mission. We know this because many contacted ICExS declining the offers and some voluntarily reported what had been done to them. Also, several of the names on the list were our people.

"They were offered everything from bribes to threats. They were expected of course to give up their own lives in the interest of whatever religion they either subscribe to or which was trying to subvert them. Some of the propositions that our ringers reported were unbelievable. Some were offered billions of dollars if they would sabotage the mission. Two of our people under instruction from us asked what they could possibly do with billions of dollars if they were aboard the sabotaged ship. In one case a person trying to subvert them just looked at him incredulously. It was as if the person who made the offer had never thought it through. In a fast recovery, they said, 'you can leave it to your heirs.' Another of our people was given the 'we know where you live' threat, which was not true because the person we sent was an orphan and had no family to threaten. For just this reason, many of the people in the organization have no family connections.

"We've had every perspective scientist under surveillance continuously from the time the names were announced until now. We know that several of them just told the people trying to bribe or threaten them to go to hell. This resulted in a lengthy lecture of how the scientist was going to hell if he or she did not do everything possible to prevent the expedition from being successful. We knew there would be problems, but we had no idea the lengths some religious leaders would go to stop the expedition. We're fairly certain that no matter who we choose, at least one and perhaps as many as two or three will have been contacted and may have been made offers they couldn't refuse. Note, I said *couldn't*, not *wouldn't*. The one exception was Dr. Jamilah Burns who contacted us very early on because of her work in desert ecology and in hydroponic gardening. She worked with the ship's designers to design and set up the onboard garden. She has been on board for many months.

"We made up a new list of scientists who will be contacted within hours of being whisked away to the training facility if they accept. All of the people on the new list either have no families or should be able to ignore any threats. But we expect some problems there too, because some of them will have almost certainly heard about what happened to their colleagues or friends and want to opt out.

"As for the crew, we have much more leeway in terms of what we can do to select them. We can choose people who are totally dedicated to the success of the expedition. We know neither of you were approached. Alexi has been on board for almost a year and a half, and I would hate to see what would happen to the person who threatened to destroy his reactor. Ian, your name was never released. The question presented to your Navy was if they would release you as an advisor only. As far as they know, that is your sole role in the project. You were followed from the moment you got your orders until you joined us at ICExS headquarters in Zürich. But you are not the only two we need.

"We need two pilots who will alternate as duty pilots during the expedition. Both of them will be shuttle pilots for flying from the *Explorer* down to the surface of Mars and back up once we are there.

"Alexi, you are going to need an assistant engineer because you can't be on duty 24/7. For the most part, things are automated, but there must be an engineer on duty at all times.

"We need a navigator or astrogator in order to keep the ship on course. That person needs to be able to recompute orbits in the event there is a need to change something while you're in transit.

"We need a communications operator who can double as an electronic specialist to operate and maintain the communications and computing equipment on board.

"We need a person to operate and control the magnetosphere that surrounds the ship to block out harmful solar radiation. That also is a job that could use a second person because, while the controls for the magnetosphere are automatic, they must be manned at all times because a failure even for a short period of time could be fatal to all aboard."

"We will need a machinist of some sort who is adept at fixing things. We wondered if we might need a master-at-arms to maintain order. But with such a small complement, it doesn't make good sense. We'll also need a doctor or physician or medic who can attend to the typical kinds of problems that might occur among twelve people over a long period of time. We have even entertained the idea of a psychologist or psychiatrist all things considered.

"If I counted correctly, I listed thirteen crew jobs that have to be filled one way or another by six people. If necessary we can add a seventh crew member and eliminate one of the scientific jobs," the director said.

"Excuse me, Director, if I counted correctly when we were doing the preliminary Book walkthrough, there are twenty accommodation berths. What are the other eight for?" Ian asked.

"I would appreciate it if you would keep that under your hat. I will explain that in due course. I'm sorry I can't go into more detail at this time," the director stated forcefully.

"Yes, sir," Ian replied. Then he asked, "How thoroughly have the personnel here at Farside Base been vetted?"

"What happened yesterday should provide part of your answer, Captain. But that is not the whole story. When the project began over five years ago, we had no idea how much of an uproar it would cause. We wanted to do a scientific expedition to a neighboring planet in search of life. What we have done is create a religious-political movement of unimaginable proportions. All of the people wearing the Ring are as reliable as it is possible to be, the exceptions being the two board members who leaked the list of scientists. Was there a reason you asked, Captain?" the director asked.

"Yes, sir, if we are looking for shuttle pilots, what's the matter with Miriam and Rachael? We had dinner with them last night and had plenty of opportunities to discuss what we liked and didn't like, what we had done with our lives, and what we would like to do. From what I gather they are the two best shuttle pilots you have and you'll not need them once we are underway. They carry most of the burden. They told us there were other shuttle pilots who ferried workers and material up and down from the surface to the *Explorer*. But the two of them are the only ones who were allowed to make deliveries of people and supplies going inside the ship.

"In addition, were you aware that Rachael is a licensed physician's assistant? Miriam has a master's degree in mathematics. I know that for naval ship navigators, the Navy used to assign people with experience in mathematics specifically in higher mathematics. Of course, now with the navigation satellites the navigator pretty much only chooses where and when, and then follows a line on the map. I imagine navigating a spaceship is not quite that simple.

"Would you consider Miriam and Rachael as two candidates for the crew? As ex-military officers in the Israeli Air Force, I can pretty much assure you that they know how to take care of themselves. We could fill four of the crew positions just from those two women alone. They are both also wearing the ring," Ian said.

"Did they put you up to this, Captain?" the director asked.

"Certainly not, Director. Do you think so, Alexi?" Ian asked.

"Perhaps, but I doubt it. We were just four people talking about life over drinks and dinner. I must admit, though, Miriam was still sort of shaken up by the bomb," Alexi offered. "Why do you ask, Director?"

"Because they are on our short list for the crew for the very reasons you gave. But as far as I know, they were not aware of that. That list is kept more secretly than the combination to the liquor locker," the director responded with a smile. "I doubt we'll find anybody more experienced as pilots and as shuttle pilots than those two. As you point out, they have several other desirable attributes as well. They were both orphaned by the Arab-Israeli war. They have been friends since they were children. They have no known living relatives. And, they are unmarried and as far as I know, have no known love interests at the moment.

"I know you intended for all crew members to do the Book. But we cannot spare them at the moment from their duties as shuttle pilots. However, we try to limit them to two flights per week each to prevent ill effects from the acceleration when they carry a big load. Let me think about how we might get around that problem. Using unknown shuttle pilots might put the expedition at risk. I'll get back to you on that," the director said. Then asked, "When do you two plan on going back up to the *Explorer*?"

"We were thinking of going back up tomorrow afternoon with Rachael. It will give us a chance to see how good a pilot she is," Alexi answered.

"Good. Let me know how you feel about it when you get a chance. Now, gentlemen, I must get back to my other administrative duties," the director said.

The next day, Ian and Alexi met Rachael at the launch facility and helped her go over the manifest by double-checking everything. After all the supplies and containers had been loaded into the capsule, Rachael buckled them in, and a few minutes later they were on their way back to the *Explorer*.

Once they reached the ship, Ian and Alexi began taking the ship apart piece by piece. They identified every piece, documented it in the Book and replaced it where it belonged. While they were doing so, they discovered thirteen sabotage attempts. Of the thirteen, twelve were known and accounted for and disabled. They had all been found by Alexi. He repeatedly checked the ship after every visit by someone delivering equipment from one of the shuttles not flown by either Miriam or Rachael. This time around, working with Ian, they found the thirteenth sabotage device wedged carefully behind one of the other twelve.

Since Alexi had carefully logged in and out every visitor, he was reasonably sure he knew who had put the thirteenth device in place. They reported the new sabotage attempt to Security and Alexi identified the individual that he thought had delivered and installed the latest piece of equipment and who would have had access to the area where the bomb was found.

Several hours later, Security notified them that the individual in question had resigned and returned to Earth shortly after the instrument had been installed. From that moment on whenever any worker who was not known to either of the men came up to install something, one of them stayed with the worker from the time of arrival until the time of departure regardless of how long it took. During this time there were no further attempts at sabotage.

In order to prevent someone boarding the ship in their absence, Ian requested and received a programmable digital lock for the airlock. He personally entered and set the code needed to open the airlock. This was more than a simple combination lock. Any time anyone even attempted to enter the ship the event would be recorded both on board the ship and to base Security. In addition to recording the day, date, and time, a video was taken of the person attempting to enter even if that person had the correct combination to preclude a forced entry. It would not be possible to take a picture of the face of the person attempting to enter because of the space helmet, but all space suits and helmets had a large number printed on the front and the back. It wasn't a perfect system, but it was really intended to be more of a deterrent than anything else. Whenever anyone attempted to gain entrance, or exit, through the airlock, the equivalent of a doorbell was rung. If the attempt was not successful, an alarm sounded.

Alexi repeatedly tested Ian at any time of the day or night with different kinds of emergencies that might possibly happen. He did this sometimes when the ship was completely dark inside. Ian returned the favor and it became a game as each tried to outfox the other. Sometimes even Jammy would enter into the game whenever the problem was in her area. By the time they were finished, Ian and Alexi could find any operational element of the ship in the dark and Jammy could find most of them. Over 100 LED flashlights were placed in easily accessible places anywhere they might be needed. They now felt ready to train the rest of the crew when they arrived.

At the end of two months, Miriam brought up a load of supplies, and the two men returned to Farside Base with her. Both Miriam and Rachael had visited the ship often to make deliveries and had frequently stayed for several hours and occasionally overnight observing the two men working on their Books. The entire process had been explained to both women and they understood the importance of having every crew member develop their own Book under the tutelage of someone who had already completed his or her Book.

The return trip from the *Explorer* to Farside Base was much more complicated than the trip up. The launch facility was fully automated and required that two other people besides the pilot enter the launch sequence prior to departure. The pilot was expected to compute his or her own launch sequence based on the total mass of the capsule and its contents. When done properly, the launch would go as it had when Ian first went up and deposited the capsule within a few hundred yards of the *Explorer*. Then the maneuvering rockets could position the capsule at the *Explorer*'s airlock. The trip down had to be coordinated with the landing facility to ensure that a landing pad would be available when the capsule arrived.

The pilot computed all of the navigational and operational elements including burn times and positional vectors. The landing facility would compute and transfer their recommended navigational and operational elements, but the pilot would be the one who entered the data into the capsule's control computer. If the recommended elements did not match what the pilot had computed, he or she could refuse to accept the data from the ground and could either request a recalculation or choose to ignore what had been given. Occasionally there are minor differences between the data from the ground and what the pilot computed. There'd only been one instance in which the data from the ground was incorrect but had been accepted by a lazy pilot whose capsule did not reach the landing facility. It crashed several kilometers away which resulted in a dead pilot and a destroyed capsule. It never happened again.

The director's assistant met them at the door to the facility. "Welcome back, gentlemen. The director sent me to invite you to lunch at 1230, which should give you adequate time to freshen up and change clothes."

"Thank you, Susan. Please inform the director we will be there within an hour," Alexi said and Ian nodded agreement.

"Greetings, Captain and Commander," the director said as they arrived promptly at 1230. "Please, come on in and have a seat. I ordered assorted sandwiches and salads."

"Thank you, sir," Alexi said. "That will be a welcome change from our freefall meals."

Ian asked, "Is it safe to talk here?"

"The office was swept for bugs just two hours ago, so we should be able to talk freely, Captain. What about this new sabotage attempt?"

"We gave the device to the Security boys as soon as we arrived," Ian said. "They did a quick check and told us it was not explosive. They're analyzing it now to see what it is. As soon as they figure it out, they'll tell us. Along that line, we are reasonably confident that there is at least one and maybe two more devices on board that we were unable to find."

They were later told the device was intended to broadcast intense electronic interference in order to disable the ship's instruments and controls and it was timed to activate at the turn over point presumably to disrupt things during a very critical maneuver.

The next topic of business was choosing and training the rest of the crew.

"It should be no surprise to you that both Miriam and Rachael have volunteered as pilots. They have been training on the ship simulator and on the Mars orbit-to-surface shuttle simulator and both have demonstrated competence to pilot either. Miriam has been studying and practicing astrogation. She has an advanced degree in mathematics as you know. She also has a degree in computer science and has practiced on the computer simulator as well but would happily give up that job if a more competent individual is found to take on those duties. She will be the primary pilot of the *Explorer* with Rachael as a backup. Because of her medical training, Rachael will be designated as the assistant medic. We have asked her to keep that to herself so that she can observe the actions of any doctor who might be appointed with the science team. In addition, she will be the primary shuttle pilot with Miriam as a backup. Since these two will be the only trained pilots, I think it would probably be a good idea to never let both be away from the ship at the same time."

"That is great news about Miriam and Rachael, Director, and I concur with your suggestion to never let them both be outside the ship at the same time," Ian said. "Now, how about the rest of the crew?"

"We talked about the possible need for a master-at-arms, but with two trained naval officers and two Israeli fighter pilots, the need for a master-at-arms was not considered essential. The choice of a sixth crew member is still undecided and might be eliminated in the interest of adding a seventh scientist," the director said.

"Keep trying, Director. Even though Miriam can act as an electronics specialist with respect to operations, we really need an experienced electronics expert in the event something needs to be repaired or replaced," Ian said.

"I see your point, Captain. You will also need someone to be responsible for the magnetosphere generator operation and repair. We will keep on looking as long as possible."

"We only have two and a half months until the optimum launch window opens," Ian said. "We need to have the full crew complement aboard as soon as possible so they can work on their Book. How soon will the final complement of scientists be selected?" Ian asked.

"I've been told they will be selected, trained, and be available within two to four weeks of launch time," the director replied.

"That's not soon enough for them to go through the full initiation process aboard the ship. Alexi and I will work on an abbreviated Book that will give them just enough time to get used to freefall and to become familiar with all the operational and safety facilities. It would be too much to expect them to be able to access and repair any malfunctions. That must be left to the crew," Ian said.

"I agree, Ian, but we are doing the best that we can do," the director said.

"Can we speed up ground training?"

"We have sped up ground training. We have cut everything that can be cut. The only thing we cannot cut is the freefall training. We have to do that to weed out the weak stomachs and those who are disoriented or incapable of maneuvering in freefall. Any other training will have to be done aboard ship and possibly en route. As we choose potential members of the science team, they will be rushed to the training facility within a very short time after the offer. We have to do that to preclude intervention by the religious fanatics.

"The planetary scientist who will be the science team leader we feel is quite safe. His appointment has not been announced, but he was picked up in secret and taken to the training facility directly. He is single and has no religious affiliations of any kind, and no record of any all the way back to his childhood. He should finish training in a few days and be brought up to the *Explorer* within the week. For the others, the choice is not quite so simple. All of them either have religious affiliations or were raised in an environment where religion governs the country. So they have to be chosen with great care. They also have to have specialties that are consistent with what they will be expected to do on Mars and/or in route.

"For example, the desert ecologist, Dr. Jamilah Burns, was raised and educated in a desert environment around Albuquerque, New Mexico, in the American desert country and has a PhD in Desert Ecology. She is also an expert in hydroponic gardening and minimal water farming. Do you see what I mean?" the director asked.

"Yes, sir I do. I had never imagined it could be so complicated. While a trip to Mars is not for everybody, I pictured people with the proper qualifications standing in line to go," Ian replied.

"They probably would be, Captain, if it weren't for the interference by those trying to block the mission. We have even lost some of those on the new list because they were contacted in anticipation of being selected and threatened with all sort of things if they accepted. We are making progress. Unfortunately, we will probably have to take potluck with respect to the science specialties."

"In any event, you can have Miriam and Rachael essentially full time immediately so they can complete their Books as soon as possible. You will need to release them to make trips to and from Farside Base when needed. That should only be once a week or so until we have ferried up the last of the crew, and the science team. Miriam and Rachael can take turns making the runs so each one will only have to be gone approximately half a day per week. We have gone over one of the capsules very, very, thoroughly. That capsule whenever it is not being used to ferry someone up from Farside Base will remain locked to the *Explorer*'s airlock. This will prevent anyone else from entering the *Explorer* except those that have been vetted and approved by ICExS Security," the director finished.

. . .

The next day, the director called on the secure line. "Hello, Ian."

"Director," Ian replied.

"Will you please ask Commander Gargorin to get on the line?" the director said.

"I buzzed him and he is on his way, Director. What is the problem?" Ian asked.

"I want to give you both the good news at once," the director replied.

Five minutes later, Alexi joined the conversation. "Good morning, Director, what's the news?"

"Gentlemen, I am pleased to tell you that we have located an assistant nuclear engineer.

His name is A. J. Kaniyar and he is from—"

"The Indian Navy!" Alexi interrupted. "That's fantastic, Director. I've met Mr. Kaniyar, who prefers to be called Ajay, by the way. Wasn't he the chief engineer on a nuclear heavy cruiser they built ten years or so ago? How did you land him?"

"Yes, Commander, he was, but the Indians wanted younger engineers to get more experience, and assigned him to train them. We have been covertly contacting everywhere there were nuclear engineers letting it be known that there was a challenging assignment for the right person. He got the word from a friend that we were looking for someone. He had no idea who 'we' were, so he sent his request through channels. We sent a Security team out to interview him without telling him what the job was. Once Security had vetted him, they sent him to Zürich for an interview.

"In the interview at Zürich, they asked him about some of the other requirements, notably machinist and mechanic. He told them he had come up through the hawse hole, whatever that is, and had been a master chief petty officer before he was made an officer and got into the nuclear side of things so he had lots of experience as a machinist and mechanic. Then we told him who we were and that we needed an assistant chief nuclear engineer. When he learned that Alexi was the chief engineer, he said he knew you, knew what you were doing, and accepted the job without asking anything more. We shipped him to our training facility immediately. He should be able to join the ship in about two weeks depending on the shuttle schedule."

. . .

Two weeks later, Ian and Alexi shuttled down to Farside Base to greet Mr. Kaniyar. "Hi AJay," Alexi said when Mr. Kaniyar stepped into the base after the shuttle ride from Circum-Lunar. "This is our captain, Ian McMichael."

"Pleased to meet you, AJay, welcome aboard," Ian said. "I'm very pleased that you decided to join us." Ian offered his hand. "We were beginning to worry that we wouldn't be able to find someone in time for the launch."

"If you would join us for lunch," Alexi said, "I will try to bring you up to speed on the *Explorer* and what the two of us need to do."

During lunch, Alexi explained about the *Explorer* and the Book. AJay nodded knowingly during the discussion.

"I am familiar with the Book concept, Commander, I had to create a Book when I was sent to the UK for training on a nuclear submarine. I think it is a great idea and I instituted it in a limited way into the training program I created for the Indian Navy. Cruisers are quite different in engineering operations from submarines. They are much more compartmentalized. I required all trainees, officers, and enlisted, to be completely familiar with the engineering facilities and able to do anything needed in the dark."

After lunch, Mr. Kaniyar was introduced to the director and then escorted out to the launch facilities for a ride up to the *Explorer*. Rachael, the designated shuttle pilot for the day, greeted AJay warmly and explained the launch procedures and what to expect on the way to the *Explorer*.

"The description of what to expect and the reality are two quite different things," AJay said as they neared the *Explorer*. "I never imagined that it would be so big. It looks almost as big as my cruiser. I am amazed."

He took two days to become accustomed to working in freefall and after that, Rachael and Miriam, who were well into the preparation of their Books, took turns guiding AJay.

A week later, an electronics specialist was found. Ichuro Watanabe, an American electronics engineer and computer scientist of Japanese descent, was just finishing a three-year assignment to the International Space Station and was considered to be a safe selection. He was transferred directly to Farside Base from the ISS and then to the *Explorer* because there was no concern about his adapting to freefall conditions during his initial training aboard the *Explorer*. Within a week of his arrival, he had almost caught up to the other three

Book trainees. From that point forward, Ian and Alexi alternated among the new crew, which sped up the process.

By the end of the month, most of the science team had been selected and isolated at the ground training facility and trained in what to expect on the *Explorer*. The names of the scientists were never announced to the public and from the moment they were chosen until they were ready to be transferred up to Farside Base and then to the *Explorer*, they were always under the close scrutiny of ICExS Security. When they reached Farside Base, Ian was notified and Miriam ferried him down to the surface. While he was meeting the science team for the first time, she personally supervised the installation of eight additional passenger facilities in her capsule. After the meet and greet in the director's office, the science team and all of their equipment were loaded into the capsule and they were launched up to the *Explorer*.

Ian and Alexi were sitting in the office of Chris Craft listening as he explained the problems in selecting the rest of the science team. "We have everyone in training except for an astrobiologist, a geologist, and a medical doctor."

"Isn't Rachael qualified as the medical doctor, Director?" Alexi asked.

"Yes, she is up to a point, but if a serious medical ability is required for some reason, it would be better if there was a qualified doctor aboard. Fortunately, we have located a husband and wife team. The husband is well qualified for the position of geologist and his wife is a doctor, a general practitioner, and an amateur geologist as well."

. . .

Lima Institute for Geologic Studies, Lima Peru
Dr. Esteban Martinova was peering into the electron microscope display of a rock sample he had collected when he heard the door to the laboratory open and a woman with an American accent asked, "Dr. Martinova? Dr. Esteban Martinova?"

"Yes, I am Dr. Martinova," he replied somewhat curtly at being interrupted at his work. When he turned and saw a woman wearing a business suit, he modulated his tone and continued, "Who are you and how may I help you?"

"I am Mary Lou Carl, Dr. Martinova. I need you to look at a rock sample my husband Edward and I collected in the far northeast corner of the Atacama near the mountains."

"Why?" he asked, again with agitation.

"Because we think it might have some diamond inclusions."

"Impossible, I know that area very well and there are no indigenous diamonds in the Atacama or anywhere else in South America." *Another American tourist with illusions of grandeur and wealth,* he thought.

"Nevertheless, could you at least look at the sample. I will pay you for your time."

"You will be wasting your money, how much?"

"Would 500 US dollars be sufficient?"

He thought for a moment and did a quick calculation in his head, almost 2000 Nuevo Sols. Too good to pass up. If she was willing to waste her money in a foolish gesture, who was he to ignore her. "Give me the sample."

He knew something was amiss as soon as he looked at the sample. It was clearly Kimberlite, a small piece about 200 grams in mass, but like nothing he had ever seen in South America. "Where did you get this again?"

"At the edge of the Atacama. Is it valuable?"

"It might be, let me look at it under the microscope. I will need to break it to see what it contains. Please have a seat while I check it." Martinova placed the rock on an anvil and taking a rock hammer, smashed it. Without even putting a sample under the microscope, he could see the telltale glint of small diamonds. He placed a sample in the mass spectrometer and started the analysis process. He watched the display as the mass-spec produced a ragged graph showing the minerals contained in the rock sample. He was not surprised when the telltale line signifying diamond and other carbon compounds appeared on the display in addition to several other minerals that are typically found near diamond deposits.

"Hmm, it would seem that you are correct. This sample contains diamonds. They are mostly small industrial quality diamonds, which are known as black diamonds and are not particularly valuable except in very large quantities. There are also a few very tiny gem-quality diamonds, which were too small to be of any value. Again, where did you find this?"

"What have you found, Esteban?" Dr. Guadalupe Martinova asked from the doorway.

"This woman claims she and her husband found diamond ore up in the Atacama," he answered his wife.

"Impossible!" Lupe exclaimed.

"Mrs. Carl, this is my wife Dr. Guadalupe Martinova who is also a geologist here at the institute." Then to his wife, he said, "Impossible or not, see the proof on the screen of the mass spectrometer, see for yourself."

"Amazing, Mrs. Carl," Lupe said, smiling at the stranger. "Call me Lupe, everyone else does.

"Would the two of you like to see the site for yourself, Drs. Martinova?" Mrs. Carl asked. "I have a helicopter standing by over at the airport that can take us there directly. It is still early in the day."

"Yes, I certainly would," Lupe said. "Esteban?"

"Of course, my dear," he replied to his wife. He was already formulating a paper on the discovery and the recognition that would result, and at the same time trying to figure out how he could cut himself and his wife into the possible treasure. Then to Mrs. Carl, "Give me a moment to gather my field kit."

During the short drive to the airport, Mrs. Carl explained that the helicopter was owned by her husband and that he was the helicopter pilot. When they arrived at the airport, Mrs. Carl performed the introductions. "Drs. Martinova, Lupe and Esteban, this is my husband Gary Carl." The helicopter was a late model used most often by law enforcement and medical services. It was comfortable and fast. Once they were all strapped in, Gary started the helicopter and within minutes they were airborne and heading east towards the Atacama.

Two hours later they spotted what the Carls called their camp, and shortly thereafter they landed amongst a cloud of fine sand stirred up by the rotor.

"Here we are, folks," Mary Lou announced as she opened the side door and stepped out of the helicopter onto the desert. She led them into the largest tent where they were greeted by a third person, a woman, who was holding a pistol. The woman could easily pass for Lupe with someone who did not know Lupe.

"What is this?" Esteban asked. "Who is this and what is going on here?"

"This, Dr. Martinova, is a person who is going to substitute for your wife on the Mars expedition."

"What Mars expedition? What do you mean by this?"

"Sit down, Martinovas," Mary Lou said, indicating a pair of canvas covered chairs, "and I will explain."

Esteban and Lupe went to the indicated chairs and sat down. "Alright, we are sitting, now what is going on and what do you mean she is going to substitute for Lupe on a Mars mission?"

"There are two competing organizations planning a trip to Mars, ours which has no name but which is known as The Cartel and the one you will be invited to join, sponsored by ICExS, The International Consortium for the Exploration of Space. Ours is a private venture whose goal is to claim Mars as a private planet owned exclusively by The Cartel. Theirs is a publicly funded organization that wishes to establish a scientific mission on Mars and colonize Mars in the name of all humanity. Ours is for profit and theirs is for glory, if you will.

"Our ships left for Mars half a year ago and because we have to take the long 'matching orbits' approach it will not arrive for another three months. Theirs is going in a ship that was built on the other side of the Moon. It will be ready to go in less than a month and the travel time will be about seven to eight weeks because they will go directly to Mars. If they are successful, they will beat us to Mars and set up a scientific mission before we even get there. But, in order for their claim to be valid, they must either return to Earth or establish a permanent scientific colony. We must not allow either of these things to happen and that is where you come into the picture.

"ICExS will be contacting you within a day or two at most to invite you as a geologist and your wife as a geologist and as the medical doctor for the mission. As you can see, our Guadalupe Martinova can pass for yours. So she is about to become your wife for the trip. She is familiar with the construction of the ship from plans that have been smuggled out from the Moon and she is familiar with the planned mission for the same reason. She has a working knowledge of geology and what she does not know will not matter because her job will be to ensure the ICExS mission fails. She is also a certified first responder as a paramedic and emergency medical technician and will be able to handle most of the medical problems that might crop up and thus allay suspicion until it is too late.

"You will treat her in every way as if she was your real wife and she has been instructed to cooperate completely with you. She will also give you instructions so you can be complicit in the failure of the ICExS mission. In the meantime, we will hold the real Lupe Martinova at our home base in Eastern Europe until you have been successful. Once you have succeeded, we will release her and return her to Lima. If you in any way give away what has happened, we will kill her immediately so there will be no proof that we have her.

"Do you understand, Dr. Martinova?" Mary Lou asked. "If you refuse to do this, we will kill both of you and bury you here in the Atacama where you will never be found and you will become just another mysterious disappearance in the desert."

"Yu, yu, yes," Esteban stammered. "Lupe, what else can I do?"

"Esteban, do we have a choice?"

"Apparently not, my love."

"Good, now that that is settled, we will return you and the new Lupe to Lima so you can be in your laboratory when the ICExS agents come to offer you the position."

"What if they do not come to us?"

"They will, we have made sure of that."

"Lupe, see amado," Esteban pled to his wife.

"Just go, Esteban. Do what they ask and return to me when it's over," Lupe said through tears. She held out her arms to him and they embraced.

A radio that was sitting in a far corner of the tent, squawked and emitted several sentences in a guttural language. To which New Lupe replied, "Da."

"It is time to go, Dr. Martinova," Mary Lou said. "The ICExS agents have arrived in Lima and will be calling upon you in a few hours. Gary will fly you back to Lima and I will stay here with Lupe. Hasta la vista, Dr. Martinova, don't fail us or your wife."

On the ride back to Lima, the new Lupe kept her gun pointed at Esteban. When they arrived, a limousine took them all back to the institute.

"I will stay with you until after you leave for the ICExS training facility," Gary explained. "Lupe will introduce me as your laboratory assistant. You are to ask about your instruments and equipment, and I will offer to prepare them and send them along later. Everything that you and Lupe will need to carry out your orders will be in the containers that will be shipped to the moon for your use on Mars. Is that clear, Dr. Martinova?" Esteban gave a slight nod and mumbled his assent.

Within an hour, two men arrived at the laboratory and introduced themselves, "Dr. Esteban Martinova, we represent the International Consortium for the Exploration of Space and we would like to ask you and your wife to join an expedition to Mars as our geology team and, of course, with your wife as the medical doctor for the mission."

"When do we leave?" Lupe asked. "And what about our equipment and instruments?"

"I will take care of that for you, Dr. Martinova," Gary, the laboratory assistant, offered. "Will that be alright?" Lupe asked the agents.

"Yes, but it needs to be done within a week if it is to get to the moon in time for the planned departure," the agent replied, then continued, "We need to leave Lima immediately for the training facility, the mission leaves in less than a month," the ICExS man explained.

After an hour of discussion where they instructed Gary what to send along, the Martinovas were taken to their home where under the direction of the ICExS agents they packed the minimum they would need for the proposed trip. Two hours later they were on the way to the training facility.

. . .

University of Edinburgh, Edinburgh Scotland

The office, like faculty offices the world over, was small. There was just room enough for a small desk, two chairs, and bookcases lined the walls. A shawl knitted in the Campbell pattern hung on a hook by the door. Dr. Gladys Campbell, a rather plain spinster in her late thirties, sat at the desk grading undergraduate term papers while wishing she was back in her equally Spartan faculty apartment knitting Christmas tams for friends and their families. She sighed as she finished reading a hopelessly disjointed paper that deserved a failing mark. But, she assigned a minimum passing mark as a gift for the effort made.

She looked up at the sound of footsteps in the hallway. A shadow of a large man appeared at the frosted window in her door, followed by a brief knock. "Come in," she invited.

The door opened revealing a tall ruggedly handsome man dressed in a casual cardigan and tan corduroy slacks. "Dr. Campbell?" he asked in a velvet-smooth baritone voice with a mild Eastern European accent.

"Yes, and you are?" she asked slightly annoyed at the intrusion on her private time.

"My name is of no consequence, but you need to talk to me, now," he replied as he closed the door and, uninvited, seated himself in the other chair.

"May I ask why I might need to speak with you, sir?"

"It is a matter of life and death; the life and death of your son, Erick. Is that reason enough, Dr. Campbell?"

"Indeed, why would that be so, if I may ask?" she replied with immediate concern.

"Sometime in the next day or two, you are going to be contacted by an agent of the International Consortium for the Exploration of Space. You will be invited to become one of the scientists on the expedition to Mars because of your area of expertise. You are to accept that invitation or the life of your son will be forfeit. Is that clear?"

"But why me?" Gladys pleaded.

"Because you are the next choice for the qualifications they need. I represent another, call it competitive, organization that wishes to insure the failure of the ICExS mission. To do this we need an agent aboard who is above reproach, and that would be you."

"How is it you know about my son?"

He opened a notebook, glanced at the top page looked up at Gladys and said, "We know everything about you and your life. We know you had a lengthy affair with your graduate student Martin Allberg and that you became pregnant. To hide the pregnancy from the University, you took a sabbatical in northern Scotland in the home of the Clan Campbell and there your baby was born. By the time the baby was born, Martin had married Molly Edelberg, one of your students and moved to London to accept a position with the government. You told him about the baby and he and Molly agreed to adopt the baby, Erick. You are Great Aunt Gladys who visits the Allbergs several times a year usually at holidays and birthdays bringing presents for Erick and his parents."

As he spoke Gladys shrank in her chair stunned with the depth of his knowledge about her.

"In about five minutes, your telephone will ring and it will be Martin calling verifying that we have Erick and that he is in a secure location. We have no intention of harming him if you do as we ask."

"What is it you want me to do?"

"Sometime during the voyage, you will receive an email from Martin, which contains the following, Erick says to 'tell Aunt Gladys hello.' When you receive this message, you are to do as follows." He drew a long, large diameter knitting needle from a cardboard tube he was carrying and showed it to Gladys. "You are to take this knitting needle, twist the knob at the top end and then press the knob. That will send a signal to us indicating you have done what we have asked you to do. As soon as we receive the signal, we will return Erick to his parents."

"That is all?" Gladys asked as she took the knitting needle and carefully placed it into her knitting bag.

"That is all, Dr. Campbell." The man paused and looked at his wristwatch and nodded as her phone rang. "Answer that, Dr. Campbell."

Gladys picked up the phone hesitantly and before she could speak, he reached across the desk and pressed the speaker phone button. "This is Dr. Campbell," Gladys said.

"Gladys, this is Martin, Erick has been kidnapped and I was directed to call you. Molly is beside herself with grief and so am I. Do you have any idea what all this means?" Molly could be heard sobbing in the background.

"I have no idea why this is happening, Martin. Only that they have something they want me to do for them and if I do it, they will release Erick. Do you know if Erick is safe?"

"He rang us up a few minutes ago and said he was safe. He said he was with some people who were taking good care of him and that we were not to worry. He said he would be staying with the people for about three months and he would call us regularly to let us know he was still all right. What is going on, Gladys?"

"I can only say that I am to do something for them after which they will release Erick and return him to you and Molly," Gladys said.

"What should we do, Gladys?"

"Nothing, just wait and pray that I will be able to do what they want me to do."

"What is it that they want you to do?"

"I am not able to tell you about that. Just wait and trust that I will do what is necessary."

"All right, all right, but we really don't like this at all. Molly thinks we should call Scotland Yard and report it."

Gladys looked up; the man shook his head. "Don't do that, Martin, please don't do that," she said.

"All right. We trust you."

"Please tell Erick that I asked after him next time he calls."

"Will do. Goodbye, Gladys."

"Goodbye to you both," Gladys said and the man pressed the button to break the connection.

"Now, Dr. Campbell, do not tell anyone we have been to see you and do not fail," the man said and stood up to leave. As he was closing the door, he smiled at her and nodded, then shut it behind him and left.

Gladys sagged in her chair and burst out crying again. She vowed she would do anything to ensure Erick came to no harm.

The next morning as Gladys sat in the kitchen of her small flat drinking her breakfast tea the telephone rang. It startled her. With shaking hands, she picked up the handset and answered. "Hello, this is Dr. Campbell."

"Dr. Campbell, this is Jenn from Dean McGregor's office. Dr. McGregor asks if you would please come to his office as soon as possible."

"Tell Dr. McGregor that I will be there in twenty minutes, is that soon enough?" Gladys tried to modulate her voice so Jenn would not know she was confused and upset.

"That will be fine, Dr. Campbell," Jenn replied and disconnected.

Twenty minutes later, Gladys entered the reception area to the dean's office. "Go right in, Dr. Campbell. He's expecting you," Jenn said.

Gladys knocked and entered the dean's office and as she did, the dean and another man rose to greet her.

"Good morning, Dr. Campbell, I'm so glad you could join us. May I introduce Dr. Walter Cartwright of His Britannic Majesty's Royal Academy of Science."

"Good morning, Sir Walter." Gladys knew of his knighthood, so she curtsied and managed to say the honorific without tripping over her words. "I am so happy to meet you."

Then, noting her obvious discomfort, Dr. Cartwright added, "Please could we all be seated."

The dean pressed a button on his telephone and Jenn entered with tea and biscuits. "Have some tea, Sir Walter and Dr. Campbell."

Once that time-honored ritual was accomplished, Sir Walter spoke. "I suppose you are wondering why you're here and probably also why I am here. Because time is of the essence, I will get right to the point. Dr. Campbell, I am one of the managing directors of the International Consortium for the Exploration of Space. Have you heard of us?"

"No, sir," she lied, but it was not much of a lie considering that less than twenty-four hours before she really had never heard of it.

"ICExS, as we call it, is preparing to launch a manned expedition to Mars. A scientific expedition designed to answer several questions. Notably, is there now or has there ever been any life on Mars and would it be possible to establish a scientific colony on Mars for future research? I have come to recruit you, if possible, as a specialist in your field of astrobiology and invite you to go along with the expedition as a member of the scientific team." Dr. Cartwright paused to let the significance of his offer to register. "Would that interest you, Dr. Campbell?"

Gladys nodded. "Certainly, Sir Walter, but why me?"

"Because, dear lady, you and your specialty are essential to the success of the mission."

"How long would I be gone? I have my classes to teach."

"Approximately two years and it will be departing in just over a month," Sir Walter replied.

Before Gladys could reply, the dean stepped in. "Don't worry about your classes, Gladys. One of the lecturing assistants can take over for you. Of course, it will not be the same as you would do it, but this is a great opportunity for you and for the university." The dean did not mention that Sir Walter had promised a huge grant for his department if Gladys accepted.

Gladys paused and appeared to be considering the offer while she was actually remembering what the stranger had told her the evening before. After a moment she managed a smile and said with feigned enthusiasm, "I would be happy to join your expedition, Sir Walter. When do we leave?"

Sir Walter beamed at the dean and said, "Immediately. You will not need to pack very much because everything and I mean everything will be provided for you. We will be leaving here within the hour to take you to a training facility to prepare you for the journey."

"Immediately?" mused Gladys. "I will need to take a few personal things from my apartment. Excuse me, but would it be possible for me to take my knitting kit and yarn? I like to pass the time knitting things for people."

"I don't see why not. My driver will take you to your apartment and will help you and advise you on what you may need to bring and she will carry your luggage to the automobile."

"Thank you, Sir Walter."

"Make us proud, Gladys," the dean said as Gladys and Sir Walter left his office. She managed a nod and hint of a smile in response.

CHAPTER SEVEN

After they arrived at the training facility and settled into their accommodations, the science team began an intensive orientation and training in the operational procedures of the *Explorer* that they could be expected to share. Ordinarily, they would not be expected to participate in the operation of the ship, but in an emergency, they had to know how to help. As the director had explained almost two months before, the science team was made up of a mixed bag of individuals whose appointments were largely political. They were all competent in their fields but had no practical experience that would benefit them on a spaceship.

Their initial experiences with weightlessness resulted in many cases of motion sickness or more properly freefall sickness. After the first week, all but one, with occasional exceptions, had adapted to the weightless environment.

The hold-out was Gladys Campbell, an astrobiologist, from the University of Edinburgh. Gladys was not the first choice. She was quickly recruited when the person originally chosen decided to back out during ground training because she was ostensibly claustrophobic. It was later determined that she was warned by an associate at her university not to take the position because it could be very dangerous to her career.

Guadalupe Martinova from Peru, the official ship's doctor, placed a scopolamine patch behind Gladys's left ear and within a few hours, Gladys seemed to be over her space sickness. Within a week, Gladys no longer needed the patch.

The biggest problem was those who were not familiar with maneuvering in freefall and were trying somewhat unsuccessfully to navigate around the inside of the ship. Like everyone else who had never experienced freefall for any length of time, they had to learn that for every motion they made, there resulted an opposite motion. Reaching for a nearby handhold resulted in a spin in the opposite direction away from the handhold. By moving the arm slowly the reaction could be minimized. For the first several days, ropes were strung back and forth across common deck to provide a means of movement by pulling hand over hand along the ropes. Each day some of the ropes were removed until nearly everyone was able to move about safely.

Once the "newbies" learned to move from handhold to handhold like a monkey, things became simpler. On the other hand, if they allow themselves to float away from the handholds it created a different problem. An awkward swimming like movement would get you to a wall and a handhold eventually. It was a learned skill that took a while to achieve. Practically, there was almost always someone close by or within hailing distance who could offer a hand and a safe landing place. Before long they were all moving around as if they had been in freefall all their lives.

The final ship's complement consisted of twelve people: eight men, and four women. The crew was made up of six experienced people—Captain Ian McMichael; Chief Nuclear Engineer Alexi Gargorin; Chief Pilot and Astrogator Miriam Steinmetz; Copilot and Principal Shuttle Pilot Rachael Perlman; Assistant Nuclear Engineer, Machinist, and Mechanic A. J. Kaniyar; and Computer, Electronics; and Communications Officer Ichuro Watanabe.

The science team also had six members, the Chief Scientist Jan Pitrasen from the University of Oslo, who was the university's planetary scientist; Environmentalist Thomas Vernon from the University of Alberta in Canada; Geologist Esteban Martinova from the Federal Institute of Geological Sciences in Lima Peru; Assistant Geologist, Medical Doctor, and Chief Cook Guadalupe Martinova, wife of the geologist; the desert ecologist and hydroponics expert was Jamilah Burns from the University of New Mexico in Albuquerque, and the astrobiologist was Gladys Campbell from the University of Edinburgh.

Once she had conquered her space sickness, Dr. Campbell asked about protection from solar and cosmic radiation.

Alexi explained, "One of the first things that were powered up after the reactor was installed was the magnetosphere. Basically, it is a large very powerful magnetic field that completely surrounds the ship to block out as much of the solar and cosmic radiation as possible. Some get through, of course, but it is no worse than what you would experience in high-altitude flight. In addition, once we are pointed away from the sun the water in the reaction mass tank will also act as a shield against some forms of solar and cosmic radiation. Is that clear, Dr. Campbell?"

"Yes, I think so," Dr. Campbell said. "As an astrobiologist, I have made a study of the effects of the radiation in various experimental settings as reported from the International Space Station and the surface of the moon. I would like to see how the magnetosphere operates sometime when you have the time to show me. Please call me Gladys, everyone."

Tom Vernon, the environmentalist, asked, "Will we be able to communicate with our loved ones on Earth?"

Ian replied, "There will be regularly scheduled tight beam laser connections with Farside Base or Earth so that you can communicate with home. Mr. Watanabe would you like to explain how that will work?"

"Yes, sir. Using regular broadcast radio or other electronic connections is fairly complicated in a moving spaceship. That is not to say that we cannot make a connection, we can. There are a number of satellites spaced around the orbit of Earth specifically to facilitate communications from virtually anywhere in the solar system to Earth or the Moon. We signal them and they relay the signals to wherever Earth is in its orbit. Right now, we can make a direct connection with the Moon because it is in our line of sight, but Earth is hidden behind it. Once we're on our way, the Earth-Moon System will move ahead of us in its orbit and it will eventually be where we will not be able to make a direct connection. When I said tight beam connection, I was referring to using the laser to carry the messages, which actually uses less energy than using radio. This means that all messages will be filtered by the computer before they are sent and by every computer in the relay system and finally by the final receiving computer before they are passed on to the recipient."

"Does that mean we'll have no privacy in our communications?" Vernon asked.

"Yes, sir, it does. Actually, it wouldn't matter very much what mechanism we used to communicate. All communication will go through our computer before it's transmitted. Likewise, we'll receive messages through our computer and they'll be directed to the individual addressed. There is no other way to do it. Nothing else on the ship has sufficient power to make a secure connection anywhere in the solar system."

Ian stepped in. "I'm sorry, Dr. Vernon. That's how it has to be." What he didn't say was that the computer was programmed to filter messages going either way for anything subversive. Otherwise, it would send and receive messages without censorship.

Clearly, keeping the science team busy and engaged was going to pose a problem. Other than studying their e-books, eating and sleeping, there was not a great deal for them to do. Therefore, all of the scientists were assigned shipboard duties they voluntarily selected from a list of necessary chores. These varied from cooking for Lupe and Rachael to maintaining the garden for Jamilah to various essential housekeeping chores shared by all. Everyone, even the ship's crew had miscellaneous housekeeping chores to do.

Ian had expected some complaints from members of the science team when they were asked to do the chores. He was pleasantly surprised when he found they all quite willingly accepted things to do because just sitting in the front of a large ship with nothing to do was not only boring, but it could lead to irritation and conflict. An old adage his grandmother often recited, "busy hands are happy hands" seemed to apply.

A variety of games had been provided for the entertainment of all aboard. Playing cards or checkers in freefall was virtually impossible because the cards and the pieces tended to drift away from where they were needed. Over

100,000 books ranging from the classics to the most recent bestsellers, fiction, and nonfiction were stored electronically in the ship's computer. Each scientist and crew member had a tablet computer capable of acting as an e-book reader or solitaire game facilitator. All of the tablets were connected electronically to the computer system so they could also be used to communicate among the members of the company.

As the departure window approached, the crew and science team were as ready as they were ever going to be. Miriam had computed departure vectors for every day of the first week of the window. Ian, having had experience before in getting a new vessel underway was eager to depart as early as possible. If there should be problems, they could hopefully be fixed in time to still make the window. At breakfast time on the first optimal day, Ian polled everyone to see if they were ready to go. He received eleven ayes, twelve counting himself.

"Alexi, how long will it take to get that teakettle of yours online?" Ian asked.

Alexi replied, "It's in idle mode, Captain, and ready to go. When we tested the rockets last week everything was nominal."

"Ichuro, notify Farside Base that we are ready to get underway."

"Yes, sir," Ichuro replied as he connected with and notified Farside Base.

"Miriam, dial up your navigation program for today and let's get this trip underway," Ian commanded.

Miriam rechecked the sightings she had made on her navigation stars, and said, "In ten, nine...."

Ian took up the count over the intercom to Alexi, "three, two, one, now, Commander!"

A low rumble was felt throughout the ship as the VASIMR (Variable Specific Impulse Magnetoplasma Rocket) rockets began to move it. To minimize stress, Alexi brought up the power gradually. Once the ship began accelerating, everything that had been drifting around loose for the past several weeks settled slowly to the deck or the table in the Common Room. Everyone watched the accelerometer as the numbers gradually increased until it indicated 0.257G at the end of an hour and then gradually began reducing the number until it stood at 0.25G exactly.

"We are at one-quarter G and everything is stable, Captain," Alexi announced over the public address system.

"Thank you, Commander. Your audience applauds you," Ian said, then, "How goes it, Miriam?"

Miriam reviewed her instruments and replied, "Everything is A-OK as they used to say."

"Are you able to give us a running commentary at this time?"

"Yes, sir, everything is automatic and we will be alerted if anything should deviate from the planned trajectory. As we pull away from the Earth-Moon L2 point, we will be headed not towards Mars but towards the Sun in order to build up speed as quickly and efficiently as possible. The ship is going to enter an eccentric elliptical orbit around the Earth-Moon system, which will give us a slingshot effect for a boost of speed."

"Thank you, Miriam," Ian said. "Just to review the details once more, we will have a travel time to Mars of about six weeks at an average velocity of 50,000 miles per hour. The distance at closest approach between Earth and Mars is roughly 55 million miles."

"Roughly, Captain? Surely it is more precise than that," Tom Vernon said.

"That's true, Dr. Vernon, but we can avoid the fine decimal places and leave them up to Miriam and Ichuro," Ian replied. "Since no one has ever done what we are about to do, there are undoubtedly some unknowns that will have to be resolved in flight. To continue, once we leave the Earth-Moon system, the *Explorer* will travel in nearly a straight line to a point intersecting the orbit of Mars at approximately the same time Mars reaches that point. Along the way, Miriam will be making continuous fine adjustments to the flight path to ensure that happens.

"This is much better than the way used by the first exploratory missions to Mars. The older way followed a long unpowered elliptical path to match orbits with a travel time that takes approximately eight months compared to our six weeks. We will have almost eighteen months at Mars before we can return again using a straight-line path."

"Miriam, can you put the view on the big screen so we can all see what you're seeing as we go around the Earth?" Ian asked.

"It should be on the screen now, Captain. Has anyone turned on the display, sir?"

"Thank you. The display has been turned on now, and the view is incredible."

Once the ship was running at full acceleration, everyone aboard was much more comfortable and able to move around through the ship without concern for drifting along in the wrong direction. In addition to making life simpler, the artificial gravity produced by the acceleration helped them to maintain body tone and good health without concern for the loss of bone mass and other medical problems. They had all been given medications that deterred the ill effects of prolonged existence at lower than normal gravity. But, they would still need to exercise regularly in order to maintain themselves, but the exercises would be far less rigorous than they would be in freefall.

The *Explorer*'s course took the ship wide around the moon headed towards Earth. It swept around Earth at an altitude of 2500 miles, close enough to get the slingshot boost but not so close that there would be any atmospheric drag slowing the ship down. The swing around Earth went quickly. The continual modification of the thrust vectors kept the two pilots busy during the passage around Earth and back past orbit of the Moon.

For the first several hours during the sweep around Earth, everyone watched the display or tried to see through the windows on the pilot deck. After that, they gradually wandered off to their cabins or sat reading in the Common Room. Miriam kept them informed of anything they might find really interesting. At closest approach to Earth, they all watched through various viewports as the ship swept by the "blue marble" that was their home. Ian watched their faces as the *Explorer* traversed the daylight side of Earth looking for any clue that might indicate anything other than genuine admiration; he found none.

The executive officer's job was to make sure everything ran smoothly. Absent an executive officer, the chore fell naturally on the captain. The crew quickly settled into their underway duties. An alternating schedule was set up for the pilots and the engineers, since one or the other had to be on duty at all times. Alexi and AJay stood their watches aft in the reactor room until they were confident that everything was running smoothly; then they could stand their watches on the control deck, which had a duplicate set of controls but lacked the proximity of being in the reactor room.

Ichuro Watanabe maintained a continuous flow of performance data through the computer back to Farside Base for analysis. This was essential, in the event something unexpected should happen so that the designers would have some idea as to what had occurred. In addition, he was receiving news reports and other televised information from Earth through the same tight beam channel. This was broadcast to the monitors throughout the ship. Everyone aboard could watch the programs from Earth or monitor the performance of the ship, or just look at the stars as seen by the television cameras around the ship. There were several channels that played the music in various genres. Everyone had a pair of earbuds that were matched to their tablets so that they could listen without disturbing anyone else and maintain privacy.

Lupe and Rachael worked out a schedule that enabled them to take turns cooking without interfering with Rachael's scheduled watches as a pilot. Surprisingly, several of the crew and scientists offered to do some cooking as all had a fair amount of experience in cooking for themselves when they were on field expeditions. The galley was provided with a plentiful supply of spices and other condiments that could be used to fix almost any kind of meal. As much of the food as possible was freeze-dried so that it could easily be reconstituted by adding water. Some of the food was in discrete meals, but most was in quantities that would facilitate fixing the meal for everyone.

There were all of the ingredients required to make bread, desserts, side dishes, pizza, and most forms of comfort food. It was not long before the cooks began posting what they called a tentative menu for the day subject to revision by anyone who offered a better idea. Like any large family, there were likes and dislikes, so no meal made everyone happy. If someone wanted to fix something for themselves, they were free to do that. At the end of the meal, the scraps were collected. Meat scraps were given to Jammy to feed to Ferd or fertilize the garden.

In less than a week, the entire complement had settled into a routine that provided maximum freedom without troubling anyone else. It was quickly discovered that there were seven people who knew how to play bridge. Not quite enough for two tables. So, an offer was made to teach anyone who wanted to learn how to play. Surprisingly, all of the five non-bridge players volunteered to learn. This provided a great deal of amusement as well as frustration for the players as they tried to teach the volunteers. Eventually, everyone could play which made it possible to have three tables but duty schedules and assigned responsibilities rarely made that possible. However, two tables were frequently made. All but one of the people turned out to be adequate social players, not competitive players, which minimized criticism when someone misplayed. There were several who knew how to play chess or Scrabble, so there was nearly always a game of some sort in progress when duties allowed.

CHAPTER EIGHT

Everyone on board wore a badge that was ostensibly to monitor exposure to radiation. It also had an electronic responder that enabled the computer to keep track of where everyone was at all times in the event they were needed. The first problem occurred when Lupe "accidentally" dropped her badge in the soup as it was boiling and left the room. What she had not expected was that the computer detected the sudden rise in temperature and set off the ship-wide fire alarm indicating a fire in the galley. It was early in the morning, and other than those who were on duty, most were asleep or still in bed.

Alexi was coming off duty from the reactor room and passing near the galley when the alarm went off. He immediately pulled one of the fire extinguishers out of the recess in the bulkhead and ran into the kitchen. No one was there. He looked around trying to find the problem and eventually looked in the pot of soup and there was the badge roiling around in the liquid. He took a spoon and picked out the badge, examined it and dropped it back into the soup and washed off the spoon returning it to the rack. By this time everyone was in the common area except AJay who was on duty with the reactors. Alexi was standing holding the fire extinguisher looking eagerly for a fire he knew was not there.

Lupe returned to the galley from the general direction of the ships fresher, looked around for the fire, and then seemed surprised that her badge was missing. She went back to the fresher looking for it, and returned to the galley to find it boiling in the soup and exclaimed loudly, "Madre de dios!" She looked around to see who was watching her then used a pair of tongs to get the badge out of the soup and finally washed it off. She said loud enough for everyone to hear, "My badge must've fallen off and gotten too close to the heating element while I went to the fresher."

Alexi had seen her show out of the corner of his eye as he was pretending to look for the fire somewhere besides in the galley. He noted the time for the record and to check against the computer. Later when he and Ian were alone he reported the incident.

"Captain, I think something strange is going on here. I had just come up from the reactor rooms when the fire alarm went off. I could not smell any smoke, so I started looking for the cause and I found Lupe's ID card in the soup. It might have been an accident except for one thing," Alexi said.

"Captain, not Ian?" Ian asked. "Okay, what is it?"

"Yes, sir, I think this a true captain thing. It is more than an accidental dropping of her badge in the soup. When Lupe returned to the galley, she said she had been in the 'fresher,' but she did not come from the direction of the fresher. So, I noted the time and then checked the log and found that there was no record of the fresher door opening and closing near that time. We have no way of knowing where she had really gone during her brief absence because the fresher would not have recorded it if someone went there without a badge."

"I wonder if she was trying to find out what would happen if the badge got too hot?" Ian asked rhetorically.

"My thoughts exactly. It could be a coincidence, but I don't believe in co-incidences," Alexi said, "We will have to keep an eye on her from now on and track her every move."

"I'll have Mr. Watanabe set up the computer to do that at least for the time being. It could've been unintentional, so I don't think we should say anything now other than to compliment her on her quick thinking in retrieving her badge from the soup."

"I agree, Captain," Alexi asserted.

. . .

Three days later, there was a beep on the intercom followed by, "Help. The ferret is lost."

Ian reacted almost immediately and went to the garden deck. When he arrived, he found the hatch was shut, so he assumed that the ferret was still contained in the garden. Ian very carefully opened the hatch just a crack to prevent the ferret from getting lost in the ship.

"Jamilah?" he asked.

"I'm here, Captain."

"Is the ferret still in here?" Ian asked.

"Yes, sir. He's up in the overhead on one of the pipes. It's safe to come in," Jammy answered.

He looked through the hatch port and could neither see Jamilah nor the ferret. He squeezed through the hatch and entered the garden. He looked around and saw Jamilah trying to climb up one of the pipes to catch the ferret.

"Jammy, stop," he said.

"Okay, then what, sir? How'm I going to get him down?" she asked.

"I'm not as worried about the ferret being lost as I am for you climbing around on the plumbing. Even at a quarter G, if you fell and injured yourself, how would we replace you? Please get down, Jammy and let's think this over."

Jamilah slowly backed down from her perch on a pipe bracket halfway up to the overhead and dropped the last few feet to the deck. At one-quarter G, it was almost as if she gently floated down. She could not imagine what might happen to her if she fell from the ceiling, but she conceded the point.

Ian keyed the intercom. "Relax everyone. It is not an emergency. The ferret got out of his cage somehow and we are working on getting him back into it." Then he stood beside Jamilah and they both looked up at the ferret who was sitting on one of the pipes 4 meters above them. Ferd was perched on a pipe at the farthest possible point from his cage just cleaning his whiskers.

Ian looked down at Jamilah who was a fully foot shorter than he and asked, "Any ideas, Jammy?"

"No, sir, Captain, but the ferret is not my fault. I always lock his cage and double-check it. You've seen me do it. His cage was locked when I left for lunch. When I got back, he was lost. He is clever, but he cannot possibly unlock his cage. Look, sir, there is a plate blocking the lock to prevent him from reaching it. Somebody had to unlock it for him," Jamilah explained. "I tried to lure him down with one of his treats, but he just ignored it. I guess the only way to get him down is to go up and get him."

"That's out. There is too much equipment down here. If you fell, you could hurt yourself. It is fully 3 meters from the deck to the overhead. That's a long way to fall," Ian said.

"Captain, I'm—"

At that point, the intercom interrupted. "What is going on, Captain? Can I help?" Alexi asked.

Ian responded. "The ferret got lost in the garden and apparently does not want to go back to his cage. We are trying to figure out how to catch him without injuring anybody in the process." Then Ian explained the problem and ended with, "Jammy is willing to climb up to catch him, but I'm concerned for her safety. She could fall and hurt herself. Do you have any suggestions?"

"Maybe, let me think about it for a minute or so, Captain. I'll get back to you. Alexi out." Jamilah waited anxiously. She did not complete what she was going to say.

A few minutes later, Alexi called back, "Captain, I have been talking things over with AJay and we think we may have a solution. We could cut off the thrust for a few minutes and Jammy could go get him in a weightless situation. As I recall, she was pretty adept at navigating in weightlessness."

As Alexi was speaking, Jamilah tugged at Ian's sleeve and nodded approval at the suggestion.

"Jammy likes that idea," Ian said and left the mic open because Jamilah wanted to say something.

"Captain, we'll have to cover the hydroponic tanks first to prevent any problems with them," she said.

"Did you get that, Alexi," Ian asked the intercom.

"Yes, sir, we'll be standing by. In the meantime, I'll take up the power problem with Miriam to see what it might do to her vectors."

"Thanks, do that. Nothing is simple on a spaceship, is it?" Ian asked rhetorically.

Nevertheless, Alexi replied, "Not like it is on a submarine with a full crew, is it?" Ian did not respond.

A few minutes later, Rachael's voice came from the speaker beside the hatch. "Captain, I helped Jammy set up the hydroponic beds. Can I help with covering them?"

Ian looked to Jamilah with a raised eyebrow and she nodded yes. Ian opened the hatch to let Rachael in. There were several of the others near the entrance. After a moment's reflection, he said, "Thanks, folks. In this case, three's a crowd, any more in here and no one would be able to move." Which was an exaggeration but was adequate to discourage any more volunteers. "So, thank you and please go back to whatever you were doing."

Twenty minutes later, the hydroponic beds were all covered and safe from damage. Ian called Alexi, "Have you checked with Miriam, Alexi?"

"Yes, Captain. She says a five-minute pause in the thrust will not create any problems requiring a major navigational shift, and she was due to make a minor correction anyway," Alexi replied.

"Great. We are ready here, so do a countdown for cutoff," Ian directed. Then to the rest of the compliment, "Get ready for thrust cutoff. Grab on to something, otherwise, you might pop up towards the overhead just from the tension in your legs needed to stand up against the thrust."

Jamilah positioned herself near the pipe she was trying to climb earlier. Rachael moved to the other side of the garden to head off the ferret if he tried to go that way.

"Okay, Alexi, we are ready," Ian said. "Go."

Alexi paused for a moment and then began a short count from five down to zero. When he reached zero, he announced, "Power off now."

Suddenly, the acceleration stopped and Ian was thankful that he had a grip on a handhold following his own advice. Because his own ordinary muscle tension caused his body to rotate around the hand that gripped the handhold near the door.

"Okay, Jammy, go," Ian directed.

"Yes, sir." Jamilah pulled herself hand over hand up the vertical pipe towards the overhead. When she had climbed to the point where she could reach the cross pipe, she pulled herself to it and began to cross the room towards the ferret. The ferret looked at her with interest, and just as she was about to reach for him, he launched himself toward the far wall and sailed across the room as if he had been doing it all his life. Jamilah was completely frustrated and emitted a few choice words in Spanish.

Ian and Rachael were doubled over with laughter. Clearly, the ferret had the best of them and could avoid them forever unless they had some way to catch him. Jamilah, also laughed when she heard Ian and Rachael laughing. She hung on to the pipe with one hand and just stared at the ferret. Then she swung, launched herself towards the captain and caught a handhold to bring herself to a stop.

Ian again called Alexi on the intercom, "Okay, Chief, you can turn the gas back on we are not going to be able to catch him that easily."

"Yes, sir, Captain," Alexi replied. The thrust was gradually, but quickly, brought to what it had been before it was cut off.

"I'm sorry, Captain," Jamilah said, looking quite contrite. "I'll sleep here tonight and hope he'll return to his cage to eat."

"Very good, Jammy," Ian said, there was no point in belaboring her with a lecture on the importance of keeping the ferret caged.

At dinner that evening, Lupe asked Jamilah, "Jamilah, that's a Middle Eastern name, isn't it?"

"Yes, Doctor, it is. My mother was an Iraqi and my father was American. They met and fell in love when he was in Iraq during the war. She insisted on giving me the same name her mother had, and my father thought that was beautiful. The Burns was from my father's side as you might expect. I was born in America over a year after they were married. Does that answer your question, Ma'am?"

"Yes, but you don't need to be so sensitive about it," Lupe replied.

"Ma'am, I have been getting that question all of my life. I am an American," she said with conviction. "You are from Mexico, why would you ask such a question?"

"Take it easy, Pajarita," Dr. Martinova said as he put his hand on his wife's arm and squeezed gently.

"Okay, ladies. That's enough. Jammy has been through enough today so let's just let it lay, okay?" Ian said.

"Sorry, Captain, I just wanted to establish where she was from," Lupe said with a sneer.

"Can we assume you have done that, Dr. Martinova?" Ian asked.

Her reply was a grim stare.

Later that night as Jamilah slept, the hatch was quietly opened, the door to the ferret's cage unlatched and the ferret escaped into the common area of the ship. The first indication that this happened was a surprised yelp from the cabin known as "girls town" because that was the cabin shared by the two pilots and Jamilah under ordinary circumstances. This particular night Jamilah, as promised, slept on the deck in the garden area. The yelp came from Rachael when she turned over in her sleep only to feel something soft and furry next her cheek. This, of course, startled the ferret who immediately took off for parts unknown.

Rachael's cry woke up everyone who was asleep and alerted those who were on duty that something unusual had happened. Rachael was not angry just surprised. She had handled and petted the ferret when she was working in the garden area with Jamilah long before the *Explorer* left the Moon. Because she smelled familiar, the ferret curled up with her. Everyone except Jamilah turned out to see what the uproar was all about. This immediately led to a search effort to find the ferret to no avail.

Ian immediately asked, "Where is Jamilah? She's not here to help search for Ferd?"

AJay Kaniyar went to get her and found her still asleep on the floor in the garden with the hatch ajar.

"Wake up, Jammy," he said. "Ferd has escaped again."

Jammy immediately checked the cage and saw that the latch had been slid back again allowing the ferret to escape.

AJay told the assembled complement that he found her sound asleep on the deck of the garden compartment near the cage, which was open.

"Sorry, Captain. It happened while I was asleep," Jamilah protested.

"We will talk about that later," Ian said. "In the meantime what can we do to catch him?"

"He likes people, Captain, you know, you've held him. He'll come out when he's no longer frightened. Please everyone, don't try to grab him, because if you grab him he may bite. He does not bite normally. He's really very affectionate, but any animal will react if they feel they're being attacked. He has been trained to use a litter box, and he always does. The best thing we can do is leave the door to the garden area open so that he can get into his cage and use it when he needs it," Jamilah explained.

"All right, let's do that," Ian ordered. "Jammy, I want to see you in my cabin, now!"

"Yes, sir," Jamilah replied and followed him into his cabin.

After Ian and Jamilah entered the captain's cabin, he closed the door and indicated a seat that had been provided for visitors. "Okay, Jammy, relax. I'm not angry with you," he assured her, "Now, tell me what happened or what you think happened."

"Captain, I don't know what happened. As I promised, I slept on the floor near his cage last night. The first I knew that anything had gone wrong was when AJay, Mr. Kaniyar, woke me up and told me. I immediately checked the cage and found that the latch had been slid to the unlocked position allowing him to escape again. When I went to bed, sir, I checked it, and I have a hook that I slipped over the knob on the latch. There is no way that Ferd could have opened that cage. I'd like to add, sir, when I was awakened, I felt very drowsy. I must've slept really hard because otherwise, I would have heard someone enter the garden and release the latch. Captain, once again, the ferret is not my fault. Oh, I guess he is because I brought him along, but he is ordinarily very well behaved. He's not any danger to anyone unless they try to grab him. He probably explored the ship, then curled up in bed with Rachael because he knew her. What do you want me to do, sir?" Jamilah asked.

"First, let me say I believe you," he assured Jamilah. "I'm not sure what's going on. But, before I went to sleep last night, I checked the hatch to the garden. It was closed and latched, and I left it that way. You were asleep on the floor. I saw you through the porthole in the hatch. I could not see Ferd's cage through the porthole because it is against the wall, but I thought I saw the outer edge of the cage door leading me to suspect it had been opened. Based on what happened yesterday, there will be some backlash from this. You undoubtedly will be blamed. Ignore it. If you get defensive, it might make you look more guilty. I will do my best to get to the bottom of this," Ian continued.

"Jammy, to tell you the truth, at this point I'm thinking of just letting Ferd have the run of the ship. I don't see how he can do any harm and as long as he won't hurt anyone. He could become the ship's mascot. Would that be all right with you?" Ian asked.

"Yes, sir, that would certainly solve the problem. Should I leave his cage in the garden area or put it in the storage area where he can get into it whenever he needs it to use a litter box?" Jamilah asked.

"Do whatever you think best. I will announce my decision to make him the ship's mascot during the morning meal. I want to see who might object," Ian finished. "You may go, Jammy. Say nothing to anyone, and thank you."

Jamilah left the captain's cabin and wondered as she walked slowly back to the common area what this was all about.

At breakfast, Ian stood up and rapped on the table for attention. "Ladies and gentlemen, I propose to make Ferd the ship's mascot and give him the run of the ship." While he was making this announcement, Ferd came scampering across the deck and jumped into Jamilah's lap.

"Jammy," Ian said, "why don't you take Ferd and introduce him to the rest of us."

"Yes, sir, I think that would be best." Jammy picked Ferd up and walked around the table, introducing him to everyone in the complement, and encouraged them to offer the backs of their hands for the ferret to smell. Everyone let him sniff their hands and petted him or scratched his head except Lupe. She announced that he reminded her of a rat and that she wanted nothing to do with him. Ferrets like most animals that are kept as pets were attuned to the emotions of the people around him and he made it clear that as far as he was concerned the feeling was mutual.

. . .

A week later, Mr. Watanabe, the communications and electronics specialist, reported that one of the cables connecting the computer to the sensor network had been tampered with. He made his report to the captain privately.

"Captain, it is supposed to look as if the cable has been gnawed, so the ferret will be blamed. But I don't think it was the ferret, sir. Whoever did it was not aware that the cable chosen is a coaxial cable which has a woven wire sheath, that acts as a ground connection, under the outer insulation. Some of the sheaths were cut through. I have a difficult time imagining that the ferret would chew on a coaxial cable, to begin with, and I am certain he would not or could not gnaw through the coaxial sheath. But just to be safe in the future I rubbed all of the exposed cables with the liquid kitchen detergent after I made sure that the ferret was repelled by it. He took one sniff and then sort of hissed like a cat and went running away. If it happens again, I will know for sure that someone is trying to sabotage our computer and communications system and that it's not the ferret. Is there anything else you would like me to do, Captain?"

"No, Ichuro. Keep it under your hat for the time being and let's see what happens. Someone aboard this ship is messing with us and I'd like to catch them in the act. Is there anything you can do with your gear to detect who it is if they try again?" Ian asked.

"Our equipment was not designed with that in mind. I'll see what I can do by using the cameras on the computer monitors to catch whoever it is in the act," Mr. Watanabe offered.

"Do that if you can," Ian ordered, and then continued, "Don't say anything to anyone. Leave it to me. At the next meal, report to me in the presence of everyone else that there was a glitch in the computer connection to the on-board sensors, but you've fixed the problem," the captain ordered.

Mr. Watanabe did as the captain asked. No one mentioned the cable nor even suggested that there might be a problem. However, two people glanced quickly in the general direction of the computer when Mr. Watanabe made his report. Ian was surprised at who they were, and he made a mental note to keep them under closer scrutiny.

CHAPTER NINE

Nineteen days after they left Earth orbit, things had been going smoothly for over a week. There was no trouble except for a couple of minor confrontations that were only to be expected when twelve people were confined in a space the size of a small home for almost three weeks. Both incidents were quelled by other members of the crew and did not require the intervention of the captain. There was an Acey-Ducey contest in progress with two boards competing, one on each side of the Common Room table. The real problem was everyone was bored.

Miriam had to make just four course corrections since leaving Earth orbit. All four were relatively minor. The exception was the adjustment necessary after the engines had been shut down in the first attempt to catch the ferret. That correction was slightly more complicated. The corrections needed to use the axillary jets to change the heading of the *Explorer* only a small fraction of one degree. The current velocity of the *Explorer* was nearly 450,000 mph or approximately 122 miles per second. Any deviation could make a fairly significant difference that required immediate correction. Even though the course was essentially a straight line from where Earth was to where Mars was going to be, in reality, it was more like a great circle route on Earth. Earth's orbital velocity is 18.25 mi./s and Mars orbital velocity is

15 mi./s. Minor, really minuscule adjustments were necessary to constantly adjust for the differences in orbital velocity. In addition, as reaction mass was used and the ship became lighter, it was necessary to constantly adjust the thrust in order to maintain a continuous one-quarter-G acceleration.

As the *Explorer* approached the halfway point, it was necessary to stop the engines and reverse the orientation of the ship relative to the course. The engines could then be used to decelerate the ship to a speed exactly matching the orbit of Mars orbit. In addition, the goal was to place the ship in the same orbit as Phobos, Mars's larger moon, which was orbiting Mars at a velocity of 1.3 mi./s at an altitude of 3700 miles above the surface. It was no mean feat to make all the adjustments necessary to bring the ship to stop relative to Mars orbit at a point 20° behind Phobos in its orbit around Mars. The navigation for the first half of the trip was fairly straightforward. The navigation for the second half would be incredibly more complex as the ship decelerated. Miriam had made fair allowance for the intended duration of the flip over procedure, but the final adjustments to the course could not be made until the actual deceleration began so she could determine the vector of the ship. There were bound to be some minor errors that simply could not be accounted for until after the flip-over operation was completed and the engines were restarted. Even a few seconds more or less could make a significant difference.

. . .

The countdown for the flip-over procedure began at T minus sixty minutes.

Ian called for assistance in preparing the ship for the maneuver. "Would you all please prepare for the flip over maneuver by securing all loose objects are not tied down or otherwise anchored to prevent them from drifting around the inside of the ship and possibly causing problems during the weightless period. To speed things up, I have prepared a list of the things to be done by each person. You are to go through the entire ship from the command module to the Reactors and check to be sure everything is secured."

After everyone had completed their other assigned chores, Rachael, Lupe, and Ichuro helped Jamilah cover the hydroponic beds and lock them in position and to generally batten down everything else in the garden compartment.

At T minus five minutes, everyone except Miriam, Ichuro, and Alexi were strapped into seats around the Common Room table. Miriam strapped herself into the pilot station and controlled the countdown in conjunction with Ichuro and the computer, which was programmed to operate the steering rockets and the ship's gyroscope to perform the flip-over maneuver. Ichuro was strapped in the electronics and computer cubicle ready to assist Miriam with computer control if necessary. Alexi was aft in the reactor room at the controls ready to shut down the thrust and then restart it once the maneuver was completed.

As T minus thirty seconds, Miriam performed a final check of all of her controls and then announced she was ready for the flip-over maneuver. "I have computed sixty predetermined corrections that can be selected from the computer to adjust the attitude and vector of the ship before the main engines are restarted. "As you can imagine, reversing the direction of a ship that masses over 100 thousand metric tonnes is not a simple process. The steering rockets at both ends of the ship will be used to rotate the ship around its central axis and its center of gravity. It will be necessary to maintain a very minimal amount of thrust until a turnover in order to keep the reaction mass at the aft end of its tank and that has to be allowed for."

Ichuro started a computer program to count down the last ten seconds over the PA system so that everyone aboard could be prepared for zero time. There were displays throughout the ship to show the countdown to avoid even milliseconds of delay between the spoken zero and the actual engine cutoff moment. Miriam waited five seconds while Alexi throttled back the engines to the predetermined minimal thrust. As the thrust was reduced, almost everyone gripped whatever was handy in a reflex action. The one thing they had overlooked was the ferret who was on his favorite perch above the galley cabinets sleeping.

When Alexi completed the cutback, he announced, "The engine room is ready for the flip-over maneuver." He was surprised when he didn't feel the rotation begin on his signal. Thinking something was wrong, he called Miriam on the intercom to ask if there was a problem. "Pilot, is something wrong up there?" he asked.

As soon as she heard his voice, Miriam began the rotation sequence. "I never got your signal, Commander," Miriam replied, "but we are still within the parameters for the precomputed corrections. There shouldn't be any problem. Mr. Watanabe is indicating that the signal was never received by the computer. Can you check things at your end, Commander?"

"I'll do that immediately," Alexi responded.

It took over an hour to find a cable connection that might have been disconnected by the deceleration. Alexi called the captain, "We have found the problem, Captain. One of the cables apparently came loose somehow."

"How could that happen, Commander?" Ian asked.

"Damned if we know, Captain. I am open to suggestions. I, we, can't think of any way the cable, which is behind an inspection panel, could have come loose. It has a bayonet connector that locks it in place. Can you think of anything?"

"Keep it under your hat, Alexi. It has to be sabotage. I doubt we will ever find out whether it was done by someone on board since we left or by someone back on the Moon. My guess it is was probably one of the scientists because I cannot imagine why anyone in the crew would do such a thing. Almost anyone aboard could have done it. Everyone has done the Book and would be likely to know where it was and, if it is labeled, what it is for. But, haven't you been using that connection to talk to the command deck all along?"

"Yes, Captain, I have, so it has to be someone aboard who did it. Why don't you have Ichuro check the computer logs for the past week or two to see if anyone besides AJay and I have been in the reactor area."

"Thanks, I'll do just that," Ian replied.

The flip-over procedure was scheduled to take almost thirty minutes. One hundred thousand tons of mass over 500 feet long, could not be swung around like an automobile doing a bootleg turn. It took time to get the rotation started, and it would take an equal amount of time to get it stopped. Once the rotation began, the steering rockets could be cut off. The ship would continue to rotate until action was taken to stop it. As the rotation approached the halfway point, the steering rockets on the opposite side of the ship would be used to gradually stop the rotation.

At the precise moment shown on her astrogation monitor in conjunction with her celestial sightings, Miriam fired the opposite steering rockets to initiate the stop procedure. It was immediately obvious something was wrong. One of the steering rockets for stopping the rotation was not firing. She cut off all of the steering rockets as the ship began to wobble and pressed the alarm button. Ferd woke up and tried to leap down from his perch, but he was not prepared for the unusual motion of the ship and sailed end over end toward the table. AJay reached up and caught the ferret and handed him to Gladys who hugged and comforted him.

Ian could feel something wrong as well. He left his seat at the table and made his way up to the pilot deck. Miriam still had her finger on the alarm button as Ian came up behind her. He took the copilot seat in the pilot station.

"What happened, Miriam?" Ian asked. "It's complicated, sir," she replied.

"Of that, I have no doubt, Major." Ian used her rank to emphasize the seriousness of the situation.

"Okay, Captain, here's what happened as I see it. The steering rocket at position 270 at the aft end did not fire, resulting in unequal forces on the rotation axes that threw the ship into a skew tumble. The tumble is very slow and I'm sure I can correct for it. To do so, I'm going to need to rotate the ship axially in order to position the steering rockets that were used to initiate flip-over to stop the tumble and complete the maneuver, Captain," Miriam reported.

"How difficult will that be?" Ian asked.

"I'm not entirely sure, sir. We are going to over rotate and will need to go around again maybe more than once before I can stop the tumble and the flip. I have about forty-five minutes to figure out what to do and how to do it. Captain, I'm going to have to do this by the seat-of-my-pants. I don't know why but no provision was made in the programming to correct this problem, probably because it was never anticipated. I would really appreciate it if I can have

Rachael up here to work with me on this," Miriam answered. As she said this Rachael put her hand on Miriam's shoulder to indicate that she was there.

"What are the chances that we can fix the problem with the steering rocket. The panel that provides access to the steering jet is one of the ones around 38-25," Ian said. "I remember looking in there when I did my Book. I'll go check it out."

Ian really wanted to stay on the pilot deck and observe what the pilots were doing. But he was smart enough to realize there were times when it really wasn't a good idea to be looking over someone's shoulder when they did something this difficult, and he really wanted to go find out what had happened.

He said, "Okay, ladies, I'll leave it up to you. Please keep me and the rest of the ship's complement informed of your progress. I would really like to ask what the consequences would be if you can't fix it, but at the moment I'm going to assume it can be stopped and leave it in your capable hands." Then Ian slid out of the way so Rachael could take the copilot seat.

"How much did you hear, Rachael?" Miriam asked.

"I came in where you were going to fix this by the seat-of-the-pants," Rachael replied with a grin.

Miriam explained the entire problem to Rachael and then asked her what she would do. As Rachael was considering her response, there was an uproar from the common area. They were unable to hear the actual words that were being spoken, but it was clear that the people in the common area were agitated and frightened and demanding information. Miriam looked over at Ichuro and shook her head to let him know she did not want him telling anyone what was going on. Ichuro closed the hatch sealing off the command deck.

It took over two hours for the two pilots to develop a plan for counteracting the complex motion of the ship. The ship was wobbling like a bowling pin out of balance and also tumbling end over end. They broke the problem down into its component parts. It was agreed that before the tumble could be fixed, it would be necessary to first stop the axial spin and the associated wobble. This was made more complicated because they could not use all four steering rockets at each end of the ship. Because the problem was caused by the failure of steering rocket 270 aft, in order to maintain symmetry they would only use the steering rockets at 0 and 180 fore and aft to counteract the axial spin.

Small bursts would be used so they would not lose control again and create a bigger problem if something went wrong. Rachael entered the necessary commands into the computer and then, Miriam and Ichuro both double-checked the entries to make absolutely sure that everything was precisely what was intended. Then they activated the program.

The large monitor that displayed a complete diagram of the *Explorer* showed that the selected steering rockets rotated in the correct direction and fired the specified amount. They waited to see if the axial rotation and wobble was slowed as expected. Careful measurement of the actual rotation speed against what was predicted indicated a slight difference between the intended effect and the actual effect. The ship was still spinning but much more slowly. To be safe, they planned to do the additional correction incrementally to avoid overshooting. The revised data was entered and cross-checked; then they activated the program again. This was done three more times with a quick check after each activation, and finally, the results were spot-on. They had stopped the axial rotation. It was also essential that when the rotation stopped the steering rockets that could be used to stop the end-over-end tumbling were positioned correctly relative to the crosswise axis of the ship.

"Miriam," Ian said through the communication system. "Commander Gargorin and I have found the correct access panel and it has been tampered with. The fuel line to the steering jet you need has been crushed so fuel cannot get to the nozzle and it is going to take a while to fix because there is not much access room back there."

"That's okay, Captain," Miriam replied. "We have developed a program using only the remaining steering jets to stop the wobble and rotation problems. Our next problem is to determine precisely when to fire the steering rockets to stop the end-over-end motion and leave the ship pointed in the correct direction for deceleration. We have two choices. We can try to stop the end-over-end motion with one continuous burn, or make multiple shorter burns like we did to stop the spin."

"Alright, Miriam, I'll leave it in your cable hands. While you're doing that, we will repair the fuel line so that you can use the entering jet in the future. Let me know what you decide to do, please."

"Wilco, Captain. We've about decided to go with the long continuous burn and hope for the best. Chances are, any problems we encounter doing this will definitely be easier to correct than what we had to start with. If we tried to make several shorter burns, it might take hours because the ship would continue tumbling between burns and it would be necessary to recompute after each burn, which would take time. On the other hand, if we use one continuous burn, it should take care of most of the problem and we can adjust if it's necessary."

"Your call; do what you think best. We never had these kinds of problems in submarines," Ian said with a chuckle. "Carry on."

"We'll have to wait about forty-five minutes until the ship's orientation is in exactly the correct position before we can fire the steering jets. We felt it isn't a good idea to attempt to stop the flip-over incrementally because if we do that, we might have to wait for extra revolutions before we could complete the process. We are planning to stop the correction just slightly before the rotation has completed. We can then make the final adjustments at the end of the next rotation. Unfortunately, this means waiting almost four and a half hours before we can make the final correction," Miriam explained.

Then the program began. The initial corrections went off exactly as planned. Before they were finished, Ian joined Miriam and Rachael on the pilot deck.

"Hi, Captain," Rachael said as he arrived. "It looks like we're spot-on with what we've done so far." She pointed to a countdown clock. "That is the time remaining before we try the final correction."

As the countdown clock ticked toward zero, the tension in the command deck was palpable. Then the steering jets started and the final correction went off exactly as planned.

"That's it, Captain," Miriam announced.

"Really? It still looks as if it is not quite right. Don't misunderstand. That was a layman's opinion, not a judgment. I trust you. If you say it is right, I believe you."

The ship was still traversing on a course that was very close to what was desired.

"Now that we have the ship pointed in the right direction and almost perfectly stable," Miriam said, "I have to take sightings on my reference stars to see what else I need to do before we can begin our deceleration." She took the sightings and then made two very minor burns. "There, we are now lined up precisely on our course and all of the residual spinning has stopped. Our next problem is to recalculate the deceleration program, allowing for lost time while we were correcting the tumbling."

The recalculations took almost two hours with inputs from Alexi. Finally, it was done and the data was entered into the computer.

"Are you ready, Commander?" Rachael was handling the communications while Miriam was focused completely on the reference stars to correct for any anomalies that might occur during the throttling up of the engines.

"Ready," Alexi replied.

Rachael counted down from five. When she reached zero, Alexi began to throttle up the engines. Rachael watched the accelerometer as the reading slowly approached the one-quarter G point. Thirty minutes later, Miriam confirmed that they were on the correct vector or so close to it she could not determine the difference.

"We will continue to monitor the positions of the reference stars over the next few days to see if any corrections are needed. But, I'll bet we are spot-on," Racheal explained.

There were some recriminations and dirty looks from some of the scientists in the common area when Miriam came in to eat dinner, leaving Rachael at the pilot station. Miriam ignored them, sitting quietly by herself. After a bit, Lupe asked, "What would've happened if you were unable to correct the problem?"

"It is difficult to describe. In simple terms, we would have continued tumbling right past the orbit of Mars and into outer space," she answered.

Later when he came off duty, Alexi went to the captain's cabin to make a confidential report. "Do you know what happened and how it happened?" Ian asked.

"Yes, sir, the inspection panel for the electronic valve had been removed and replaced.

There were scratch marks in the paint near the screw heads."

"There are always scratch marks on the panels," Ian replied.

"True, but after we did the final run through before we departed, I sprayed paint on all the scratch marks to make everything look shipshape. The panel in question is right next to a bulkhead former that hides the panel unless you are looking right at it. When you sent me to check the valve, there were new very faint scratch marks that could only be seen from a certain angle. What's more, the screws used to retain the panels are a quarter turn, square-hole Robertson-head screws that require a special screwdriver to turn them. Whoever had turned the valve off knew what they were doing because I checked all the other access panels and the one covering the valve was the only one that had been tampered with."

"Seriously?" Ian asked. "Someone purposely opened the panel and turned off the valve?"

"Yes, sir."

"This poses a real problem, Commander. Chris was right; there is a saboteur on board. Well, what he said exactly was that we might have one or more saboteurs on board. I'll bet my stripes that it's not a crew member, but the sabotage had to be done by someone with detailed knowledge of the ship or at the very least a set of blueprints and they are only accessible to crew members. Furthermore, whoever did it, had been told what to do and when to do it to cause the most harm.

"Do you trust the whole crew, Alexi, even Ichuro and AJay both of whom were relative unknowns when they joined us?"

"AJay is unlikely because no one knew who he was until ICExS picked him out of a roster of possible candidates. Ichuro is a different issue because he was a volunteer from the ISS crew who came highly recommended by his supervisor, but he was shipped up to Farside within hours of volunteering, so it is unlikely anyone could have gotten to him and also filled him in on what needed to be done."

"Okay, so what does that leave?" Ian asked again.

"Well, I seem to remember that a set of blueprints for the ship went missing for most of a day about a month before the scientists, except for Jammy were chosen. They were later found in a different filing cabinet than the one they were usually kept in and the incident was passed over as a clerical error. They could easily have been copied and sent to whoever wanted them, probably the Cartel. Anyway, whoever selected the time and place for the sabotage had to know what they were doing and what we would be doing at the time designated. That is really frightening, my friend."

"Yes, sir, it certainly is."

"What can we do to insure nothing like this ever happens again?"

"Institute a daily inspection program, and a comprehensive inspection program before every maneuver from now on."

"Let's do it," Ian ordered.

. . .

There were no further incidents during the remainder of the trip to Mars. Miriam had made a dozen course corrections and speed adjustments in as many days as they neared the point where they would enter Mars orbit. These were necessary to correct for the delay caused by the flip-over the incident. The last thirty minutes during the approach required some fine-tuning that could not have been foreseen during the original course planning. In the end, she nudged the *Explorer* into orbit exactly as planned.

They were still decelerating slowly when Miriam announced, "Main engine cut-off." Followed by, "Captain, we have arrived in orbit as planned. There will still be some adjustments to be made for a perfect orbit, but we need to take some measurements and analyze the data before the final adjustments can be made. Actually, I suspect we are pretty close right now, so waiting an orbit or two will be fine and I would prefer to be on the sunny side of the orbit when any final adjustments are made."

"Well done, Major" Ian replied in congratulation. "Secure the flight deck and join us for dinner."

As Miriam floated down to the common deck everyone in the room applauded and congratulated her.

"It's back to covered trays and freefall eating," Tom observed. "What's on the menu today?"

"Where's Phobos?" AJay asked. "I looked for it out the viewport and all I saw was the surface of Mars and some stars."

"We are 20 degrees behind Phobos in its orbit, so it's not very close," Miriam explained. "In addition, the ship will be apparently doing a continuous end-for-end rotation as we circle Mars."

"Why?" AJay asked again.

"The ship will not actually be rotating. In fact, it will always be pointed at the same reference star initially all the while we are here in orbit. In effect, we will do one flip-over per orbit while we are actually standing still relative to the universe," Miriam answered. "Let me try to show you what will be happening." She picked up a pencil and said, "Watch." With that, she pointed the pencil at one of the lights and began to move around the table while continuously pointing the pencil at the same light. "Notice that the pencil seems to do one rotation as I walk around the table, but it is actually always pointed in the same direction.

"The final fine-tuning I'll have to do will be to have it pointed at Phobos when we're in the middle of a daylight cycle. In the middle of the night cycle, it will still be pointing in the same direction but will face away from Phobos, relatively. It is all nothing but Newton's First Law in action on a grand scale. I could have it always point at Phobos, but that would require more or less continuous use of the steering jets and that would be a waste of fuel. Got it?"

"Got it," AJay said with a smile as he bumped his head with the heel of his hand. "Dumb, me. I never took any astronomy courses at university."

"Not so dumb," Gladys Campbell said. "I had the same question for the same reason." There were several nods from around the table as the others grasped the concept.

"One final thought, if the *Explorer* is pointing exactly at Phobos at the middle of the current orbit, where will it be pointing relative to Phobos half a Mars year from now?"

"Aha, celestial navigation, right?" Ian asked.

"What about it, Captain? What does celestial navigation have to do with this?" Gladys asked.

"Back in the dark ages when I was a midshipman at the Naval Academy we went on a summer cruise. While on that cruise, every midshipman has to shoot the Sun at exact noon to get the latitude and then a set of three stars late at night to get the longitude. The star I could see at Christmas, for example, would not be visible six months later because the Earth would be in the way and I would have to use a different star. We had a book of tables of position of every bright star for every day of the year and were required to use a different set of stars every night. The captain and the training officer decided which stars we would use each day so we could not cheat and compute our position in advance."

"I'll be damned," Ichuro said quietly.

After the meal, there was an excited conversation about the upcoming work to be done before the scientists could be ferried down to the surface and begin their work.

As Ian watched the panoramic sweep of the Martian surface through the portal in his cabin, he pondered what the next problem might be. He still had no absolute proof as to who might have been the person or persons who caused the prior problems. He had gone over the problems time and again ever since the first incident where the ferret was released and an attempt was made to blame him for gnawing on a cable in the communications cubicle. The only conclusion he could come to was probably more than one person was involved.

Ian prepared a report to Farside Base notifying them that the *Explorer* had arrived in orbit behind Phobos as planned and all was well. He pondered whether to include descriptions of all the incidents. He had informed Farside Base of each one as it occurred but put no stress on the severity of the problems until the flip-over incident, which had to be explained. He reported the events of the day every day in clear. Today, he decided to use his secret personal code to ask if it would be possible to initiate a deeper background check of everyone aboard. He could rule out himself and he was absolutely certain that Alexi had not caused the problems, and that neither of the pilots had been involved. But he took no chances and requested that everyone on the ship except the ferret be rechecked. He smiled at that because, in reality, the ferret had brought a great deal of levity to the trip.

As Ian was preparing his report he could hear everyone exclaiming over their rediscovery of weightlessness. There were no cases of motion sickness; they were acclimated to that. But a full collection of bumps and bruises were earned as a result of misgauging the effects of moving too quickly or without foresight. From the sounds he could hear, there seemed to be a fair amount of gaiety. Mostly the scientists were eager to go down to the surface of Mars and set up camp as soon as possible.

PART TWO

CHAPTER TEN

"May I have your attention, please," Ian addressed the company. "Now that we have settled into a stable orbit, I know you are all eager to begin your work, especially the scientists, but I suggest you take a day and do some planning or just taking it easy. You all need to reacquaint yourselves with living and working in freefall before unpacking your equipment. To facilitate that, I have asked the crew to string rope in a network throughout the forward module around and between the important locations. So, be careful and take your time. We have eighteen months to do what we came to do."

Within a few hours, they were swimming around without running into each other or any obstacle and no one was getting space sick.

"Captain, we've been taking it easy for eight weeks. We want to get busy now," Tom said.

"Yes, but you haven't been taking it easy in a weightless environment and that makes a big difference. Moving containers that weigh up to several hundred pounds is a tricky process in weightlessness. Just moving yourselves now that we're weightless again has proved to be difficult at times. I ask you to consider how you might start a 500 to 1,000-pound container moving and once you did that how you would get it stopped. It is not as simple as being weightless suggests. The containers may be weightless in the broadest interpretation of the term, but remember, they still have mass. Believe me, when I say, it can result in sprains and broken bones. Then, once you begin unpacking, there will be all sorts of things drifting around in the storage deck. So, even the unpacking will have to be planned and executed carefully."

"Rachael and Miriam assisted by Commander Gargorin and myself transferred the containers from the Lunar Shuttle into the storage area, stacked them and tied down each one individually. For example, the six containers containing the primary elements for construction of the surface shelter and the base were the last ones loaded and, except for the containers with your personal items, are the ones easiest to access. They will need to be moved out of the way and into the Mars Surface Shuttle before most of the other containers can be accessed. Before they can be loaded onto the Mars Shuttle, the Lunar Shuttle will need to be undocked and moved to the aft airlock, then the Mars Shuttle will need to be moved from its attachment point to the forward airlock."

"Why couldn't that have been done while we were in route, Captain?" Esteban Martinova asked.

"Rachael, would you like to answer that one?" Ian asked.

"Yes, sir. While we were on the way, Dr. Martinova, the *Explorer* was under constant Acceleration, so moving the shuttles would require them to be under constant acceleration as well and matching acceleration between two ships is a very difficult process," Rachael replied.

"Then, why couldn't it have been done before we left the Moon?" Dr. Martinova persisted.

"Because, sir, until we actually began our departure acceleration, there was a very real chance that we might need the Lunar Shuttle in the event there were any problems. And, before you ask, no, we could not have used the Mars Shuttle instead because it was not designed for travel between the *Explorer* and the Moon," Rachael replied.

Before Martinova could persist, Ian interrupted, "People, before we actually left the Moon, we needed the Lunar Shuttle and now that we are here, we need the Mars Shuttle. It was planned that way from the beginning, so there is no use in trying to second-guess the designers after the fact. Now, who is going to do what to rearrange the shuttles?" Ian asked.

No one had left the ship since leaving the Moon, there had been no reason for a spacewalk up until now. When everything was ready to make the first trip out of orbit down to the surface, Miriam spoke up and asked, "Captain, may I have permission to move the shuttles?"

"Rachael, do you have anything to say in this case?" Ian asked.

"No, Captain, Miriam and I discussed the rearrangement process. Your order that both of us cannot leave the ship at the same time means essentially that one of us do the arranging because whoever does it, will have to do a spacewalk to get to the Mars Shuttle. We drew cards from the deck, and Miriam won. Subject to your approval, Miriam will be the one to actually do the rearranging."

"Okay, but Miriam, first tell me how you plan to do that," I said.

"First, I will undock the Lunar Shuttle from the forward airlock and move it to the aft airlock at the reactor compartment. Then I will do a space walk around the superstructure of the *Explorer* to reach the Mars Shuttle. Then, I will undock it from the superstructure and move it around to the forward airlock."

"Alright, I agree with your plan. If you have problems, there will not be anyone to help you, because of the rule that both you and Rachael cannot both be off the ship at the same time, understood?"

Both women nodded their agreement and said, "Yes, sir."

Miriam crawled into her space suit with help from Rachael and Tom Vernon. They attached the oxygen supply to the space suit, checked to make sure the oxygen was flowing properly, then connected the power module.

"Ready?" Rachael asked.

"Ready," Miriam replied, then entered the *Explorer*'s airlock.

Rachael sealed the airlock behind her and cycled it and scavenged the air from the airlock into the storage tanks. Miriam then opened the shuttle airlock and entered the shuttle.

"I'm doing the shuttle checklist now," she reported and she could be heard as she read out and verified each checklist item. When she had finished, she said, "Everything is working correctly after eight weeks of cold storage. Disconnecting, now."

There was the usual *thunk* as Miriam disconnected. She could be heard over the ship-to-ship radio as she reported, "All systems are working properly."

There was no way to see exactly what she was doing because the only real windows were the ones facing forward on the pilot deck and the small viewport in the airlock door.

Rachael was looking through the small viewport in the airlock and saw Miriam fire the steering jets to move the lunar shuttle to the back and confirmed that everything seemed to operate normally.

Shortly the listeners in the Common Room heard Miriam as she was docking at the rear airlock. "Commander Gargorin are you ready for me to dock?" It was a formality that was strictly adhered to ensure there would be no errors as the airlock mated.

"You are lined up slightly forward of the airlock mechanism," Alexi reported. "Can you back up about half a meter?"

"Can do, Commander," Miriam said as she gently manipulated the steering jets.

"Perfect," Alexi said a moment later. "Come on in." Then added, "docked" as the connecting mechanism engaged.

"Lunar Shuttle out," Miriam said as she shut down the shuttle systems and then entered the Reactor Deck.

Ten minutes later Miriam swam back into the storage area towing her space helmet. Rachael helped her check all of her personal equipment was in proper working order. "Okay, you are cleared for the space walk to the Mars shuttle," Rachael said. As she led Miriam once again to the forward airlock. "Be careful out there," she admonished as Miriam cycled back through the airlock in the storage area and after attaching a safety line to a connection point outside the airlock, she began the space walk to the nearer Mars Shuttle.

Once again, after she entered the Mars Shuttle, she read the checklist aloud and Rachael verified each item as it was reported. Then Miriam reported, "Checking steering jets." Followed by her reporting, "They're all responding normally. Disengaging now." Miriam disconnected the Mars Shuttle from its dock on the side of the *Explorer* and maneuvered it slowly back to the forward airlock at the storage area and reconnected with the *Explorer*. Then she reported, "Docking completed, ready to receive air into the shuttle."

"Roger, matching air pressure with the *Explorer*," Rachael said as she adjusted the air pressure between the two vessels. Then, "Ready."

This procedure was a little different because air pressure between the Mars lander and the storage area of the *Explorer* had to be the same so that the equipment containers could be moved from the *Explorer* to the shuttle without the need to constantly adjust the air pressure.

When this was finished, Ian took command, "Let's have lunch before we move the containers to the shuttle."

After lunch, the six containers containing the pieces of the surface base were loaded and strapped down for the trip to the surface. As part of their training program on Earth, Tom Vernon the Canadian Environmentalist and Jan Pitrasen the Chief Scientist practiced assembling the initial buildings for the surface base.

"Are you ready, Tom?" Ian asked.

"Yes, sir. But I think it would go quicker if Jan went down too," Tom asserted. "I know I was designated as the person to actually assemble the habitat, but I practiced with Jan and it will go much quicker if we work together. Jan?"

"I agree," Jan Pitrasen said.

He put on his space suit and ancillary equipment and entered the surface shuttle. Rachael resealed the airlock to the storage area and waited while the air from the shuttle was pumped back into the storage tanks and then she sealed the shuttle airlock. Everyone was watching on the large monitor as the shuttle undocked and prepared for its first trip to the surface. Rachael waved from the shuttle's forward window and began the trip to the surface.

The location for the Martian surface base had been chosen with care, the area was flat, relatively low in altitude, in the lee of a very tall cliff, which would tend to shelter them from any wind or sandstorms, and in an area where it would receive the maximum amount of sunlight possible.

Flying the shuttle down to the surface of Mars was not greatly different from flying the lunar capsule down to the surface of the moon. The main difference was there was a vestigial atmosphere on Mars that could be used to help slow the shuttle during the final stages of the descent and landing process. In general, the time to begin the descent was a ten-minute window out of each eight-hour orbit around Mars. Rachael was in position and ready to go as soon as the window opened. She fired the retro rockets and began the descent. Slowing from the 1.33 mi./s orbital speed to a zero speed on landing required a combination of rockets and atmospheric drag.

Mars atmosphere was not dense enough to actually fly in except at a very high velocity so that it would be necessary to use braking rockets to land. Twenty minutes later, Rachael called to inform the *Explorer* that the landing had been successful and was at a position almost exactly at the intended location. Everyone breathed a sigh of relief when they heard her.

The plan was for them to be on the surface for twenty-three hours. During that time, they would set up the buildings of the base and connect the power unit and the air supply. They would set up the main shelter first, so they could rest in the shelter, before assembling the rest of the buildings and completing the work required to prepare the base for the scientists. Right on schedule, they lifted off the surface and ascended back into orbit in a near-perfect match with the position of the *Explorer*. A few minutes later, they were docked at the storage area airlock and after re-pressurizing, the two scientists rejoined the group.

"Piece of cake," Rachael said, grinning at Miriam. Then turning to Ian, she said with a salute and undue formality, "Captain, sir, I am here to report that the landing went exactly as planned and the preliminary construction of the surface shelter has been completed."

Ian replied with equal formality and a happy smile, "Well done, Major!"

For the next six days, Miriam and Rachael alternated taking loads of supplies and equipment down to the surface. By the seventh day, the scientists were ready to begin their work on the surface. The first two down were Tom Vernon and Esteban Martinova. Rachael took them down and made sure they were in the shelter and that the shelter was functioning correctly before returning to the *Explorer*. Next Miriam took Jan Pitrasen and Jamilah Burns. Finally, Lupe Martinova and Gladys Campbell were taken down by Rachael and the decision had been made for Rachael to remain on the surface with the shuttle for a day in case there should be a need for someone to return to the ship.

The crew remaining on the ship went into repair mode and fixed everything that they could find that needed fixing from one end to the other. They inventoried supplies and checked to make sure things left on the ship were ready and available should they be needed. Ichuro Watanabe maintained a continuous flow of communication between the *Explorer* and Farside Base.

In time, a lengthy message marked "Captain's eyes only" in code was received, printed, and turned over to Ian. Ian deciphered it and read it as he did so. When he was finished he went back and read it through again. It was a report from Security detailing further investigations of all of the scientists and crew. Nothing new or revealing had been found. Ian was disappointed because he had hoped that a deeper check would tell them who was causing the various sabotage incidents.

For two weeks everything went according to plan. At the end of two weeks, the plan called for the scientists to return to the ship with whatever samples they might have found and file a report for Farside Base. There had been relatively constant communication between the *Explorer* and what was now called Ares Base whenever the *Explorer* passed overhead.

Then suddenly, the day before the scientists were due to return, Ichuro reported to Ian, "Captain, I am unable to raise Ares Base on the radio."

"What? Why?" Ian replied.

"Sir, communication with Ares Base was lost between the last two passes. I have no idea what happened. I tested all the ship's radio equipment on all frequencies with no response."

"They're due to return on the next pass, right?"

"Yes, sir. All we can do is wait and see. Maybe the equipment at Ares Base failed somehow, or they lost electric power. It is only about eight hours until they are due to return."

"Captain," Miriam said, "I can wake up the second shuttle and go down to see what the problem is, sir."

"No, Miriam, you know as well as I do that we have to keep one pilot aboard the *Explorer* at all times."

"I know, Captain, but—"

"No buts. We will stick to protocol and give them time to fix the problem on their end and then decide what to do. If you should have a problem, we would be without a pilot to get us home and I cannot let that happen. Let's wait and see what happens."

"Yes, sir," Miriam replied.

Then as scheduled, Rachael ferried up the three women scientists to the *Explorer*. When the shuttle drew near the *Explorer*, Rachael called using her space suit radio to announce their arrival. A few minutes later the shuttle docked and the women were all aboard.

Lupe was the first to talk after she had removed her helmet. "What happened up here? We have not been able to communicate with you for at least a day."

The other three women confirmed what Lupe had said. Rachael said, "We tried everything we could think of to contact you. We checked all the equipment and could not find anything wrong. But as we approached the ship, I could hear you calling us. I could not tell whether it was my helmet radio or the shuttle radio with the problem. I figured it was least likely to be my helmet radio, so I waited until I was within hailing distance to call you to let you know we were arriving."

"Ichuro, do you have any ideas about what might be the problem?" Ian asked.

"No, sir, but I think we should check to see if the shuttle radio works properly before we draw any conclusions. Normally, it should put out enough power to reach the ship clearly from the ground," Ichuro responded.

The airlock between the shuttle and the *Explorer* was still open. Rachael had removed her space suit, and said, "I'll check it, sir." She did the weightless swim back through the airlock into the shuttle and keyed the radio. "*Explorer*, can you hear me now?" Her voice was heard weakly through the speakers on the command deck, and there was static.

"I hear you, Rachael," Ichuro responded. "But the signal is very weak and there's a lot of static." He turned to Ian. "Captain, there must be something wrong with the shuttle antennas. I need to go outside to look things over."

"How comfortable are you with that idea, Ichuro?" Ian asked.

"Sir, I went external on the ISS several times to do maintenance on the electronic equipment. But we can do this either of two ways. We can have Rachael disconnect and maneuver the shuttle up toward the nose of the *Explorer* so we can look at it through the windows. Of course, I'm not sure how well we could see things anyway, and if something is wrong, I'm going to need to go out and fix it anyhow."

"Okay, how would you go about it?" Ian asked.

"There are two possibilities, Captain. I could go into the shuttle with Rachael, have her disconnect and then go out and have a look, or I could go out through the reactor deck airlock, connect a long line to an anchor point, and go hand over hand on the handrail from there to the shuttle," Ichuro replied.

"Which do you prefer?"

"Out through the airlock, sir. I think it will be quicker and less risky."

Ian decided to give him the go-ahead. "Let's wait until the next daylight pass so you can see what you're doing."

Ichuro tied his space suit, the oxygen tank, the other controls, and a toolkit he had taken from under his desk in the communications cubicle and towed them through the command deck and back the to the reactor deck. Alexi and AJay helped him put on his space suit and cycled the airlock for him. Ichuro kept up a constant chatter with the command deck as he progressed the length of the ship up to the shuttle. Once there, he connected himself to an anchor point and began to check over the shuttle.

Within a few minutes, he reported, "Got it! The antenna has come loose and is hanging on by its cable. I will remount it and you can do a radio check," he said, and then, "What the hell? Captain, this was no accident, someone deliberately broke it loose from its base. I think I can repair it. Give me a minute. … Okay, try it now."

Rachael was already in the shuttle, she keyed the radio, and her voice was received loud and clear.

"That appears to have done it, Ichuro. Is it secure?" Ian asked.

"Not exactly," Ichuro replied without further explanation.

Twenty minutes later, he arrived back in the Common Room, having removed his space suit. "Captain, I need to speak to you in private," he said where everyone could hear.

Ian led Ichuro into his cabin and closed the door. Then Ichuro made his report. "Captain, I don't know what actually happened, but I can tell you that the three screws that hold the antenna proper in its base had been removed. The screws could have been removed at any time, but the antenna also connects to its base with a bayonet connector. When the screws were removed I cannot guess, but the bayonet connector should have kept the antenna in its base anyway. I think, whoever removed the screws was counting on atmospheric drag to pull the antenna out of its base and when that didn't happen they disconnected it by hand while the shuttle was on the ground. Because that is the only time they could have done it. No, one has gone outside in a space suit except, Miriam when she woke up the shuttle and moved it from its dock to the airlock, and me just now. I will go out again tomorrow and replace all the screws."

"Thank you, Ichuro. I agree with you and I approve your suggestion to go external tomorrow and fix the problem," Ian said. "As before, I do not want you to say anything more to the others. What you found about the screws had to have been done while the *Explorer* was still at the moon. Whether or not the antenna worked loose or was removed from its base by someone at Ares Base is anyone's guess, but I think you're correct. It was probably done while the shuttle was on the surface. Excuse me for a moment, please and stand by." When Ichuro left his cabin, Ian called Alexi and asked him to come to his cabin.

When Alexi arrived, they spoke briefly and then Ian invited Ichuro back into his cabin. "I have not discussed this with anyone but Commander Gargorin, Ichuro, but there is at least one saboteur on the *Explorer* or perhaps on the surface at the moment. I have been trying to figure out who it is with no success. I think someone is trying to put the focus on Jamilah because of her Arabic ancestry, but I don't think she's the one. Please keep this to yourself and tell me if anyone tries to get the details out of you."

"Yes, sir!" Ichuro replied. "Why don't I check the badge movements database to see if anyone could have done it?"

"Do it. But I do not hold out much hope of that doing any good."

"Neither do I, but just to make sure." Ichuro returned to his station in the communications cubicle and checked the database where the movements of the complement were recorded based on signals from their ID badges. He was unable to find where anyone actually left the ship except Miriam when she woke up the shuttle and himself as he went out and back to repair the antenna on the shuttle. He was still engrossed in the search when there was an explosion that was felt as well as heard throughout the ship.

Everyone aboard came immediately to the common area and there were lots of questions being asked. AJay was the last to arrive, having had to come from the reactor room where he was standing watch.

• • •

When Ian arrived the first thing he asked was "Is anyone hurt?"

As he looked from person to person they all replied: "No, sir."

Ian retrieved the operations manual from its place in his cabin and they proceeded to go through the checklist item by item to determine what might have happened. Alexi and Ichuro were going through the computer and checking every sensor on the ship.

In short order, Alexi exclaimed, "Got it! It was in the reaction mass tank, Captain."

"Are you sure?" Ian asked unnecessarily.

"Yes, sir, I am absolutely sure. We are losing the reaction mass to space and the CO_2 that is used to keep the tank pressurized. There's a hole in the tank itself and in at least one of the reaction mass bladders. We won't know which one until somebody goes in the tank to find out. That somebody should probably be me because I've been with the ship all through the latter phases of the construction and I am pretty familiar with how things are in the reaction mass tank."

"Hadn't you better have somebody with you?" Ian asked. "You know the rules; we should always work in pairs. The only exceptions to that are the pilots."

"Yes, sir, I know. I think I would like to have Mr. Watanabe help me. He has the next most external time after mine," Alexi replied.

"Ichuro, I know it's not in your bailiwick, but are you willing to help Commander Gargorin?"

"Yes, Captain, I'll go," Ichuro replied.

As they were getting into their space suits, Alexi asked, "Ichuro, have you been back or down to the reactor room yet?"

"Yes, sir, I was there while I was doing my Book and when I went out to fix the antenna."

"Good, just do what you did then and use the handrail to pull yourself along, You did use the handrail then, didn't you?"

"Not all the time, Commander. We sort of had contests to see who could use a single pull and flip over to go all the way and still land correctly."

"This time, just follow me. We could use the elevator, but it is not really very useful in weightlessness. Just remember to go slowly."

"Yes, sir," Ichuro replied.

After they put on their space suits, they headed for the tunnel from the command module to the reactor room.

"There are three access panels from the tunnel into the reaction tank. Did you check them when you did your Book?"

"No, sir, they were not on the list we started with. We checked the other panels in the tunnel that provided access to various control systems and plumbing."

"Okay, they are spaced equally down the tunnel. One at each quarter of the distance. I think we should check the access panels first to see if any have been tampered with since the ship was finished."

There were no scratches on the screw heads on any of the panels.

"That gives us some hope, that nobody has been inside the tank since the panels were installed. So let's open the aft one since we are here," Alexi said, handing the electric screwdriver to Ichuro. "Remove the screws slowly and only along the two long sides, and the aft short side. Loosen but do not remove the screws along the forward short side."

Ichuro did as instructed. "That's it, Commander, now what?" he asked.

"Now, we open it lengthwise very slowly just a couple of centimeters using the screws on the forward side like a hinge. If there is any air loss, it should be almost impossible to open. I want to look and see if there is a booby trap before we pull the cover off completely. I would suggest that you go into the reactor room while I do that, but I don't have enough hands so we'll just have to take a chance. You hold me while I give it a look," Alexi explained. "Okay?"

"Okay," Ichuro answered. He held Alexi steady while Alexi pried up the cover. He began to ask, "What—" when Alexi interrupted him.

"Damn, I can't see with this helmet on. Go see if AJay has an inspection light and camera," Alexi said.

"I've got one in my kit, Commander."

"Can it be used while wearing a space suit?"

"Yes, sir, I can connect it to my tablet computer so we will be able to see it easily."

"Good, please go fetch it."

"Here it is, Commander," Ichuro said when he returned. "You slide the business end under the panel and we can take a look together."

They looked at the display as Alexi slid the business end farther into the area above the panel. "Damn, there it is. See this shiny line across the opening from corner to corner, that's a trip wire. It's booby-trapped alright. Just screw the corners in to hold it in place."

They decided to try the first access panel next using the same procedure. It, too, was booby-trapped.

"Well, that only leaves one choice, Ichuro, doesn't it?" Alexi observed as he moved towards the middle panel.

They very carefully removed the panel to check for booby traps. There was a trip wire there as well.

"Now what?" Alexi asked.

"Commander, since we're not losing air, may I suggest that we exit the ship through the airlock in the reactor room and go around the outside just to be safe? I can't imagine how anyone could set a booby trap outside, can you?"

"Good thinking, let's do that, but not tell anyone," Alexi replied. "Unless there is someone watching the all-ship display, no one will know that we went out through the rear airlock," Alexi continued.

The two men pulled themselves along the handrail back down the tunnel to the reactor room. Once there Alexi closed and locked the airlock between the tunnel and the reactor room. The reactor room airlock to the outside was large enough for two, so they both cycled through at the same time. They took a quick look along the side of the reaction mass tank that was easily visible from the area of the airlock and saw nothing unusual. They pulled themselves along the handrail past the fattest part of the reaction mass tank, looked forward and back and saw nothing. Then they used the circular handrail around the waist of the reaction mass tank, and from there Alexi could see water vapor escaping from an area near the forward end of the tank and on the side opposite the airlocks.

"Let's go take a closer look," Alexi said. They pulled themselves along the tank until they saw a hole more than two meters in diameter through which water vapor was escaping. The hole was partially blocked by one of the four bladders in the tank but based on where the explosion took place at least two bladders had been ruptured.

Alexi placed his helmet against Ichuro's and with the radios turned off said, "There's nothing we can do here. I have an idea we might try, but we had better go back inside and tell the captain before we try it." Ichuro nodded agreement.

They retraced their path to the rear airlock and reentered the ship. Still wearing their space suits and helmets as a precaution, they traversed the tunnel and returned to the storage room. When they arrived, they were met by the rest of the complement.

"Any luck, Commander," Ian asked as they removed their helmets.

"Yes and no, Captain," Alexi replied. "Can we speak with you in your cabin, sir?" The rest looked on in surprise when still wearing their space suits, they followed the captain to his cabin to make their report.

"If there is a hole, why didn't you feel air escaping when you removed the hatches?" the captain asked.

Alexi thought for a minute and then asked to see the plans for the ship that the captain kept in his cabin. They carefully checked the plan in the area of the access panels and Alexi spotted the reason why they did not feel air escaping. "Captain, there is sort of an informal airlock between the tunnel and the reaction mass tank. Each of the access panels has a sealed bubble over it so that someone can remove the access panel, go into the bubble, and then have the access panel replaced temporarily by someone in the tunnel. That done, the bubble seal is released providing access to the inside of the tank. This is probably because the workers needed some way to go from the ship into the reaction mass tank without having to pump all the air out of the ship to prevent its loss."

"Damned good thinking on somebody's part, I'd say. So what do we do now? Don't we need to be concerned that all of the reaction mass will leak out?"

"I don't think so sir. The ice and bladder are pretty much plugging the hole. Like I said, there is just a little water vapor escaping at the moment and that will probably stop eventually."

"I think I may have a solution for that, Captain," Ichuro interjected. "There was a fair amount of free time on the ISS and I am a reader. Someone had brought up a complete set of C. F. Forrester's novels. Most of them were about the sea and about a naval officer named Hornblower."

Ian nodded and replied, "Yes, I've read several of those. They had some process they used when the ship was holed below the waterline. Is that what you're thinking?"

"Yes, sir. They had a technique where they placed a sail or a piece of sail over the hole to keep the water out. They did something to the sail beforehand, but I don't remember what it was. It wasn't perfect, but it worked until repairs could be made. In any event, I don't think we need to do that. If we could find a ground cloth or tarpaulin at least 8 feet square, it should cover the hole. There are miles of duct tape on board and we could use that to secure the cloth to the tank," Ichuro said.

Alexi looked at Ichuro with admiration and gave him a pat on the back. "There are the tarpaulins that were meant to be the ground cloth for the second round of buildings down at Ares Base. We will have to go through the manifest to see what container they are in."

"Do it!" the captain ordered.

"I'll search the manifest, Commander, while you get together a work party to shift the containers around."

"Yes, sir," Alexi said with a grin and a hotshot salute.

An hour later they had located the containers with the tarpaulins in them and had found one that was 12 feet square And fifty rolls of duct tape, which was far more than they needed. Ichuro also located fifty self-drilling screws and washers large enough to be used through the grommets around the edge of the tarp. Once again they made their way back to the reactor room, out through the airlock, and over the surface of the reaction mass tank to the location of the hole.

The first thing they did was anchor the tarp to the structure with a line so it could not drift away. Then Ichuro began along one side to put the screws and washers through the grommets and into the surface of the tank. There was still some water vapor leaking out, but by the time he was done screwing the tarp to the tank most of it had stopped. They still used four rolls of duct tape, taping down all the edges and crisscrossing the tarp in every direction they could until they ran out of tape. Long before they ran out of tape, the hole was effectively sealed. After checking all the way around to ensure they had gathered up everything they had come with except the tarp and the tape, they made their way back into the ship tired but delighted with the effect of their repair.

When they returned to the Common Room where everyone was present, crew and scientists. "Tell all of us what happened. How serious is the damage to the ship? What did you do to repair the damage, and what we can expect now?" Ian directed.

Alexi began, "An explosive device was apparently placed inside the reaction mass tank at the point farthest from the airlocks and access panels where it was least likely to be seen. I suspect it was placed on the inside surface of the tank and was probably attached to the hull itself where it could do maximum damage. I doubt it could be seen from anywhere once the reaction mass bladders were installed."

The captain asked, "How much of the reaction mass do you think we lost, Commander?"

"At best, I can only guess until we can get inside the shell and actually check. If my estimate is correct, I think it was placed right at the point where bladders Number 2 and Number 3 are closest together. That place would insure maximum damage to both the reaction mass tank and the bladders. How much is left? I can't say yet. I can tell you this, the very nature of how the reaction mass is used means that more than half of it was used on the way from the Moon to Mars. Remember from the moment we left the moon, we had to not only push the ship with a thrust from the rockets but also the reaction mass itself. So we use reaction mass to move reaction mass and that's why we used more than half before we ever got here. Also, I could see pieces from two of the four tank bladders near the hole, and I suspect a third one may have been damaged. The fourth one is on the side of the tank farthest from the hole. It may survive. Ichuro's suggestion of a way to keep any more water from escaping worked."

"My thanks to both of you," the captain said. "Now I want to say something to all of you. Someone on this ship detonated that bomb. From what

Commander Gargorin told me earlier, someone also booby-trapped all of the access panels to the reaction tank to prevent us from being able to get to the damage from the inside. That is why Commander Gargorin and Mr. Watanabe had to patch the hole from the outside. So, I have to tell you what you have probably already guessed—we are stranded in Mars orbit until we can fabricate a fix and find water for reaction mass."

CHAPTER ELEVEN

"I think she did it," Lupe said angrily, pointing at Jamilah. "She's an Arab and they are out to stop any progress at any cost in the name of Allah or Jihad or some such. She and that damned ferret are the problems, Captain. She has access to the tunnel from the garden deck and she often works down there alone. It would not be difficult for her to do the job without anyone ever knowing about it. I suspect that some of those chemicals she uses in her hydroponic tanks could be used to make an explosive. Fertilizer and oil are all that it takes to make an improvised bomb."

All eyes turned towards Jamilah. Some in accusation, some in inquiry, and some in disgust.

Jamilah reacted immediately. "I am not an Arab, I am an American! I was born in America, I was raised in America, and my mother was an Iraqi Christian. I was raised an Episcopalian. I have never been to an Arab country, and I have no interest in going to one. Just because my mother was an Iraqi does not make me a spy or a saboteur or a religious fanatic." She was furious.

"Calm down, Jamilah. No one is accusing you of anything," Ian said.

"She did," Jamilah replied angrily, pointing back at Lupe.

"To begin with, as Commander Gargorin explained, no one aboard could possibly have placed the bomb in the tank once the bladders were filled," Ian said, then asked, "Mr. Watanabe do you have the results of that search I asked you to do the other day?"

"Yes, sir, I do," Ichuro answered. He went to the communications cubicle and picked up a port-A-disc and returned. "Here it is, sir, and here is also the list of all the communications we have received since we lost communications with the surface."

"Before I begin, I want you to know that the saboteur, the one who detonated the bomb, is here aboard this ship now. If the saboteur steps forward right now it would be best for all of us," Ian said, looking around the room expectantly. When no one stepped forward, he continued, "I didn't think you would. So we will have to do this the hard way."

Ian inserted the port-A-disc into the Common Room terminal and selected the large display. "Mr. Watanabe, can you trace the movements of everyone aboard the ship since the shuttle returned?"

Mr. Watanabe began by displaying the ship's diagram on the large monitor in the Common Room. "What you see here is the location of every person on the ship or more properly their ID badges at a specific moment. We do this so, should the need arise, we can find everyone aboard wherever they may be. Every snapshot has a day, date, and time signature In the upper left-hand corner of the screen, and the snapshots are taken every second. So the system takes 86,400 snapshots per day and they are kept for ten days before they are written over unless they are saved as they have been on this port-A-disc. So, we can show the movements like a movie. If I showed them at the rate of twenty-four frames per second, it will take an hour to see what happened in an entire day. Captain?"

"At various times since the beginning of our mission when we left the Moon, I have asked Mr. Watanabe to save certain days," Ian said.

There was an immediate uproar from a number of the scientists, all except Tom and Jamilah.

"Have you been spying on us all along, Captain?" Jan asked. "And you too Mr. Watanabe?"

"No, just being careful. There has been a series of minor problems ever since we departed and we needed to know who was causing them. Mr. Watanabe has only been following orders."

Esteban Martinova at the instigation of his wife continued the accusations. "Captain, surely that's not legal. I demand that those discs be destroyed before anything more is done to embarrass us. You are acting like a dictator and you have no right to do that."

"That is where you're wrong, Dr. Martinova. Life aboard a ship, any ship in the ocean or in space is not a democracy. It is an absolute monarchy where I rule life aboard the ship. Most of the time, you have not even been aware of that. Which is how it should be."

"You can rule the crew, but we are passengers and we are not subject to your orders," Esteban continued.

"That, sir is where you are wrong," Alexi jumped in. "As far back in history as it is possible to go, Dr. Martinova, the captain is the absolute ruler aboard his ship. It cannot be any other way. As for passengers versus crew, you are just cargo to be carried from one point to another. You have no say in how the ship is run. As for the crew, have you noticed that there is a rank system in place here? There are three department heads, myself for the reactors, Major Steinmetz for the pilots, and Mr. Watanabe for communications and electronics. In addition, Dr. Burns is an honorary crew member because of her responsibility for the garden. Each of us reports to the captain on a regular basis, but it is done so seamlessly that you probably never noticed. When necessary, Captain McMichael gives a direct order but because we work together like a well-oiled machine, it almost always sounds as if he has made a request rather than giving a direct order."

There was more grumbling among the scientists and some angry looks were directed at Jamilah, but it quickly died down into a sullen, arm-crossed silence.

Ian waited until everyone quieted down except for the dirty looks that were being directed at him. Then said, "Thank you, Commander I appreciate it." Then, looking at the assembled company, he continued, "Most of what you said is simply not true. The only times I have looked at this data was when there was an incident of one sort or another on the ship. It is essential when one is managing a ship that is over 500 feet long and which carries twelve people each of whom has their duties and moves about the ship in the execution of those duties that we know where everyone is at all times. I want you to know that I did not review these records until the second time the ferret apparently escaped.

"The first time could have been an accident, but the second time, I personally checked to see that his cage was locked before I went to bed. Because this was a relatively minor issue and no harm was done, I did not investigate but asked Mr. Watanabe to retain the recordings. Mr. Watanabe, would you please bring up the recordings of the day when the ferret first escaped from his cage and show the movements without names associated with them."

Mr. Watanabe entered some data into the terminal and suddenly twelve dots, one representing each person aboard were shown at various locations on the ship. He set the time to two hours before it was discovered the ferret had escaped and then ran the sequence for four hours showing all motions of all twelve people at that time. What it showed was someone, who was in the garden deck up until a few minutes before the ferret was presumably released, had left the garden deck to use the fresher. It also showed that someone else left the Common Room and went into the garden deck, did something there, and returned to the Common Room. The person who had gone to the fresher returned to the garden deck. And immediately began moving quickly around the garden.

Within minutes it showed several people converging on the hatch to the garden deck. One of these people entered and appeared to be in close association with the person who was there. "You all know what happened at that time and the next few minutes will show me helping Dr. Burns recapture the ferret. Now, Mr. Watanabe would you please show the sequence when the ferret escaped from the garden deck," Ian requested.

The next sequence of images showed the time during the night when the ferret escaped. It showed two badges in the garden deck not moving for several hours. It also showed the garden deck hatch being opened, but with no ID badge being associated with the opening. Presumably whoever opened the hatch released the ferret. That person also failed to close the hatch to the garden deck thus allowing the ferret to escape into the forward module of the ship. What followed was presumably the ferret leaving the garden deck, wandering around apparently aimlessly, perhaps looking for something to eat, then going into "Girl's Town" and curling up in bed with another badge.

"It is very common for animals or pets to wear a collar. If you will look at the ferret on Jamilah's shoulder, you will see he is wearing a collar. He has worn the collar since she brought him aboard the ship. After the first incident when he presumably escaped from his cage, I had Mr. Watanabe embed a tracking chip in the ferret's collar so we could keep track him as well whenever we needed to know where everyone, including the ferret, was on the ship. The only people who knew that chip was in the ferret's collar were me and Mr. Watanabe—oh and Dr. Burns," Ian said. "You know what happened next; Rachael screamed when she found the ferret in bed with her."

"Now, if you will show the sequence when the computer cable was presumably gnawed by the ferret," Ian directed.

This sequence showed almost everyone in their cabins except the duty pilot, the duty officer in the reactor room, and the ferret. But the movements of the ferret were somewhat different than they were when he typically roamed about. The ferret went directly from the place where he was sleeping to the communications cubicle where he presumably gnawed the cable. Then he returned directly to where he had been sleeping and stopped moving.

"There, that shows that damned ferret was the one who gnawed the cable!" Lupe declared in a shrill voice.

"No, that shows that someone who was not wearing a badge picked up the ferret and carried him to the communications cubicle. Once there he was placed in Mr. Watanabe's chair where he curled up and went back to sleep. But the chair was pushed out of the way and the ferret's badge moved away from the kneehole of the desk in the communications cubicle. How do we know that? Because we have several days recorded of how the ferret moved when he moved around the forward module and he never moved in a straight line more than 2 feet at any time," Ian asserted firmly.

"It also shows that one of the badges did not move during that time. Some of you, as was suggested when you were given the badges were to keep them clipped to your clothing at all times even when you're sleeping. Not all of you do that. Likewise, some of you only clip the badge to your clothing when you are awake and moving around. We know which is which, that is to say, we know who commonly wears the badge at all times and who removes it when sleeping. I heard what was said when you accused us of spying. But until these incidents occurred, no one ever looked at the recordings. The only reason we did look at them was to determine what had happened and who had done it. By a process of elimination, we have determined the person or persons responsible for the ferret incident are among the scientists."

Lupe jumped up and screamed, "Who gives a damn about the God-damned ferret. What about the bomb? And what gave you the right to keep track of us?"

"Shut up and sit down, Pajarita!" Ian said in his best command voice. "In case you were not aware of it, Pajarita," Ian emphasized her childhood name again. "As I told you a while ago, this is not a democracy. As the captain, I am responsible for the complete operation and security of this ship. I am allowed to do whatever I deem necessary in fulfilling my duties, whether you like it or not. If you doubt that authority, ask Commander Gargorin. And for the record, Dr. Martinova, your husband called you Pajarita during the ferret incident."

Lupe gave him a startled look and drifted back down into her chair. Then started to get up again but thought better of it and stayed where she was, glaring at Ian.

Jamilah knew exactly what Pajarita meant in Spanish. She was startled by the tone of Ian's command to Lupe. She started to say something and then stopped.

"Yes, Jamilah, I know your childhood nickname too. Yesterday we got a congratulatory message which, as you know, we posted on the display board. There was a strange sentence in that message and it read, 'Grandpa says, hello to Little Bird' I am sure all of you saw it. It was completely out of context with the rest of the message which was filled with general news including the media reports of our arrival in orbit around Mars. So we had the security people do a little searching to see if they could find out who Little Bird was.

"We were surprised to find out that little bird could be either Jenna or Pajarita. Jenna is a little bird in Arabic. Pajarita is little bird in Spanish. After the explosion and while Mr. Watanabe and Commander Gargorin were patching the damage done by the bomb, we determined it was a coded message directing Little Bird to sabotage the ship."

"I knew it, I knew it! She's the one, it must be her," Lupe said, pointing once again at Jamilah.

"No, Dr. Martinova, it was not Dr. Burns. And we know it was not you either. While our security was checking to find out who 'Little Bird' was and what Pajarita meant, they also found out that they were not the first to seek something that could be used as a key to pass a message to the saboteur and deflect the blame to either you or Jamilah," Ian said.

As he said it, Dr. Gladys Campbell started to move away from the table towards her cabin until she saw Alexi blocking the way.

"Sit down, please, Dr. Campbell," Ian said in a very level voice. "We have already searched your cabin and removed the very small transmitter you used to send the signal to the bomb as well. You had hidden it well in your knitting kit and it took us a long time to find it. We also found a pill I presume you were supposed to take to suicide if you were caught."

Dr. Gladys Campbell, astrobiologist, from the University of Edinburgh broke down and cried in great sobs. When she once again regained control, she said between gasps, "They had my son. Eighteen years ago, I married one of my students who were much younger than I. We were happy for a while and then for whatever reason he sought solace in the arms of another. By that time I was pregnant with Erick. My husband stayed with me until our son was born and then offered to plead for custody when we applied for divorce. I agreed to that.

"My ex-husband and I have been divorced for sixteen years. His new wife adopted Erick shortly after they were married. My son thinks of her as his mother and of me as a kindly aunt that visits several times a year during the holidays. He calls me, 'Aunt Gladys.' But they—and I have no idea who they really are—found out about Erick and threatened to kill him if I did not do exactly as they told me. They found me literally hours before I was picked up to go for training. They showed me evidence that they knew all about Erick. They had his birth certificate, our divorce decree, and recent pictures of him at school. How they found out I don't know. But they were very explicit about what I was to do and how I was to do it.

"They provided the transmitter and they told me everything was in place and all I had to do was turn on the transmitter and push the button. I had no choice. I apologize for what I have done to all of you and for the fate my actions have condemned you to. But, it was my son."

As she confessed this, everyone else looked at her in disbelief. She was everybody's grandmother or maiden aunt, or a nice old lady next door. One could not help but love her she was so sincere and genuinely caring. She never failed to offer help to anyone that needed it for whatever they might be doing. She did not enter into the games that the others played. She preferred to read or knit or sometimes just sit and watch the others play the games. She took a turn at cooking a couple of times during the first week, but after tasting what the others could make, she stopped trying.

"Thank you, Dr. Campbell, for your candor. We will send a coded message immediately to our Security team and they will do their best to find and recover or protect your son. You really don't have any idea who 'they' were?"

"No, I'm sorry. I am not accustomed to these things. I had to take them at face value. They were not mean or evil-looking, they were just the man who came to my office at the university and told me about my son and gave me the knitting needle, and a woman who knocked on my door when I was expecting to be picked up by the ICExS people to remind me of the consequences if I failed. They told me not to ask any questions and to tell no one they had been there. I was so frightened I could do nothing. What are you going to do with me?" she asked in a toneless voice as if she was anticipating the worst.

"There's not much we can do with you, Dr. Campbell," Ian replied, then added in a quiet tone of voice, "I can't hang you, or keel haul you, push you out an airlock, or any of the other punishments meted out to mutineers or saboteurs and I am not sure I would if I could anyway. I think the worst I can do is to make you suffer the same fate as the rest of us as a result of the sabotage."

"Thank you, Captain," Dr. Campbell said equally quietly. "Will you let me know what they find about my son, please?"

"Yes, I'll do that," Ian replied.

Captain Ian McMichael looked slowly around the room and made eye contact with everyone there. Then he said, "We still have not resolved the issue of the ferret."

Lupe looked at him venomously and demanded, "Who cares?" As she said that, to the surprise of everyone, the ferret flowed from Jamilah's shoulder onto the table and, gripping the green felt tablecloth with his claws, walked over and faced Lupe Martinova, rose up on his hind legs, and hissed at her.

"I guess he does," Ian said as he looked at Lupe. "Dr. Martinova, meet your accuser. Before you say anything, we know it was you who released him to start with. Then you went back and released him again so he could get into the forward module and, as I am sure, you hoped to do something which would condemn him."

"I hate him. When I was a little girl, I had a gerbil as a pet. I took him along when our family visited some friends in Wyoming. I took my gerbil out of his container and was playing with him in front of the house. The gerbil was just looking for seeds when a wild ferret ran out of the bushes, killed my pet, carried it off, and ate it. I have hated them ever since," Lupe said vehemently.

"I would say the feeling is mutual, Lupe!" Miriam said from behind her. "How did you manage to take him out to the communications cubicle if you dislike him so much."

"I lured him into my laundry bag with a piece of meat. Once he went in, I closed the bag, carried it out and put it in the chair. I tried to damage the wire with a nail file and nail clipper in a way that it would look as if he gnawed on it. When I was done, I took him back, opened the bag and put it down to let him out. He hissed at me then too."

"Where did you get him from?" Rachael asked.

"As usual, he was sleeping with you when he wasn't sleeping with Jamilah. I just waited until he was with you because you were nearest to the communications cubicle and because you are a very deep sleeper," Lupe replied. "When I was done, I put the open bag on the foot of your bed and as soon as he ran out of it, I took it back to my cubicle. As the captain has already surmised, I was not wearing my ID badge. I left it on my pillow." As Lupe was making this confession, her voice became quieter and quieter until at the end she could only barely be heard.

"Does anyone else have anything to say or confess, if so let's do it now because from this moment on we have to focus on how to fix the damage in a way that will allow us to get home," Ian said.

No one said a word.

. . .

The next order of business was to determine how badly the ship was damaged. But before they could do that, it was necessary to remove the booby traps in the access panels to the reaction mass tank. Dr. Campbell explained that she did not put them there, but she knew they were there. She was told if anyone tried to remove or disarm the bomb they would be killed by the booby traps. She had no idea how they worked nor how to disarm them.

Alexi and Ichuro took on the task of hopefully disarming the booby traps. Dressed in space suits, they entered the tunnel and had it depressurized, then they removed all three of the access panels. The area of the access panel openings was large enough for a man in a space suit to pass through if necessary. But with a trip wire running diagonally across the opening, it was impossible to take a look at the booby trap while wearing a space helmet. Very carefully using a mirror and a fiber-optic camera, they checked the construction of the booby traps. Clearly, the booby traps had to take a fair amount of vibration or they would've been set off by the explosion. After looking them over and photographing them from every possible angle, they reported back to the captain in the Common Room where everyone could hear. There was a time for secrets and a time for openness. With the fate of all of them in the balance, Ian judged openness was what was called for.

"They are very primitive, Captain, and we cannot be sure they are actually functional," Alexi reported. Then with a nod toward Ichuro, he said, "Mr. Watanabe has a theory. The booby traps are primitive and depend upon a wire strung between the device itself, and an anchor point diagonally across the opening, a screw that had no other purpose. They must have been installed during the final phase of construction but after the final inspection. Ichuro took some very careful measurements and thinks that we may have the materials necessary to attach to the device itself and simulate the anchor point. Then, if we detach both ends again very carefully we should be able to remove one of them without setting it off. Once we do that we can look it over and determine how we can defeat the others."

"Ichuro," Ian said, looking intently at him, "how confident are you?"

"I can't say, Captain. There is going to be a risk no matter what we do. I can't think of any other way other than to go out to the hole made by the explosion, crawl in and try and worm our way over to the area of the access panels and attempt to disable them from there. Frankly, sir, that idea scares the crap out of me. Not knowing how messed up the bladders are, we could get lost or trapped in there, and besides, we have sealed the blast hole and we agree, it would not be a good idea to reopen it," Ichuro said, then continued, "Like Commander Gargorin said, the mechanism does not look too complicated. Here are the pictures we took.

"As you can see it looks very primitive. I don't really see why they didn't go off as a result of concussion due to the explosion. So I think, no I hope, that it would take a pretty good yank on the trip wire to set it off. Shall we say the equivalent of pulling the pin out of a hand grenade. We are going to have to work in space suits, although I'm not sure why because if we set one off it won't make much difference. However, whatever we do we have to plan on doing it while wearing space suits."

"Wait a minute," Alexi interjected, "that pseudo airlock above each of the access doors should prevent the air from leaking out of the tunnel while we work, shouldn't it?"

Ichuro Watanabe uncharacteristically slapped his forehead and said, "You're absolutely right, Commander. I'm an idiot for not having thought of it."

"Don't beat yourself up, Ichuro. I just remembered them myself."

"Then maybe we don't have to wear space suits after all. I doubt that anyone on the ship planted the bomb or the booby traps. It had to be done before we ever left the moon. Still, neither one of us is small enough to get above the booby traps by squirming up through one corner of the opening," Ichuro said with a shrug.

"Am I small enough, Ichuro?" Jamilah asked. Every eye in the room turned toward Jamilah as she continued, "I'm five foot two inches tall and weigh only ninety-five pounds. I'm fairly flat from top to bottom… unfortunately," she said as she looked down at herself. "I can bind my breasts, such as they are and be completely flat. Oh, and I did gymnastics in high school and college."

Everyone tried to speak at once, but Ian silenced them with a gesture. "Jammy, you don't have to do this," Ian said.

"Captain, it sounds as if it would be better if someone could get up past the trip wire and check things out. I'm in the same ship as the rest of you. If Commander Gargorin and Ichuro can use me, then I volunteer," Jamilah said.

"We gratefully accept your service, Dr. Burns," Alexi said. "Let the three of us get together and go over the photographs and discuss what needs to be done." The statement was directed at everyone as a tactful way of saying leave us alone and let us work. An hour later they were ready to tackle the booby traps. Alexi and Ichuro removed their space suits while Jamilah went off with Miriam and Rachael who helped her bind her body. Then the three of them went into the tunnel and closed and sealed the hatch.

"Why don't we work on the one farthest from the forward module just in case? Alexi suggested as they pulled themselves down the tunnel.

All of the access panels were stacked and secured out of the way. When they were under the third access opening, Alexi took charge.

"Since we're in freefall, stabilizing ourselves is going to be a major problem. So I suggest that I hold on to your legs, Jammy, and position you so only your head is through the opening. You grip either side of the access opening to keep from accidentally bumping the trip wire. I want you to look around very carefully and think about what you're going to do once you're in the access airlock," Alexi said before pointing at a nearby hand grip. "Ichuro, you hold on to my belt and that hand grip for stability."

"Yes, sir," Ichuro replied, getting into position as directed.

"Are you frightened, Jammy?" Alexi asked.

"Yes, sir, I am. I'm nervous and I'm concerned about what might happen if I do something wrong. But, Commander, have you ever tried to do a back-flip on the gymnastic rail for the first time? Nervousness and fear, when they're channeled properly, can help one do what one is trying for the first time. So, sir, let's be about it," Jamilah said with a conviction that was not felt by the others.

Jamilah stepped into Alexi's open hand and, putting her left hand on his head slowly straightened up until she could grip the side of the access with her left hand. She pulled herself up until her head was right at the lip of the access opening, then removed a small lantern from her coveralls pocket, pressed a button to turn it on, and carefully placed it inside the access area. Then gripped the side of the access opening and slowly pulled herself up while Alexi kept her under firm control.

"Okay, Commander, I can see it just like in the pictures. It's a small box being held in place by what I think are magnets. There is more than enough room for me to maneuver once I get into the access area. I'm confident I can get up without touching the wire." She began to pull herself up with her right hand and stopped. "Commander, please rotate me a bit to the left. That's it, a little more. Stop. Now push me up through the hole, slowly. Stop as soon as my elbow is past the lip of the opening. Okay, stop while I change grips. Now as you stabilize me, I am going to bend at the waist as I go through the hole so I can get my bottom through and so I do not hit the pseudo airlock." Alexi continued to gradually push her through the hole, and as she had said, as soon as she could, she placed her left hand on the short side of the opening, bent at the waist and pulled herself the rest of the way into the access space with Alexi guiding her feet to prevent them from touching the trip wire.

"I'm in. Ichuro, don't we have a piece of rope or an anchor line that I could use? There are several anchor points in here. I am holding on to one of them now to keep myself as far from the device as possible. There's actually quite a lot of room here, or at least there is if you're my size."

They chuckled at her joke and then passed her up a short length of line that Ichuro extemporized into a safety line by bending clips on both ends. He also passed her a small tool belt she could put around her waist to clip on to the safety line. She spent about twenty minutes roaming around the inside of the access area and told them everything she saw.

Finally, she said, "I don't know anything about such things, but there is no way they armed this thing after it was put in place. You'll have to trust me on this. It looks as if to set it off, you'll actually have to pull on the trip wire. It doesn't appear to be a very clever job. They probably hooked the ring on the wire to the far corner first and then pulling the wire taut put the explosives in place. Isn't the tunnel an alloy aluminum? The reason I ask is there appears to be a metal plate here that was glued to the outside of the tunnel wall and then the box with the explosives was placed on it and held in place with a magnet. Please pass me a pry bar, and then move as far away from here as possible. I can't see anything else to do but pry up the explosives box without pulling on the wire."

They handed her up a pry bar and as they did, Alexi said, "It would not matter where we are in the tunnel if it explodes. So we will stay right here in case you need something else. Go slowly, Jammy, take your time and tell us step-by-step what you are doing."

Jamilah started to argue, then realized she was outranked. So she said, "Yes, sir." And did what Alexi had asked. She put the tip of the pry bar under the edge of the explosives box and tried to pry it off the metal plate. She forgot about the leverage problem in weightlessness and had to position herself with one hand on an anchor point and the other on the pry bar which was positioned under the edge farthest from the anchor point. Then, by way of informing them, said, "I'm ready, sir."

"Wait, Jammy. I am going to lift Ichuro up so that he can get a grip on the explosive box when you pry it loose. We don't want it to go banging around in that space up there once it is lifted off its metal plate," Alexi said.

"Yes, sir," Jamilah said. Then she watched as Ichuro's hand came over the lip of the access entry and grasped the box.

"Okay, Jammy," Ichuro said.

Jamilah pressed down on the pry bar. The magnets were stronger than she expected, so she warned Ichuro and increased the pressure. The box lifted off the plate suddenly. Ichuro held on to it and then it was all over. Jamilah pulled herself over to the far side of the access entrance and unhooked the ring and passed it down to Ichuro so it couldn't catch anything. Then she unhooked her safety line and slowly flipped through the access hole and into Alexi's outstretched arms.

"It looks like you were right, Jammy," Alexi said as he placed her where she could grasp a handhold.

"I'm still shaking, Commander."

"You're not the only one," Ichuro said and Alexi endorsed that with a nod.

The remaining two booby traps were removed by the simple expedient of cutting the wire and then prying them loose carefully. When they were finished, they screwed the access panels back in place. Then they went back to the Common Room where Alexi held up the one with the ring still attached to show everyone.

"Jammy figured it out and removed them from the access space," he said. "I'm not sure what we should do with these," he added. "We have no way of disposing of them. We can't throw them out of an airlock because they would still be in the same orbit as we are and might cause us problems later."

Jamilah stood red-faced as everyone applauded and gave her a cheer.

Ian smiled and said, "Jammy, if you were in the military I would see that you got a medal, but the best I can give you is a hug of appreciation."

"I know what to do with them, Captain," Rachael said. "We can take them down to the surface and dispose of them there. Until then, I think it will be a good idea if they were put under lock and key."

"I agree with all of that," Ian said. "Now we have to get on with the business of determining how much damage was done by the explosion."

CHAPTER TWELVE

The next morning, Ian called the crew together to discuss how they were going to evaluate the damage. "Ladies and gentlemen, I trust you all slept well and are ready to tackle our problem," he said, looking at the ensemble. What he saw were blank faces that told him nothing. "Alright, I didn't do any better myself. So, here is what I think might work best; we'll have a one-hour brainstorming session. All ideas are welcome no matter how ridiculous they might seem. So let's begin. Miriam, would you please write the ideas down so we have some record of what was suggested?"

"Yes, sir," Miriam said, picking up her tablet computer and a stylus.

After a slow start, ideas began to flow, faster and faster. At the end of the hour, Ian took the tablet from Miriam to look through the list.

"We have thirty-five suggestions, some are duplicates or near duplicates and some are outright wild; some are either impossible or impracticable. Ichuro, can you send the ideas to every tablet so we can review them?"

"Sure, Captain," Ichuro said as he did as directed.

"Okay, we'll go down the list one at a time, and I want comments from all of you on each suggestion. First, we'll throw out any suggestion that is clearly impossible and see what's left."

Fully two-thirds of the possible solutions involved extra vehicular expeditions by one or more crew members. Everyone agreed that the problem was getting enough equipment and tools to the damage site and maintaining them there while the crew members entered the reaction mass tank through the hole made by the explosion.

"Captain, might I make a suggestion that is a combination of three of the other suggestions?" Rachael asked.

"Go right ahead."

"Thanks, sir. May I suggest that I take a few people in a shuttle over to the damaged area and somehow anchor there. The shuttle could act as a base of operations for exploring the damaged area, and if possible, going into the shell to see what is damaged. It seems simpler than going in through the access pseudo airlocks and working our way to the damage from the inside."

"That sounds reasonable if you're sure you can maintain a position there while they work. Who would be willing to go?"

There was no shortage of volunteers to go help with the work, but Lupe abstained.

"Thank you all for volunteering, but certain protocols have to be maintained. Only one pilot is allowed to be off the *Explorer* at any time."

Rachael said, "Captain. We would not exactly be off the *Explorer* —"

"Sorry, Rachael, if someone is outside the confines of the ship, even on the outer hull, they must be considered as being off the ship. If something should happen and both pilots were lost we would be stranded, not to mention that the scientists down on the surface would be in even worse straits. Risking even one pilot is not a good idea because if there is only one pilot, getting the scientists from the surface up to the ship would mean that our only remaining pilot would be required to leave the ship to rescue them. In addition, only one nuclear engineer can be off the *Explorer* at any time for essentially the same reasons," Ian replied.

Jamilah started to volunteer, but before she could say anything, Ian cut her off. "Sorry, Jammy, none of the scientists have any experience working outside the ship in a space suit in a weightless environment."

After a long debate, it was decided that Ichuro and AJay were the only ones who could be spared and Rachael would be the pilot.

Alexi tried to object because he did have experience with working in a weightless environment in a space suit, and AJay did not. "Sorry, Commander, you built the propulsion system and have the most experience with it, so I cannot allow you to be risked."

Tools and equipment were loaded into the shuttle, Rachael, Ichuro, and AJay suited up and boarded the shuttle. It had been decided that it would be best to limit communications at least initially to just between Rachael and the two men to keep the others from becoming panicky.

"I don't think you folks need to strap in," Rachael said when they were all in the shuttle. "I will only be using the maneuvering jets, so just grab a handhold to keep from drifting around the inside. I'll strap in because I need both hands to maneuver the shuttle. Ready?"

Rachael released the shuttle from the airlock and began to slowly maneuver to the position of the hole made by the explosion. Once there, she rotated the shuttle so that the airlock pointed at the ship. She carefully killed all motion of the shuttle with respect to the *Explorer* so that it could maintain that position indefinitely. The only one who could see outside the shuttle was Rachael.

It took a few minutes before she realized the shuttle was drifting away from the wound in the reaction mass tank. The two men were ready to exit the shuttle when she stopped them. "Hang on a minute, gentleman, we have a problem. I will not be able to maintain position over where you are working without constant maneuvering. We are maintaining a constant distance from the *Explorer*, but she's rotating very slowly out from under us. It was not rotating before the explosion. I think the outgassing and the escaping water put a slow spin on the *Explorer* that no one has noticed for the past couple of days mainly because we've been busy on the inside and we thought everything was stable. I think we better go back."

"Wait, Rachael," Ichuro said. "What about the idea that we were going to anchor you here? We can go out and install some anchor points around the hole and tie the shuttle down."

"That was a good idea when we thought everything was stable relative to the *Explorer*. You're right, you could anchor the shuttle, but that would cause a problem. The shuttle masses about 20 tons fully loaded. No matter how you connected it to the tank there would be a tendency to throw our whole system out of balance. We started from the storage area airlock and our position there was part of the change in motion affected by the explosion in the outgassing. Here we are at a different distance from the axis and the physics would make it impossible to balance. Therefore, as captain of the shuttle, it is my decision that we go back and get the ship stabilized before we try to do this."

"Okay, Rachael, as you say you're the boss. So let's go back and start over," AJay said, speaking for both himself and Ichuro, who nodded agreement.

Rachael switched to the command channel and explained the problem to the captain and the rest of the ensemble and said they were coming back.

"Okay, Rachael, we'll keep the door open and the lights on," Ian said, mimicking a popular commercial for accommodations. Then he switched off the microphone and spoke to the people waiting to find out what would happen. "Miriam, you'd better go take some readings to see what the rotation is, and to determine if we also have a wobble, which I suspect might be the case."

Thirty minutes later after a tense period of very careful maneuvering by Rachael, the shuttle reattached to the airlock. As soon as they reentered the *Explorer*, Rachael removed her helmet and said, "Sorry, Captain, you saw how tricky it was to redock just now, there was no way I would be able to hold position over the explosion site. Anchoring the shuttle at the explosion site could possibly put everything out of balance, which is essentially what happened when we departed and why it was so difficult to reconnect."

"Miriam," the captain called, "what have you found?"

"Captain," Miriam replied, "I don't think it's as bad or worse than we originally thought. We definitely have some unanticipated motion. I don't have all the parameters of the motion, yet. What I do know is the ship is spinning slowly at about one rotation per hour, but it wobbles because the water in the reaction mass tank is no longer balanced along the longitudinal axis, or let me put it another way... the longitudinal axis no longer runs down the exact center of the ship because the CG has shifted. In addition, the ship is also precessing around its new center of gravity and I've not been able to establish the rate or angle of precession. What we have, Captain, is a…." Miriam paused, searching for a word and settled for "…mess."

"Believe it or not, when Rachael undocked, I'm sure it also had an effect on the CG. The shuttle masses 20 tons and the forward airlock is a little over 200 feet from the normal center of gravity. That much mass at the end of a 200-foot lever has a definite effect on the motion of the ship. It's going to be very difficult to stop the rotation with the steering jets because they'll have to be applied centrally as the ones on one side of the ship are farther from the new centerline than those on the other side. Stopping the precession is going to be a whole different problem. I'm concerned that if I use the steering jets to stop the rotation, I may exacerbate the precession."

"Why, didn't we have that problem when we moved the shuttle from its attachment point or when we launched and recovered the shuttle when it went back and forth to the surface?" Ian asked, then said, "Sorry, it's been a long time since I took elementary physics. And, we don't have spin problems or major CG problems on submarines. Yes, sometimes they get slightly out of balance fore and aft, but the diving officer corrects for that by pumping water from the heavy end to the light end. Most of the time the only one who knows we're out of balance in a submarine is the diving officer who makes minor corrections as part of his job."

"Actually, sir, it's not as simple as it might seem. When we moved the shuttle from its attachment point to the forward airlock, if you recall, we swapped it with the lunar lander. But that didn't really make much difference either. When we stabilized in orbit, there was no spin on the ship. Yes, we do one apparent end-over-end rotation each time we orbit around Mars so the ship is not always parallel to the surface. But that is one rotation every eight hours, and only on one axis and it only affects our attitude relative to the surface. We always have the airlock perpendicular to the lengthwise axis. When the ship is in balance, matching up when the shuttle docks is simply a matter of having it at the right attitude with respect to the ship. It is essentially a one-dimensional problem. The precession and wobble are a completely different issue."

Miriam demonstrated the problem using a spoon from the kitchen. She tried unsuccessfully to make it spin and process in the weightless environment. "Well, you get the idea anyway," she said. "We were lucky today when Rachael took the guys over to the explosion site. If things were much worse than they are, she might never have been able to reconnect with the airlock.

"So, the first thing we have to do is establish where the new center of gravity is and I have no idea how to do that. The way the wobble is occurring tells me that at least one and maybe two of the water bladders are still intact, and of course, there might still be some water in those that were ruptured. But one thing we can be sure of is that the two that we know were ruptured are both on the same side of the ship, which throws things way out of balance. Because we were in freefall when the explosion occurred, the water in the intact bladder or bladders can be anywhere in them, but the effect they have on the CG is based on where they connect to the hull. Sorry, sir, that's how it is."

"One of the first rules of command on a ship is that the captain is always expected to know what to do no matter what happens. In reality, that means he is probably the most experienced officer on the ship with the exception of the chief engineer. There is also a chain of command so if the captain is killed or put out of action the next one in line steps up and becomes the new captain. If it all goes to hell, you abandon ship which is not an option here. Another rule is the captain always has staff officers on hand to advise him, and a smart captain makes extensive use of them. You are all my staff officers, including scientists. So I'm open to suggestions or advice," Ian said as he moved his hand to include everyone present.

"Sir, as I said before," Miriam said, "I think the first thing we have to do is to establish the new CG, which we might be able to do by deduction from the motions of the ship. Then we have to do what we can to correct for that. To be safe I'm going to need at least one whole day and maybe more to establish our new motions relative to the originals. The reason it takes so long is the only way I'm going to be able to establish the angle and rate of precession is by sighting on specific stars which is what I did for navigation on the trip out. The difference is, we're not always pointed toward stars for which I have ready data. I wish I could say I could do it faster, but I'm not even sure I can finish it in one day. That's my input as pilot and navigator."

"Thank you, Miriam, do the best you can, but take all the time you need. Do any of the rest of you have any other ideas or suggestions?" Ian asked. When he received no replies he said, "Okay, that's it, then, for Miriam. Commander Gargorin, I'm going to have to ask you and Mr. Watanabe to open up the access panels again and see what you can find out about the condition, position, and contents of the water bladders."

"Can I work on that too, Captain?" Jamilah said. "There's not much space in the area above the access panels. Being small helped before. It might be easier if I was able to do the initial work to open one of the pseudo airlocks and prepare the way for the Commander and Ichuro. I also took three years of math and physics before I switched to biology so I might be able to help Miriam too."

"Why am I not surprised?" Ian said, laughing to himself. "I'm sure Commander Gargorin and Mr. Watanabe would welcome your help in any way you can give it. And, from the hopeful look on Miriam's face, I suspect that any help you might be able to give to her will be equally welcome. Thank you, Jammy. If no one else has anything at this time, let's be about it. Meanwhile, I have to go prepare a report for Farside Base."

. . .

Once again, the tunnel was sealed and in a vacuum, Jamilah, Alexi and Ichuro were all wearing their space suits. Alexi and Ichuro were looking up into the entrance holding lanterns to provide light for Jamilah who was trying to release the mechanism of the pseudo airlock so they could enter the reaction mass tank.

"Commander, the release mechanism seems to be stuck," Jamilah said. "Do you suppose it would do any damage if I gave it a whack with my wrench?" she asked.

"Leave it be, Jammy, let's try the middle one," Alexi said.

"Okay. Look out, Commander," Jamilah said as she did a slow, headfirst flip out of the access area and landed gently on the opposite tunnel wall. Ichuro caught her hand to keep her from rebounding. "Thanks, Ichuro."

They moved to the middle access point, removed the cover, and Jamilah climbed up Alexi into the space above. A moment later, she announced, "Got it! It won't open all the way, something is blocking it, but there is enough room for us to go through."

Ichuro came next followed by Alexi. As Alexi who was the largest went through the opening, it suddenly opened completely.

"There was some of the bladder blocking the way," Jamilah said. "Wow, this is big. The light just fades away."

"It takes a lot of space to hold enough water to get us here and back," Alexi observed as he came up behind Jamilah and Ichuro. "What you're looking at, Jammy, is the space between two of the bladders and it should not be anywhere near this big. These two must have been ruptured by the explosion, which is why we have all the space here and that is why the access was blocked. Ichuro, put a marker light here near the access area, it will make it easier for us to find our way back if we get disoriented while we are in here. We are right in the middle of the water tank and we are facing forward. The bladder to the right is Number 1, and working clockwise while facing the nose of the ship, the next one is Number 2 and so forth so the bladder that was on our left when we started is Number 4. See where the bladders are all bunched up over there?" Alexi said, pointing forward and to the right. "That should be where the patch is. Let's go check it out."

With Alexi leading the way, they found the place where the damage was. "We can't actually see where the patch is because pieces of the two ruptured bladders that had blocked the hole from the inside are in the way," Alexi said. "Let's work our way around the blockage. The bladder material is fairly thick and it will be stiff, but do your best to just push it out of the way. Under no condition should you become separated from the rest of us. So don't try to worm your way between the bladder and the hole because you would be out of sight and could easily become disoriented."

Alexi maintained a continuous narrative for the benefit of the captain. "The damage is pretty extensive, Captain. Ice seems to be completely blocking the hole so we are no longer leaking to space. We are passing under the blockage. We can see that the forward ends of bladders 1 and 2 are completely shredded for 10 to twenty feet. Now, we are going to look at bladder 3. Oh, oh, this is bad. From what I can see, bladder 3 has been ruptured but not as bad as the other two. There is a large tear and I can see water droplets and globules floating in the space between the bladders. I am going to work my way aft between 2 and 3 for as far as I can go without losing touch with Ichuro and Jammy."

Alexi worked his way aft towards the point where the gap between bladders 2 and 3 was narrowed. He pushed the water in the bladders out of the way as he went. He pushed alternately on the material of 2 and 3. The wall of bladder 2 just moved away from his hand when he pushed, but number 3 seemed to resist his thrusts. When he was well past the midpoint of the tank it was clear that bladder 3 still contained some water.

When Alexi rejoined Ichuro and Jammy he said, "Number 2 is empty or nearly so, but Number 3 still has some water in it. How much I can't tell. But it is far less than it should be. We can probably get past Number 3, but let's go back around and check Number 4." He led the way back under the patch into the space between Number 1 and Number 4. Because of the damage to Number 1, the space between 1 and 4 was large, but there was obvious damage to bladder 4. Again, Alexi went aft punching the bladders as he went. When he was just aft of the halfway point the contents of Number 4 clearly resisted him, but curiously, the water was all against the outer shell of the tank.

"Okay, let's go give them the bad news and see if anyone has a suggestion for how to mend the damage." As they went back into the tunnel, Alexi said, "Why don't we leave the lantern where it is. We're undoubtedly going to need in the future."

Ten minutes later they were back in the Common Room dressed in their normal clothes. Alexi explained the situation to Ian and the others. "It is bad, very bad," he said. "If I had to guess I would say we only have 10 or maybe

15% of the reaction mass we would need to go home. You were right, Miriam, the spin, as slow as it is, has caused the water in bladder 4 to be against the outside wall of the reaction mass tank causing the problem. Normally, when we are under power, we draw from the bladders in rotation in order to maintain the balance. So all four had approximately the same amount when we arrived.

"If we had some way to patch the others I might be able to redistribute the water equally to reduce the wobble. Bladders 1 and 2 are heavily damaged and I'm not sure there's any way we could put water back into them. At the moment the water in the area of the explosion is frozen and effectively plugs the hole. In order to maintain the water in liquid form and under pressure, we circulate warmed CO_2 throughout the tank. The pressure of the CO_2 serves to compress the bladders and our acceleration ensures that the water is in the aft ends of the bladders."

"Commander," Gladys asked, "is there any way to patch the bladders?"

"We have a couple hundred small patches about the size of your hand for repairing holes caused by micrometeorites. They are peal and stick type patches. If we get hit, which we were a couple of times before we left, someone goes into the tank through one of the access holes finds the puncture puts a patch on the outside of bladder and on the inside of the tank. Typically these holes are no bigger than the end of your finger, and most of the time the impact is absorbed by the tank and the bladders are not punctured," Alexi explained.

"I have been going through the manifests ever since we got in this predicament thanks to me," Gladys said, "and I found the boxes of small patches you described. I also found a record of ten larger patches that are described as being a meter square and ten very large patches that are described as being three meters square. And, there are three gallons of rubber cement as well. Is there any way we might be able to use those?"

Alexi pulled himself around the table to Gladys, gave her a big hug, and said, "Madam, your sins are forgiven!"

He continued, "Captain, with patches that big we might be able to cut away the damaged parts of bladder 2 and patch it. If all we did was patch number 2 and pump some of the water from number 4 into it to balance the mass, we might be able to correct for the wobble. Miriam, what do you think?"

"If you did that, Commander, you might be able to move the CG back near where it is supposed to be. But what about the water in bladder number 3?" Miriam asked.

"I see what you mean," Alexi replied. "It would be almost impossible to pump the remaining water out of number 3 without patching it first. The hole in number 3 is a long slit. I think that could be patched by cutting up one or two of the larger patches then we could pump that water into number 2. But it appears to me that simply pumping the water around so that it is equally distributed between bladders 2 and 4 is not going to correct the CG. We may have to use some acceleration to force the water to the rear of the bladders where it will be equalized radially around the longitudinal axis, but that is also going to move the CG aft from where it has been since we entered orbit and that will undoubtedly affect the parameters of the precession."

"Yes, sir, it would," Miriam said, "I've been thinking about that and I think the first thing we have to do is stop the spin, then worry about the precession."

"Okay, the first-order business will be to get the ship back in balance. Then stop the spin and the precession," Ian ordered. "Commander, you and your team need to have something to eat, and a good night's sleep. While you're doing that, we will locate the patches for you. What are you going to need to cut the bladders?"

"I won't be able to answer that until we try. If you would round up everything you can find that will take a good edge, we'll just try them one by one until we find one that will work," Alexi answered. Then asked, "What is being done about the scientists stranded at Ares Base?"

"We haven't forgotten about them. We're doing nothing at the moment since their radio equipment doesn't work," Ian replied. "We've talked about having Rachael do a rundown to the surface to bring them up. But considering the docking problems she had yesterday when she took you over to the damage site and tried to return, I think we had better wait until we see if we can correct some of our motion problems. However, when we're at sea and operating under radio silence, the way we talk between ships is to use Aldis Lamps to send the code back and forth. What do we have that we might be able to use to at least signal them that we're still here? Do we have a really powerful spotlight?"

"Yes, sir," Alexi replied. "There are four very strong spotlights around the front of the ship. We can turn them on in hopes that someone on the ground will look up and see them. You might try sending code, but considering our gyrations I don't see how they could be pointed at Ares Base long enough to send a message, and we don't know if any of the people down there know Morse code."

"Thank you again, Commander. We'll try that," Ian said.

For the next two days, Ichuro and Jamilah tried various knives with minimal success because the material the bladders were made of was very tough, designed to resist tearing. At the same time, Alexi was having no success applying strips of patches to the tear in bladder 3. Finally, as they were having dinner on the second day, Jamilah said, "Commander, would it be easier to close the tear in number 3 if I got inside and used a couple of strips to pull the edges of the cut together?"

Before Alexi could reply, Gladys asked, "have you thought of sewing the edges together?"

Alexi looked at Jamilah and then at Gladys and said, "those are both great ideas and the best way might be to do both. We have a battery-operated electric drill that should be able to drill through the material, then have Jammy inside to pass the needle back and forth as we try to stitch it up." Then he said with a twinkle in his eye, "but that might leave Jammy on the inside. How do you feel about that, Jammy?"

"Whatever it takes, Commander," Jammy replied with a laugh.

"Okay, it sounds like a plan," Alexi said. "But what are we going to use for a needle? There is some waxed twine in the shop, but I can't think of anything that would work as a needle. I suppose we can just try and push the end through the hole."

"Will this do, Commander?" Gladys asked as she held up a 4-inch long plastic needle. "I use it when I stitched the parts of my knitting together. The eye is large enough for my fattest yarn, so your waxed twine should fit through just fine."

"Captain, may I say that I am very glad we brought women on this expedition?" Alexi asked.

"Me too, Commander," Ian replied.

It took three days to stitch the slit in bladder three together. They tried several kinds and sizes of drill bits before they found one that would penetrate the bladder material. They could only drill about four holes before the bit went dull and had to be re-sharpened. In order to drill holes, Alexi had to place his hand on the inside of the material and press the drill against the outside in order to develop the pressure needed to puncture the material. There were actually four bits approximately the same size, two metric and two in inches. As each bit became dull, Ichuro would take it over to the access area and exchanged it for one that AJay had resharpened in the shop.

Try as they may, they could find no way to tie knots while wearing a space suit. While Alexi and Jamilah stitched, Ichuro trailed behind them squirting rubber cement from a catsup container borrowed from the kitchen. When they were 3 feet from the end Jamilah squirmed through the gap. The slit was almost 15 feet long. When they were finished the joint wasn't perfect and it probably wasn't watertight but it was closed up enough that pieces from one of the larger patches could be used to cover it and seal it. They perfected their bladder patching technique on bladder 3.

Patching bladder 2 was a completely different problem. When Ichuro wasn't taking drill bits back and forth, he worked at cutting away the rough edges around the hole. The damage was uneven, which enabled leaving a longer flap on one side of the damaged area. They folded the flap over, sealed it with the cement and then used pieces of the larger patches to make sure it was airtight and watertight. Finally, after all the damage to the bladders had been repaired and the ice was chipped away from the hole they very carefully applied a large patch over the hole on the inside of the tank to make it as airtight as possible. When they were finished Alexi slowly injected CO_2 into the tank to pressurize it. He checked continuously for any drop in pressure that would signal a leak, and to the surprise of everyone found none. The tank was once again airtight. Completing the repairs took a week.

During that time Miriam with Rachael's help worked continuously trying to determine the parameters of the ship's various motions. None of the solutions were adequate enough to determine how to correct the rotation and precession of the ship. When the repairs were completed and the tank pressurized, they were ready to transfer the water.

"Alexi took charge. "First the water remaining in bladder 3 will be pumped into bladder 2 a little at a time so that any changes to the center of gravity will be made very gradually." It took several hours for the rotation to cause the water in bladder 2 to move away from the center and out to the side of the tank. "Now we will begin transferring some of the water from bladder 4 into bladder 2 to try and balance the ship. The problem is we have no idea how much water is in bladder 4. My best guess is a little less than half of what was left when we left the Moon. I know how much water was pumped from bladder 3 into the bladder 2. So we will pump enough from bladder 4 to even up the mass." Within four hours, Mariam was able to measure the change in the wobble and watched it slowly disappear as the ship was rebalanced.

"Miriam, are we back in balance?" Ian asked.

"Yes, Captain, if not, we are very close and won't notice it. The spin is still there, of course. It was caused by the explosion and the outgassing of the CO_2 and the water that escaped. I will try to stop it using the steering jets." Miriam very carefully fired the steering jets in small bursts and watched the spin slowly come to a stop and the precession reduce as well. "Sir, the spin has stopped, however, some of the precession is in effect residual spin and it continues. It will take a while to eliminate it if I can."

"Nice work, Miriam, thank you," Ian said.

It took another day of carefully timed bursts from the steering jets to eliminate the precession as well. Once again the ship was stabilized in its orbit around Mars.

"Rachael?" Ian said.

"Yes, Captain. I think it is safe to go down and get the other scientists. I'm ready to go as soon as we're back on the sunny side of our orbit."

"Captain," Ichuro began. "May I have permission to go down with Rachael and see if I can fix the radios."

"Yes, that's really necessary if we are to stay in orbit any longer."

"Captain, do you think that's wise? If something should happen to him, we would be without an electronics specialist," Lupe said with emphasis. "I am concerned about his going. Wouldn't it be better just to bring the others back to the ship and see what we can do to get back to Earth?"

"We are going to be here for a long time, Doctor," Ian replied. "From what Miriam tells me, we will not be in the position to leave orbit for Earth for over a year. So we should just keep on doing our jobs until it is a time to depart. That goes for the scientists as well as the crew."

"But, sir—"

"The issue is settled and I've made my decision, Dr. Martinova."

Six hours later, Rachael and Ichuro departed for Ares Base.

The three scientists were outside in their space suits when Rachael landed.

"We're so very happy to see you, Rachael. We saw the spotlights on the front of the ship and deduced from the strange motions they were making that there was a problem up there," Jan said.

"We're happy to see you are safe as well," Rachael said. "We brought you a new radio."

"Do you have any ideas what could have gone wrong with your radios?"

"We're not sure that anything is wrong with them," Ton Vernon said. "We simply could not send or receive on the ship's frequency. We could use our suit radios to talk to each other if we were very close together, but there was a lot of static," Tom said.

"Ichuro, is here to see what we can do to fix the problem."

Ichuro used a frequency sniffer and found a jammer in one of the containers outside the habitat.

"This is what was blocking your radios," he said, holding up a small blue box with an antenna sticking out of the side.

With that fixed, they waited until the *Explorer* completed an orbit and would be in position to receive them when they returned. When the *Explorer* floated into the intercept position, Rachael took them back up to the *Explorer*.

. . .

When everyone was assembled in the Common Room, Ian explained the bad news. "Ladies and gentlemen as some of you know already we have a problem. What you may not know is the seriousness of that problem. The explosion in the reaction mass tank cost us an enormous amount of our reaction mass. The original contents of the tank were enough to get us from the moon to Mars and put us in orbit, leaving enough to provide for the trip back. For the moment, we are stranded. The crew has been going through various scenarios on the computer to determine if there was any economical orbit or path that we could use to get back to the Earth or the Moon with the reaction mass we have left."

"We have identified several possibilities but all of them involve very long elliptical orbits that are essentially comet paths. The fastest alternatives would allow us to depart Mars and swing out beyond Mars orbit in a very large elliptical path and coast like a comet down towards the Sun and when we were on the far side of the Sun just skim Venus, which would give us a gravitic boost or sling-shot maneuver to provide the velocity needed to match the orbit of the Earth. Realistically, none of the alternatives would enable us, in the interest of safety, to exactly match the speed or position of Earth in its orbit.

"None of them would match the timing and speed differential required to put us back at the L2 point over the far side of the moon. In a few of the alternatives, ICExS would be required to send a 'tug' or rescue ship out to meet us and provide us with assistance to achieve Earth orbit. In over half of the cases, we would have to abandon the *Explorer*, transfer to the rescue ship and allow the *Explorer* to eventually spiral down into the Sun. These possibilities are all several years in duration, and the optimum time or times for departure are from two to three years away. There is no possibility that ICExS can build a ship and come out to Mars to rescue us. It took almost ten years to build the *Explorer* and the Barsoom Explorer 2 is still at least two years away.

"We have sufficient food and supplies for the original trip as planned and a comfortable reserve in case we needed to do an alternative. If you do not mind becoming vegetarians or vegans, Dr. Burns says she has adequate chemicals for her hydroponic garden to go on indefinitely with careful recycling. The original plan was for us to remain in Mars orbit for approximately eighteen months and then to take a direct route straight back to the Earth, in essentially the same way we did when we came to Mars."

The captain had waited until everyone was back aboard the *Explorer* before he laid out the full details of their predicament. When he was finished speaking, the only sound that could be heard were the fans in the air circulation system running. Except for the few who were completely involved in the attempts to repair the damages caused by the explosive, this was the first time all the details had been laid out before them. Only Miriam, Alexi, and the captain had been completely aware of their true situation with respect to returning to Earth prior to the captain's announcement.

"Is ICExS aware of our predicament, Captain?" Jan Pitrasen asked.

"Yes, Dr. Pitrasen. We have informed them; we have transmitted all of our data to them, and they have done their own computations in an effort to determine if there were any other alternatives. So far, they are in complete agreement with what we have computed here. They are continuing an effort to find a way to help us. Short of sending us several hundred tons of water, which is completely impossible, there is no way they can help us. I truly wish there was," Ian replied.

"Yes, I'm sure you do, Captain," Dr. Pitrasen said quietly. "Do you have any suggestions of what we should do, Captain?"

"Only, that we carry on as we have been, and continue to do our jobs, both crew and science team, to the best of our abilities. That's about all we can do at the moment. You scientists have your agendas. I suggest that you follow them. Gather your data to perform your experiments and we will transmit the results back to Earth. Sitting around here wringing our hands with concern is not going to do any of us any good. Doing the jobs we were sent here to do is what we owe those who sent us," Ian said.

The silence was broken when several of the scientists all tried to speak at once. While the three women scientists may not have been completely aware of the details of just how bad their situation was, they had been on the ship when the explosion occurred and while the repairs were being carried out. Other than what had been told to them when Rachael went down to Ares Base to retrieve them, the men were unaware of the seriousness of the situation.

Dr. Pitrasen tapped his pipe on the table for silence. When he had everyone's attention he said, "Thank you, Captain. Your advice is well taken. I think I heard someone say as far as they were concerned we didn't owe anybody anything because they had not allowed for the situation. Whoever said it is wrong. The people who built and equipped the ship provided us with everything we would need under normal circumstances and with provision for things we might need in case we had serious problems. There is no way they could have foreseen what has happened."

"That's bullshit, Jan, and you know it," Esteban Martinova announced loudly. "This whole expedition has been screwed up from the time they began. Religious fanatics from all over the world did everything they could to prevent us from coming. And, I, for one wish they had succeeded."

Dr. Pitrasen sighed and replied, "Then why did you come, Esteban? Nobody forced you to come. There were plenty of other qualified candidates. What made you accept the offer?"

Dr. Pitrasen was answered by silence. Gladys Campbell, who had been advised that her son was rescued and in protective custody, sat quietly at the table sniffling into her hanky. Dr. Lupe Martinova sat beside her husband whispering into his ear. Dr. Esteban Martinova stared accusingly at Dr. Campbell while the muscles in his cheeks showed that he was clenching his teeth in anger. Dr. Thomas Vernon sat quietly looking at his hands, which were clasped in his lap. The only scientist who was not exhibiting any reaction at all was Dr. Jamilah Burns who sat in the lotus position floating in the air above the end of the table while holding hands with Ichuro Watanabe.

No one of the crew said anything. They all sat silently watching the captain. "Have you received any further orders from ICExS, Captain?" Dr. Pitrasen asked.

"Just what I have passed on to you, sir. The essence of which was, 'carry on,'" Ian replied.

"I concur, Captain," Dr. Pitrasen said.

"Now just a damned minute, Jan. Who made you the boss?" Esteban Martinova asked.

"ICExS did, Esteban" was the quiet reply.

"Well, I for one, object!" Esteban asserted in angry tones.

Dr. Jan Pitrasen was well-known in scientific circles for being unflappable. "What do you suggest, Esteban?"

"I suggest that we choose a new leader right now!" Estevan said deliberately.

Dr. Pitrasen looked thoughtfully across the table and nodded. "And who do you suggest Esteban? You or one of the others?"

"I have far more experience at leading scientific expeditions then you do, Jan. I have led groups all over the Peruvian Andes and the Chilean Atacama Desert. In some cases with twenty-five to thirty members. I have more experience than anyone else here. What have you done?" Esteban demanded, holding his head back at an angle so he was looking down his nose at the others.

Jan Pitrasen took in a slow deep breath and let it out. He had no ego tied up in his appointment. He knew why he had been asked and he knew why he had accepted. One of the reasons sat glaring at him from across the table. He had been warned about Esteban Martinova's ego and ambition. He weighed the replies he could make and considered carefully how he could deal with Esteban's egotistical attitude and still retain control over what could turn into a dangerous situation. He sat silently for a full minute considering his options, then replied, "Well, you have me there, Esteban. I have never led a large scientific expedition anywhere, and I have never led any scientific expeditions in western South America. I have led numerous small expeditions into the Arctic and Antarctic. But this is not about that, is it Esteban?"

"What you mean by that?" Martinova snarled.

"Does it really matter which of us has led more expeditions where? If you doubt my competence as the scientific leader of this expedition, why didn't you say so before now?" Pitrasen replied evenly.

The captain watched the interplay and started to say something. As he looked up and started to speak he saw Tom Vernon across the table give a very slight shake of his head. The captain accepted the signal and cleared his throat instead, choosing to leave the politics between the scientists with them.

"Nobody asked me before now," Martinova said. He wasn't sure what had happened, but he knew he had lost control of the situation.

"Would you like to take a vote, Esteban?" Dr. Pitrasen asked.

Dr. Esteban Martinova glanced around the table at the other three scientists. He was sure of his wife's vote in addition to his own, but he did not really know how the others might vote. He said, "No, not right now. We'll settle this later."

"All right, Esteban, if that's how you want it, then that's how we'll leave it," Dr. Pitrasen said.

"What have we decided to do about our situation, Jan?" Tom asked.

"We'll leave the solution for the problems with the ship to the captain and the crew. As for the scientists, we will do as we have been asked to do, 'carry on,'" Jan replied.

"That suits me just fine," Vernon said. He had some experience with Martinova's attitude while they were down on Mars at Ares Base and he wanted no part of his being in control. He knew that if a vote had been taken, it would have been two in favor of Esteban Martinova, himself and his wife, three in favor of Jan Pitrasen, and one abstention, Jan.

"Now, Captain, what are we or, more appropriately, you planning to do about the other problem?" Dr. Pitrasen asked the captain.

"All I can tell you at this time, Dr. Pitrasen, is that we are working on it and we will keep working on it. I can't make any promises. I wish I could. I have the best crew that I could wish for and I am confident that given time, we will find a solution. Does that answer your question, sir?" the captain replied.

"It does. If there is anything any of us can do to help, you please let us know and I am sure we will be happy to do it. Now, what's for dinner?" Dr. Pitrasen asked with a smile.

CHAPTER THIRTEEN

After additional equipment and supplies had been loaded into the shuttle, Miriam took the scientists back down to Ares Base. They unloaded the shuttle quickly, and Miriam was able to relaunch and meet the *Explorer* on its next pass even though it meant docking in the dark. She wanted to get back aboard and continue working on the problem, but she also really wanted a chance to fly the shuttle again.

While Miriam was gone, the captain was quietly concerned because he had no idea what he would do without his Astrogator. When she returned, the captain called a meeting of the entire crew. "Well, folks, you know the worst of it, do any of you have any ideas, wild or any other kind?"

"I've been thinking about that, Captain. Of course, I have," Rachael said with a laugh, "who hasn't? I keep wondering about that ten trillion ton rock sitting over there just 3000 kilometers away. We've all read what is in the database, but aside from a hat full of statistics what do we really know about it?" she asked rhetorically, then offered some answers. "It has a mean density of about 2 grams per cubic centimeter. Water has a mean density of one gram per CC. So Phobos's masses not quite twice that of water. Earth's moon has a mean density of about three and a half grams per CC. So Phobos is only about half as dense as our moon and twice the density of water. It makes me kind of wonder what kind of 'cheese' Phobos is really made of. I propose that we take one of the shuttles over there and check it out."

"Holy Moses, Rachael, you have a very good point there," Miriam said with genuine admiration. "That's just the proverbial hop, skip, and a jump from here. It shouldn't take us more than four or five hours to get there and what have we got to lose?"

Ian tried unsuccessfully to keep from laughing. "Do it! If you find anything even remotely interesting that we can make use of we will probably have to send one of the geologists over there to take a look."

"Really? Captain. That means one of the Martinova's. There has to be someone else who can tell one rock from another, isn't there?" Rachael asked.

"I think you'll find Dr. Pitrasen lists geology among his other accomplishments," Ian replied.

"Thank God!" Rachel exclaimed.

"We have to wait until Phobos emerges into the daylight side of its orbit," Ian said. "I want to insure that the shuttle will arrive at Phobos when it was in sunlight in order to avoid unexpected consequences as much as possible and I want two people in the shuttle for safety. Rachael, you will be the shuttle pilot and, AJay would you please accompany her?"

"Yes, sir, I would be happy to," AJay replied.

Ian looked at Miriam and saw the look of disappointment on her face. "Miriam, I know you want to go too, but I cannot risk you again if we are to have any hope of finding our way back to the Moon."

. . .

The *Explorer* was just twenty-four minutes behind Phobos when it passed the terminator. Rachael disengaged the shuttle from the airlock and was drifting parallel to the *Explorer*. She activated the forward television transmitter so the people on the *Explorer* could see what she could see.

"Ready?" Rachael asked AJay as she watched the countdown timer approach zero.

"Ready!" AJay replied, wondering what she would've done if he had replied, No! He was fully aware that he was essentially deadweight as far as assisting in any way with the piloting of the shuttle, but he also knew that he was vital to the mission. He was given the task of watching the approach radar and keeping Rachael informed as they neared Phobos and to be able to do that he had to be close to the pilot station which meant floating freely inside the shuttle.

At zero, Rachael said, "Hang on, Ajay," and fired the rockets to begin their journey. She gradually accelerated to 1200 kilometers per hour, then cut the jets. As planned, at that speed and allowing for the deceleration, they would overtake Phobos in just over three hours.

As they approached the midpoint, she said, "Get a grip again, Ajay, I'm going to fire the braking rockets to begin the deceleration. Keep a sharp eye on Phobos so I don't overshoot," she said unnecessarily.

"Aye, aye, Ma'am," he replied. During the deceleration, AJay called out the distance to Phobos in declining increments while Rachael focused on the stars she needed for navigation.

At a distance of 60 kilometers, Rachael cut the engines and used the residual velocity for the final approach. Ajay called out the distances and Rachael used the throttles with a fine touch.

As AJay said, "Fifteen kilometers," Rachael brought the shuttle to a stop relative to Phobos. Not quite four hours after departing the *Explorer*, Phobos loomed large in the forward view screen.

"Not bad, eh?" she said as she high-fived AJay, which pushed him across the cabin.

"No, not bad at all," he replied as he rebounded.

Rachael kept the *Explorer* continuously informed of their progress except for the last few minutes during the deceleration when she was totally focused on tight piloting. Of course, they could hear AJay as he counted down the distance.

"Are you seeing this?" Rachael asked the viewers on the *Explorer*.

"We see it, Rachael," Ichuro replied. "It looks exactly like the pictures in the database. Someone once described it as a huge potato, and that's what it look like, but we can also see it's rotating slowly."

"According to our instruments, it has two axes of rotation. End over end due to gravity lock with Mars and equatorially as well," Rachael replied.

"How is everything with you?" Ian asked.

"We're fine, sir," she said after receiving a confirming nod from AJay.

"Do you think the equatorial rotation is going to cause you any trouble when you land on it?" Ian asked.

"I don't think so, Captain. The rate of rotation is slow enough that I should be able to match it long enough to land."

"I won't say 'be careful,' because I know you will. Have a nice nap," Ian said.

The plan was to just stay in position while they followed Phobos in its orbit around through the night side and back into daylight before they attempted a landing on the surface. The plan was also that they were to take a nap during this period, but they were both too excited to nap and spent the time watching Phobos. Even when on the night side, they could see its outline as it blocked the starlight and some of its surface features, which were illuminated by starlight.

After what seemed like an endless four hours, they came back into the sunlight and could see the detail of its surface. Phobos has a very low albedo, much lower than Earth's moon.

"Captain, as planned, Stickney Crater looks like the best place to attempt a landing. We'll sneak up on it from behind relative to its rotation and follow it around as we do our final approach."

Stickney Crater is the largest feature on the surface of Phobos, it is very deep and might provide access to the interior where there might be water in the form of ice. Phobos was rotating between three and four minutes per revolution or at an equatorial speed of about six miles per hour. Rachael approached Phobos at a speed that would match the rotation as she approached on a tangent. Phobos did not have enough gravitational attraction to pull the shuttle to its surface very quickly.

"As we suspected, there is no practical way to just dive into the crater. We will have to constantly maneuver to stay in position once we're over the crater.

I am not going to give you a moment-by-moment narrative of the approach because I will be rather busy," Rachael said.

She slowed to let Phobos's rotation bring the monolith to her. She was "flying" backwards so she could see what was coming as the moon turned. The surface of Phobos was very irregular, so it was difficult to maintain a constant distance from the surface except by hovering fairly high. As she saw Stickney come over the horizon, she gradually decreased her altitude and settled into the crater.

"Nice, job, Rachael," Ian said.

"It's not over yet, Captain," she said. "We're about to land, but I think until we are somehow anchored, I'm going to have to almost constantly stay on the throttles to maintain position."

Rachael lowered the landing skids and gently kissed the surface stirring up some dust. She turned the steering jets up and used the lowest setting to push the shuttle against the surface of Phobos.

"Okay. Ajay, are you ready?" she asked.

"Okay," AJay said as he opened the airlock and clipped a safety line to an anchor point on the outside of the shuttle and stepped out onto the surface of Phobos. He had practiced placing a grappling hook while he was in freefall aboard the *Explorer*. Any effort to push on the hook to keep it in place resulted in his moving away from the position, so he had to develop a technique of placing his hand in the crack next to where he intended to place the hook, then use a twisting motion to anchor the hook. It wasn't going to be nearly as easy on Phobos as it had been on the *Explorer*.

After a few minutes, AJay could feel the very slight gravity that Phobos provided. "If I even lift my foot quickly, I drift away from the surface. It is very much like being in freefall. I think if I tried hard enough I could jump right off into orbit." More to keep himself focused than to inform anyone. "I'll try a slow shuffle like we did on the moon. It's not much better and will go very slowly, but I see a place where I can tie off one of the anchor lines. And once I have that, I'll have a way to maintain surface contact."

He tied the first anchor point around a rock jutting out from the surface. Within ten minutes, he located two other places around the shuttle where he could jamb a hook into a crack. A hard tug with his feet on the surface gave a satisfactory anchor point. The three lines were attached to the shuttle and pulled tight.

"That should do it, Rachael, try killing the jets," AJay said.

She stopped the jets and the shuttle settled onto the surface of Phobos. They were down.

Rachael picked up one of the long safety lines they brought and, anchoring herself to the shuttle, stepped out onto the surface. She immediately bounded off the surface and had to use the safety line to pull herself back down.

"Go very slowly," AJay said as he pulled himself over to where she stood. "Progress is going to be very slow, but it is doable."

"So I see," Rachael observed.

They had several 100 meters or longer safety lines which, if placed properly, would give them a large radius of operation as they explored the surface.

"I see a dark area over that way," AJay said, pointing. "I'll go over that way, and you go over there." He pointed toward another feature.

They were both connected to the shuttle so there was no risk of drifting away from the vicinity of the shuttle. The escape velocity of Phobos was so low any unintended movement could cause one to drift off the surface and only settle back very slowly. They proceeded in opposite directions to the limit of their safety lines and made a sweep around the shuttle looking for anywhere they might be able to penetrate the surface.

Photographs of Phobos that were taken years before by survey satellites showed the surface inside Stickney Crater as relatively smooth. It had been estimated that Phobos had a dust covering that might be as much as 100 meters deep. There was indeed dust, but the surface felt fairly firm as they did their sweep of the area around the shuttle. Both bounced off the surface several times before they developed a technique for moving without risking loss of traction. They found numerous places where the rock from which Phobos was formed projected above the apparent surface. Using these, they created a series of anchor points surrounding the shuttle with a web of safety lines.

Their safety lines allowed them to cover a fair amount of territory in their sweep. Several times the anchor lines snagged on a projecting rock. The first time Rachael's safety line snagged, without thinking she tried to flip the line off the snag. Her quick motions left her 30 meters above the surface with the line still snagged or she would've been far higher.

"AJay!" she called, hoping for help. "What do I do now?"

AJay looked around for her and saw her drifting above the surface and laughed. "Just pull yourself down slowly. I did the same thing a few minutes ago myself."

"It's not funny," she said, then began laughing herself. "Why didn't you warn me?"

"Some things have to be experienced. They cannot easily be explained, besides, I have my own problems."

"You're right," she said. She very slowly pulled herself down to the snag and the surface, then lifted the line carefully over the snag to continue her sweep. She looked around for AJay and could not find him. "Where did you go, AJay?"

"It's difficult to explain where I am," he replied. "I tried to descend into one of the smaller craters inside Stickney. My line was too short so I am currently drifting above the surface of the lower crater where you cannot possibly see me from where you are. I'm going to try to pull myself back towards the shuttle," AJay said as he began to pull. "Damn! That didn't work very well. I'm going headfirst towards the wall of the crater ahead. I'm not going very fast so I doubt I will damage my helmet.

"I'm going to try to flip myself over so I land feetfirst." He reached down the line with one hand and pulled slowly until he was going feetfirst. "Yes, that did it, what a relief. I'm almost there. Wait a minute, I think I see something." As he turned he saw a large crack in the wall of the crater only a short distance away from where he was going to land on the other side of the crater. Hey, I found a way in I think."

"Where?" she asked.

"Just follow my safety line."

"I'm on my way," Rachael said. When she reached the lip of the crater she looked for AJay. She could see where his safety line went over the lip of the crater but the immediate area was in shadow and she could not see where the line went after that. "Where are you?"

AJay could see her when she reached the lip of the crater. "Over here," he said as he turned to face her and shine his helmet light in her direction.

Rachael saw a light and floated over the edge of the crater. "Got you," she said. Then using his light for guidance, she pulled herself over to him.

"Look, I think it's a crack," he said, pointing to an irregular darker area. "We might explore it. What do you think?"

"I think we should advise the captain before we do anything that might be difficult to undo."

"I heard him, Rachael," Ian said. "Does it look dangerous to either of you?"

"We're working ourselves around the inside of the crater for a closer look, Captain," Rachael replied. They pulled themselves from rock to rock around the inside of the crater until they reached the dark space. "Okay, Captain, it is an irregular crack or cave. The entrance is two meters wide and maybe 10 meters high. It runs from the surface down to a spot below where we are at the moment."

"Are you both comfortable exploring it?"

Rachael looked at AJay. "How do you feel about it?"

"I don't see any problems. There is no evidence of rock slides or any damage to the cave."

"Then go ahead. I should say, be careful, but I won't," Ian said, a smile in his voice.

"Yes, sir," Rachael replied. Then to AJay, "Okay you found it, you lead the way," she said, pointing into the darkness.

They moved slowly from point-to-point using cracks and outcrops for fingerholds. They entered the cave where the trend was generally downward at a slight angle. When they were at the limits of their original safety lines. AJay asked, "More?"

"Sure, why not? We have plenty of lines if we stay together and connect them end to end," she replied. "Lead on."

AJay led them another twenty-five to thirty meters where they were forced to stop. "There's no way we can squeeze past that; it's too narrow," he said, pointing toward a very narrow place in the crack. What do you think we should do now?"

"Why don't you chip off a piece of the rock here so we can take it back to the *Explorer* for analysis."

AJay took the rock pick attached to his belt, braced himself with his back against one wall and his feet against the opposite wall and chipped off a piece of the wall. "Okay, let's go back to the shuttle, my oxygen is getting low. You lead the way."

They worked their way back up to the crater floor collecting the line as they went. When they emerged into the crater, darkness was approaching as they returned to the shuttle.

Rachael called the *Explorer* to give a report of what they had done and what they found. "Captain, we went about 150 meters into the surface of Phobos and all we found was rock. AJay took a sample, and as far as we can see, it looks pretty much like what we've seen in samples of stony meteorites. What we did not find was any ice. We have four more days of oxygen here and plenty of rations, so we would like to take another look around here and then move to another location before we return."

"Your call, Rachael, as long as you and AJay agree on what to do, you have my blessing."

"Thank you, Captain. I think we should take a nap while we're behind Mars and wait until we're on the day side for further exploration." She looked to AJay for confirmation, which he gave with a nod. "And, AJay agrees."

"Do it," Ian ordered, unnecessarily.

"Okay, we can probably get out of our space suits if the heater works. We'll be much more comfortable using our sleeping bags," Rachael said, then activated the shuttle's heater and waited for it to warm the cabin. After half an hour, they looked at the internal thermometer, "It looks like it's not going to get much warmer than minus 10, Ajay. What do you want to do?"

"They're the best sleeping bags you can buy; they should keep us warm," AJay said.

"I'm not suggesting anything, but wouldn't we be much warmer if we zipped the sleeping bags together?" Rachael asked. "We'll have our uniforms on," she added.

At the next light, they found nothing more of particular interest over their first location. They did pick up samples of various kinds of rock in hopes that someone more knowledgeable in geology could determine what they were. They retrieved the grappling hooks and anchor lines and stowed everything. Then Rachael, using as little thrust as possible, gently lifted them out of Stickney Crater and away from Phobos about 500 meters.

"Better safe than sorry," she explained to AJay. "I would not want to be bumped by that big rock as it turns." She moved them slowly towards what on the map looked like a relatively featureless plain or flat spot at what they called the North end of Phobos's major axis.

"I don't see anything of interest out there," AJay said as they drifted up the side of the Martian moon while watching it rotate slowly.

"Just more pits and craters of various sizes," Rachael replied.

They traveled very slowly taking their time to look everything over as they went. When they reached Phobos's North Pole, Rachael moved them into position above the plain and they began searching for a spot to land.

"I can't tell if it's covered with dust. We'll just have to go down and find out, but if it is covered with dust 100 meters deep, I have no intention of landing," Rachael said.

There was nothing that suggested there was any one place that seemed better than another.

"Do you see any rocks or whatever that might be good anchor points?" Rachael asked.

"No," AJay replied. "It looks pretty flat in the middle, what do you think?"

"It's as good a place as any," she replied.

Rachael used a little thrust to start them descending and just let the shuttle settle slowly to the surface. When they reached the surface they found themselves slowly sinking into dust that was everywhere. She cursed and immediately fired the steering jets to lift them off again. This blew the dust everywhere making it impossible to see.

"I hope we're going straight up, but there isn't a clue that I can see."

"We should be pretty safe at this speed, shouldn't we, Rachael?"

"I hope so. Can you get any readings on the radar?"

"Only that we are moving away from the surface, but nothing to show how fast we're going."

Slowly the dust spread away from them and became thinner. After a few minutes they could see, not well, but it was obvious they were moving away from Phobos. They had to go out almost a kilometer from the surface before the dust no longer occluded their vision. They floated there above Phobos and asked for instructions.

"You heard?" Rachael asked the *Explorer*.

"We heard," Ian replied. "You are just about to enter the night side of the orbit. Why don't you take some time, take another nap, and think about what you would like to do next."

"Wilco, Captain," Rachael replied.

Four hours later when Phobos emerged to the daylight side of its orbit around Mars, Rachael was prepared to discuss the situation with the Captain. "Captain, we are not sure just what to do about Phobos. For comparison purposes, the surface area of Phobos is approximately one-third of that of Israel. In my opinion, trying to search over 2400 square miles for something useful to us with two people in a shuttle is just not feasible. I thought it would be possible to identify a few possible candidates and when we get back, we can all review the pictures we recorded of the areas that we traversed or passed over as Phobos rotated around its axis. But we think that it's rather pointless to try further searching for water or ice without doing considerable research for sites first."

"How's your fuel supply, Rachael?" the captain asked.

"It's getting pretty low, sir. That last bit trying to escape from the dust field used up a lot. We have enough to get back to the *Explorer* and an adequate reserve," she reported. "I can probably make—"

"Rachael, look," AJay interrupted as he pointed through the vision screen. "Look at the debris that's in orbit ahead of Phobos's path."

"Excuse me, Captain, I'll get back with you in a minute," she said into the microphone. There was a double-click in her earphones indicating the captain had heard.

Rachael followed where AJay pointed. There was indeed a debris field that extended as far as they could see in orbit ahead of Phobos. She said, "That looks a lot like the ring the astronomers thought should be in the same orbit as Phobos but was never photographed. What do you suppose is out there?"

"I have no idea, but there are things spinning and tumbling out there that sparkle in the sunlight," he said. "If it sparkles it must be something shiny. It's just a guess, but it could be ice left over from a collision between a small asteroid or comet that settled into this orbit."

"I think you're right," Rachael said as she looked through the binoculars that up until now had been useless. Then she reported the new findings to the captain. "Captain, AJay just spotted some debris, shiny debris in orbit ahead of Phobos. He thinks it might be ice left over from a collision."

"Do you have enough fuel to comfortably make a pass out over the debris field and see what you can find?"

"No, sir, as much as I would like to go for a look-see, I think I'd better come back and refuel before I try," Rachael replied.

"Your call, but I agree. Come on back and you two can go out again tomorrow or the next day after you get some good food and rest."

. . .

Five hours later, after a freefall shower, and some clean clothes, Rachael and AJay were having dinner with the rest of the crew as they planned how to explore the debris field.

"Once we get past Phobos, which we can do just by coasting. I can slow the shuttle so that we would be going at the same velocity as the debris. We talked it over and would like to give it a try."

"Do any of you have any objections or suggestions?" Ian asked.

"Only that I wish I was going, Captain," Miriam said.

"I know you do Miriam, but—"

"No 'but' necessary, Captain. I'm just indulging in wishful thinking. I understand the reasons and can't disagree with them."

"I think we should advise the scientists about the potential of the debris field before you go. They may have some ideas of what to do and how to do it," Ian said.

The captain radioed to the scientists at Ares Base the next time the *Explorer* passed over. He explained to Dr. Pitrasen what Rachael and AJay had done while they were searching Phobos and their discovery of what they thought might be ice in a debris field in the orbit of Phobos.

"Thank you for the update, Captain. In the interest of keeping everyone informed, I left the microphone open and played your comments through the speakers in here. That is an amazing discovery, Captain. What do you plan to do—" Dr. Pitrasen was interrupted by shouting in the background.

"Jan, gimme that Goddamned microphone!" Esteban Martinova shouted. There was a brief scuffle and then Martinova addressed the Captain. "Captain, I demand that we be returned to the ship so that we can go on the exploration of the debris field. I'm taking over as leader of the science team, which I should have done when we were still aboard."

The captain could hear the heated discussion between Esteban Martinova and the other two men in the habitat. He waited patiently for it to be resolved. There was little else he could do from orbit. He, too, had left the speakers on so everyone aboard the ship had heard what was going on at Ares Base.

"Look you little Peruvian…," Tom was heard to say in the background as he enumerated various behavioral and hereditary characteristics real and fictional of Esteban Martinova for almost a minute without once repeating himself. Then he continued, "Get it through your head, Esteban, Jan is the designated leader of the science team. If you try to take over again, I will personally take great pleasure in demonstrating my abilities in the martial arts. Do you understand that?" A grunt was heard after which Vernon repeated his question spacing out his words in emphasis, "Do. You. Understand. That?"

"Si, si comprendo," Martinova said in Spanish in a tone of voice that indicated he was in pain.

"Sorry, Captain," Tom said into the microphone. "We just had a vote among scientists and Dr. Pitrasen is now and will continue to be the leader of the science team." Then as he returned the microphone to Dr. Pitrasen he said for all to hear, "Here, Jan, he won't mess with you again."

"Captain, are you still there, sir?" Dr. Pitrasen asked.

"Yes, Dr. Pitrasen, I'm still here. I take it things have been sorted out there?" the captain asked.

"Yes, they have. I'm sorry that you had to be witness to that," Jan Pitrasen said. "Is it your opinion, Captain, that any of us could be of help in the exploration of the debris field?"

"Not at the moment, Jan. The first thing we're going to do is have Rachael and AJay go back and look things over. That will take several days. While neither of them has anywhere near the expertise you have when it comes to ice, I am confident they can recognize it when they see it. Do you have any advice for them?" Ian asked.

"I think your plan is sound, Captain. Tom Vernon and I are the only ones here that have any extensive experience with ice. But that is with the kind of ice that is found in the Arctic and Antarctic. It is my guess and I think that is seconded by Dr. Vernon that the ice they will find will not be what I would call, 'normal' ice. Not to deliver a lecture on ice, I can only say that ice has several forms or phases depending on how it was formed and how cold it is. Unless the collision or whatever else might have created the ice in the debris field happened very recently, the ice, if any, will be stable and will resist evaporation due to sunlight or it would have disappeared a long time ago. Do you think there is any way they could capture some of the ice?" Jan Pitrasen asked.

Rachael looked at AJay, shrugged her shoulders and extended her hands palms up to indicate they did not know if they could capture any of the ice. Then she said knowing that the microphone was still open, "Captain, as it stands right now, it's impossible to know if what we saw was ice, or if we can capture some pieces. We have no idea how big or small the pieces are. I suspect that if a piece was too small it would melt very quickly and not tell us very much about its phase. On the other hand, if the piece is much bigger, I cannot think of any easy way to bring it in through the shuttle's airlock. We really have to go out and look first and we will need something to store any ice we might capture."

"Bravo, Rachael," Jan Pitrasen said. "Use your judgment, if it is ice, and it is easy to collect some without risking the shuttle, give it a try. No matter what kind of ice it is, we should be able to analyze it to see if it is usable as reaction mass. At this point, we have no idea what contaminants it might contain."

"What is the plan, Captain, if it is ice and it can be used?" Dr. Pitrasen asked.

"If it is ice and is usable, and its orbits are stable, we will have to move the *Explorer* over into the debris field in order to be able to effectively collect a sufficient amount for use as reaction mass," Ian replied.

"I, excuse me, sir, we concur," Dr. Pitrasen said. "Godspeed to you, Rachael and AJay. We will anxiously await your findings. In the meantime, we'll get on with our work here." There was a click as the microphone at Ares Base was turned off.

Rachael and AJay were rested and refreshed when they disconnected the shuttle from the *Explorer*'s airlock. Unlike for their original exploration, they disconnected on the night side and went directly to Phobos just as it was about to cross the terminator into the daylight. They passed Phobos 15 kilometers outside of its orbit as measured by the approach radar and began to approach the beginning of the debris field.

"Do you see anything interesting, AJay?" Rachael asked. She was totally focused on the area immediately in front of the shuttle in case she needed to evade anything that might be on a collision course with the shuttle and thus had a limited view of the debris.

"Just dust and really small stuff that may or may not be ice. I can't tell. We're going to have to go farther along to the area where we spotted what looked like ice from Phobos," he replied.

"Okay, I'm going to start us drifting along. Speak up if you see anything worth considering." Rachael used the steering jets to start the shuttle moving at a comfortable pace over the debris field. It took over an hour to move to where they could see what were clearly larger pieces.

"Let's stop now and take a good look at what is here," AJay said. "I don't have any way to guess at the size of the pieces., what do you think?"

"Only the very largest pieces produce an echo on the approach radar, but that only gives their distance, not their size," Rachael replied. "Let's stop here and see if we can get some idea of how big that stuff is."

Rachael brought the shuttle to a stop relative to the first cluster of debris large enough to make it worthwhile checking.

"How close are we to the debris?"

"It's hard to tell, but I would guess several kilometers. We are going to need to move closer."

"Right. I'm going to try to get into the cluster." She then chose a path very carefully into what she guessed was the center of the cluster. "I'm going to move slowly through the area, say, at about ten kilometers per hour. Shout out if you think we're close enough to some pieces to capture them. "The debris is spread out more than I thought it was. Do you see anything of interest? From what I can see of it, it looks as if at least some of it is ice. What do you think?" she asked AJay.

"It looks as if it's mostly ice," he replied. "As for size, I'm just guessing but most of it is very small, cricket ball sized or smaller. There are a few larger pieces that are about the size of a soccer ball and some up to a meter or more in diameter. Here take a look," AJay said, handing Rachael the binoculars. "They get bigger the farther I looked. As a rough guess some of the pieces as far ahead as I can see, might be as much as a kilometer in diameter, but that is just a guess because I don't have any way of telling how far away they are. What does the radar say?"

"The radar is essentially useless at any distance. I'm getting muddled readings because the amount of debris overwhelms the distance readings," Rachael replied. "Your call."

"Thanks," AJay said. "It's hard to determine whether the larger ones I can see around us are in fact ice. Almost everything I can see around us might be some rocks as well."

"Are you going to feel comfortable going out there and trying to snag one of those?" Rachael asked.

"Yes. Nothing is moving very fast nearby, so I'm not afraid of being hit by one. As you get near the next one that's about soccer-ball size can you slow down and stop relative to it?"

"Yes, I can. Go ahead and open the airlock and hook on. I'm not sure how close I can get so you're probably going to have to push off in order to catch it in your net. I'll do my best to get within 10 meters of one. Be careful," she said.

"I'm always careful," he said as he was screwing together pieces of rod that were to become the handle of the net. Then he continued, "Nuclear engineers always have to be careful. Oops, is not a word you want to use close to a reactor."

Rachael maneuvered the shuttle so that its speed was zero relative to three soccer-ball-sized chunks. When she was sure everything was stable, she left her pilot seat and took a loose grip on AJay's safety line. He carefully eyed one of the pieces and pushed off in its general direction. He tried unsuccessfully to get one of the pieces. Rachael slowly pulled him back to the shuttle.

"Damn, this is much harder than it looks. I used to be a pretty good cricket fielder, but I was on the ground and had a stable place to stand to catch the ball. Let's try again, and this time I will not push off so hard."

Rachael helped AJay get set and watched him push off again as she fed out his safety line. She tried to govern his progress by controlling the line, but this just made things worse. They repeated this procedure five times before he successfully netted the smallest of the pieces.

"Got it," AJay exclaimed. "Reel me in."

Rachael gave a brief tug to get him started back to the shuttle and deftly guided him to where he could get a grip on a handhold.

"Okay, now what are we going to do with it?" she asked. "We didn't plan for that. The net handle is about 5 meters long, so where are you going to be when you pass the catch to me?"

"You hang on to me, and I will pull the net end to me and then hand it to you. Okay?" AJay very slowly pulled the net towards himself hand over hand up the handle. "Ready? he asked.

"Ready," Rachael replied, holding out her hand. She missed it on the first try. "I'll bet you never had to catch a cricket ball while wearing a space suit."

"I can't say that I did," Ajay replied, laughing. "Here try again."

Rachael grasped the net handle close to the net itself and brought it into the shuttle. "Can you hang on while I transfer the ice to the storage bin?"

"Yes," he said, holding the net handle in one hand and a handhold with the other. He watched as Rachael wrestled with the net, the ice piece and the container that was to hold it. After a busy minute, she succeeded in storing the piece of ice.

"I need to find a better way to do the transfer. That thing was so cold, it nearly froze my hand inside the space suit glove," Rachael said. "Do you want to try for another one?"

"Yes," AJay said. "One of the others is drifting slowly towards us or we are drifting towards it, but it should be easier to catch."

He lined himself up carefully and pushed off very gently towards the approaching piece of ice. He had intentionally launched himself so that he would be between the shuttle and the piece of ice. He netted it on the first try. Rachael pulled him back to the shuttle, took the net from him and put the second piece in the storage container.

"That ought to do it. Let's not push our luck," Rachael said.

Rachael helped AJay disassemble the net handle and the net and stowed them inside the shuttle while he unhooked and came back through the airlock. As they were doing this they, felt and heard a bump as a piece of debris collided gently with the shuttle.

"That's not good," she said. "But it was so slow no damage was done. I hope." Rachael quickly strapped herself back into the pilot seat, and began the delicate process of leaving the debris field without hitting anything else. Half an hour later, they were 15 meters away, out orbit from the debris field and ready to go home.

"Hello, *Explorer*, your errant crew is on its way back home," Rachael announced over the radio. "We have what we came for. It's not much, but it is ice. We'll be home in time for dinner."

"Well done, errant crew, we'll leave the lights on so you can find your way back, you'll be late for dinner, but we'll save some leftovers or you," Ian joked.

"Gee, thanks, boss!" Rachael replied in kind.

When they returned to the *Explorer*, the ice container was removed from the shuttle and placed in the freezer that was used to contain frozen food. The whole process start to finish had taken just over twelve hours. They had neither eaten or slept during that time because they were wearing space suits so they could open the shuttle airlock and leave it open when they retrieved the ice.

While Rachael and Ajay slept, Alexi and Ichuro chipped several small pieces of ice off the specimens and performed an improvised set of tests to determine the quality and nature of the ice from the debris field.

Rachael and AJay were awake and in the Common Room when they were finished with the tests. Alexi reported to the assembled crew. "It looks good, Captain. One of the pieces had a small grain of rock of some sort in it. That is not a problem because we would normally filter the water before we put it in the reaction tank anyway to avoid clogging an injector. After filtering out any solids that might be included, it is fit to drink."

PART THREE

CHAPTER FOURTEEN

The results of the expedition to capture some of the ice from the debris field were reported to the scientists at Ares Base by the Captain. "Rachael and AJay went past Phobos to take some samples of the ice and to evaluate the feasibility of restoring our depleted reaction mass with the ice. The samples they took show promise. They are all pure H_2O with the exception that one sample had a small amount of rock in it. Nothing that we cannot filter or so I am told."

"That is wonderful, Captain," Dr. Pitrasen said. "What is the plan to capture more of the ice?"

"We are going to move the *Explorer* from its current position to a position above the ice field and try to determine how much there is and how we can exploit it."

"Please keep us informed, Captain," Pitrasen said. Some grumbling was heard in the background about not being included in the analysis of the ice. "It would appear, Captain, that we are not in complete agreement with how to proceed. However, I can see no other choice so good luck."

Ian double clicked the microphone switch to indicate agreement and to avoid further discussion.

Sixteen hours later with Miriam at the controls and Rachael observing, they began the relocation. "Captain, we think that we should flip the ship so we can observe directly where we're going," Miriam said. "We could fly over there backwards using the video image from the aft cameras, but we would be more comfortable if we did the reversal."

"If you think that would be best, proceed," Ian replied.

"We'll use the steering jets to do the reversal and to move the *Explorer* to a new orbit 20 kilometers out beyond Phobos orbit so we can pass Phobos with a comfortable margin. Its mass is not great enough to attract the *Explorer*," Rachael explained, keeping the captain informed. "Once we're in position for the transfer, we'll use a short burst from the center main nozzle to move us over to the ice field."

It took two hours for the reversal and the movement to the outer orbit. "We are in position for the main engine thrust, Captain," Rachael announced over the intercom. "It would be a good idea to hang on to something. We do not expect there to be a problem, but we would rather not be surprised. Ignition in 5…." Rachael continued the countdown to ignition and at zero, Miriam started the engine. The burst was so brief that it was impossible to actually feel the acceleration before it was finished.

Ten minutes after the main engine burn, Miriam announced, "We are on our way. According to our instruments and the computer, our velocity is very close to what we planned. The actual transit time will be 83.5 hours to the point where Rachael and AJay took the samples. Our velocity is about 30 kilometers per hour. We will really be creeping when we get there. Stopping by using the steering thrusters will be relatively easy and maneuvering should be fairly simple."

"Very well," Ian said, then added, "All things considered, I think the difference in time is irrelevant, especially since we have no specific destination other than the vicinity where Rachael and Ajay found the ice."

Miriam and Rachael took turns in the primary pilot seat in four-hour shifts. The other members of the crew were stopping by the pilot deck off and on to find out how the movement was going until the captain put a stop to it. He requested that the pilot coming off duty from a shift make a brief report to him and to anyone else who wanted to hear it. For the pilots, there was not much to do except watch and use the navigation scope to sight on the stars and observe the angle as they approached Phobos. The Common Room display showed their progress for all to see and everyone was interested as they approached Phobos because only Rachael and AJay had seen the moon up close. Once they passed Phobos, interest waned until they approached the beginning of the debris field.

"Deceleration to a relative stop is going to take about four hours, and 80 kilometers, Captain," Miriam said.

"Rachael, you've seen the debris field, what do you suggest?" Ian asked.

"It all looks the same. I can't be certain, but I think we're nearing the point where AJay and I collected the samples," Rachael said. "I suggest that we begin deceleration now but not stop relative to the debris. We should maintain a very slow drift. I think we are far enough out that we are in no danger of collision with the ice. There is not too much of interest here, we need to go farther until we catch up to some of the larger pieces we spotted. I also think we should maintain our present orbit and not get into the debris until we sight something of interest. Then we can take the shuttle down to look things over."

"Miriam, what is your opinion?" Ian asked.

"I think Rachael is right. Let's stay in this orbit for the time being. We probably need to do some mapping of the debris to see what is there," Miriam replied.

"Does anyone else have an opinion on the subject?" Ian asked the rest of the assembled crew. After a few moments of discussion, all agreed with the proposed action.

"Miriam, you may begin," Ian said.

"Deceleration started, sir. You probably won't be able to feel the deceleration because the steering jets do not provide a lot of thrust. If you watch the big screen, you might be able to see us slowing down relative to the debris. I have reset the program to slow us to 5 kilometers per hour. When we need to come to a relative stop, it will only take a few minutes," Miriam said.

Four hours later, the *Explorer* gradually slowed to what seemed like a full stop. Careful viewing of the large screen showed they were still moving, actually creeping along. They drifted above the debris field for several hours until several larger pieces of debris were sighted and mapped. Then Miriam gradually reduced their speed using the steering rockets until they were effectively at a full stop relative to the debris. After the congratulations and high fives were finished, the captain called them to order.

"All right, what do we know? Are any of those pieces of ice something we can use? I'd like some estimates of the mass of each of the medium-sized and smaller ones. Ignore the real little pieces."

It took almost a day to complete the calculations on everything that was even remotely usable. The size was mostly estimated using the radar images that were captured.

Rachael described the situation, "There are several hundred pieces that vary in size from the size of an automobile to the size of a house and one that is the size of a football stadium. I think we can probably snag some of the automobile-sized pieces and tow them up to the Explorer using the shuttles. But to do that we're going to burn one hell of a lot of shuttle fuel. An automobile-sized piece that is, for example, six meters in diameter would only give us a little over 113,000 kilos of water. A house sized piece that is, for example, 12 meters in diameter would give us about 900,000 kilos of water. And that isn't enough, plus there is no place to store the water.

There is one relatively spherical piece that measured out to approximately 30 meters in diameter, that would give us about 14 million kilos of water which is almost what we started with but again, there is nowhere to put it.

They sat around the table talking it over for almost an hour. No one seemed to have any suggestions of what to do to solve the big problem. Small pieces could be melted and used to fill bladder 2 with as much as it would hold and then balance that by adding water to bladder 4 so that they were equal. That would only give them slightly over 3 million kilos, less than half of what was needed. It might be enough if they took one of the long elliptical paths that took almost ten months to match the orbit of Earth, but that might not leave them with enough to maneuver when they arrived. Finally, the captain stopped the discussion and asked. "Does anyone have a workable suggestion?"

Ichuro Watanabe replied, "How about this, Captain? Why don't we take the thirty-meter-diameter piece home with us? We could make a hole in it that would fit the forward part of the ship."

For three or four minutes, there was absolute silence among the crew while a couple of them did some hasty calculating on their tablet computers. Finally, Alexi looked up after performing a couple of additional calculations and said, "That just might be doable. That's nearly the mass we had when we left the moon, subtracting the volume of the *Explorer* we would have more than enough."

Several people began to talk at the same time and they all had the same question. Ian looked at Alexi and said, "Hold it. Commander Gargorin has the floor. Go ahead, Alexi."

"For the trip out to Mars, we had to balance a number of things. We wanted to get here as fast as possible—that was a given. The ship was designed to contain a given amount of reaction mass when we left. We had to design the trip in such a way that we used only a little more than half of our reaction mass water on the way out. When we started we had about 17 million kilos of water. In order to take the shortest path possible in a straight line between Earth and Mars, we had only fifty-four days in which to do it. During that time with the mass we had at turn-over we used up almost 10 million kilos of the water and maintained a constant acceleration of approximately 1/4 G. As we used up the water, we were able to very gradually throttle back the engines and still maintain the one-quarter G acceleration. Because we had less mass, it took less power to maintain the acceleration.

"I assume that you are all familiar with one of the most basic formulas in physics, $F=Ma$. Force is equal to mass times acceleration. In simplest terms, if we double the mass and want to keep acceleration constant we have to double the force. I believe I can do that." Then with a smirk, he finished with, "There is just one small problem: How do we get that giant ice ball up here where we can use it and somehow attach it to the ship? We can't drag it behind or even if we could, the plasma from the main engines would simply melt it away and do it very quickly."

Rachael squinted at Alexi and said, "You're right, Commander. We can't tow it, but could we push it? That's what we would have to do all the way home no matter where it was attached to the ship except behind, of course. Navigating down there in the debris field is fairly tricky. But as we are now we would be going at virtually the same speed as the debris around us. And yes, there are irregularities in the orbits of the pieces. When AJay and I went down there, we got bumped by a piece but it wasn't going very fast compared to us so no harm was done."

Miriam took up the baton and asked, "Commander, I remember from the countless trips I made hauling water up to fill the reaction mass tank that there are five rocket nozzles. Is that correct?"

"Yes, that is correct," Alexi replied.

"When we moved the *Explorer* from where we were to where we are now, we only used one nozzle, the center one, right?"

Alexi began to get the drift of what Miriam was getting at. He replied, "Yes, we only used the center one to get us up to the speed we needed to coast over here and not so fast that you could not stop us using the steering jets. If you wanted to know if the nozzles can be used independently, individually, or in some combination, the answer is yes. Are you thinking of trying to steer the *Explorer* using the main engine nozzles differentially? As I'm sure you saw, but for the benefit of everyone else, the five nozzles are arranged as a plus sign with one nozzle at each tip of the cross pieces and one in the center.

"I don't remember the precise dimensions, but I think the plus sign is 10 meters or about 40 feet across. They were spaced out that way so the exhaust from one engine wouldn't interfere with another. They were never intended for steering the *Explorer*. When everything is balanced perfectly, using one of the outer nozzles, your vector diagram is a triangle 8 meters long on the short side and around 80 meters long to the CG with another 80 meters beyond that, with a total mass of well over 25 million metric tons."

"I wasn't thinking of using the main engines for maneuvering within the debris field and up to our selected ice ball. I was wondering to what extent they could be used for maneuvering when we were pushing the ice ball since we can't pull it," Miriam said.

"How are you planning on pushing it?" Alexi asked.

AJay was peeling an orange when Alexi asked his question. Rachael reached across the table, took the orange, and stuck a ballpoint pen right up into its centerline. "Like this, sir. We could embed the *Explorer* nose first into the ice ball. That would move the center of gravity considerably forward from where it is and give your nozzles a longer lever arm for steering."

"*Give me a lever long enough and a fulcrum on which to place it, and I shall move the world,*" Ian said quoting the ancient Greek philosopher Aristotle. "What do you think, Alexi?"

"It's the damnedest idea I ever heard of, and it just might work. We will have to do everything in the seventeen months between now and when we would start back to Earth if we wanted to go by the shortest path. At the moment, I have no idea how we would go about it, but I can't think of a better team to come up with something workable. Rachael, if I was wearing a hat, I would take my hat off to you," Alexi said, bowing from the waist.

The eyes of everyone around the table were focused on Rachael. Six minds all started working on the problem. Basically, they were confronted with two related problems. The first was how to bring the *Explorer* near to the ice asteroid. The second was how to excavate a hole in it large enough to contain the command module on an axis through the center of gravity of the asteroid. After those two problems were solved there was still the issue of how to leave orbit around Mars and position themselves to make the trip back to Earth as quickly as possible.

Ian radioed the plan to the scientists at Ares Base, he finished with, "That, ladies and gentlemen, is the best thing that we can think of to do. If you have any suggestions we are open to them."

"For once, sir, you appear to have left us speechless. Let us discuss it and we will let you know what we come up with on the next pass," Jan Pitrasen said.

"We will do that, Dr. Pitrasen. We would like to hear anything you can think of that will enable us to do this, or any alternatives you can think of no matter how outlandish they may seem," Ian said.

When the Explorer was again within radio distance of Ares Base, Dr. Pitrasen spoke. "Captain, that is an incredibly bold plan. We have discussed among ourselves and only have one thing significant to advise you about. The temperature of the ice in your ice ball is not going to be at zero degrees Celsius. It could be as cold as minus 325 degrees Celsius. At that temperature, it will be as hard as iron."

"We hear you, sir. The samples that were brought back from the exploration mission to debris field were just ice," Ian said.

"If I remember correctly, the ice was in the container for over four hours on the trip back from the debris field and you haven't said how long it was in the freezer before the samples were taken. Ice at minus 300 degrees Celsius will absorb heat very quickly, and we think it did. Space suit gloves are made to protect the wearer from the severe temperature differentials that can be experienced in space. So Rachael and AJay were protected and likely did not realize how cold the two samples they brought back were when they put them in the storage container. What you plan to do is going to be very difficult, but… not impossible. We wish you well and if you need us to help, please come and get us and we'll be happy to oblige," Dr. Pitrasen said and the other scientists endorsed it from the background.

"Why didn't we think of that? For myself, I have been in submarines all my life, and they don't operate in temperatures of minus 325 degrees," Ian said to the assembled crew.

"Captain, my teakettle, as you have so aptly dubbed it, is capable of producing almost unlimited power. That power can be transformed into heat one way or another. In fact, thanks to Miriam's suggestions, it might be possible to back into our ice ball and run one or more of the nozzles at reduced power. The temperatures at which the plasma exits the throat of the engine is measured in millions of degrees under full power. To keep from melting the nozzles, plasma has to be contained within a very strong magnetic field. If it touched any part of the ship it would destroy that part in an instant. That's one of the reasons we have to maintain a constant watch in the reactor room when we are under power. The system is designed to shut down in picoseconds if one of the magnetic fields should collapse," Alexi said.

"Captain, the scientists are right about the temperature on the shady side of anything in space. We balance the temperature here in the command module as well as the rest of the ship, including the reaction mass tank by pumping coolant from the Sunnyside to the Shadyside continuously. We had to do the same thing on the International Space Station to balance the temperatures and we were well insulated. Once we make a hole in the ice ball big enough to begin to insert the nose of the *Explorer*, we will probably have to use the same system to warm up the outside all the way around using the excess heat from the reactors and that should insulate us from the extreme cold of the ice," Ichuro Watanabe said.

"Right! Would you, Ichuro, and AJay and Rachael start working on a scheme for melting the ice in an ice ball and dealing with the extreme cold? Miriam, please draw up a plan for moving the *Explorer* down to the vicinity of the ice ball. Commander, would you work with Miriam to determine how much and how little throttle control we have over each individual plasma jet whether for steering or for melting into the ice ball or how the controls can be adapted for that purpose?"

Ian was reminded once more of how lonely command could be. He had not needed to give many direct commands so far because the team worked well together. This was different, someone had to manage the process and as captain, the responsibility fell on him. He had to maintain a command distance from everyone in the crew with the possible exception of Alexi, who was a personal friend, but even there it had to be formal except when they were alone.

Alexi was as much or more aware of what Ian was facing as the captain than most of the rest. He took great care to not cross the boundary between being a friend and being a subordinate at any time except when they were alone, and even then he was very careful. The two pilots had been captains in the Israeli Air Force and were accustomed to taking orders and carrying them out to the best of their ability, and they had been shuttle pilots on the moon and were subject to the demands of the job and their superiors. Mr. Watanabe had experience with command when he was aboard the International Space Station even though he was not in the military chain of command. AJay was smart enough to accept command authority without argument and took a cue from Alexi.

Several hours later, Alexi knocked outside the door to the captain's cabin and asked, "Have you got a minute, Captain?"

"Come in, Commander, and please close the door behind you," Ian answered. "What do you need, Alexi? I'd offer you a drink if I had something worth drinking besides this damned powdered orange juice."

"I thought you might need a drink too," Alexi said as he reached into the pocket of his coveralls and brought out two small plastic bottles of Stolichnaya Vodka. "Try this in your orange juice, Ian. I had been saving these for a special occasion and I can't think of anything any more special than where we are now."

"Thank you, my friend," Ian said.

Ian poured the vodka into his orange juice and figuratively touched glasses with Alexi who had seated himself on what would be the bed if they didn't have to sleep in net hammocks. Alexi acknowledged the salute. He preferred his vodka straight. He sipped from the bottle while they sat together silently. The shared moment with a friend is what they both needed. Neither spoke again until Alexi stood to leave. He put his hand on Ian's shoulder, gave a slight squeeze, and said, "I'm damned glad you are in that chair. I can't think of anyone else I have ever worked with who is better suited to handle this situation than you. You know you can count on me."

Ian put his hand on top of Alexi's and said, "Thank you for that."

With that Alexi left the captain's cabin and shut the door quietly behind him, leaving Ian to his thoughts.

. . .

The next few days were filled with endless discussions between and among the crew. Finally, Ian called for a meeting to discuss the progress being made. "Miriam, would you please go first. Without your input, we are stuck right here."

Miriam began, "Captain—"

"For the moment," Ian said, "let's avoid the rank issues and just talk as if you were my advisors. You are not just addressing me, you are addressing all of us."

"Yes, Captain," she said, "I know that, but I think we all would prefer to never forget that you are the captain, sir and unless that was an order, I will continue to address you as such."

Ian looked at Miriam trying to decide how to proceed, then at the rest and finally at Alexi who gave a brief nod and said, "Captain." That settled the issue.

"Please continue, Major," Ian said, returning the ball to her court with a canard he knew would cause her to wonder.

"I was a captain, sir," she responded, picking up on the canard.

"Yes, you were, but on any ship, there can only be one captain, so all people with the rank of 'captain' in any other branch of the service are honorarily addressed as 'major' while aboard ship. A naval officer of equivalent rank to you would be a full lieutenant, and the next rank above that would be a lieutenant commander," Ian said, smiling.

Miriam started to respond and saw he was teasing her and continued with her report. "Captain, I have been following the orbits of everything bigger than a golf ball, and I think we would be safe if we just slowly moved down into the debris field and up to our ice ball. We will undoubtedly collide with a number of pieces of all sizes, but we will be going so slowly relative to them that we are not likely to incur any damage. I have no idea how long it will take, but I would guess a day at least because I would like to do the maneuvering during the daylight periods so we can see what we're doing in addition to the radar. We'll be using the steering jets to do the maneuvering and we're going to run the risk of depleting their fuel reserves. So we'll have to be very careful with how we use them."

Alexi indicated he had something to say bearing on Miriam's report. "Captain, I think we can probably help out with the fuel for the steering jets. They use hydrogen and oxygen that is kept under very high pressure in auxiliary tanks aboard the *Explorer*. The quantities of both are adequate for the work of regular shuttle missions, but not for what we are proposing. We work with high pressure as a matter of course in the reactors and the main engines. As I said before, we also have a virtually unlimited supply of electrical power.

"We can use electrolysis to break water apart into hydrogen and oxygen and compress them under sufficient pressure to replace the fuel in the shuttle tanks and reserves. The same fuel is used by the steering rockets. The designers may not have had in mind our manufacturing additional fuel when they designed the steering rocket fuel system, but there are pipes that run from a high pressure retort in the reactor area to the steering rocket fuel tanks and to the station where we recharge the oxygen tanks for the space suits."

"That's excellent, Commander. What about the problem of throttling the main engines so they can be used to help excavate the hole we'll need to embed the *Explorer* into the ice ball? Have you made any progress in that area?" Ian asked.

"Yes, Captain, we have. AJay and I have made several small runs at the lowest possible setting, which is way below what the designers intended. The runs were brief on the order of a second and were coordinated with Major Steinmetz, who has had to do some minor maneuvering with the steering jets for the past day to correct for them. I doubt that most of you were even aware we were doing this testing. We were very successful. By manipulating the strength of the magnetic fields that contain the plasma jet and reducing the velocity, pressure, and therefore the temperature of the plasma to the absolute minimum, we can allow the plasma to flare outward as widely as we need to and, thus, essentially eliminate the thrust problem or at least minimize it. This will allow us to produce a great deal of heat and not require much effort from the steering jets to hold us in position. Also, I believe Major Purlman and her team have some ideas that may even eliminate the need for the steering jets once we are in position," Alexi reported.

Ian turned to Rachael, and said, "Major?"

"Yes, sir," Rachael replied. "What we would like to try is to melt a series of small holes around the area we wish to excavate and embed anchors in the Ice Moon. We have a couple dozen 100-meter safety lines that are nylon covered steel cable. We have not been able to find anything about the breaking strength of the safety lines but suspect it is on the order of several thousand pounds. If we use enough of them at low angles to the ship we would be able to anchor the *Explorer* to the ice ball. We have no idea how many of these lines might be required so we think we should use as many as possible to be safe. AJay is a machinist, and he has assured us that there are sufficient materials in the machine shop to create the anchors and we have half a dozen grappling hooks still aboard the *Explorer* as well. Once it is anchored, Commander Gargorin can use the center jet of the main engine at the very low setting he described and we should be able to melt a hole in the Ice Moon without the risk of drifting away from it.

"The ice that's melted should just evaporate and more or less blow out of the way as steam. As for balancing the heat and cold once we embed the command module in the Ice Moon, we recommend delaying that problem until we have solved the problems at hand. We think we can just alter the operation of the current heat disposition system, but we won't know until we can actually try it. If that doesn't work, we're working on a couple of less ideal solutions that are not yet ready for discussion."

Ian paused for a few moments to gather his thoughts before he spoke. "You've all done a phenomenal job. I can't begin to explain how impressed I am with what you've accomplished. You've done something that most people are unable to do—you found a way to think outside the box. Now as two of my favorite fictional characters, Jean-Luc Picard and Honor Harrington would say, 'make it so, Number One' and 'let's be about it, people.'"

· · ·

The next day was spent fabricating anchors for use to hold the *Explorer* in position when they reached the ice ball.

Miriam waited until they were fifteen minutes from the terminator between the nightside and the dayside in the orbit. She had pre-positioned the *Explorer* at the optimum angle for changing orbits inward before she began. Then, right on the mark, she began the descent into the debris field. It took almost four hours before they actually entered the debris field in an area where there were no large pieces. The steering jets were used to slow the movement to a stop relative to most of the surrounding debris. During the next four hours as they circled around the nightside of Mars and back into the dayside, they heard rather than felt some small bits of debris collide with the *Explorer*.

The difference in visible light between night and day was not great, but it was sufficient for maneuvering. For another four hours, the *Explorer* slowly descended until it was in the center of the debris and about 30 kilometers behind the target in its orbit. Observation of the ice ball had shown that it was spinning about its axis at one revolution every nine hours and ten minutes. In addition, it was also tumbling very slowly about a secondary axis just a few degrees away from the primary axis at a rate of about one degree per hour. The result was a slight wobble around the center of gravity. The angle of the primary axis inclined slightly more than 10 degrees relative to Mars's axis of rotation but processed slowly due to the tumbling. Like everything in Mars orbit, the inclination and direction of the axis was constant relative to the stars giving the Ice Moon a synchronous rotation with respect to its path through one orbital period or approximately eight hours.

"Are you ready to approach the target, Major?" Ian asked.

"Yes, sir, I propose approaching as slowly as possible to minimize any collisions with the other pieces. We will have to 'push' a couple of pieces out of the way before we can approach the target, but I think that can be done with a shuttle. Rachael?"

"There is only one piece that is really worrying me," Rachael replied. "It is about four meters in diameter and would mass around thirty kilotons if it was water. We have no idea what the mass might be of high-density ice, but even so, as you observed, Captain, 'give me a lever,' etc. It shouldn't take too much to push it out of the way. We will have to be very careful about where we want it to go once we start it moving, though."

. . .

The next two daylight periods they spent inching forward in orbit towards the ice ball. While they were approaching, Rachael and AJay took the shuttle out and prepared to push the errant piece to a lower orbit.

"AJay, what do you make of that thing?" Rachael asked.

"Your guess as to the size is pretty close, but it is extremely irregular in shape. I think we might do better if we pulled it out of the way instead of pushing it."

"Really?"

"Yes," AJay replied. "I will go out and try to find an anchor point on it, a crack or a hole we can use to attach the cable."

"Are you comfortable with that, Ajay?"

"I don't see why I shouldn't be. It is not gyrating very much so if you can get close, I should be able to just push off from the shuttle over to it and see what might be possible."

"Please be very careful, AJay, I don't want to lose you," Rachael said, surprised at herself. She suddenly realized that if something were to happen to AJay she would be deeply hurt.

"I will, my friend. I will be very careful," AJay replied, his emotion evident as well.

Rachael swam across the small cabin of the shuttle and hugged AJay space suit and all and said, "Go get it, Yekiri."

AJay smiled, nodded, squeezed her arm, started to say something, nodded again, and entered the airlock.

Rachael watched as AJay pushed away from the shuttle very gently and drifted toward the large piece of debris. They were so close that his safety line was almost a hindrance. AJay landed on, or more properly collided with, the piece of ice. He managed to find two projecting features that he could use to hold his position.

"What do you think, AJay?" Rachael asked.

"There are many little crevices I could push an anchor rod into but how would I hang on while I pushed? I think I can wrap a line around it but how secure it would be I cannot even begin to guess."

"Are there any spots I could poke the nose of the shuttle into so I could push it? It doesn't matter much which way I push it as long as it is neither towards the *Explorer* nor the ice ball."

"Give me a minute," AJay said as he clambered from point to point on the rough surface of the piece. Then he continued, "If you can bring the shuttle around to the top or up orbit position, there might be a place for pushing."

Rachael played the shuttle's controls gently as she used the steering jets to maneuver the shuttle to the point where AJay was.

"AJay, I don't want to use the nose to push the piece, because it might damage the radar antenna, but I can use the body of the shuttle and do the pushing sideways. What do you think?"

"How are you going to see where you're going?" AJay asked.

"You're going to be my eyes and talk me in, okay?"

"Okay."

"You are going to have to stay out of the way as I approach otherwise you might get crushed between the shuttle and the ice."

"I'll be careful, I promise."

His sincerity brought a smile to Rachael's face. It took an hour of careful adjustments so the ice was firmly positioned between the shuttle's hull and one of the winglets.

"Okay, Rachael, that's as good as it gets. Give it a push, a short blast to make sure everything is secure and to see what it does."

Rachael did as AJay suggested, then asked, "How is it?"

"Good, it will be a little skewed, but it should move out of the path of the *Explorer*. It might take several hours before it is safely out of the way unless you want to give it a really hard push. I'm going to hang on to the radio antenna on top of the shuttle so I'm am out of the way."

"No, gently does it," Rachael said, then aligned the steering jets appropriately. "Ready?"

"Give it a shove, Rachael, I am out of the way."

Rachael gave a two-second blast of the steering jets to make sure that everything was in position, then followed that with a ten-second blast that apparently accomplished nothing."

"Damn, how much do you think I need to use?"

"No more. Believe it or not, it's moving. I can see the movement when I align a star with some point on the piece. It will be out of the way in a couple of hours. By the way, it is also now rotating as well, so you might back off so it doesn't affect anything on the shuttle."

"Got it," Rachael replied. "Now, please come back inside so we can return to the *Explorer*."

"On my way."

When they returned to the *Explorer* they were congratulated and teased.

"You could probably get a job as a tug boat operator with a little practice." Was the worst of it coming from Miriam. Then Miriam glanced at AJay who was talking with Alexi then back at Rachael with a raised eyebrow. "Yekiri?" she asked quietly.

Rachael replied with a nod.

When the *Explorer* was within five kilometers, Miriam positioned the main axis of the ship such that it was parallel to the principal axis of the Ice Moon.

"That's as close as I want to get it, Captain, until we know more about it," Miriam reported. "We might have to allow for the tumbling once we're attached, but it is so slow that I don't see a problem if we can align with the polar axis."

"Rachael and Ajay, are you two ready to go over and have an up close look-see?" Ian asked.

"Yes, Captain, we are," Rachael said baffled by the question since they were in their space suits.

"Have you refueled the shuttle?"

"Yes, Captain, we have or, to be more specific, Commander Gargorin did it for us," Rachael replied again, wondering why the captain seemed unsure.

"Good, then there is nothing more to say except, be careful."

"Captain, are you unsure about this?" Rachael asked. "You seem concerned."

"Just cautious, just cautious."

Rachael accompanied by AJay took the shuttle over towards ice ball. It had been determined that the only way it would be possible to attach the *Explorer* to the Ice Moon would be at one end or the other of its principal axis of rotation. It was so massive there was no practical way to stop its spin around its axis and anchor anywhere else on its surface.

"AJay, what is our distance now?" Rachael asked as they approached what they thought of as the south end of the Ice Moon first.

AJay read off the distance from the approach radar. Rachael "parked" the shuttle so that the nose was pointing towards the ice ball.

"The light is really bad, Rachael, I can't make out any significant features. Frankly, it looks like a mess to me," AJay said. "I think it would be a good idea to use the spotlight."

Rachael reached to her left and found the spotlight switch. When the light came on the scene was chaotic. There were jagged points everywhere. "What a mess. Oh, well, let's get on with the mapping, although I think it will be a waste of time. There is no way we can land in that."

As they approached, AJay took pictures continuously with the digital camera and they sent continuous high definition television to the *Explorer*.

"Can you all see this?" Rachael asked.

"We see it, Rachael can you get any closer.?" Miriam asked.

"Yes, but I don't want to get too close in case something went wrong, I would not like the shuttle to be brushed by that stuff."

Miriam double clicked the mic button indicating that the message was received.

Rachael stopped moving closer when the approach radar indicated a distance of 100 meters from the surface. If left unguided the shuttle would also perform one synchronous rotation per orbit, and thus would alternately point towards and away from the ice ball, so Rachael used the steering jets to put it in a slow rotation that kept the nose pointed at the Ice Moon.

"That's as close as I want to go right now. Do you agree, AJay?"

"Yes. I do," AJay replied.

Up close and well lit, the surface of the south pole was not as jagged as it seemed at first. It clearly was not smooth, nor was it particularly uneven. It showed some pocking from collisions with other objects, but it looked otherwise acceptable.

"Okay, *Explorer*? We have a detailed map of the surface. We are now going to relocate to the north pole."

The distance from the south end to the north end was just over 35 meters. But to maneuver around the Ice Moon leaving no room for error, Rachael decided to back away from the it 500 meters. As they were backing away, Rachael saw something move out of the corner of her eye and made a quick adjustment in an attempt to avoid colliding with a sizable piece of debris. It did not look very large from a distance but as it approached it seemed to be about 2 meters across and very irregular in shape and it was tumbling.

"Hang on AJay, we've got company."

"Where?"

"Over my left shoulder," she replied nodding to the left. Then she fired the steering jets trying to maneuver out of the way and to rotate the shuttle so the collision would be with the bottom of the craft. "It's going to hit us. But I hope only a glancing blow. I'm going to try and match its speed to minimize the impact."

They felt the collision as a more-than-gentle bump, which caused them to spin slowly away from the point of impact and away from the ice ball. The debris broke into pieces which moved in the opposite direction.

"Shuttle, are you alright? We saw the collision and heard the sound," the captain asked over the radio.

"Yes, sir, we are fine, no damage done, at least not anything that is immediately obvious," Rachael replied. She thought to herself that if she had been in an automobile and felt that same bump she would have a badly dented fender.

Rachael quickly stopped the spin of the shuttle and began once again on the path to the north end of the ice ball. She did a large swinging maneuver which kept the nose pointed towards the Ice Moon at all times until they finally came to a relative stop pointing directly at the north end of the ice ball.

"Hey, that was some pretty fancy flying, Rachael," Miriam said. "You'll have to show me how you did it some time."

"Nothing to it; I could do it in my sleep!" Rachael quipped back.

"Uh-huh."

Once again they approached the Ice Moon very slowly until they were an indicated 150 meters away. They spent another hour taking photographs and televising what they saw.

It was easy to see that the north end was probably the best bet for connecting the *Explorer* to the Ice Moon and for excavating a hole in which to park the command module. There was a crater about 15 meters in diameter and perhaps half that deep centered almost exactly on the axis of rotation at the north end. The area surrounding the crater appeared to be firm ice which should be easy to drill into and attach anchors.

"What do you think, AJay?" Rachael asked.

"It looks about the same as the floor of that big crater on Phobos, smooth and fairly level. It shouldn't be too difficult to anchor the *Explorer*. The worst problem would be any other debris that might come along and hit the *Explorer*; it makes a very big target."

"I agree, but it's our best hope."

When they were finished mapping the north pole, Rachael flew the shuttle back to the *Explorer* and docked. The reception when they entered the *Explorer* was very gratifying.

"Great job, you two!" Ian said with a huge grin on his face. "That was some of the fanciest flying I've ever seen, not that I have seen all that much, you understand. You have clearly paved the way to connect the *Explorer* and the ice ball, now all we have to do is drill the hole."

CHAPTER FIFTEEN

While Rachael and AJay had been locating a spot to attach the *Explorer* to the Ice Moon, the rest of the crew kept an eye on the video feed from the shuttle while they worked on solving the problem of drilling into the ice and what to use for anchors. The bigger issue was how to drill a hole in minus 325-degree ice into which an anchor point could be firmly attached. Various options were suggested and discussed and there were two possibilities that seemed to be workable.

The first was to create a drill bit using pieces of steel and the welding equipment in the workshop.

"Has anyone ever used an arc-welder?" Alexi asked. "We have an arc welding unit that could be used to weld a piece of steel to a shaft." Receiving no answer other than blank stares, he continued. "I've seen it done and I'm willing to give it a try. As I remember, striking an arc isn't too hard, but making a really good weld takes skill and experience."

"I've used one a time or two," AJay's voice erupted from the speaker. "I'll see what I can do when we get back to the ship."

"Right," Ian said. "Thank you AJay."

"Our other possibility is a hybrid oxyacetylene unit also in the shop. It can reach and sustain much higher temperatures than are possible with the arc welder," Alexi explained. "I have some experience with that one, not much but some. Who could have known that we might need to actually weld something when they were equipping the ship?"

"So, assuming we can actually manufacture drill bits and anchors, there is the other problem," Ian said. "Remember the scientists warned us that ice at the ultra-low temperatures of outer space can be as hard, if not harder than rock or even steel. Do we actually have anything that hard aboard?" The question was rhetorically intended to start them thinking about how to solve that problem.

"Ichuro, can you come and help me see if we can build a drill?" Alexi asked.

"Sure, Commander."

Alexi and Ichuro went to the shop to see what could be done with the equipment they had.

"Can we just use one of the larger drill bits from the tool kit?" Ichuro asked.

"We probably could, but let's keep that option as a last resort. Those bits are designed to drill through mild steel and I suspect they have the wrong type of tip for what we need. You could not drill through rock with one without breaking it or ruining the tip. The rock bits I have seen have just a flat blade with a broad point and carbide tips."

After several practice efforts on some scrap, Alexi successfully arc welded a piece of steel to the end of a steel rod. "Let's try it on a piece of aluminum first to see if we can drill through it."

"How are we going to put pressure on the bit in freefall, Commander?" Ichuro asked.

"I've been thinking about that. If I can get a grip on the workbench with one hand, I might be able to hold the drill and apply the necessary pressure. Ready?"

"Ready."

Alexi tried the first arc-welded bit first. It began to bite into the aluminum grabbed and broke immediately. "Damn, the job was not good enough. Let's try the oxyacetylene bit."

Ichuro replaced the bit and handed the drill back to Alexi. The bit drilled through the thin aluminum but was quickly dulled, then deformed when Alexi tried it on the side of an anvil. "Well, that's that," Alexi said. "Apparently, drilling using manufactured bits is not practical. Do you have any other ideas?"

It was AJay who suggested using the oxyacetylene torch to drill directly. "Commander, what if we used the oxyacetylene to drill the holes. We could use the torch in essentially the same way as we planned to use the plasma from the main engine nozzles to heat and melt the ice leaving a hole. If we did that, we wouldn't have to worry about getting a good grip on something for leverage like we would with a drill bit."

"That's genius, Ichuro, absolute genius. The only obstacle I can see is we only have a very limited supply of acetylene. What you see in those two bottles is all we have. Oxygen is not a problem because it can be produced by using electrolysis. There is no way to produce acetylene," Alexi said. He opened a channel to Ian. "Captain, Ichuro came up with a great idea for using the welding torch to drill the holes but that has some problems. What else could they do?" Alexi asked.

For the next half hour, various other ways of producing enough heat to melt the ice were suggested. Finally, someone asked if it would be possible to use electricity to heat a tool to a temperature that would allow it to be used to drill into the ice?

Alexi thought for a moment, and replied, "That's not a bad idea, but I have no idea what we could use as an electrode. We might be able to bend a piece of rod or pipe into a U shape and connect the ends across the electrical output of the reactor. It would mean we would have to run a heavy electrical line from the reactor out through the airlock to the site where the hole was to be drilled. I'm not sure we have enough heavy electrical wire to do this. Anything but the heavy wire will also heat and could melt the insulation causing the short circuit. I think we better put that suggestion on the table for later consideration."

"Do we have any other suggestions to consider?" Ian asked.

Finally, Miriam asked, "How hot is the output from the steering jets when we're burning an oxygen-hydrogen mixture? If it's hot enough to produce thrust might it not be hot enough to melt the ice?"

"Of course," Ichuro mused aloud. "We could fill one of the empty gas tanks in the workshop with compressed hydrogen and give it a shot. I don't remember enough of my basic chemistry, but what I do recall suggests that might be a very hot mixture. They use that as rocket fuel from the surface of Earth up to the International Space Station because it's nonpolluting."

"That's the best idea I've heard yet," Alexi said. "We'll give it a try."

They emptied a workshop oxygen bottle and exposed it to vacuum in the aft airlock to insure there would be no danger of an explosion when the bottle was refilled with hydrogen under pressure. The bottle was filled with hydrogen under the maximum pressure that could be produced by the compressors in the reactor room.

"Hadn't we better mark the hydrogen tank so there will be no mistakes?" Ian asked.

"Yes, sir, Captain." Ichuro replied. "But I can't think of anything to use except one of our markers and that wouldn't be easily recognizable, would it?"

"We need something that we can wrap around the tank so it can be seen no matter how you look at it," Miriam said. "But what?" she asked, then answered her own question. "Adhesive tape. There's an adhesive tape in the medical supplies. We could wrap that around the tank and then mark it with one of our markers."

"Do it," Ian ordered unnecessarily as he saw Miriam already moving toward the medical equipment locker.

While the hydrogen tank was being labeled, Ichuro went to the computer and looked up the use of a hydrogen oxygen mixture. "According to this, an appropriate mixture can produce a temperature as high as 2800° Celsius. That should melt almost anything known to man. That high temperature can only be achieved by mixing the two gases at precisely a two to one ratio. This will ensure both gases will be consumed in the flame. Apparently, any other mixture other than that will result in a flame that is not as hot."

Alexi said, "Getting exactly that mixture with the coarse control valves on the oxyacetylene torch is going to be nearly impossible. Furthermore, for testing aboard ship, we need to make sure that the mixture is oxygen-rich so that we do not release any hydrogen into the environment. Is there anything in what you're reading that indicates how fast the temperature falls off from the maximum when the mixture is safely oxygen-rich?"

"No, sir, Commander. But the temperature would have to fall off a lot to make the flame not usable for melting ice. We can fiddle with it once we're on the surface of the ice ball and see which settings works best. It's the best shot we have, sir," Ichuro replied.

. . .

When Rachael and AJay returned to the *Explorer* and had a cup of tea, they showed a slide show of the pictures they took. AJay provided narration for the slide show. "We can skip through the pictures of the south end; notice how irregular the surface there. Now for the pictures of the north end. First the stills and then the video. As you can see, there is a fairly large crater on the north end," Ichuro explained. "We have far more pictures and video of that." The crew watched in silence as AJay described what they were seeing.

"As you can see from the most distant shots, the crater is not exactly centered on what we assume is the axis of rotation. However, it's big enough that with a little work we can modify its shape to suit our needs. There's no way to tell when the crater was made. But if you look at the detailed photographs we took as Rachael circled the crater, you will see that there are radial cracks in the surface, which appear to have healed to some extent. Those might provide some of the places where we can position our anchor points without the need to drill down into the ice. However, once the anchor point is positioned, I think it will be necessary to inject water into the crack and let it freeze the anchor in place. The videos show some of what I just mentioned but without telephoto lens, we couldn't get close enough for the videos to show the same detail as the stills."

Then Rachael said, "The sooner we move over there where we can work on it the better. Once the anchor points are in place, the actual anchoring will have to be done very carefully because we will want the *Explorer* and the Ice

Moon to function as one unit as quickly as possible. I assume that some consideration has been made to the effect that attaching the *Explorer* to the Ice Moon is going to drastically change the center of gravity of the system. We will need to be certain that the axis of the *Explorer* is exactly aligned with the CG of the Ice Moon.

"I was able to maintain what appeared to be a constant position relative to the ice moon by continuous maneuvering. It only does an apparent synchronous end for end revolution once every orbit. While we are placing the anchors, the *Explorer* can remain at a comfortable distance from the Ice Moon. It would be better, of course, if it will be possible to move the *Explorer* in and out and expand the excavation of the crater before we try attaching them together. I know you can't maneuver a 500-foot long ship of this mass as easily as I can maneuver the shuttle. Somehow we will have to solve that problem."

"We have part of a solution to that problem, Rachael," Miriam exclaimed. "The Commander has told us that with the electrical power that is output from the reactor, he can produce oxygen and hydrogen by electrolysis. That means that within reason we have an unlimited supply of fuel for the maneuvering jets. That also means that we have the capability of drilling the holes for the anchors by using an oxygen-hydrogen mixture through the nozzle of the acetylene welder from the shop."

"Will there be enough oxygen and hydrogen for the maneuvering jets of the shuttle?" Rachael asked.

"I don't see why not," Alexi responded. "The fuel mixture used in your maneuvering jets is ignited electrically, so it should work. It'll take some testing to get everything right, but that should not be too difficult."

"That's fantastic," AJay said, reverting to the lilting accent of his native land in his excitement. "When do we start?"

"Having solved the problem of how to drill the holes, the next problem that we've been working on is what to use for anchors," Ian said. "If you have any ideas, please tell us about them."

"Nothing comes immediately to mind, Captain. I started my professional life as a machinist so the best thing I can do is help make the anchors in the machine shop," AJay said.

Making the anchors to be embedded in the Ice Moon was a different sort of problem. Every piece of metal that could possibly be used to create an anchor point for a safety line was taken to the workshop. This included steel, aluminum, copper, and some other pieces whose makeup could not be determined but which Alexi said is known as pot metal. The most interesting pieces were the grappling hooks that were still in storage aboard the *Explorer*. Each consisted of four hooks welded around a central rod that had an eye on the end to which the safety line could be attached.

"AJay, do you think you can disassemble the grappling hooks?" Alexi asked as he examined one. "The welds were obviously made by machine, they are very regular and even."

"Commander, I suggest that the best way to deal with the grappling hooks is to simply cut off the hooks as close to the central rod as possible. Then we can use the torch to heat the hooks and straighten them. Next, we will need to weld the straightened hook to a piece of steel rod. We should also use the torch to heat the ends of the rods red-hot so they can be bent into an eye so the safety line can be clipped to them."

There were five grappling hooks including the one that was on the shuttle. That provided twenty handmade anchors.

While the anchors were being made in the shop, it was decided to move the ship closer to the Ice Moon and to begin the effort to widen the crater. If they couldn't do that, then all the rest was for naught. The plan was to position the *Explorer* with the main engine jets pointing towards the north end of the ice moon. Alexi and Miriam experimented with keeping the *Explorer* stationary by balancing the thrust from the steering jets against the thrust that was produced by the central nozzle of the main engines when its jet was allowed to flare the way it was judged best for melting the ice. They were satisfied that they could do this without a great deal of difficulty through some judicious programming of the computer to maintain position. This was necessary because the Ice Moon was revolving around its axis.

"How are you planning to widen the crater?" Ian asked.

"Well, sir, we're planning to use the axial rotation of the Ice Moon as if it was on a lathe. We will hold the ship relatively steady at an appropriate distance from the surfaces and flaring one of the main engine nozzles whenever an area of the crater to be removed passes under it," Miriam said. "We will program the computer to maintain position and control the nozzles by hand. It might be a little crude, but it should work."

Miriam repositioned the *Explorer* 500 feet away from the north end of the Ice Moon and, in the process collided with several small pieces of the ice debris. Alexi watched the Ice Moon rotate under the rear of the *Explorer* through the windows in the floor of the main engine room. They did a dozen dry runs for practice in maintaining position. Each time they moved a little closer to the surface of the Ice Moon. On the last practice, the intent was to maintain position 100 feet above the end of the Ice Moon.

As the *Explorer* backed slowly towards the Ice Moon, Alexi suddenly said, "Stop! Go forward."

Miriam reversed the maneuvering thrusters and used them to slow the ship and then pull away from the Ice Moon. As soon as everything was stable she asked, "What happened, Commander?"

"Take us back out to where we guessed we were about 500 feet away, please," Alexi said. "Then meet me in the Common Room and I think we should include everyone."

A few minutes later when everyone was once again in the common area, Ian said, "You have the floor commander."

Alexi explained the problem. "As you all know intuitively, the *Explorer* was never meant to go backwards except during deceleration in open space. That means we have no way of knowing how close we are to the surface as we backup. I was watching through the window in the floor of the main engine room and suddenly I realized I had no reference point that would tell me how close we were. We have been doing the positioning exercises without anything that will tell us how close we actually are to the surface. If we should collide with the Ice Moon while going in reverse no matter how slowly we run the risk of damaging the main engines. At this point, we don't even know how close we have to get in order to actually excavate the surface around the crater. I need something that I can use that will tell me how close we are."

Rachael said almost to herself, "Of course, they would not think to put an approach radar on the backend of the Explorer. Who could have guessed we might need it?" Then she continued, "How precise does it have to be, Commander?"

Alexi replied, "I'm not sure. As we do this there may be times when inches matter. But that won't be until we're ready to do the major excavation."

"How about to the nearest foot, Commander?" Rachael asked.

"As long as we moved in dead slow, that would probably be enough. But we have to be able to pull away quickly if necessary," Alexi replied.

"Commander, the approach radar on the shuttle is accurate down to a foot, I think. I've never done anything that needed anything that precise. I suppose we could calibrate it to see just how accurate it is. We'll need some means to actually measure the precise distance," she said as she chewed her cheek.

"How will that help, Major?" Ian asked.

"Well, Captain, I don't know for sure. There is one approach radar in the nose, and one in the bottom of the shuttle. We might be able to use the one in the nose," she replied.

"How?" Ian asked.

"What if I moved the shuttle from the airlock off the storage area to the aft airlock off the reactor room. I'm pretty sure I can lock onto that airlock in almost any position. If I lock on with the nose of the shuttle pointing to the rear I might be able to provide some readings that would tell Commander Gargorin how close we were to the surface."

Miriam, who had been wondering to herself where Rachael was headed said, "That just might do it, Rachael. How do you think you would go about calibrating it?"

"I don't know," Rachael replied. "But I'm confident we'll be able to figure something out. But first, we have to find out how close the nose of the shuttle is from a plane across the rear surfaces of the main engine nozzles and then go out from there. As far as I know, the approach radar on the nose of the shuttle increases in accuracy the farther away you are from what you're scanning to a point. If you get too close, you're approaching the wavelength of the radar or at least how the bounce of the signal returns to the receiver antenna. The actual distance seemed about right when we were surveying the Ice Moon. But I never got closer than an indicated 50 feet as indicated by the radar readout."

"How close do we have to be, Commander, in order to have the jet effective in melting the ice?" Miriam asked.

"I can't be sure," Alexi responded. "When we are running full throttle, the plasma can be seen out to a distance of almost 500 meters. But when it's running full throttle we couldn't use it to melt the ice because we wouldn't be able to control the motion of the *Explorer*. Even one nozzle running full throttle develops an appreciative amount of thrust and there's no way that the maneuvering jets on the *Explorer* could hold her in position. It's impossible to see through the portals in the floor of the engine room how far the flame goes out at minimum throttle. If I had to guess I would say as much as 10 meters or 30 feet approximately."

"Okay," Rachael said. "How about this? I will attach the shuttle to the aft airlock with its nose pointing aft. Then you and Miriam can do your balancing act and back slowly up to the asteroid, while I run the approach radar to see how close we are when the flare from the jet touches the surface of the asteroid. I will also have a better view looking through the forward view screen of the shuttle than you do looking through the portals in the floor of the engine room.

"The reactor room is about 30 feet in diameter that gives us a 15-foot radius, the rear airlock extends outward from the wall of the reactor room about 8 feet, and the hull of the shuttle is about 10 feet across at the point where the shuttle airlock would connect to the reactor room airlock. That would place me about 30 feet out from the center line giving me a better angle for viewing when the flare touches the ice, and I could take the radar reading then. If we do this very carefully, I'll be able to tell you when the flare touches the ice and begins to melt it."

"That sounds like a plan," Ian said. "Let's do it next daylight side of the orbit. In the meantime let's have dinner and a good rest and I'd like to make a suggestion," Ian said.

"You have the floor, Captain," Alexi said.

"We keep calling that thing out there an Ice Moon. It is certainly ice, but it is most definitely not a moon. Can't we come up with a better name for it?"

Various names were suggested and discussed but no one name appealed to everyone. Finally, Ian suggested, "Well, it was probably part of an icy asteroid that collided with Phobos, so why don't we call it an Iceteroid?" There were nods all around so Iceteroid was adopted as the name of the ball of ice.

Six hours later Rachael moved the shuttle from the forward airlock to the aft airlock and with help from AJay when she docked. The normal way the shuttle docked with either airlock was with its nose pointing forward. The designers had placed approach lights on the hull of the *Explorer* that were used to properly orient and guide the shuttle for docking facing forward; there were no lights to guide when facing aft. AJay looked through the window of the shuttle airlock and directed Rachael while she attempted to dock. In the end, the actual docking was more like a controlled collision with no harm done.

When everything was secure, the two airlocks were opened and a new set of measurements were taken that established the nose of the shuttle was approximately 14 feet forward of the floor of the engine room making it about 44 feet forward of the exits from the nozzles. Once docked, Rachael tested communications from the shuttle to the engine room and to the pilot station. Once three-way communication was clearly established, the test began.

"Before we actually begin, Commander, my approach radar indicated we were 585 feet from the asteroid when I docked. Now it's showing 586 feet. For what it's worth we are drifting very slowly away from the Iceteroid. Since the approach radar is only accurate to the nearest foot we may have moved anywhere from 6 to 12 inches. How's that for precision?" Rachael asked.

"I would say that is excellent, Major. That reminds me, communication will be much simpler if we drop titles and simply use first names. I haven't been a Commander in the Navy in a good many years, so the title is in effect honorary. But I suppose much like the myriad of people in the US and Commonwealth countries who call themselves 'Colonel' the titles sometimes remain long after you have left the service," Alexi said.

"Yes, sir, Commander," the two women said in chorus and laughed.

For the next two hours, they reran all of the tests that Alexi and Miriam had done before. This time the approach radar readouts provided hard evidence as to how fast they were moving in which direction. They used this as a baseline for everything else. Once they knew the effect of the maneuvering jets for moving the *Explorer* towards the Iceteroid, and how much minimal throttle and maximal flare counteracted the movement, they were ready for the final test of closing in on the Iceteroid.

Miriam began a rearward approach at 2 feet per second based on the input from the radar. As they approached, Rachael read out the distance continuously. It had been decided that the closest they were going to go to the Iceteroid would be 100 feet as reported by the radar.

As they passed 200 feet, Alexi said, "Okay, Miriam, I am going to start the engine at the minimal setting at 3, 2, 1, now."

"The *Explorer* is slowing nicely," Rachael reported. "We are coming to a stop, now. We are at an indicated distance of 125 feet from the surface of the Iceteroid. As far as I can see, the flare from the engine is not touching the surface, but there might be some apparent melting. There is now a shiny spot where there was none before."

"Miriam, set the steering jet thrust to the lowest setting possible and give me a five-second shot that should let us slowly back up to the Iceteroid," Alexi said. "I'll tell you when to stop with a reverse shot."

Miriam started the steering jet thrust, and after five seconds, cut it off. She waited a minute before asking, "That was the minimum thrust possible. Are we making progress yet?"

"Yes, we are," Rachael reported. "Nicely done. We are moving at approximately 2 feet per minute. Stand by, I'll talk you in." Rachael reported the distance as they got nearer to the surface of the Iceteroid. At 80 feet, she reported again, "We are 80 feet from the surface. The flare is actually touching the ice and visibly vaporizing it."

"Alright, Miriam, stop us now," Alexi said.

Miriam's reply was a five-second shot bringing the ship to a virtual stop relative to the Iceteroid.

"Good, that did it," Alexi said. "Let's wait a few minutes to see if we have it right. Rachael, let us know if you detect any drifting one way or the other."

"Yes, sir," Rachael replied. After a few minutes, she announced, "We still have a slow drift, the radar is jittering between 72 and 73 feet from the surface," she announced.

"Because of the irregularities in the surface, I think we should wait through one full revolution of the Iceteroid and see what the radar tells us. Rachael, keep us informed, please. I know it is like watching paint dry, but it is necessary."

As the Iceteroid revolved behind the *Explorer*, Rachael gave a running commentary. Finally, when the Iceteroid completed a revolution, she reported. "According to the radar, the highest points are only 6 feet closer than the lowest points. We may still have a slight drift, but it's nothing to worry about."

"Perfect," Alexi said. "Now, Miriam, can you hold us here within a 10-foot range using the steering jets when I fire the center jet of the main engine?"

"I think so, Commander. Ichuro has a new program for the computer that should do that using the inertial movement instruments," Miriam replied.

"Wonderful, thanks to both of you."

Thus began the leveling of the north end of the Iceteroid. After six revolutions the northern surface of the Iceteroid was approximately level with the bottom of the crater. They had a very good idea of how far the flare would spread at the 80-foot distance. They also knew that the closer they approached the surface, the smaller the area of the flare would be and the deeper the hole it would make.

"Are we done for a while, Commander?" Miriam asked. "The fuel reserves for the maneuvering jets are getting low."

"We are finished for the time being, so why don't you give the main engine a shot and move us out to a distance of around 250 feet. Then use the steering jets to stop us. Finally, check for any appreciable drift."

"Yes, sir," Miriam replied and began the process. When she was satisfied that there was no appreciable drift she stopped. "That's it, Commander. Final distance 266 feet give or take a few inches."

When the crew had assembled in the Common Room, Alexi reviewed what had happened, then reported their current status. "The diameter of the circle is close to 50 feet. Now, we can begin phase two of the excavation. First, we have to complete the anchors, then we have to use some of the pictures we took during the leveling process and decide where to put them in the surface of the Iceteroid."

Once the fuel for the maneuvering jets both on the *Explorer* and the shuttle was replenished they were ready to embed the anchors and start the serious excavation of the Iceteroid. AJay volunteered to be the one to try embedding them. The oxygen and hydrogen cylinders were loaded into the shuttle along with several anchors. The plan was to first set two anchors while Rachael hovered and then use those anchors and a safety line to secure the shuttle to the surface of the Iceteroid. It was easier planned than done.

Rachael gently settled the shuttle on the surface of the Iceteroid inside the cleared area. AJay opened the airlock and prepared to lower himself to the surface. First, he clipped his safety line to the anchor point at the airlock exit, and then attached a safety line for the oxygen- hydrogen cylinders to keep them from drifting away.

"I'm ready, Rachael," he said.

"Good luck and be careful," she replied. She could not help him without leaving her pilot seat and she could not do that until the shuttle was secured to the asteroid.

He used a pair of geologist's picks to pull himself the 10 feet from the shuttle airlock to the nearest edge of the circle. Then working them against each other to chip out a place to anchor himself. He used a short piece of line pulled tightly between the two rock picks as his anchor. When he was sure he was secure, he pulled the gas cylinders over to himself, very slowly. They might be weightless, but they still massed about 125 pounds and he did not want to start them moving towards him without any way to easily stop them. Rachael watched from her pilot seat and held her breath as he moved himself and the equipment into a workable position.

"Now, let's see how this is going to work," he said as he struck the spark to light the mixture at the welding nozzle. He immediately drifted out from the surface. "I didn't expect that," he said. "The torch is producing enough thrust to make things difficult. I'm going to have to hold on with one hand and hold the torch in the other while I work."

"I'd help if I could, AJay," Rachael said. "It should be better after you set the first two anchors."

"Yes" was his reply.

He shut off the torch and began to work backwards under the line between the two picks so he could prevent his feet from moving. When he had done that, he relit the torch. He pointed the flame towards the surface and began to make a hole for an anchor.

"This is not going to be as easy as we hoped," he said. "The ice is refreezing as fast as I melt it and it is hard to keep my grip."

"Why don't you use the torch on the geologist picks and use the heat to embed them more solidly?"

"Hmmm, good idea. I hadn't thought of that," AJay replied. He pulled himself over to the pick nearest the shuttle so Rachael could see what happened. Five minutes of playing the flame up and down the pick end of the tool and it visibly sank into the ice. He held it in place and in less than a minute, it was firmly embedded in the Iceteroid. He pulled himself over to the other pick and repeated the procedure. "That worked great, Rachael. Now to try it on the anchors. Say, did you just take a flash picture?"

"No, why?"

"I think I just saw a flash of light over towards the shuttle."

"It wasn't me," Rachael said. "Hang on, let me check with the ship." She changed channels and called Ichuro on the ship and asked about the flashes.

"I was listening in, Rachael. Nobody here is taking any pictures. Different question, do you think the new technique will work to embed the anchors well enough to hold the ship in position?" Ichuro asked.

"Okay on the flashes. Maybe a reflection of sunlight off the ice. As for the anchors, he is trying now, but it's not going as fast as it did on the picks. I'll let you know how it goes," Rachael replied, then switched back to AJay and reported, "No one on the ship took any flash pictures. Are you seeing things?" She laughed at the thought and then asked Ichuro's question. "The ship or actually Ichuro wants to know if the heating technique will work on the anchors."

"The anchors do not have as much mass as the picks. No matter how much I heat it, it only goes in about 18 inches. After that, I assume the heat is carried away from the metal as fast as I can heat it. Whether it will hold is anybody's guess. The ones that were made from the hooks will have a little more grip from the barb on the hook. Maybe we should suggest they bend the ends over a little," AJay said. Then continued, "I'm going to have to move the picks from site to site as I go. I can't exert enough pressure on the anchor. I'm trying to embed without being anchored myself. Damn, there goes another flash."

Rachael relayed AJay's comments to Ichuro. "He says, the anchors are only going in halfway. He has no idea if they'll hold. He also says he just saw another flash."

Then she saw a flash out of the corner of her right eye and it was reflected across the inside of her helmet's face mask. It was inside her helmet. She turned her head slowly and looked towards where she thought it was. There was nothing there. "AJay, I just saw a flash and it seemed to be inside my helmet. There goes another outside the helmet over the control panel." She immediately called the ship, "*Explorer*, may I speak to the Captain?"

A moment later, Ian replied. "This is the Captain, Rachael, what can I do for you?"

"Captain, I think we have a problem. I am seeing flashes now too. One was definitely inside my helmet and another was over the control panel. Any suggestions, sir?" she asked. "Miriam just said she saw one too. I think it would be best if you two returned to the ship as soon as possible."

"Yes, sir," Rachael replied. "AJay is just finishing an anchor now. Oh, my God, he is surrounded by the flashes!"

"Do they seem to be harming him in any way?"

"No, sir, they're not bothering him other than being there and distracting him."

"Tell him to drop what he is doing and come back aboard here now."

"I cut him into the circuit, Captain, he heard you. He's gathering his stuff and will be back in as soon as he can—"

"Go get him, Major, and leave the mic open," Ian said.

Rachael could not remember the captain giving a direct order before. Reflexes trained by eight years in the Israeli Air Force took control as she automatically lifted the shuttle away from the surface and headed for AJay as she replied, "On it, sir."

Her reply was the customary two clicks indication reception and an end to the conversation.

She moved the shuttle sideways toward AJay very slowly so as not to overrun him. She brought the shuttle to a stop less than 10 feet from where he was. "Can you get in, Ajay?"

"Coming," AJay said as he was pulling himself towards the shuttle using his safety line, towing the welding tanks behind.

"Are the tanks anchored to something, AJay?"

"Yes, to one of the picks. Why?"

"Leave them, and get aboard. Be sure to unhook the safety line to the tanks as soon as you get into the airlock and yours as well. Then get aboard and hang on. The captain said now and he meant it."

A moment later, a clang as the outside door of the airlock shut and locked. Rachael could see him in the space between the inner and outer airlock doors as she lifted off the surface of the Iceteroid and headed for the ship. A quick fifteen minutes later, she docked with the forward airlock, matched air pressure and they swam into the *Explorer*.

The rest of the crew were in the Common Room when Rachael and AJay arrived. "Hook up," the captain directed pointing to two empty positions at the table.

As they took their places, Rachael and AJay could see the others following the flashes around the room and the ferret was jumping from perch to perch apparently trying to catch one.

"Can you grab him?" the captain asked Rachael. "After Dr. Burns, he seems to like you best."

Rachael held up her hand in a fist and made clicking sounds with her tongue. The ferret stopped at the sound and taking careful aim jumped towards her arm and fist in a very slow leap. She opened her hand at the last second and caught him gently. As she brought him to her shoulder, the ferret continued giving his danger call. She scratched him behind his ears and made soothing sounds while the rest waited patiently.

"Okay, Captain, I think he's calmed down now," Rachael said.

The ferret continued to watch the flashes while making his equivalent of a growl deep in his throat.

As the captain started to speak, the lights went out and the emergency lights came on. No one said a word.

CHAPTER SIXTEEN

The captain reacted quickly and said, "Commander."

"On it, Captain," Alexi replied as he immediately started towards the reactor room gathering up Ajay with a look as he went.

"Any ideas, people?" the captain asked as he looked around the table at the other three who were doing their best not to make eye contact. Then he added, "A very good friend of mine used to say in unusual situations, 'we are in deep yogurt.' I think this is one of those situations. Does anyone have a spoon?" This elicited the laugh he expected and broke the tension.

"What are these flashes?" Ian asked.

"They are Sprites, sir," Rachael offered.

"What the hell is a Sprite, Rachael?" Ichuro Watanabe asked.

"I don't know. The name just sprang to mind when the captain asked. Years ago, the meteorology folks described unusual lightning flashes that occurred in the upper atmosphere above really intense storms as Sprites. They only last a few milliseconds and had all kinds of interesting effects."

"It's as good a name as any, and much better than flashes, so, Sprites it is," Ian said. He wanted to continue to release the tension. A tense crew who did not know what to expect next was a dangerous crew; dangerous to itself and dangerous to others. He continued, "Okay, now we have a name for them.

Since we are not above a really intense thunderstorm they must be caused by something else. What are they? Brainstorm." It was intended as a suggested strategy, but he realized as he said it, it almost had a double meaning which was immediately evident as everyone chuckled and the tension evaporated.

For the next few minutes, suggestions flew around the room. In true brainstorm fashion, no idea was too wild and no one interrupted or contradicted anyone else. Miriam wrote them down as fast as they came. When the flow of ideas ground to a stop, she handed the list to the captain who started to read the list aloud.

"Excuse me, Captain," Rachael interrupted. "Has anyone besides the ferret noticed the number of Sprites has dropped off over the past few minutes? Ferd has stopped growling and has settled down. He is still watching, but apparently does not feel as threatened as he was before."

Ian saw the ferret had curled up on Rachael's shoulder. As she said, he was still alert and scanning the room but much more calmly. Ian took the pen from Miriam and added, *why is Ferd calmer?* and *why are there fewer Sprites?* to the brainstorming list. They discussed the items on the list one by one and after half an hour the only two remaining were the last two for which no one had a suggestion or an answer.

Just as they were finishing the brainstorming session, Alexi and AJay returned.

"Well, Commander, give us the bad news," Ian directed, indicating that he wanted everyone to hear it.

"Captain, I don't have any news good or bad. We cannot find anything wrong, but the reactor will not run," Alexi reported.

"How can that be, Commander?" Ian asked.

"Damned if I know, sir. We checked every switch, connection, and circuit. We checked for the flow of fusion fuel, we checked the flow of reaction mass and we checked the lasers used to fire the fusion, everything is in first-class working condition, only it will not run or generate any power. We have more than adequate reserve power in the battery so we are at no risk of a complete shutdown for a very long time."

"Thank you, Commander. Did you notice fewer Sprites in the reactor room?"

"Sprites, sir?" Alexi asked, then, "Oh, I see, is that what we have decided to call them?"

"Unless either of you have a better suggestion," Ian said.

"Not me, sir," Alexi said.

"Nor me, Captain," AJay said.

"We have been brainstorming, here while you were in the outback. So far all we know for sure is the ferret is calmer and there are fewer Sprites." The moment Ian said that, he sensed a change in the room.

While Alexi and AJay were absorbing that piece of information, the ferret sat up, crept slowly down Rachael's arm to the table and began looking around the room. When he stopped, he was looking towards the hatch to the storage area. A single Sprite came slowly through the hatch and approached him. He watched quietly as it came towards him. He had his ears laid back indicating he was not too happy, but he stood his ground. The Sprite slowed to a stop an inch from the ferret's nose and paused for a moment. Then it entered the ferret's head. Four more Sprites came into the room and began circling the ferret. Ferd did not move while this was happening. Then Ferd turned to face the Captain, walked slowly up to him, stood on his hind legs and held out his forepaws towards the pen the captain held.

There was not a sound in the room as Ian handed the pen to the ferret. Ferd put the pen in his mouth and turned to Miriam who quickly laid the tablet she was holding on the table. Then Ferd walked over to the tablet and stood upright on it. He took the pen awkwardly in his forepaws and tried to make a mark on the paper. But, the second he walked onto the tablet, he no longer had the tablecloth to hold on to so as he pushed the pen to the paper, he just naturally floated up away from it. He squirmed in the air performing his usual weightless acrobatics trying to control his movements and get back down to the paper. Miriam reached over and caught him gently in her hand and pressed his tail first onto the tablet. She held him by his lower body and kept him in position on the tablet.

With infinite slowness, Ferd drew a ragged square. Then he tried to move farther down the page and Miriam, sensing this, moved him. When he was satisfied with his new position, he drew a small but passable triangle. Everyone looked on with amazement. When he was finished, he turned and handed the pen back to Ian and Miriam passed the tablet to the Captain.

Ian looked around at the crew and asked, "What do you suppose I should do?"

"Captain, why don't you draw a square and a triangle alongside of his?" Ichuro said.

"Okay," Ian said as he drew the symbols. Then he slid the tablet back to Miriam and handed the pen back to Ferd.

Miriam again placed Ferd on the tablet and responded to his movement efforts placing him farther down the page and a little to the right of the drawings of the square and triangle.

This time, the ferret drew a triangle and square overlapping with the triangle above the square. He then moved to the left and drew a triangle above and overlapping another triangle. When he was finished, he tried to give the pen back to the Captain, but the captain refused it indicating the ferret should continue.

Miriam moved Ferd to the far right side of the page. He drew a triangle above a square above another square with all three overlapping. This was followed by a slight move to the left where he drew a triangle above a square above a triangle with all three overlapping again. He followed this by a triangle above a triangle above a square again all overlapping and finished with a triangle above a triangle above a triangle all overlapping. Then he looked at Ian again, holding out the pen.

Ian started to refuse again when Ichuro gasped behind him and said, "Oh, my God, it looks like binary numbers. The top square is zero and the triangle is a one below it. The two symbols, side by side, below that are combinations for 3 and 2 in binary, below that are 4, 5, 6, and 7 with 4 on the right and 7 on the left. May I, Captain?" Ichuro reached for the pen and rapidly drew eight sets of symbols in stacks of four squares and triangles. As he drew he explained,

"Eight on the right followed by 9, 10, 11, 12, 13, 14, and 15 to the left." When he was finished, he handed the pen back to the ferret who stood holding it.

A moment later, the Sprite left Ferd and danced briefly in the air before departing the way it had come followed by the other four.

"What the hell did we just see?" Ian asked. It was more of a reaction than a question. "Communication, sir," Ichuro replied. "Communication between two drastically different species using the universal language of mathematics."

When the Sprites left him, Ferd went limp in Miriam's hand, his tongue hanging out of the side of his mouth. She handed him to Rachael who held him in her arms like a baby. A few minutes later, he came back to life, nestled into her arms tucked his nose in the bend of her elbow making himself more comfortable and went to sleep.

"Well, that is certainly a beginning, but where do we go from here?" Ian asked. "Why did they pick squares and triangles?"

"They are just symbols, sir, and as such, they are probably as good as any other symbols providing they are understood for what they represent and they are easy to draw. I think we got lucky, Captain. I can't imagine what else they could have done that would have established that they are intelligent," Ichuro said.

"You have a good point, Mr. Watanabe. Thank God for computers and those who know how to work with them."

Then the lights came back on.

As soon as the normal lights came back on, Alexi and AJay headed back towards the reactor room. Fifteen minutes later they returned to the Common Room to report. "It all works again, Captain."

"Great, thank you, Commander and AJay," Ian said.

"Does anyone doubt that the Sprites are the ones who caused the problem?" Ian asked.

A brief discussion followed in which everyone basically agreed with the proposition the captain suggested with his question.

"This began as Rachael and AJay were putting the anchors in place on the Iceteroid. Is it safe to assume that the two actions are connected in some way?" Ian asked.

"I think that is a very safe assumption, Captain," Alexi replied.

"May I make a suggestion, Captain?" Ichuro Watanabe asked.

"I wish somebody would," Ian said. "What do you have in mind, Ichuro?"

"I think we need to find a way to enable the Sprites to work through a computer instead of the ferret. The ferret is probably smarter than the average computer but, the strain on him is obvious and his limitations prevent him from helping the Sprites to communicate much beyond what they did with the binary numbers. We have lots of tablet computers, and we can slave them to the display here in the Common Room. Then using the drawing app that comes with most of those computers, I can duplicate the binary number communication and display it. I have no idea whether or not the Sprites can see, but somehow they were able to control the movements of the ferret's muscles, thanks to Miriam so that he could be used to draw the symbols. The drawing apps for the tablets allow the user to use a stylus or a fingertip or almost anything that will make an impression on the sensitive glass surface to produce a drawn image on the face of the tablet. If we can get the Sprites back in here I can perhaps find a way to teach them how to use the tablet to communicate," Ichuro explained.

"Mr. Watanabe, if that works, you just earned your pay for the past month," Ian said.

"Thanks, Captain, I'll hold you to that if it works," Ichuro said with a grin.

"I have a personal tablet, Ichuro," AJay said. "It's an older model but it works fine for me. I've never tried the drawing app that came with it, but it's yours if you think it would be useful."

"Will whoever is keeping track please add AJay to the earned pay list," Ian said, then added, "Why don't we stop and have lunch before we go any further. I don't know about you, but I am suddenly famished."

Immediately after lunch, Ichuro slaved AJay's tablet through the computer and onto the large screen. Then using the drawing app duplicated the binary numbering system demonstrated by the Sprites.

"Okay, Captain, I'm ready to proceed as soon as the Sprites return," Ichuro said.

Either the Sprites had been observing, or they could read minds because shortly after Ichuro announced he was ready, one of the Sprites returned to the Common Room.

Ichuro was ready to give the Sprites a demonstration of how the tablet could be used. He placed it face up on the table and first using the stylus and then using his finger he added a crude drawing of an eight-pointed star. Then having no idea of what to do next he pointed to the tablet computer and with a sweeping motion of his hand invited the Sprite to try.

For the next two hours, Ichuro repeated the invitation over and over to no avail. "It doesn't get what you are trying to teach it, Ichuro," Miriam said.

"What else can we do?" Ian asked. "Does anyone have an idea."

When Rachael started to answer Ian said, "It wasn't really a question, I was just expressing frustration."

"Look," AJay said, pointing at the tablet.

The Sprites danced in the air, then they made some very precise squares, circles, and triangles. As they did, Ichuro took the stylus and drew the same symbols on the surface of the tablet. Then the Sprites began a system of trial and error attempting to duplicate Ichuro's motions. They tried to re-engage Ferd in the process, but he just growled and snuggled deeper into Rachael's arms.

Eventually, a Sprite actually touched the surface of the tablet. On the first touch, the screen went blank and the tablet shut itself down, the software had obviously crashed. The Sprite immediately retreated away from the tablet. Ichuro rebooted the tablet, located the images he had drawn with the app and looked to the group for suggestions.

"Do any of you have any idea how we can do this so that their energy doesn't overwhelm the electronics of the tablet?" Ian asked, then added, "That wasn't meant to be a rhetorical question. I really need another brainstorming session that will help to figure this out."

The Sprite hovered patiently while the issue was discussed. There were not many ideas and none that were suggested were really practicable. In the end, it was the Sprite that solved the problem. It was clear that it understood how the tablet could be used and it apparently had noticed that in several instances when Mr. Watanabe was actually drawing images on the tablet surface he was not actually touching the tablet surface. The receptivity or sensitivity of the glass actually extended out almost a quarter of an inch from the surface. At least it did for people.

The Sprite began circling slowly above the surface of the tablet from about a foot away and as it did so it spiraled down until it was about an inch and a half from the surface at which point a spot appeared on the screen. The Sprite stopped as soon as the spot appeared. As it hovered in place above the tablet the size of the spot grew slowly. Then the Sprite moved slowly away from the tablet until the spot stopped growing.

Ichuro reached over and erased the spot. When he removed his hand, the Sprite once again descended toward the surface of the tablet this time in minute increments until a single dot appeared on the screen. Then maintaining its distance above the screen it slowly drew the square and the triangle that the Sprites had chosen to use for the values of zero and one and stopped.

"Bingo!" Rachael exclaimed.

"Let's hope so," Ichuro said. "Now for the tough part what's my move? That also is not a rhetorical question."

It was the captain who offered a possible solution. "Why don't you draw a zero and a one alongside the square and the triangle and see what it does?"

"Thank you, Captain, that sounds like a great idea," Ichuro said as he slid the tablet out from under the Sprite and did as suggested. When he had finished he slid the tablet back under the Sprite.

In a totally surprising move, the Sprite quickly drew the values for the binary equivalents of the numbers from 0 to 15 using the zero and one characters of the humans and stopped.

"Now you can say bingo, Rachael!" Ichuro said. "But now what do we do? Again—"

"Simple arithmetic might work," Ajay interrupted.

Before he could reach for the tablet, the Sprite wrote in binary a one followed by an unknown symbol followed by a one followed by another unknown symbol followed by a two. Then a one followed by a third symbol followed by a one followed by the second symbol followed by another one. And stopped.

This time Miriam reached across the table for the tablet. "May I?" she asked taking it. Then she wrote on it "01 + 01 = 10 followed 01 * 01 = 01" and returned the tablet under the Sprite.

The Sprite immediately picked up on the symbols Miriam had used and rapidly ran through a sequence of sums and products that made it completely clear that the Sprite understood what was meant. For the next hour, Miriam and the Sprite went back and forth doing simple arithmetic.

"Miriam, I lost track of the ones and zeros almost an hour ago. It might be a good idea to determine if the Sprites notation is only binary or if they use some other number base," Alexi said.

"Okay, Commander, but I want to try something else first. Drawing all these ones and zeros is driving me crazy too. I'm going to try and introduce the Sprite to the screen image keyboard and see if it can pick up on that."

Being very careful as she altered the procedure, Miriam showed what she was doing and what the result of the change was on the screen. She typed very slowly "01 + 01 = 10" followed by "01 * 01 = 01." Then she pressed the return key and immediately below what she had typed, she typed "1 + 1 = 2" followed by "1 * 1 = 1" followed by the return key.

The Sprite paused before replying and was joined by three others. To the amazement of all, the Sprite picked up on the keyboard and after conferring with its fellows typed the following: "1 * 2 = 2" then "2 * 1 = 2" followed by the return key. Then it typed "1 + 2 =" and stopped.

Miriam reached over and pressed the 3 key followed by the return key. The Sprite typed "1 + 3 = " and stopped, waiting.

Marion reached over and pressed the 4 key followed by a return. Then she typed the digits from 0 to 9 and stopped.

The Sprite quickly typed the sums and products of one and all the numerals up to six.

Then it typed the sum of "1+ 6 = 7" followed by "1 + 7 = " and waited.

"Okay, guys," Miriam said. "Now what do I do? I have two choices, clearly, it understands the meaning of the symbols we use for digits from zero through seven, I can show the sum as being the digit 8, or its octal equivalent 10 which is the octal representation of the digit eight?"

"Your guess is as good as mine," Ichuro said. "Give decimal a try. You've already shown them the digit symbols so do 1 + 8 = 9, and 1 + 9 = 10 and see what they do with that. Let's hope they are smart enough to understand and are able to compute in decimal. If they are it will be a whole lot easier than if we have to convert everything to octal. We can use the computer to do it for us if we have to, but it will end up being very clumsy. But better clumsy and continuing to communicate than otherwise."

"Miriam?" Ian said.

"Right," she replied and did as suggested.

For the next several hours, they did simple arithmetic which the Sprites duplicated and embellished.

"That's enough for now," Ian said as he picked up the tablet and turned it over. Apparently, the Sprites got the idea and left the Common Room and presumably the ship.

Ichuro Watanabe was sitting at the computer console dozing when an alert beep brought him to attention. The system requested a single-use data chip be inserted in the appropriate slot after which it wrote the incoming message to the chip as it was received. For several minutes, the message came in slowly on the tight beam laser from, he assumed, Farside Base or through one of the relay points. When the message receiving light went out, Ichuro took the data chip to the captain's cabin/office. He knew the captain was sleeping so he knocked and waited.

"What is it?" Ian asked.

"Excuse me, sir, another coded message just arrived. The trailer said, give it to you immediately, sir," Ichuro said.

"Just a minute, Ichuro, until I get out of this damned hammock," Ian said. "Now what is the rush?"

"I don't know, sir. The complete trailer said, 'Captain ICExS *Barsoom Explorer*, secure, eyes only, private code.'" Then as he handed the captain the data chip he continued. "This is a one-use chip, sir. It self-destructs after you have decoded it and read the message.'"

"That's a new one," Ian said. "Thank you, Ichuro."

After closing and locking the door, Ian activated his personal tablet and inserted the chip. He looked up the code key formula for the day, checked the day, date, and time it was sent and using those numbers, computed the actual key and entered it into the reader App. This was a new procedure he had not done before. He had received messages before addressed with the "eyes only tab," but never one on a self-destruct data chip with secure, "eyes only" and private code flags. The tablet paused and requested he enter part two of the code; then the message began to scroll up the screen. He skipped the header which was just a formal address typical of all military messages to the captain of a vessel.

Sir,

Ian, there are all sorts of bits and pieces to send you, hence the secrecy.

1. Father Sabatino who is the person who facilitated the meeting in Moravia, has been killed, poisoned in his office. His office was ransacked, presumably by the killer. I did not tell you this before because there was nothing more to report. It seems that Father Sabatino was not operating solely out of his alleged religious convictions. He left a coded message to be opened in the event of his death. There were three copies, of which we have recovered two. The gist of the message is he was seduced and bribed by a very skilled female operative working for a corporate cartel that wanted to prevent our mission to Mars. In the interest of peace, we have not told the religious activists of his perfidy to avoid another backlash of being accused of trying to tell them what to believe. It will all come out eventually anyway.

2. The Cartel is a group of eastern European Oligarchs and corporations, and possibly others, that want to claim Mars and all its resources for itself. One way or another, either through the

religious smoke screen they created or through direct action, they have been behind all the bribes and threats made to the original selectees and the workers who contributed to the sabotage here at Farside Base. As you doubtless know, they even got to people who were "ringed" members of ICExS at all levels. Two board members were guilty of revealing our primary choices for the scientists and have been disciplined. One did it for money and the other for personal reasons. Neither was aware of the other which we assume was for purposes of cross- checking the information. One way or the other, nearly every scientist who was qualified was contacted and either threatened or bribed, some by the religious zealots and others by direct influence of the companies in the Cartel threatening to cut off their funding or harm their close relatives. The scientists who were finally selected were on a very secret list which was never released. Even so, somehow the cartel figured out that Gladys Campbell might be selected and kidnapped her son as you know.

3. Before I go any further, please be advised that Thomas Vernon is an ICExS agent who is also completely qualified for the scientific work. He is an ex-SAS Command Sergeant and is completely reliable. Because he had only been working at the university for two years and had not published, he was not visible to either the Cartel or the zealots. From something you reported earlier, he has already acted to stop Esteban Martinova from taking over from Jan Pitrasen. Not that it would take much stopping because Jan can handle himself when necessary. He was trying to remain low-key which is his natural demeanor.

4. This brings me to some really bad news. The woman who is known to you as Guadalupe Martinova is not actually Dr. Martinova. They got to the Martinovas before we did and probably threatened to kill Guadalupe unless Esteban went along with the substitution. I can offer you no guidance with regard to Esteban,

but we would consider him dangerous. We were informed earlier this week, that the body of the real Guadalupe Martinova was found by a scientific team exploring a remote part of the Atacama Desert. She was partially buried in a dry wash. Because of the nature of the Atacama, her body was almost perfectly preserved, desiccated but recognizable. One of the Martinova's students was in the team who found her and she identified the body.

5. Now for the really bad news. The Cartel launched a Mars mission of their own from the Capustin Yar launch facility long before the *Explorer* left. The reason we did not detect the launch, is it was described as a survey satellite insertion. Then they reported that they had lost contact with their satellite, which was now on a path towards the sun and the launch was a failure. It was launched from the opposite side of the Earth from the Moon and took a path that kept it essentially behind the Earth for the first part of the trip. After that, it was detected and appeared to be on a course towards the Sun. Therefore, it was just considered to be one more piece of space junk. The reality is, they used the Sun to do a slingshot maneuver much like you did around Earth at the beginning and they are on a cometary orbit which will bring them out to Mars in about two months. They may be able to do some maneuvering and I would consider them to be very dangerous. We are assuming that they are on a one-way trip as there have been other satellite launches with essentially the same result that we assume are supply ships. We assume that Esteban Martinova and the substitute wife whom we have not yet identified, are under orders to take over the scientific mission and if possible the *Explorer* and be waiting for the arrival of the Cartel's vessels. The Cartel's ships went quick and dirty, they will have to land via retro-rockets and parachutes from Mars orbit and will have no means to return to Earth unless they take over the *Explorer*.

6. I get periodic reports from Tom Vernon piggybacked on your normal traffic. He reports that he found a beacon on the far side of a hillock near Ares Base. It was broadcasting a signal which we assume was a homing beacon for the approaching ship so it can plan when and where to land. The only scientists who have gone over that way were the Martinovas in doing their geology on a supposedly interesting outcropping. Apparently, the Cartel's plan is to take over the habitats and other facilities we brought to Mars after declaring that our mission was a failure thus leaving them as the sole claimants to Mars. We have kept very quiet about the progress of our mission since discovering this so we would not tip them off and to the best of our knowledge, the Martinovas have not been able to communicate with either the ship or the Cartel on Earth without revealing what they were doing. They don't have the power or a tight beam laser like we do. If they tried to send a radio message, we would intercept it as well so they are forced to play a waiting game until the other ship arrives.

7. Which brings me to this. How are things going as far as embedding the *Explorer* in the ice ball? We would advise you to expedite that effort as much as possible and then to move the *Explorer* out to the L5 LaGrange point and park it until it is time to come home. We suggest that because Mars will block any radar signal that might be used to locate you until it is too late for them to do anything about it. We know it means abandoning much of the scientific side of the mission, but we would rather have your crew and the other scientists safe than risk the Cartel people having the ability to harm any of you or the *Explorer*.

8. We recommend that you bring the scientists up to the *Explorer* as soon as possible. Since it is what they wanted to do anyway, we suggest leaving the Martinovas on the surface with a habitat and survival equipment to avoid any problems they might cause if they got back in the ship. In all likelihood, Esteban will probably

not survive to meet the Cartel's ships, but that is probably true if they got back aboard the *Explorer* as well.

9. We have reviewed the manifests of the equipment that the scientists brought along, and there are chemicals in the Martinova's kit that could be used to create explosives as well as sarin gas. The list of their containers is appended to this message. We would advise you to have one of the pilots take the containers that are still aboard the *Explorer* down to the surface and leave them there.

10. Anything you can do to foil the Cartel's plans without risk to either yourself or your crew would be highly appreciated. We thought about having your pilot move the homing beacon and the Martinovas as far as possible from the site of Ares Base to prevent them from having access to anything you are forced to leave behind. We suggest that you destroy the facilities and equipment you leave behind. We leave that decision up to you. It will probably mean risking one of your pilots to have her in the same shuttle as the Martinovas. We want everyone who is not involved with the Cartel to come back safely.

11. Finally, I remind you unnecessarily that the *Explorer* is not a warship. There is only one weapon aboard and you know where that is. Use it if necessary.

We have dumped a lot on you that was never part of the original plan. All I can do is wish you good luck.

Chris Craft for David Palmquist, Managing Director ICExS

When Ian was finished reading the message, he went through it again twice more to memorize the salient points and then called Alexi to come to his cabin. When Alexi arrived Ian had him stand behind and read through the message with him. Ian could not pass Alexi the tablet because it was necessary for him to keep his thumb over the tablet's fingerprint sensor, the instant he released the tablet, the chip would be destroyed. Alexi read through the message once, looked at Ian with raised eyebrows and then indicated he wanted to read it again. As Alexi read the message the second time, he was mumbling Russian expletives under his breath. When he finished, he nodded to Ian and Ian released his thumb. The only indication that the chip was destroyed was the message disappearing and the chip was no longer being recognized by the tablet.

"My God, Captain—" Alexi began and then looked at Ian again and revised his comment. "My God, Ian, what have we gotten ourselves into?"

"Yes," Ian said. "What have we gotten ourselves into?"

"What are you going to do?"

"I have not thought it through completely yet. When I do, I will give you a call again and go over it with you," Ian said. "Thanks, Commander."

Alexi took his cue to leave and as he did, he put his hand on his friend's shoulder once again and said, "As I told you before, I am glad it is you sitting in that chair, Captain."

Alexi closed the door behind him and returned to his cabin after checking that everything from the reactor to the command deck was functioning properly.

The next morning, Ian decided that there was no way to implement the requested actions or his plans without the input and support of the entire crew. He called for a crew conference and informed them of the essence of the message, then explained his decisions.

"What I have decided to do is as follows. I would like to go all the way through it first and then ask for any ideas you might have to help make it work or any objections that might make it not work," he said. "There are only a couple of options that I can take. I see no alternative other than to leave the Martinovas on the surface and to bring up the rest of the scientists immediately. I have thought about the suggestion that we move the Martinovas to another location along with their beacon and I have decided to do exactly that. We will leave them with one of the spare habitats, a water, and oxygen generator, and sufficient food to last until the other ship arrives. After that, we will dismantle Ares Base and return it to the *Explorer*.

"While we are doing that, I need for you to continue to try to establish contact with the Sprites so we can explain what is happening and what we need for the trip out to the L5 point and ultimately to go home. If we cannot establish adequate communications with the Sprites, then we will have to use the remaining reaction mass we have to move the *Explorer* out to the L5 point anyway and wait for the window to do an unpowered return. If they can, I feel confident that ICExS will send a ship to meet us with additional reaction mass, or to rescue us and or take us off the *Explorer*. Now, any questions or suggestions?"

Alexi responded first. "I agree with everything except using our remaining reaction mass. As you suggest, there is probably, enough reaction mass left to get us on our way. Note, I said probably enough for the move and to start us home, but I, for one, would like to have some left over for contingencies that might come up. Why don't we just do whatever it takes to take over the Iceteroid from the Sprites?" The last was a planted question that he and Ian had decided upon before the meeting.

"Commander," Ian began, "I hear what you say, but as far as I am concerned the human race has to stop just taking what they want from whoever has it. In North America, the people took the land and resources away from the Native Americans in the USA and the First Nation peoples in Canada and either killed them directly or indirectly by letting them starve. In Australia, we did essentially the same thing to the Aborigines. I, for one, don't wish to be part of any such action here. The Cartel may think they can just take what they want without consequences, but not us. Might I add that the Sprites shut us down before when we tried to appropriate their home and I have no doubts they could do it again to us or the Cartel."

"I agree," the two Israeli pilots said simultaneously and then laughed at themselves.

"I, too, agree, Captain," Ajay said. "I come from a country that was taken from my ancestors by a conquering nation. It took us over 100 years to get it back, and they left a lasting imprint on our culture that is far more than the language we use."

Ichuro Watanabe looked at the captain and nodded his assent.

"I would not write off the Sprites just yet, sir," Miriam said. "I am gaining ground rapidly in communications. It may be only mathematics so far, but they are showing me as much as I am showing them. There is one peculiar thing, though. Whenever I make significant progress with whichever one is with me at the time, several others show up and seem to be conferring with our contact before it responds. They can use the tablet now for their part of the exchange. I still have not figured out how they get what I'm showing them, but it works so I'm just going with it. The next thing I planned to do was to present a drawing of the solar system and identify Earth and Mars respectively and see how they react. Somehow, I don't think it is going to be a big surprise to them. As soon as I get that far, I think maybe I should show or tell them about the other ship or ships that are coming and I don't think that will be a surprise either."

"That is fantastic, Miriam. Keep up the good work." Ian was temporizing while the rest of the crew digested what he had said, and what Miriam just revealed.

"Yes, sir," Miriam replied. "Ichuro has been working with me to see if there is some other way we could communicate using the ship's electronics equipment."

"Excuse me, sir," Rachael said. "How do you suggest we take over the Martinovas and move them to another location? I can't fly the shuttle and keep them at bay. Even if we strap them in, I will still have to release them when we get to wherever I take them. May I ask if you have another way to relocate in mind?"

Ian had expected the question and had an answer prepared. "I was looking at the map of the surface and I think the best place would be in the rocky highlands. Where is the map display?"

"Coming up, sir," Ichuro said as he had the computer display the map on the Common Room monitor.

Ian took a moment to orient himself and find Ares Base, then pointed to a location nearly 700 miles north and west of Ares Base. "Right there. It should present a difficult landing spot to the incoming ship and get them out of our hair. Then, to answer your other question, I am going to accompany you down to Ares Base and I will be armed. In addition, we will pick up Tom Vernon and take him with us when you actually fly them to the other location. Between the two of us, we should be able to control them. But, I expect some sort of fight nonetheless.

"Miriam, I want you and Ichuro to continue your efforts at communication while we take care of this rather revolting problem. Commander, if you or Ajay can add anything to their efforts, it would be appreciated as well."

PART FOUR

CHAPTER SEVENTEEN

"Rachael, when will the shuttle be ready to go?" Ian asked.

"It is fueled and ready to go now, sir," she replied.

Everyone pitched in to help locate and load the shipping containers with the explosive and sarin gas components into the shuttle. The storage area was closed off from the rest of the ship and the air was pumped into a holding tank. Then the airlock was opened to the shuttle, which was at zero pressure. This was a precaution while they inspected the contents of the containers just in case they were booby-trapped. There were no booby traps, but it was clear that the containers had been moved from where they were originally placed when they were brought aboard. There may have been some things missing from the containers, but it was impossible to determine without completely unpacking them. They also loaded the reserve habitat and the water and oxygen generator. It had been decided to take the material to the new location and unload it before picking up the Martinovas, just to be safe.

When everything was securely packed in the shuttle, Ian and Rachael went aboard. Once the airlock was closed and sealed, Ian reached into the cargo pocket of his space suit and took out an automatic pistol that had been adapted for use either in a normal environment or while wearing a space suit. He placed the gun in a storage space in the flight deck area.

Rachael looked at Ian in surprise and said, "A gun, Captain?"

"I am taking no chances with the Martinovas. From what I have been told, Mrs. Martinova, whoever she is, would not hesitate to kill everyone in order to accomplish her mission. The nice thing about a pistol in a vacuum or very low pressure is, you do not have to actually hit someone with the bullet to put them down. Just putting a hole in the space suit will accomplish that nicely," Ian replied.

Fifteen minutes later, they were on the ground at the new location. It took the two of them some time to unload everything. The material was scattered around the area but was accessible from the newly inflated habitat. They also took the time to connect and test the generator so the habitat was immediately usable.

"Why all the setup, Captain?" Rachael asked as they finished.

"I just want to isolate them, not kill them. So, I figured if we set things up first, we would not have to stay here and help them set up, and risk ourselves unnecessarily."

"Thank you, sir."

"Okay, let's go get the Martinovas," Ian said as he led the way to the shuttle.

Rachael lifted off and flew a ballistic path to Ares Base in Gale Crater. A ballistic flight was a good choice because they coasted most of the way of minimizing the fuel required. When they landed, it was night, and they were over one hundred yards away from Ares Base. Sound does not travel well in the thin Martian atmosphere so it was unlikely that anyone would have heard their approach. The intent was to surprise the scientists and not give the Martinovas time to prepare for their arrival. The first clue the scientists had was when the airlock of main habitat cycled and woke them up. When he stepped into the habitat Ian had the gun in his hand with the safety off.

"Good evening, ladies and gentlemen," Ian said. "We are here to pick up the Martinovas and relocate them. So Esteban and whoever you are 'Ms. Martinova' please get into your space suits immediately," he ordered.

Tom Vernon marshaled Gladys, Jamilah, and Jan Pitrasen to the opposite end of the habitat and then stood behind the Martinovas as they unzipped their sleeping bags. As she stood up, it was clear Mrs. Martinova had something in her hand. Then she moved toward the other scientists.

"Drop whatever you have in your hand, Lupe," Tom said.

Lupe Martinova then turned and lunged at Ian and Rachael holding what looked like a knife. "You can't do this to us!" she screeched.

Ian and Rachael moved out of the way as Tom grabbed for Lupe's hand. She avoided his grip and slashed him with the instrument in her hand, then turned quickly away and slashed into the outside wall of the habitat. The wall of the habitat was nearly half an inch thick and made up of many layers including a layer that contained a chemical that would seal any leaks. The cut was over a foot long before anyone could react.

"You will all die before you can do anything to me," she screamed through the rapidly thinning air.

Ian did not hesitate, he took careful aim and shot her in the leg. Lupe dropped the knife and collapsed to the floor screaming in pain and hurling obscenities at Ian. The bullet had passed through Lupe's leg and through the wall of the habitat adding another hole to the one from which the air was already escaping. Tom grabbed Lupe in a chokehold from behind with his injured arm and pressed her carotid arteries with his good hand until she passed out. Then he turned to Esteban and said, "Don't move or I'll do the same to you."

Jan Pitrasen sprang into action and was prepared to patch the cut in the habitat wall. Rachael had immediately backed up to the cut and blocked the hole with her body to slow the loss of air. Jan reached behind her and working quickly pulled the edges of the cut closed at the center with a strip of duct tape. He did this twice more above and below the first tape before he staggered and began to collapse from lack of oxygen. The tape slowed but did not stop the loss of air. Gladys opened the environmental equipment locker and turned the valve to the oxygen tank on full in an effort to keep the air breathable before she, too, passed out. Ian eased Jan aside and applied several overlapping patches effectively sealing the cut. Then, almost as an afterthought, also put a small piece of the patching material over the bullet hole.

It took a few minutes for everyone except Lupe to recover once they had breathable air. Tom patted Lupe down without the niceties of care for her gender. He found a small pill box in her brassiere which he removed and a razor blade in the seam of her overalls. The pill box contained two razor blades, several pills of assorted colors and a folded piece of paper. Then he regained his hold on Lupe waiting for her to recover.

"She's faking, Captain," he said. "I can feel her heartbeat and the blood pressure in her carotids. Lupe, I know you're awake and I am going to hold on to you for the time being. If you try anything, I will not hesitate to break your neck. Do you understand me?"

Lupe nodded but was still tense and ready to spring into action the moment she was able. "Do you understand me," Tom asked again.

"Yes," Lupe said as she relaxed loosely into Tom's arms.

"I know what you're doing Lupe and if you want to try it go ahead, but you will not like what happens next," Tom said.

Ian reached out and while Tom held her, pushed Lupe to the floor. Then he said, "Rachael, sit on her. Watch out, she looks tough or thinks she is."

"So am I, Captain," Rachael said. "Israeli Army commando training was required of all pilots. It's been a while, so I might not be as adept as Tom or as I once was." Then she said to Lupe, "if you so much as move your hand, I will put you out like a light."

"Jew bitch," Lupe said through clenched teeth.

"Tom, would you please check Lupe's and Esteban's space suits for weapons or anything that might be usable as a weapon," Ian ordered.

"I'm on it, sir," Tom said still recovering from the lack of air.

"Sorry, Sergeant, take a minute to catch your breath first," Ian corrected the order.

Jan and Gladys were both still gasping from the near disaster, but the color was returning to their faces. Jamilah still lay on the floor but was clearly breathing. Jan helped Gladys up and into one of the camp chairs. Then turned to Ian and asked, "What was that all about, Captain?"

Ian explained about the Martinovas and the incoming Cartel ship. Then he laid out the plan for moving the Martinovas to the other location.

As he was checking the space sits, Tom said, "Jan I found a radio beacon, which I assume, was to guide the incoming Cartel ship to Ares Base."

"You're serious, aren't you?" Jan asked incredulously.

"Yes, I am serious. I reported it to the captain right after I found it."

"Why didn't you tell me about it?"

"Sorry, my friend, I wasn't sure how you might react and I didn't want to tip off the Martinovas before the captain decided what to do with them."

"I understand, Tom, you were probably right. I don't know how I might have reacted either, but I would have been very angry, and I am not good at hiding my feelings when I am angry," Jan said.

While he was talking with Jan, Tom continued to search the Martinovas' space suits and other equipment. When he finished, he displayed two additional items he had found that could be used as weapons.

"Okay, Rachael, you can get off of Lupe now," Ian said as he helped Rachael up. "Would someone please dress Lupe's wound. I can see it is only a grazing wound and not too serious."

"Let me do that, Captain," Jan said as he fetched the first aid kit.

When Jan was finished dressing the wound, Ian said, "Lupe, you and Esteban are to get into your space suits immediately after which we will be moving you to another location. Tom, I want you to come along just in case either one of them tries anything again."

Tom dragged the Martinovas' space suits into the living area and dropped them at their feet. "Get into the suits," he said.

"You can't intend for us to go dressed like this do you?" Lupe asked indicating the coveralls that were the standard dress when in the habitat.

"I expect you to go exactly like that," Ian said, "and, if I thought it might be safer, I would have made you strip to the skin before entering your space suits. We are taking no chances with you. I will warn you again, for the last time, I will not hesitate to shoot you if you cause any more trouble."

Lupe glared at Ian but began to get into her space suit. "What exactly are you planning on doing to us?"

"We are going to take you and the beacon to another site we have prepared for you. We will leave you there with everything you need to survive until the Cartel ship arrives. You had better hope it comes in on the homing beacon, otherwise, you are going to have a very long walk to wherever they do land."

"You can't do that to us. It is illegal and inhumane."

"I am the captain of this mission, Lupe. If we were at sea in earlier times, I could have you walk the plank or keel haul you or strand you on a desert island for endangering the lives of everyone on the mission. It has been over 200 years since that was a common practice, but it is still possible to put you off on a deserted island to fend for yourselves, and that is exactly what I am going to do. Since you will be left with adequate supplies until the next ship arrives, I doubt that any court would take exception to that," Ian said.

Amazingly, Esteban remained silent and made no complaint as he got into his space suit.

Finally, he asked, "What about my wife, Captain?"

"She's dead, you Peruvian idiot," Lupe shouted. "Did you really expect us to babysit her until we returned?"

Gladys paled at that comment, thinking about her son and what would have happened to him if he had not been found when he was.

"Captain?" Esteban asked.

"She's right, Esteban. A survey expedition found her body in the desert a week or so ago," Ian replied.

"Was she—"

"I don't know any more than that. There was no mention of any identifiable mistreatment, but it is probably quite difficult to check that on a body that has been in a place like the Atacama Desert for any length of time," Ian replied. "However, I would keep a very careful eye on her," indicating Lupe, "until the Cartel ship arrives. It will be here in about two months."

"It will be here in two weeks!" Lupe screamed.

"But, Captain—" Esteban started.

"I appreciate it that they threatened to harm or even kill your wife if you did not play along with her," Ian said, pointing to Lupe. "What is your name anyway?" he asked of Lupe.

"Catalina Druvescu, mein herr," Lupe replied, dropping the Spanish accent.

"Okay, Catalina, if anything happens to Esteban between now and when the Cartel ship arrives, you will bear the blame," Ian said.

"He is an incompetent idiot," Catalina said.

"That may be so, but he is also a scientist who is much admired by his peers. The only reason he is being exiled with you is you will need another pair of hands in order to survive."

Catalina mumbled what Ian assumed were Romanian curses under her breath. Tom Vernon, helped her with her helmet and then helped Esteban.

As they went out through the airlock, Rachael first followed by Esteban then Tom then Catalina and finally Ian, Catalina said, "Captain, it is dark out here. Do you plan to go now?"

"Right now before you have time to plot some payback. We got here in the dark and we can go back in the dark," Ian said.

"Jan, can you hear me?" Ian asked Jan Pitrasen over the radio. "Yes, Captain, we hear you" was the reply.

"We will take them over to the new site and then return to the *Explorer* to refuel before we can come for you. I will call you from the *Explorer* when we get there to let you know all is well. Rachael will come for you in the morning. I think it would be safer for the time being if we were all on the *Explorer*. Please assemble your belongings because that may be our last trip to the surface. We need to begin preparing for departure as soon as possible. For safety's sake, I don't want anyone to be on the surface when the Cartel ship arrives because we have no idea what their plans might be," Ian said.

"Captain, we would prefer to stay down here as long as possible. We have made some real progress in our experiments so far. A little more time would definitely be worth the effort. As I see it, Rachael can come down and get us anytime we are on the same side as Phobos, Apparently whether daylight or night it does not seem to make much difference. So the worst we would have to wait for recovery would be four hours or so. That would give us time to button up and shut everything down. I see no reason why we can't just leave our equipment and habitation right where it is until things are resolved."

"You're sure, one and all?"

Both Gladys and Jammy nodded enthusiastically. Gladys said, "Captain, we have found life. It is not much, but it is a start. So we would like to continue as long as possible."

"Rachael? Is that alright with you and what you would have to do to retrieve them?"

Rachael gave him a thumbs-up, then led the way to the shuttle. They entered the shuttle in the same order they had exited the habitat. Once aboard, Esteban and Catalina were strapped securely to acceleration couches and checked by both Tom and Rachael. Then Tom wrapped some duct tape around them as well to keep them completely secured with their arms at their sides.

After double checking to be sure everything was ready, Ian gave Rachael a nod, and they lifted off. As before, they flew a ballistic trajectory and landed at the new site. Once they were down, Tom unwrapped the tape from around Esteban and Catalina and they all exited the shuttle in the same order again with Esteban between Rachael and Tom, and Catalina between Tom and Ian. They were led to the habitat and ushered in through the airlock. Ian made a quick check of the controls to insure the water and oxygen generator were both working.

"We are going to leave you now. I'll be the last one into the airlock and I will have the gun aimed at you, Catalina. You will remain in your space suits until I cycle the airlock after which you may turn on the air and remove your space suits or do as you please. I'm going to leave the outer door open to prevent your exit without closing it. Oh, and by the way, all of your chemicals have been disposed of, so don't think you can rush out and do us any damage," Ian said.

After Rachael and Tom left, Ian backed into the airlock, closed the hatch and cycled the airlock. Thirty minutes later, they were back aboard the *Explorer* and being welcomed by the rest of the crew.

When the three of them came through the hatch into the common area Miriam, said, "Welcome back, Captain." Then, "Look out, Rachael."

Ichuro added, "Hi, Tom."

Rachael turned in time to see a small furry missile sailing slowly across the room towards her. She held out a hand catching the ferret gently. "Thanks, Miriam," she said as she put the ferret on her shoulder.

"He has been hunting for you ever since you left," Miriam said.

A moment later, Alexi and AJay arrived from the reactor room. "Everything go as planned, Captain?" Alexi asked, extending his hand.

"Yes, for the most part. I had to shoot, Mrs. Martinova, who is actually one Catalina Druvescu, by the way. We hustled them out of there as fast as possible. I did not even give them time to gather their things completely. Once Ms. Druvescu pulled a knife and tried to attack me, cut Tom and then cut a slit in the side of the habitat before she could be stopped. I had to shoot her to stop her. It's just a flesh wound in her leg. She'll recover. Jan dressed her wound and she was able to walk out to the shuttle. It will hurt like Hades for a while, but I have no doubt she'll get over it. Once we subdued them, we had them get into their space suits. Tom actually taped them to the acceleration pads for the trip to the new site to prevent any further attempts to interfere. We pulled their face shields down before we lifted off too, so I doubt they have any real idea of where they are now. They will know it is north of Ares Base because of the angle of the sun, but that's it," Ian informed the assembled crew. "Oh, in case you were wondering, Jan also dressed Tom's cut, which Tom said was routine."

The only comment anyone made was when Alexi raised his eyebrows, shrugged his shoulders and asked, "Too bad. Did you have to aim so low?"

"Yes," Ian replied. "If I hadn't, we couldn't be sure Dr. Martinova would be able to survive at the new site and I was certainly not going to bring him back up here. It really does take two to keep things running and stay alert for problems. I don't pity what he will have to put up with until the Cartel ship arrives, but she will be as dependent on him as he is on her, especially so until her wound heals," Ian replied.

"What of Jammy and Gladys and Dr. Pitrasen, Captain?" Miriam asked.

"They asked to stay down on the surface and continue their work. It would appear that some of what they have done was successful, Gladys even said she found life. She did not say what life she found, but she was quite enthusiastic about staying."

While the others were talking, Rachael asked Miriam, "I wonder how Jammy is going to feel about Ferd's attachment to me. He's been sleeping with me ever since Jammy and the rest went down to the surface. He was taking turns with us before that depending on who was on duty and who was in their hammocks."

"I wouldn't worry. He's been searching for Jammy in her compartment as well," Miriam replied.

As promised, Ian called down to Jan the next time the *Explorer* passed over Ares Base. "Dr. Pitrasen, we have relocated the Martinovas to some rough terrain or is that Aresain? We left them with what we brought down which included adequate supplies and equipment to comfortably tide them over until the Cartel ship arrives. It should make for an interesting landing when it does arrive. We thought we had two months until that event was expected but now, based on what Ms. Druvescu said we may not even have that long. If there is to be a confrontation, we plan to avoid it to protect the ship. To do that we have to move out to the L5 point before they arrive for safety's sake. That might be anything from immediate to two months."

"We are still doing productive work here, Captain," Dr. Pitrasen replied. "If we could stay until the last minute it would be appreciated. You did not say when you were here, are we to leave the supplies and equipment here or not?"

"No," Ian replied. "We should remove all trace of our having been there or at least as much as possible just in case they are more maneuverable than expected. If you could pack up as much as possible, it would be a big help. We will help you when the time gets short."

"I am getting nods and smiles from the ladies, so I assume that is an acceptable plan that we will execute while we continue with our work. We have some quite astounding things to report, but that can wait too. Thank you,

Captain, we will be in touch. But we should probably only talk through tight beams so nothing leaks out for others to hear."

"Agreed all around. Oh, and tell Jammy that we have an anxious ferret here awaiting her return," Ian ended.

"How are you doing with your attempts to communicate with the Sprites?" Ian asked Miriam and Ichuro while pointing at the resident Sprite.

"We're getting there, I think," Miriam replied. "You Ichi?"

Ichuro took up the baton. "I, we, think we have gone as far as we can with the mathematics, Captain. Miriam went through some trigonometry very quickly. She tried calculus, but they do not seem to be able to relate to it as we know it. I think the hang up was the symbology used to represent the Calculus operations. The light has not lit, if you know what I mean, sir. We are trying to figure out what to try next. Since we don't even know how they perceive what we are doing, we don't know where to go next. Any ideas would be welcome."

"Have you thought about chemistry and physics?" Tom asked.

"Yes we have, but physics without calculus is messy, and chemistry is always messy."

"What about astronomy?" Ian asked.

"We tried drawing a diagram of the solar system on the tablet, but it got way too complicated," Ichuro replied.

"What all is in that computer of yours? Isn't there an encyclopedia with diagrams in there?" Tom asked. "I was playing with it some on the way out just to pass the time, and found animated diagrams of all sorts of things."

"That's what we need, animation!" Miriam said. "I've never looked in the encyclopedia for it. I wonder what it has on the solar system?"

Ichuro launched himself over toward his computer desk and began typing happily away with Miriam looking over his shoulder kibitzing. The resident Sprite hovered above them maintaining a safe distance so as not interfere with the electronics. They found an animated diagram of the solar system and sent it to the big monitor in the common area. Within seconds, five more sprites arrived and positioned themselves in front of the monitor.

"Ichi, send it to the tablet too," Miriam requested, "and slave the tablet to the monitor like we did before."

Ichuro did as requested. The planets revolved slowly around the Sun on the diagram. Miriam moved to the tablet and used a stylus to press on the icon for Mars which caused the one on the monitor to be highlighted. The Sprites danced in front of the monitor but made no other move to indicate they understood beyond that.

"Can you zoom in on that?" AJay asked.

"Sure," Ichuro said as he zoomed in with the Sun in the center with Mars as the outermost planet shown.

The diagram was so complete that it showed the orbits of the two Martian moons and the moons themselves. When Miriam highlighted the orbit of Phobos, one of the Sprites dipped down and, touching the tablet, placed several dots ahead of Phobos that roughly coincided with the positions of the Iceteroids. Ichuro zoomed in still further until only Mars and its moons filled the screen. The Sprite responded by dipping again and by picking very carefully drew a rectangle that coincided with the position of the *Barsoom Explorer*.

"Yes!" Ichuro and Miriam exclaimed. Then, when they looked at each other, Miriam asked, "Now what? Zoom back out and show Earth again," she suggested.

When the diagram once again showed all of the inner planets, Miriam highlighted Earth with the stylus. Then she drew a line from the Earth to Mars. The Sprite dipped down and drew a representation of the ship on the line and went back up to hover at eye level. "How do I respond to that?" Miriam asked.

"Try drawing a line from Mars back to Earth and see what happens," Ian suggested.

Miriam drew the line with no response from the Sprite. Then she said, "Ichi, zoom in so that Earth and Mars are shown, please."

Ichuro changed the display as requested. Still no reaction from the Sprite. Miriam redrew the line from Mars to Earth changing the Mars end to include a line from the *Explorer* to the nearest iceteroid and then to Earth. Within seconds, six other Sprites joined up and slowly circled above the drawing. The resident Sprite dipped down and tried to change the drawing, but the result was just a confusing image.

"He does not know how to manipulate the drawing," Miriam said.

CHAPTER EIGHTEEN

For the next two weeks, Miriam and Ichuro worked to increase their communication with the Sprites. Ichuro drew a diagram showing the *Explorer* nose into an Iceteroid. The Sprites demonstrated no interest in that drawing. Various other images and drawings were shown with the same results. An attempt was made to interest the Sprites in using the tablet with no response. Finally, one afternoon, the ferret wandered into the area near the table. The resident Sprite went over and hovered as before in front of the ferret's nose.

As the Sprite moved slowly closer to the ferret, the ferret hastily left the room. Miriam and Rachael seriously considered bringing him back but decided that he had shown how he felt about welcoming a Sprite into his head again. Then the Sprite did something different, it went over and hovered two inches in front of Rachael's face and Rachael instinctively backed away from it. The Sprite made no attempt to follow her. It went next to Miriam. She considered inviting the Sprite in when the captain intervened.

"No!" the captain said. "Do not let it into your head, Miriam. And that goes for all of the crew. The six of us are the absolute minimum required to navigate the *Explorer*, I cannot risk having one of you disabled by the experience. Try to find another way. Think outside the box."

Miriam backed away from the Sprite.

"Captain, we have tried everything we can think of to no avail," Ichuro said. "How about one of the scientists?" Then he looked at Tom. "Tom?"

"No thanks," Tom replied.

They sat belted into their seats discussing and discarding other possibilities with no new choices beyond trying to draw some different diagrams on the tablet or computer. Ichuro went over to the computer and began looking for other images or animations that they might use. Then the computer emitted the sound indicating an incoming message. He scanned the header, inserted a disposable chip in the slot and transferred the message to the chip.

"It's for you, Captain," he said. "It is a short one and it's in the private code again."

Ian took the chip into his cabin to decode and read it. Ten minutes later he was back in the Common Room, looking very concerned.

"Bad news, ladies and gentlemen," he said. "The Cartel ship appears to be under power and is expected to arrive almost three weeks earlier than originally expected and they are probably armed. We have less than three weeks to pack up and leave. Ichuro, can you contact Ares Base right now?"

Ichuro looked at the clock and said, "No, sir, Captain. We entered the radio shadow about thirty minutes ago. It will be about four hours before we can talk to them."

"Will they be in daylight when we're able to talk to them?"

"No, sir, it will be near midnight when we come out of the radio shadow," Ichuro replied.

"Rachael, can you get ready to take the shuttle down as soon as possible. I hate to ask you to land in the dark again, but we are in a hurry."

"The shuttle is ready now, Captain. I checked as soon as you got that message. I just looked at the navigation data, sir. It will be a long approach, but I can manage. If it can wait an hour, it will be almost optimal."

"Good, wait the hour. Tom, will you go along to help take down the facilities. I want everything useful brought back to the *Explorer* and everything else hidden or destroyed and it has to be done as quickly as possible," Ian said. "You will arrive before we can call Dr. Pitrasen, so extend my apologies, tell him what is happening, and tell him we have to hustle. Got it?"

"Got it, sir," Tom replied. "Rachael, what can I do to help to get ready?"

"Nothing since we won't be taking anything down," Rachael said. "We'll suit up in about forty-five minutes, Between now and then, I can't think of anything we need to do."

"Meanwhile, would the rest of you please continue with the effort to communicate with the Sprites, we are going to need it sooner than we thought," Ian said.

. . .

Rachael disconnected from the *Explorer* a few minutes early and began the descent to Ares Base on schedule. The trip to the surface took just over fifteen minutes. As soon as they were able to raise Ares Base on the radio, Tom called ahead to warn the scientists of their approach and when to expect them but told them nothing more. It was two hours before midnight, Mars local time when they landed at Ares Base.

When Rachael and Tom entered the main habitat, everyone was awake and tea was brewing on the stove. Tom explained the situation to the scientists and told them why they needed to leave immediately. Then he said, "I suggest we all go to bed now, we can wait until daylight to start packing."

"How do you suggest we go about destroying or burying what we're leaving behind?" Jan Pitrasen asked.

"I don't have a good answer for that, Jan. The captain wants to leave nothing useful. Farside Base says the Cartel was planning to take over whatever we had done assuming we had beat them to Mars. This was why the Martinovas planted the beacon to guide them in. Assuming nothing much has changed since I left, we only need to deal with the habitats and the support equipment. We'll take the food, any scientific samples you have, and any useful equipment. The rest will have to be dealt with somehow," Tom replied. "We can't burn it because the Martian atmosphere will not support combustion. I would like to take it all, but disassembling the habitats will take longer than it did to assemble them, and I believe the captain doesn't think we have time to do all that."

"I have an idea," Jamilah said. "Could we dump everything in the cone of the mountain in the center of the crater?"

"That is over fifty miles away. How do you propose to get it there?" Jan Pitrasen asked.

"Can Rachael fly it there? It wouldn't be easy, but we could just push it out through the airlock and let it fall, which should smash it up pretty good," Jamilah replied.

"I could only make two trips at most, and hovering while you push it out of the airlock would eat up a lot of fuel. Good idea, Jammy, but not too practical. It would almost be easier to take it up into orbit. I could do most of it in two trips and we have enough fuel for that on the *Explorer*," Rachael answered. "Let's sleep on it."

The next morning they worked steadily packing up what they could and loading it into the shuttle. Rachael had talked to the captain and presented the suggestion of hauling everything possible back to the *Explorer*.

"Captain, there is just no way to destroy what we have to leave behind because there is no way to burn it," Rachael said.

"Yes, there is!" AJay shouted from the background. "Why not bring what you can and then go back down with the Oxy-Hydrogen welding torch and burn or at least scorch as much as possible whatever is left?"

"That would work," Rachael said. "What do you think, Captain?"

"I think it would mean another trip to do it, and all the risk associated with that," Ian replied. "We cannot afford to risk you, Rachael. So, just abandon what you cannot bring back.

"I'm willing and AJay is good with the torch—" Rachael began.

"I'm sorry, Rachael, but I don't think it is a good idea. We have enough troubles getting away from here without taking any other chances."

"Yes, sir," Rachael acknowledged the captain's order.

Jan Pitrasen signaled that he wanted to speak to the captain so Rachael handed him the microphone. "Captain, I think we can be done by tomorrow afternoon our time, so expect us for dinner," he said.

"We will look for you then, Jan," Ian said.

The next afternoon, the shuttle returned to the *Explorer* for the last time. When it docked, the storage space was depressurized. As soon as the airlock to the shuttle was opened and the seal was assured, the pressure in the storage area was returned to normal so that everyone could welcome the returning scientists. The reunion was perhaps somewhat more enthusiastic than one would normally expect, but considering the circumstances, it was needed. There were three especially warm welcomes, the ferret came whining and bouncing from one point to another and into Jamilah's arms, at almost the same time, Ichuro wrapped his arms around her and finally, AJay and Rachael exchanged an embrace. The whole company pitched in to unload the shuttle with Sprites hovering and presumably watching the process.

As they were securing the containers and loose equipment, Ian asked, "What did you do to the things you left behind?"

Jan Pitrasen replied, "We decided to bury it."

"You did? How?" Ian asked.

"It was Rachael's idea. We piled everything that was left behind into one big pile, then she flew the shuttle back and forth slowly over the pile using the steering jets to stir up the sand. It worked very well. The result was to hide everything and cover it with sand to hide it well," Pitrasen replied.

"Good on you, Rachael," Ian said.

Jamilah came into the Common Room holding a package, which she carefully secured on the counter in the cooking area near the sink.

"What do you have there, Jammy? Did you find anything interesting down on Mars?" Miriam asked before anyone else could.

"We sure did," Jamilah said. She carefully unwrapped the package. "I brought this back inside my space suit," she said as she showed the company a small foam cup from which a green leaf extended above the rim. "This is Martian soil. I grew this using only Martian soil and artificial light. The plant's seed came from the desert of the American southwest in an area that is very arid and where there is a high proportion of iron in the soil much like that of the Martian soil. I planted it about two weeks ago. Because it is a desert plant, I gave it very little water, only a couple of CCs, and it grew. So, life is certainly possible on Mars."

Ian watched Gladys beaming at Jamilah with motherly pride. "And, what did you find Gladys?" Ian asked.

"Life!" she said.

"Life," several people said at the same time. "What kind of life?"

"Didn't you tell them, Tom?" Gladys asked.

"Hell no," Tom replied. "It's your story to tell, Gladys."

Gladys took three small jars from her coveralls pocket and set them firmly on the table which did not stop them from drifting slowly away as she released them. "The jar with the yellow label contains bacteria-like organisms and the red label contains an organism similar to an amoeba and one with the green label contains an organism similar to a nematode. In all three cases, I doubt that they are even remotely similar to what I suggest as their counterparts from Earth, but that is a handy way of thinking about them. The only way to determine the similarities or differences will be to do DNA tests if they even have DNA and not some other evolutionary equivalent. I brought plenty of them so testing can be done without risk of losing the samples."

"My God, do you know what this means?" Miriam asked rhetorically.

"Yes, we both do," Jamilah replied. "It is most certainly going to cause the Earth-only creationists to have to revise their beliefs."

"But, I doubt it will cause more than a brief sensation before the conspiracy fanatics attempt to disprove the findings as fakes and blame us for trying to plant phony specimens, much like the disparagers of Darwin did when he returned from the voyage on the *Beagle*. These will revise the entire scientific understanding of life as we know it. I also fully expect to have these specimens stolen as soon as they are revealed in order to prove that they do not really exist," Gladys added.

"We will have to find a way to keep that from happening, won't we?" Ian said.

CHAPTER NINETEEN

At the suggestion of the captain, the whole company was assembled around the Common Room table. They were exchanging gossip when the captain took his place at the head of the table. The look on his face was enough to silence them immediately.

"Ladies and gentlemen, we have a serious problem. The Cartel ship is less than three weeks from arrival and Farside Base has cautioned us to be prepared for them to be armed. I received another message from Farside Base this morning explaining why it took so long to find them and describing their approach. It would appear they are coming in above the ecliptic and will probably enter an eccentric elliptical orbit using Mars's gravity to provide braking. They are expected to enter orbit around Mars at a slight angle and will probably go around several times spiraling in and slowing before they attempt a landing. They have a shuttle-like vehicle that will actually make the descent to the surface and later land the whole vehicle so it can be used as living quarters and a base.

"Farside Base was not sure which of their two vehicles is armed and what they are armed with. It is suspected, but not confirmed, that they have some sort of guided missile although a gun would work just as well against the Explorer. It has been suggested that we leave orbit and move out to the L4 or L5 point as soon as possible. It will take a while to get there as it is about 60 degrees ahead of Mars in its orbit and we can expect to find some Jovian asteroids there. The sooner we can leave orbit around Mars, the sooner we will be away from the threat from the Cartel ship. There is another possibility, and I will let Miriam explain it."

"What the captain is referring to are the Sprites. So far they seem to be benign discounting when they shut us down. They have been throughout the ship and there are several 'resident' Sprites here now, including the one we call Sparky although we are not sure it is always the same Sprite," Miriam said, pointing at the Sprite hovering above the table. "They seem to understand some of what we do and Ichuro and I have had some success in communicating with them. We think they are like bees or ants, social creatures. Which is to say, they work in groups, not as individuals. Whenever we have shown Sparky a new concept, several other Sprites join him and after that he makes a response of some sort and the others leave.

"We are not sure what to do about the most recent thing they have done. The first real progress was when one, which we assume was Sparky went into Ferd's head and drew what Ichuro recognized as a binary numbering system representation. They used symbols that were strange to us, squares and triangles. Both were equilateral and seem to us to represent what they considered to be perfect objects. Ichuro responded to them with more binary numbers using the squares and triangles and then wrote out binary numbers using ones and zeros beside their figures. They adapted to that notation instantly after which we taught them arithmetic using our symbols for arithmetic notation. We went on through Algebra and Trigonometry. Every time we showed Sparky something new, some others would appear after which he responded."

"How did he respond, Miriam?" Gladys asked.

"We taught him how to use a tablet computer. He responded by touching it lightly to activate a pixel and then drew whatever was needed to communicate his side of the issue," Miriam replied. "We showed him an animated diagram of the solar system and pointed out Mars. Then we zoomed in until we only displayed the solar system out as far as Mars and again, he recognized the diagram. Then we zoomed in even further until the display was limited to

Mars and its two moons. We drew in the ice and rubble ahead of Phobos, and he drew a recognizable image of the *Explorer* in its current position. That is where it sits at the moment."

"We, both sides, were at a loss when it comes to what to do next. I know you were not all here when he used the ferret, Ferd. Ferd held a pen, with help, and while I held him in position, he drew the binary stuff. When it left the Ferd's head, he collapsed in apparent exhaustion. Rachael helped Ferd to recover and it looks like no permanent harm was done. A couple of days ago, the Sprite wanted to try again. It approached Ferd and Ferd ran away from it. Then it approached us one at a time and hovered about two inches away from our foreheads as if asking to be allowed to enter one of us to communicate. Rachael volunteered—"

"I stopped it," Ian said. "We have a bare minimum crew and if anything had happened to Rachael, I have no idea how we could have recovered you or how we could operate the ship without her or without anybody else in the crew."

"And there it sits," Miriam finished.

"What if one of us volunteered," Dr. Pitrasen asked.

"Well, you are not crew and are not essential to the operation of the ship. But, how can we ask one of you to do it if none of us can?" Ian asked.

"I see and I understand the dilemma. I do not wish to trivialize it, but frankly, we are expendable in the interests of everyone else," Dr. Pitrasen said.

"I'll do it," Jamilah and Gladys said at the same time.

"Jammy, I appreciate your offering, but I think the responsibility lies with me," Gladys said. "I am the reason we are stuck here, or at least, I was the one who set off the bomb that cost us our reaction mass. Yes, I had my reasons, but those reasons are no longer pertinent. I have very little to lose if it does not work and a great deal to gain if it does. Ferd survived it, so perhaps I can as well. I am not trying to be a martyr, or maybe I am, but if it needs to be done, I will do it. And, besides that, I am the Astrobiologist and as such, I am supposed to be the one who interacts with aliens. Okay?"

They all looked at Gladys and then looked quickly away. Each happy that he or she did not have to be the one, and each feeling guilty that they were relieved that Gladys would do it.

"Dear lady, I give you another hug," Alexi said as he moved around the table and hugged Gladys. "You have atoned through what you have done since that unfortunate incident, but I salute you for what you are about to try."

"Thanks, Commander. Believe it or not, I am not afraid of what might happen to me. If the ferret could survive, then there is a very good chance that I will survive as well. When do we want to do it?"

"As soon as possible, Gladys," Ian replied. "Time is of the essence and if they can help us get away from here we need to find out how soon we can go and how it will be done. We have sufficient reaction mass to move the ship to either the L4 or L5 point and when the conditions are right to take the long way home to Earth. I suggest we all sleep and recover from the day before we begin with the Sprites."

"Excuse me, Captain," AJay interjected. "I know this is not a ship in the classic sense and that you may not be a ship's captain empowered to do the things old-time ship's captains could do, but I, we," he said, looking at Rachael, who nodded, "would like to become married and share a married couple's cabin before there is danger to us all. Is that possible?"

"I don't see why not. I am not sure I can come up with the words, but I'm sure that I can provide the intent," Ian responded.

"I may be able to help with that too, Captain," Gladys said. "I have a copy of the Church of England Prayer Book and the marriage ceremony is in it. Would that do?"

"That would do nicely, thank you, Gladys. Marriage is more about commitment than about ceremony anyway. I will report that I did it to Farside Base, and let them deal with the legal technicalities," Ian said, smiling.

"In that case, Captain," Ichuro said, "can we make it a double wedding? Jammy and I would like to be joined as well."

"In for a penny, in for a pound," Ian exclaimed. "I see no reason why not. We have three cabins suitable for married couples. Would you like to do it now, tonight, or tomorrow morning?"

"Tonight, Captain," both couples said. Ichuro finished with, "We have no idea what tomorrow may bring. So, let's get married right now."

"Gladys, the Prayer Book, if you please."

Gladys found her Prayer Book and the proper place in it for the ceremony and handed it to the captain.

"Gladys, will you be the Maid of Honor, please?" Jamilah asked.

"I would like that too, please," Rachael said.

Gladys burst into tears but nodded in agreement. Tom agreed to be Ichuro's best man and Alexi agreed to be the best man for AJay.

Ian took the prayer book and in the best tradition of the rite read the marriage ceremony without the religion-based overtones, asked the correct questions as specified in the prayer book and finished with, "By the powers vested in me by ICExS, I hereby declare you to be men and wives."

As if by magic, Alexi produced a bottle of wine. There were some problems getting it from the bottle into the freefall cups but once it was done a toast was offered to the newlyweds. Miriam and Alexi offered to stand double watches for Rachael and AJay, and things slowly returned to normal.

Alexi moved next to Ian and said under his breath, "We are getting old, my friend." Then he went back to the reactor room.

The entire company was gathered around the table the next morning in support of Gladys's offered reception of the Sprite. She seemed settled and composed and ready for whatever might happen. The resident Sprite, Sparky, was hovering above the table as usual. Gladys made a "come here" gesture and repeated it several times before Sparky caught on and began to approach her. He stopped about five centimeters from her forehead, as it had for the others, and paused. Gladys placed the index finger of her right hand on her forehead in invitation. Still, Sparky hesitated. She moved her left hand behind the Sprite as if to push it into her head. The Sprite moved very slowly up to the point where it was touching Gladys's forehead and seemed to hesitate.

"I can feel it, but that is all," Gladys said. "It is barely touching me, but I can feel a slight tingle. Come in, little fellow." She finished the gesture and ushered the Sprite into her head. "Ooh, I can tell it is inside my head. There is no pain and so far that is all. But, it is doing something in there. Do any of you have any suggestions of what I might try?" she asked.

"The Sprite had Ferd hold a pen while I held him in place above a tablet. Would you like to try that?" Miriam asked, then she added, "The writing, not the holding," she finished with a chuckle and then assumed a serious demeanor.

"Yes," Gladys replied as she accepted a pen from Ian and a paper tablet from Miriam. They all waited in suspense and nothing happened. "Damn, I thought that would do it."

Rachael said. "Gladys. try writing your name."

Gladys wrote her full name on the tablet and lifted the pen away from it. "Now, I can feel it trying to control the movements of my arm and hand. I guess reflexively, I am resisting. I do not mean to, but I cannot seem to help it."

"Have you ever done automatic writing with the intention of having a spirit guiding your hand?" Jamilah asked. "Just rest your forearm on the table and hold the pen loosely, and relax as much as possible."

Gladys did as suggested which resulted in pushing herself away from the table. She tried gripping the table with her right hand but even that did not keep the pen on the tablet.

Ian reached over and tightened Gladys's seat belt. "Does that help?" he asked.

"Yes," she replied in an ethereal voice.

"Gladys, close your eyes and take a deep breath," Rachael suggested.

"Yes," Gladys said as she complied with the suggestion.

Her hand slowly began to move after a few moments. The drawing was the same triangle and square as before, but it placed a zero beside the square and a one beside the triangle. Next, the drawing was enlarged. The Sprite drew several stars by drawing lines that crossed followed by an equal sign followed with a one. Gladys opened her eyes, saw what she had written and pulled her hand away from the tablet.

"Same as before," Ichuro observed. "No, wait, we never had the stars with the equal sign before. Suggestion, Gladys, take a stylus and use the tablet computer to write on."

Gladys put down the pen, picked up a stylus and pulled the tablet computer closer. At the same time, Ichuro slaved the display to the big monitor. Again the stars and equal sign were drawn."

"The many equals one seems to confirm they are social beings," Tom offered "And, here comes the cavalry," he said when six more Sprites came into the room and began to circle Gladys's head.

The new Sprites circled slowly and as they did, they moved closer to Gladys's head. At this point, she appeared to be completely relaxed. She took her hands and made it clear that the Sprites were to enter her head. "That was a combination of me and movement stimulated by Sparky," she said.

The new Sprites entered her head and she stiffened in her chair. This was followed immediately by a series of rapidly changing facial expressions ranging from a smile to a frown to anger. After a few moments, she seemed to relax. "The Sprites are all in the cavity inside my brain, at least that's the impression I have. They are feeling around and stimulating various parts gently so as not to hurt me. That's how they did the writing thing through me. It is very strange or weird and is causing conflicting emotions which I am endeavoring to stifle."

"That explains a lot," Tom said.

"Now, they seem to be exploring my sensory system because I am getting tingling feelings in my limbs and various places on my body." Then, she made a sound like no one present had ever heard before. "That was them too. They are stimulating my senses. It was as if I could hear a combination of sounds, then some smells and tastes, and—I am blind."

"We need to call this off, sir," Ichuro said.

"No," Gladys said, "I can see again they were just testing my vision and now they are causing various images of all kinds to be brought from my memory and appear to be what I am seeing. It is like a disjointed movie, and it is still going on. Oh, my goodness, that is something I have never seen before."

"What is it?" Ian asked.

"I think it is a view of the outside of the *Explorer*. I have seen it from a distance through the shuttle window, but this is much closer and from a strange angle. I could never have seen this when we were coming and going in the shuttle," she said. A few moments later, another Sprite entered the room and hovered near the ceiling. "Now, I am looking down at the table from above. Miriam, move your hand, please. Yes, I am seeing it live from the viewpoint of the new arrival. I'd give anything to know how they are doing this."

"You and me both," Alexi said.

"I am tired and I have a bit of a headache," Gladys said and as she did so, the Sprites left her head. "That is much better, thank you."

"Do you still have the headache?" Rachael asked. "I can get you some analgesic for it."

"Thank you, no. I feel better now. I am still tired and need to rest, but I am confident I will be right as rain after a nap," Gladys said.

"Do you want to continue later?" Ian asked.

"Oh, yes, Captain, I would not miss out on this for anything. It was a bit of a strain, don't you know. But now that they have figured out how to communicate, I doubt it will be so trying later," Gladys said as she unfastened her seat belt and pushed off towards her cabin.

"I had better stay with her, Captain. Just in case," Rachael said.

"I agree," Ian said.

"Gladys, wait for me. Why don't you sleep in 'Girl's Town' tonight, and I'll stay with you?" Rachael said.

"Thank you very much, Rachael, I will do just that," Gladys replied.

Gladys went to sleep almost immediately upon lacing herself into the weightlessness sleeping net. AJay offered to keep Rachael company until it was his shift in the reactor room. They played chess with a magnetic chess set and talked quietly. When AJay was preparing to leave, the resident Sparky came into the cabin and began to hover over Gladys.

"I see that Sparky is back," AJay observed.

"I suppose he or it is keeping an eye on Gladys too," Rachael replied.

Once she was alone with Gladys, Rachael turned off the light and sat watching the Sprite. As Rachael watched, the Sprite above Gladys descended slowly towards Gladys and then went into her head. Gladys gave no sign that she was aware of this. Her breathing remained even and she did not move.

A few minutes later, another Sprite came into the room and began hovering in front of Rachael. She stared at it for several minutes without moving. She felt a calmness come over her like nothing she had ever experienced before. She knew the captain had ordered her to not take any risks, but she had a mystifying feeling there would be no risk. She recalled the old military adage when you were about to do something out of the ordinary; it is easier to ask for forgiveness than to get permission. Slowly she moved her hand up behind the Sprite and gently pushed the Sprite towards her forehead. The instant it entered her head, she knew what Gladys meant when she said, "I don't feel any discomfort, but I know it is in there." She sat very still strapped into the chair waiting to see what would happen. Then she began to see images like very sharp photographs.

The first image was of the rear of the *Explorer* with the shuttle attached to the aft airlock and she could see her face looking out of the windshield. Slowly the image began to change as if a video camera was panning around until she was looking at AJay on the surface of the Iceteroid trying to set the anchors.

"Rachael, wake up. It's your watch," Miriam said. "You really dropped off, didn't you?"

Rachael awakened slowly and looked around the cabin. Gladys was still wrapped up in the sleeping net much as she was the last time Rachael looked. "My watch?" she asked. "What time is it?"

"It is 0400 and you're on duty," Miriam replied.

Rachael looked at the clock on the wall and was surprised to see that almost six hours had elapsed since she and Gladys went to bed and four hours since AJay left for his duty watch. "I'm sorry, I must have needed a nap," she said.

"I wouldn't be surprised, considering," Miriam said.

At breakfast time, the entire company was assembled in the Common Room. Gladys looked rested and very contented.

"Gladys, what can you tell me about your communing with the Sprites?" Ian asked.

"Well, Captain, once they got the inside of my brain sorted out, I saw a series of pictures or images. I know I was not actually seeing them. The Sprite was causing my optic nerves or my visual cortex to act as if I was seeing them. They were mostly just pictures of the inside of the ship. I could not really talk about them last evening because of the strain of the initial contact. But then I had some very vivid dreams of all sorts of things."

"What things?" Ian asked.

"To tell the truth, Captain, I cannot really describe them. I need time to process the images and organize them into some meaningful description. To back up a little, sir, I do know that when the other six Sprites went into my head they very quickly identified which parts of my brain do what. I cannot clarify that at this moment."

"Of course, take your time," the captain said.

"There is something else too," Gladys said with a look of concern on her face.

"Like what?" Ian asked.

"I have a very strong feeling that I or we are not the first intelligent beings they have contacted."

"What?" several people asked at the same time.

"It is only a feeling. They have not shown me any pictures of aliens, they have just given me the feeling."

"Captain, if I may interrupt, I think I can shed some light on what Gladys is trying to say," Rachael said. Then Rachael described how the Sprite had re-entered Gladys's head after AJay left to go on duty. "When it went into her head, she never even moved, sir. Then a little later, six more went into Gladys's head."

"Go on," Ian said.

"The next part you are not going to be too happy about, sir."

"That you fell asleep, I am not too surprised at that. It was a stressful day."

"No, sir, there is more. After Sparky went into Gladys followed by the other six, another Sprite appeared and seemed to ask if it would be alright if it entered my head."

"You didn't. I expressly ordered you not to take any chances."

"I didn't feel as if I was taking a chance, Captain. I felt completely at ease. It waited patiently for several minutes and then I showed my willingness for communication by pushing it into my head. Not literally, sir, I simply put my hand behind it and slowly moved my hand towards my forehead like Gladys did and tried to welcome the Sprite by thinking peaceful thoughts. My initial experience was much like Gladys's first time, except it was much quicker. I experienced some initial disorientation for a few seconds and then I began to see images much as Gladys has described. The next thing I knew, Miriam was waking me up for my duty shift."

"Do you remember any of the images?"

"Yes, sir, the first few were pretty much what Gladys described. After that, I think I fell asleep. I have memories of what I saw, but until I can sit quietly and try to recall them, I cannot describe them. But I also had the feeling that we were not the first contacts and that the first contacts were not human at least as we think of human."

"That is very much like what I felt and remember, Captain," Gladys said. "Actually, sir, I think Sparky is still with me because I get flashes from time to time. It seems to be working very hard to find a simpler way of communicating besides mathematics and so forth. Yes, that is exactly what it is doing. I just felt as if it was said. Language is going to be the barrier, but I think we can make some progress now that Rachael has encountered a Sprite as well."

"Gladys is right, sir. It just needs some time," Rachael said.

"Time is what we are short of with the oncoming Cartel ship," Ian said.

"They are aware it is coming, Captain," Rachael said. "I just got a very strong feeling to that effect."

"I did as well, Captain," Gladys said. "Nothing more, just that they know it is coming."

"How are we going to get them to understand that we are the good guys and are or were trying to set up a research station on Mars in hopes of colonizing it?" Ian asked.

"Gladys, you have a little more experience than I do with the Sprites. Do you have any ideas?" Rachael asked.

"They seem to be aware that you and I are different and that our views of what has happened and is happening are different as well. I am a scientist and you are a pilot with military experience. I think that we need to talk and have the rest of you talk to us. Perhaps they will be able to pick up on our use of language. They have a connection with the visual cortex; if we talk, we will engage the parietal lobe of the brain. Based on what we feel or hear and how our brains react to it may help them to understand our language."

"What do you suggest we talk about, Gladys?" Tom asked.

"Oh, I don't know, but I doubt it's astrobiology," Gladys replied, winning a chuckle from the group.

CHAPTER TWENTY

After the conversation the previous night in which attempts were made to find a means of communicating verbally with the Sprites, Ian, Alexi, and Ichuro were gathered around the table discussing other possibilities for communication. Suddenly Rachael burst out of her cabin and came flying into the Common Room.

"Captain, I just had the weirdest dream if it was a dream," Rachel said. "I saw what I suspect was the Cartel's ship and something I assume was the equivalent of our shuttle broke away from it and began heading towards us."

"So did I, Captain!" Gladys said as she came out of the cabin on Rachel's heels. "It was clear as a bell, Captain. I was not completely asleep when I saw the image as if it was in front of my eyes. It was much like what we were experiencing the other day only much clearer."

"Ichuro, see if you can see anything with the radar. Just take a quick peek to avoid revealing our position," Ian said.

Ichuro moved to the communications station and activated the radar in passive mode. He immediately picked up a signal from outside the ship in the supposed direction of the Cartel ship. "I've got a signal, Captain. They are painting us or they're trying to. I would say from the direction they're coming in and from which the signal came that they know exactly where we are."

"How the hell can that be?" Ian asked. "As far as we know, our position was never sent from the ship and I don't think it could have been sent from the surface accurately enough to pinpoint us considering we're in an eight-hour orbit. Any ideas?"

"Just one, Captain," Alexi said. "There's a beacon aboard that's leading them in."

"You're probably right, Commander. Where do you think it might be?"

"It might be almost anywhere, but I would start in the Martinova's cabin."

"We cleaned it out, Commander," Ichuro said. "Or at least I think we did."

"Do you have a broadband signal detector, Ichuro?" Ian asked.

"Yes, sir, Captain, I'll get it," Ichuro said as he started looking through his equipment for the signal detector. "It's gone, Captain. It was in this equipment locker, sir and it's not there now. I can try and cobble something up, but I can't make any promises. A lot will depend on what frequency is being used. What would you like me to do, sir?"

"Get your tools and go into the Martinova's cabin and take everything apart as quickly as you can. I would suggest having someone help you, but there is just barely room enough for two to sleep in there so you would probably get in each other's way."

"Yes, sir."

Ichuro gathered his tools and went into the Martinova's cabin. He began to disassemble the cots when he noticed a scratch on a screw in the light switch cover. "Captain, I think I found something."

"What is it?" Ian asked.

"I think someone has been messing with the light switch. I'm going to remove the cover to see what's inside besides the wires," Ichuro said.

"Wait!" Alexi said. "It may be a booby trap; she was very sneaky. Is there any way to look in there without completely removing the switch cover?"

"I have the fiber-optic inspection camera that I can use when I'm looking around inside the computer and that we used to see inside the inspection panels. Is that what you have in mind, Commander?"

"Yes. But to be safe, why don't you remove the cover from the light switch in your cabin first so you can see what it looks like inside. Then use your fiber-optic camera to look if possible as you loosen the screws," Alexi suggested.

Ichuro went into his cabin and began removing the cover of the light switch. It only took a moment before he realized that the screws were very short. It would not be possible to loosen them enough to get his fiber-optic camera inside without removing the cover. "It won't work, Commander; the screws are too short," Ichuro said as he replaced the light switch cover.

"Captain, doesn't the Martinova's cabin adjoin one of the empty cabins, sir?" Gladys asked.

"Did you hear that, Ichuro?" Ian asked.

"Yes, sir, as soon as Gladys asked I went over and checked. But one of the screws is scratched here too," Ichuro said.

"I would say that just about guarantees a booby trap, Captain," Alexi said. "I can shut off power to the lights from the breaker box in the workshop. Hang on a minute, Ichuro, I'll go check."

Alexi went to the workshop and checked the breaker box. "There are no marks on the screws for the breaker box. Ichuro, get out of the way in case there is an explosion," Alexi said over the intercom.

"I'm clear, Commander," Ichuro said from the intercom in the Common Room.

A moment later there was a muffled explosion from the cabin area. Ichuro immediately turned and went back into the Martinova's cabin. "It was booby-trapped, sir. The light switch covers on both sides of the partition are damaged and I wouldn't be surprised if the lights are shorted out. I am going to try and remove the cover from the Martinova's side of the partition. I don't know what else to do now if we're going to find out."

"Ichuro, be careful," Jamilah said as she came in the Common Room, rubbing her eyes from having been awakened by the explosion. "What's he doing anyway?"

"It's a long story," Ian said. "He is and has been being careful. We're trying to find a signal beacon that's hidden aboard the ship somewhere. We were pretty sure it was in the Martinova's cabin and that's where the explosion came from. But he was not in there when the explosion occurred. Please stay here, Jammy and let him do his work. I'm hoping that there is no more risk, but if we don't find and disable the beacon we may be in for more trouble from the Cartel."

"It's open, Captain," Ichuro said. "I can see inside the partition using the fiber-optic camera. Something is down about eighteen inches inside the wall. My guess is, it is the signal beacon. I'm going to need a tool of some kind in order to fish it out. It is still connected to the electrical system so I hope that by shutting the electrical system off we have also shut off the beacon. But I won't know until I get my hands on it."

"Rachael, would you please go back to the workshop and see if Commander Gargorin has a tool that could be of use here?" Ian asked.

A few minutes later Rachael and Alexi returned to the Common Room. Alexi was carrying a long flexible tool that was basically a cable with a plunger on one end and a four-clawed grappler on the other end. "This tool is used for exactly what Ichuro wants to do, fishing out something that can't be reached any other way," Alexi said, taking the tool into Ichuro, and a short time later they returned with a small box no bigger than a bar of soap, which it was painted to resemble.

"Here's what I found, Captain," Ichuro said. "I have no idea what it is, sir, as you can see it's all sealed up except for where the electrical was connected to it."

"Whether or not it is a signal beacon, we probably need to do something to avoid contact with the Cartel ship," Ian said.

"Captain, let me check and see if they're still trying to find us with their radar," Ichuro said. He went to the communication station and checked the radar in passive mode. "We are in the shadow of Mars, sir. So I can't tell if they have changed their radar watch. We'll come back into the area we were in before in about two and a half hours."

"Can you figure out how much of our orbit we're in view of their radar?" Ian asked.

Miriam answered, "Based on no more information than we have, the best I can give you is a wild guess. All things considered, if they were coming in on the ecliptic, we would probably only be visible as far as radar is concerned for about a third of our orbit. Coming in as they are above the ecliptic and without any idea what their angle of approach is, the best guess is about the same, but it could be more and it could be less. The possibility exists that in part of our orbit we are in the shadow of Phobos."

"Ichuro, did what you saw of their radar pulses give you any idea how far away they might be?" Ian asked.

"No, Captain. I can't even tell you where they were other than somewhere in the general direction where the radar antenna was pointing. If I had painted them I might be able to tell you, but in my considered opinion, painting them wouldn't be a good idea now that we've shut off their beacon. Depending on the capability of their radar it could tell them exactly where we are and how far away we are from them."

"Thank you, Ichuro," Ian said. "Ladies and gentlemen, we need a plan. Any and all ideas will be considered."

For the next two hours, the entire complement came together in the Common Room. Even the duty pilot and the duty nuclear engineer left their stations to participate. The captain allowed forty-five minutes for brainstorming ideas. Then they struck almost all of the ideas they knew were impractical from the list. The obvious choice was to move the *Explorer* away from where the Cartel thought they were to somewhere less obvious. The move had to be made when the *Explorer* was in the radar shadow of Mars, which gave them about a five-hour window in which to accomplish the move. It was Rachael who suggested moving the ship into Stickney crater on Phobos. It was generally agreed that the only problem with the suggestion was it was too obvious of a place to hide. Phobos itself made one revolution per orbit. That did not rule it out, but it would severely limit their mobility if they were attacked.

"Captain, we are coming into the area in our orbit where we might be discovered on their radar," Ichuro said.

"We can't do anything about that at the moment. So, let's see what we can do to find out where they are. Turn on your passive radar, Ichuro, and let's see if we can determine accurately when they can and cannot see us," Ian said.

After a tense twenty minutes, Ichuro said, "There they are. They have increased the frequency of their pulses, sir. So I suspect they are aware the beacon to guide them is no longer operational so they're going to need their radar to find us. We should be making a pretty big blip on their radar screen," Ichuro said.

"Miriam," Ian called to the command deck. "How soon can we be ready to move?"

"I brought all the systems online as soon as our electrical problems were resolved, Captain," Miriam replied. "So, we can move any time."

"I want to move as soon as we are no longer visible to their radar. Apparently, we will have approximately five hours in which to accomplish the move. I don't think we want to leave orbit yet because being able to hide behind Mars is very useful and minimizes our exposure. Can somebody tell me what the position is of Stickney Crater from their point of view?" Ian asked.

"Captain, since Phobos rotates synchronously as it orbits Mars, Stickney Crater always faces towards the surface. It is in the middle of the western edge of Phobos's face. It is about nine kilometers in diameter and nearly two kilometers deep. There is actually another crater inside of Stickney. It's nearer Phobos's north pole. It is almost two kilometers in diameter itself and maybe 500 meters deep. I'm doing a quick check, but I think if we go deep into the inner crater the only time we would be visible to them is briefly just before we enter the radar shadow of Mars and that's when that face of Phobos is in the brightest sunlight.

"The rest of the time the best view they will have is an oblique one, at least until they are right upon us. So if we get in the crater deeply enough, I don't think they would be able to see us from the direction they're coming. There is always some risk of exposure, but I think it would be pretty hard to pick us out from the background of Phobos's reflection even if they were looking straight at us unless they have a very powerful telescope," Marion explained. "I'll set up a program to take us to Phobos as soon as we're out of their radar picture."

"Then that's what we'll do. Now, once we get in there what's going to keep us there?" Ian asked.

"When AJay and I were checking it out, we found that it has a very small gravitational attraction. If we can snuggle right up to it, we should be able to stay in position. However, I would suggest that we put out a couple of anchors just like we did when we were in Stickney," Rachael replied. "There are cracks all over the place where we can wedge in what's left of our grappling hooks and anchors. But if they are bringing in a shuttle, they will be able to attack us eventually."

"Do we have any idea how far away their shuttle is?" Ian asked.

"Without pinging him, there's no real way to tell, Captain," Ichuro answered.

"Since it is pretty safe to assume they know where we are at the moment, I don't think a ranging ping will create any problems. So go ahead and ping him. Don't leave it on any longer than you have to."

"Yes, sir," Ichuro answered as he activated the radar. After a few minutes, he reported." At the speed he is going, Captain, he is almost thirty-six hours away. The readout does not show that he is accelerating at the moment. He probably makes corrective maneuvers every time we're visible because he will want to come into our orbit at a point where he is relatively close to us. Depending on what he's going to do. That is, of course, subject to change."

"Excuse me, sir, could I make a suggestion that should provide us with as much protection as we are going to get?" Rachael asked.

"Of course, Rachael, go ahead," Ian directed.

"What if we disconnect our shuttle from the ship before we move to Stickney and leave it in place as a target for their radar. We're not likely to need the shuttle again soon so we could leave it."

"How would you get to the ship after it departs, Rachael?" Miriam asked.

"We still have the moon shuttle docked at the anchor point where the surface shuttle was attached. I will take you around to it then you can fly it back and anchor at the aft airlock. Once the surface shuttle is set up and operating, you can come get me and carry me back to the ship. I also think we should use the shuttle's radar to paint them as they approach to give them the impression we are using the one on the ship." Rachel explained, then asked, "What do you think, Ichuro?"

"They are on the same frequency so that should be no problem. There might be a problem keeping the radar aimed at them," Ichuro answered.

"I don't think so. The shuttle is designed to use its stabilizing gyro to maintain position and attitude while using minimal thrust from the steering jets. If we top off the tanks, it should be adequate for as long as a week."

"Okay, if you get everything set up in the shuttle, we'll do a switch from the *Explorer*'s radar to the shuttle radar right before we move the ship," Ichuro mused.

"Will that work, Captain?" Rachael asked.

"If you two think it will work, do it. Things can't get much worse than they are, can they?" Ian responded. "I have a suggestion, though. On the sea, smaller vessels use a radar reflector so they show up bigger on the radar of other ships. Is there some way we can create a reflector that will give the impression that the shuttle is the *Explorer*?"

"I know what you mean, Captain," Ichuro said. "I was brought up in the LA area and have seen the radar targets you're talking about. Basically, they're just three intersecting planes at right angles to each other. They are not typically very big, but my guess is, bigger is better. AJay, can you make something like that from what's in the shop?"

"Does the material of the panes have to be solid, or can it be a mesh of some sort?" Ajay asked.

"Solid is better, of course, but almost anything that gives a big radar return should work, the more angles the better," Ichuro responded.

"I'll go see what I can find," AJay said.

"Is there anything we may have overlooked?" Ian asked.

There was a brief discussion among the company and no one was able to bring up anything that had not been addressed. Then Ichuro observed, "Murphy says, if a thing can go wrong it will go wrong, sir. But that would be true for the *Explorer* as well. It would be best if we monitored the shuttle radar ourselves so if something goes wrong we can go fix it," Ichuro said.

"Agreed," Ian said. "I had hoped we had left Murphy behind, but considering how things have gone so far, he is undoubtedly a member of the ship's company albeit an invisible one. Say, Gladys, is or are your Sprites still with you? Do they know what is happening?"

"Yes, sir. They know and they are keeping me aware of what the Cartel shuttle is doing. It is still coming."

Rachael and Alexi immediately set to work filling the shuttle's maneuvering jet tanks. Once the tanks were filled, Rachael and Miriam suited up. Rachael flew Miriam around to where the lunar shuttle was docked. Miriam transferred over to the lunar shuttle and ran through the checklist to test that everything worked since it had been anchored in place for many weeks, idle. Checklist complete, Miriam flew the lunar shuttle to the aft airlock and docked while Rachael docked at the forward airlock. Then they joined the rest of the company to make final preparations. AJay was just finishing his report on making radar target reflectors as they arrived.

The Sprites were present in abundance presumably observing what was happening.

"I am sorry, Captain, but there is nothing I can find that would make an adequate reflector," AJay reported. "The shop is just not equipped to make anything like that. I even went into the cabin area to see if I could remove one of the spare bunks. I can, but they are made of composite materials and have little or no metal in them. Almost everything removable is composite."

"Alright, you tried, thank you," Ian said.

"Captain," Ichuro said, "we are moving back into the radar shadow of Mars, their radar signals just faded. I said signals because now, I can detect two distinct signals. One from the main ship and one from their shuttle. If I can see two of them, I think it is safe to say that they will be able to see two of us very soon, so if we are going to move to Phobos, it better be on this orbit or the next while the local clutter makes the resolution of their radar signal fuzzy." Then he turned to Gladys and asked, "Gladys, do we have any aluminum wrap in the kitchen area?"

"Yes, there are two rolls. Why?" Gladys asked.

"It's an old trick, but during World War II, Allied bombers carried shredded aluminum foil, which they dumped when they were in the area where they could be detected by the German radar. It caused all sorts of problems with the German radar. Frequencies are a lot different today, but might that create a larger target area if we surrounded the shuttle with a cloud of it?" Ichuro asked.

Ian answered, "It might work. Do any of you have any suggestions for shredding it?"

"We won't have to shred it, Captain. We can just unroll it, cut it into large pieces, crumple them a little and set them adrift around the shuttle in sort of a cloud. If we are careful, it should not drift far enough away from the shuttle area to be detectable as multiple targets."

"We have two rolls of twine in the shop and lots of duct tape. Perhaps we could tape them to the shuttle at various places and let their natural drifting provide the target," Ajay said.

"Fantastic," Ichuro said. "That would be even better. Gladys, get the aluminum foil and let's cut it into five- or six-foot lengths." Then he turned to see the captain frowning. "Oh, sorry, Captain."

"No need to apologize, Ichuro. I was just trying to envision what you're planning. For this project, you have command. Go to it. How can I help?" Ian asked.

"Help Gladys cut up the aluminum foil if you will, sir."

"Done."

The Sprites continued to observe the team as they prepared for the oncoming Cartel ships.

The whole team worked on creating targets from the foil. Each roll was originally 100 feet long and eighteen inches wide. Cut into five-foot lengths, the full roll provided twenty targets and the partially used roll another fifteen. Each piece was carefully crumpled and then partially flattened to create as many surfaces and angles as possible. Several pieces were left in irregular shapes as big as possible. Each piece was taped to a length of twine and as it was finished, Rachael moved it into the shuttle.

"We cannot tape them in place until Rachael sets the gyroscope to stabilize the shuttle," Ichuro said. "Then we will have to work fast. We will have only five hours while we're in the shadow of Mars in which to set this up, and at the same time, Miriam has to move the *Explorer* as close to Phobos as possible as quickly as possible. We'll be moving back into the visible part of our orbit in about thirty minutes."

One of the Sprites hovered over the Radar Set as if watching the read out on the screen. "I have them on the scope, Captain, and it is several minutes earlier than I expected, I now have two distinct targets. The main ship is still on its approach to orbit while the Cartel shuttle is approaching faster. Assuming they're coordinating their radar readouts, we will have lost several minutes where we cannot be seen. So, if we're going to do this, it has to be as soon as we move back into the shadow," Ichuro said.

"Miriam?" Ian asked.

"I'm ready, Captain. If I push it we can do the move in four hours at least to the point where we will be in the radar shadow of Phobos."

"Rachael?"

"Ready, Captain. All I have to do is cast off and move out of your way while Miriam makes the move. As soon as you're safely out of the way, I can stabilize the shuttle and begin taping the targets in place. Once that is done, all I have to do is sit there and wait for Miriam to come and get me."

"Good. Who is going to work with Rachael?" Ian asked.

"I am, sir," AJay replied. "If you remember, we are a team in more ways than one, Captain."

"Sorry, AJay, of course, you are. I've been trying to think about several things at once and your team sort of slipped through the cracks," Ian said, then, "Okay, Ichuro, give us a countdown to entering the radar shadow, please."

The next two hours were very tense as they awaited the time to move. Rachael and AJay put on their space suits and entered the shuttle as the time approached for action. They were surprised to see that they had a Sprite with them. With minutes to go, Rachael cast off from the *Explorer* and let the shuttle slowly drift away.

"Update, Captain, we are in the radar shadow of Phobos as far as the main ship is concerned. That should help if there are any problems," Ichuro announced. Then a few minutes later, "the radar from their shuttle is fading. Ready, now!"

On, the word "now" Rachael used the maneuvering jets to back farther away from the *Explorer* and out of any possible path of the main engine exhaust. Miriam gave the main engines a quick blast and then let the *Explorer* drift for several minutes as it began moving towards Phobos. When there was no longer any risk to the shuttle, Miriam engaged only the center nozzle of the main engine as before and moved the *Explorer* towards Phobos.

Rachael maneuvered back into space previously occupied by the *Explorer* and stabilized the shuttle at zero relative motion. Then she and AJay began unloading the aluminum foil targets and taping them to every protuberance on the shuttle, away from any possible interference with the maneuvering jets that were necessary to keep the shuttle in place and pointed at the incoming Cartel shuttle. They even attached several targets to the rear of the shuttle and at the end of long strings to provide a longer target image.

For an hour and a half, the *Explorer* moved towards Phobos, then Miriam said, "Okay everyone strap in, we are now going to flip over so we can decelerate. I am not going to try to drive us right into Stickney. We will come to a relative stop about three miles out and compute the final approach when we have a very good idea of where we're going to park this beast."

The flip over went perfectly and ninety minutes later, they were stationary relative to Phobos. They looked over the surface around Stickney Crater and picked a spot inside the smaller crater as their destination. Using only the maneuvering jets, Miriam inched the ship closer to Phobos. At the last minute, as she tried to stop the approach, the gravity of Phobos took over and began to pull them in.

"Shit!" she said. "We may hit a little harder than I intended."

"How much harder?" Ian asked.

"That's hard to say, Captain, but I do not expect to do the nice gentle docking I had planned," she answered.

"Carry on, Major. Do your best, the first time is always the hardest."

"Oh, thanks, Captain," Miriam said as she tried to control the big ship in the close presence of a much bigger attraction.

Suddenly, the *Explorer* just came to a stop and settled into the crater just as planned. "Nice job, Miriam," Ian said.

"I wish I could take credit, Captain, but it wasn't me. I think the Sprites took over and guided her in," Miriam replied.

"Really?"

"Really!"

Once the *Explorer* was away, Rachael and AJay worked feverishly decorating the shuttle with the target reflectors. When they were finished they re-entered and sealed the shuttle, activated the radar and waited. Right on time, the Cartel shuttle appeared on the radar screen.

"Well, Priya, what do you think?" AJay asked.

"Priya?" Rachael asked.

"Sweetheart," he replied.

"I like it, thanks so much," she said with a smile. "What do I think? I think we have used up almost twenty-four of our thirty-six hours before that guy arrives," Rachael continued. "Let's check with the *Explorer* and see if they're receiving our radar signal. Do you have them in sight so we can use the laser connection?"

"Yes, Mera Pydra," he answered, again in Hindi then explained. "Yes, my love."

"I would give you a hug and a kiss and more if I didn't have this damned space suit on," Rachael said with a smile.

They tried several times before they managed to make the connection with the *Explorer*. "What is going on over there?" Rachael asked.

"We're down and holding while the captain and the commander are out setting the anchors. Have we got a story to tell you when you get here," Ichuro answered.

"We can hardly wait," Rachael said. "Are you getting the radar relay?"

"Not exactly. I'm standing on the top of the rim of Stickney while I set up a secondary relay to the *Explorer*. We're down in the 'hole' and there is no direct line of sight from the *Explorer* to you," Ichuro said. "I doubt we have any worries of the Cartel finding us. I can't even see us from here, so I don't see how they could. We'll have to be careful with the laser alignment, though, so nothing leaks past the relay."

"Okay, we can see your beacon and we have you in our scope so the connection seems to be secure," Rachael said.

"I hope so," Ichuro said. "Miriam said she would be over to get you as soon as we're in the radar shadow again. Okay?"

"Okay. Out and listening," Rachael replied. Then she turned to AJay, "Now, about these space suits…."

"Let me help you with that."

. . .

"Rachael, Rachael are you there?" Miriam's voice came from the console speaker.

Rachael awoke with a start and immediately jumped up and went to the console and replied, "We're here. We were napping. What's going on?"

"According to the radar, the Cartel shuttle has fired a missile at you. Check your radar readout," Miriam said.

Rachael went to the radar display and could see the larger blip of the Cartel shuttle and the smaller blip that was moving faster and was unquestionably aimed at her shuttle. "When did that happen?"

"About ten minutes ago."

"Seriously? Whatever it is, is certainly coming on fast from what I can see," Rachael said. She pointed to the radar screen when AJay joined her at the console. "Look," she said. Then she asked Miriam, "How much time do we have?" As she asked this, the resident Sprite drifted over and positioned itself in front of her forehead. Rachael used her hand to usher the Sprite into her head.

"The computer says it will get to you in less than an hour," Marion replied. "I'm coming to get you."

As soon as the Sprite went into her head, Rachael saw the image of the incoming missile. She was not sure what to do. She focused her mind on the image of the incoming missile and thought *Danger*. Then, she said, "My resident Sprite just showed me the image of the missile. From what I am seeing and receiving, it's going to be a lot less than an hour before it gets here. You won't have time to come and collect us."

After she had finished speaking, Rachael again made an effort to convey the danger to her Sprite. From her years as a fighter pilot, she had seen many missiles up close and had a pretty good picture of what they could do. She had seen fellow fighter pilots shot down by surface-to-air missiles. Her wingman had been hit by one and she watched as his plane exploded not fifty feet from her. He had tried to eject but the explosion happened too fast and he was caught in the fireball. So she had a very good image of what such a missile could do.

She kept repeating the scenario of the incoming missile hitting the shuttle and destroying it.

Send it back, send it back, send it back, she thought repeatedly while she said it aloud.

Another Sprite moved up in front of AJay and hovered in front of his forehead. "Go ahead and invite it. In won't hurt you."

AJay did as Rachael had done and brought his hand up to his forehead and pushed the Sprite into his head. He froze. After a couple of minutes, he relaxed and nodded his head. "I see what you mean. I have no fear of it. It's showing me the image you described to Miriam."

"All we can do is hope," Rachael said. "Keep thinking send it back and let's see what will happen. If that doesn't work we don't have long to wait." Rachael reached out her hand and grasped his hand and squeezed it affectionately. "Can you think of anything else we might be able to do to show the Sprites what we want them to do. If they could shut down all the electricity on the *Explorer* they should certainly be able to do something to prevent the missile from hitting us," Rachael said all this with a microphone open so they could hear her on the *Explorer*.

Less than a minute later the missile began a long U-turn. They watched as the missile turned back towards the Cartel shuttle. Then it continued to turn back towards them.

"Shit," Miriam exclaimed. "It looks like the problem was fixed. But this missile must be programmed and it's coming around right back at you."

Rachael continued to visualize the effect of a missile hitting aircraft while Ajay continued to chant, "Turn it back." The missile was still too far away to be seen but according to the radar, it was coming straight for them again. AJay pulled Rachael gently over to himself and put his arm around her. "Well, it was not a very long marriage, but it was certainly a pleasant one. Thank you."

"Don't give up, as some opera-goer observed many years ago, it ain't over until the fat lady sings, and I can't hear her singing," Rachael said.

As they watched the radar screen the blip for the oncoming missile suddenly disappeared. She looked out through the windscreen in the direction the missile was approaching and saw the results of an explosion. Within seconds of the explosion, the Cartel shuttle launched two more missiles. Their blips had only barely separated from the shuttle blip when they disappeared and so did the shuttle. They looked out to see if they could find what had happened and there was nothing there.

"Did you see that, Rachael?" Miriam asked.

"Yes and no. We saw on the radar what you saw. The Cartel shuttle launched two more missiles. But looking out in the direction from which the shuttle was coming there is no debris. It just disappeared," Rachael replied.

"I'm coming over for you anyway. The captain wants both of you back here with us with the Cartel ship still coming on. I'll be there in less than an hour so pack up your ditty bag and get ready to come home," Miriam said with a laugh.

"Right!" Rachael and AJay said together and ended laughing as well. "We'll be ready," Rachael said.

> To: Chris Craft, ICExS, Farside Base
> From: Capt. Ian McMichael, Barsoom Explorer
> We are under attack by the Cartel ship. He has launched guided missiles at us which have been dealt with.

When he finished writing the message, Ian converted it to the private code and asked Ichuro to send it to Farside Base immediately by tight beam laser.

"It will have to go by relay, it's going to take almost ten minutes to get there, Captain. It will be all over before they get it, sir," Ichuro said.

"Send it anyway, and let me know if and when we get a response."

"Yes, sir."

Thirty-five minutes later, the response was received, also in code.

> To: Capt. Ian McMichael, Barsoom Explorer
> From: Chris Craft, ICExS Farside Base
> Report damage. Can you send details about how you evaded the missiles?

Ian's reply was very terse.

> To: Chris Craft, ICExS Farside Base
> From: Capt. Ian McMichael, Barsoom Explorer
> No damage. We hid behind Phobos. Increase the ration of Vegemite for the next mission.

CHAPTER TWENTY-ONE

"Welcome home. Have some coffee," Tom said as he greeted Rachael, AJay, and Miriam and handed out coffee containers.

"Thanks, Tom," AJay said.

"Is there anything interesting to report on the progress of the Cartel ship?" Miriam asked.

"Only that they don't seem to be decelerating at the rate for orbital insertion, or at least they weren't when last we saw them on radar before we went into the radar shadow," Ichuro answered. "I fed the last radar data into the computer for analysis and the computer says if they keep going as they are, they are going to go past orbital insertion. They came out on a cometary path that should have been at minimum velocity with Mars at the far end of the ellipse. When they launched the shuttle to attack us, it changed the mass parameters enough so they will go farther out before they begin the swing back. Either that or they were going to have to do one hell of a deceleration maneuver three hours ago. Alternatively, they might be planning on going into a retrograde orbit around Mars after they swing by. Even then, they're going to need to do some fancy maneuvering at apogee or they'll head back towards Earth. We will not know until we can see them again, which should be pretty soon."

"What did you see when the Cartel shuttle went off the radar?" Ian asked.

"Nothing, sir, absolutely nothing. We saw the blip disappear and looked up immediately expecting to see the aftermath of an explosion like we did when the first missiles exploded. There was nothing there besides empty space. It's as if they were just gone," Rachael replied.

"Does anyone think that they are planning on swinging by because they detected our ruse with our shuttle. If they did would they get a better look at Phobos and possibly spot us from the other side?" Ian asked.

"About spotting us, sir," Miriam said, "when we returned to the *Explorer*, we knew where it was, but we couldn't see it. It was almost as if it was camouflaged. We could see Stickney Crater alright and the smaller crater where the ship is parked too, but that was all. Once we got close, we could see it, of course, but not from any distance."

"Do you suppose—" Ian began.

"The Sprites, sir? Yes, I do," Rachael said. "My Sprite just showed me the view from 30 kilometers out and the ship is not visible."

"Unbelievable," Ian said.

"Yes, sir," Miriam agreed.

"The Cartel ship should be visible in a minute, sir. They're in the radar shadow of Phobos at the moment," Ichuro said, then a few minutes later, "Got 'em. They haven't changed speed or maneuvered as far as the computer reports."

Miriam was in the process of entering data into the navigation computer when she said, "My God! If the computer is right, they're going to go pretty far out before they swing back in. The computed orbital path has them going out far enough before they start back that they're going to miss Mars completely. I wonder what they're planning to do."

The discussion was interrupted by the sound of a bell from the radio indicating an incoming signal. Then a voice, "*Barsoom Explorer*, this is *Mars One* calling."

Ian reached past Ichuro and picked up the microphone. "This is Captain Ian McMichael, *Mars One*, what can I do for you?"

"This is Captain Darfor Slovanovitch. You can start by explaining what the hell is happening to my ship and what happened to my shuttle. You intercepted the first missile and detonated it. After that what happened?" Captain Slovanovitch asked in a vaguely Eastern European accent, offering no apology for the missile attack. He continued, "Then our shuttle crew suddenly appeared back aboard my ship and the shuttle disappeared. Now, I have no power except for electricity."

"Yes, that is what we saw happen, Captain, except for the return of your shuttle crew and I am sorry for your lack of power," Ian replied, offering no explanation.

"I demand an explanation!" Captain Slovanovitch shouted.

"Sorry, Captain, I am cannot give you an explanation. You made an unprovoked attack on my ship and you want me to explain how it was prevented? What do you take me for?" Ian said. Then he heard quiet applause and turned around to see where it was coming from. The ship's company were all smiling, applauding and making gestures of support.

"That is unacceptable," the radio blared.

"That is too bad, sir. Did you have anything else you wanted? Are you going to explain why you tried to attack us?" Ian asked.

"We have a prior claim to Mars. We were defending that claim. We left Earth before you did and that gives us a prior right to claim it."

"Really? We have been here for several weeks and aside from a flag we left on the surface we have staked no claim to Mars," Ian said.

"I see our beacon on the surface, that gives us prior claim."

"Sorry, sir, but we placed that beacon, so you could find your agents when you arrived. When you find it, you will see our flag on the antenna. We were here first, Captain, and we helped your agents set up their camp," Ian said.

"You must know that Dr. Martinova and Catalina have just been returned to our ship as well," Captain Slovanovitch said.

"Thank you, sir, it is a big relief to us to find that all of your people arrived safely. Now, if you have nothing more, sir, it is dinnertime here and I really must sign off. *Explorer* out!" Ian said as he signaled Ichuro to cut the connection. "Leave the alarm on Ichuro, just in case they have something else to say, but I doubt they will once the Martinovas tell their story."

"Let's hope that we won't have any more trouble from *Mars One*," Ian said.

"Captain," Ichuro said. "According to the computer, *Mars One* is sending a very long message to Earth and it's not in code. We only got the part of the message, but it seems they are accusing us of using a secret weapon on them in an unprovoked attack."

"I'm not particularly worried about that," Ian said. "We have the entire radar record saved so they can say anything they want, but they're going to have a hell of a time proving it."

. . .

> To: Captain Ian McMichael, Barsoom Explorer
> From: Chris Craft, ICExS Farside Base
> The Cartel ship has reported you used a secret weapon on them and destroyed their shuttle that was approaching you with peaceful intentions. The Cartel is demanding an explanation. They are also claiming that you are interfering with the navigation of their ship and they will not be able to enter Mars orbit because they have been forced to return to Earth in a very long cometary that will take over a year. They have claimed a prior right to colonize or exploit Mars and that you have interfered with that as well.
>
> Do you have any explanation that we can offer them? What are you going to do now?

> To: Chris Craft, ICExS Farside Base
> From: Captain Ian McMichael, Barsoom Explorer
> No explanation at this time.

We are trying to recover from the damages that were done to the *Explorer* by the agents of the Cartel; recorded confession on file. As it stands, we are unable to continue the scientific exploration on Mars. We are trying to work out a plan for returning to Earth. I will keep you advised.

CHAPTER TWENTY-TWO

The next morning, the company was gathered around the Common Room table to discuss the problems of returning to Earth. The brainstorming session lasted for almost an hour, but no really useful suggestions were produced.

Miriam explained the problem. "The relative positions of Earth and Mars at this point in time means it could take us as long to get back to Earth as it will for the Cartel ship unless we can find a way to produce more thrust. Even then the best we could do would take almost six months because we have to chase Earth around its orbit and come in from behind."

"Thank you, Major," Ian said. "Is there any way that we can produce the required thrust that would be needed for a minimal duration trip?"

"Captain," Alexi said, "as it stands we only have barely enough reaction mass to get started on the long orbit. Even if we could fill our tanks with all the water they can hold there is a second problem. In order for the fusion reactor to produce the power needed for the thrust to move us into such an orbit, we would need more deuterium oxide or heavy water. We don't have enough. We have enough to get started but probably not sufficient to decelerate when we reach Earth orbit. The maneuvering we have done here has consumed most of our reserve of heavy water. Originally, there was enough for the round trip, but that was assumed to be forty-five days of constant acceleration, not six months or so even of reduced acceleration."

"Heavy water?" Tom Vernon asked. "What is it needed for, and is there any way to make it?"

"As you all know, there are two reactors on the reactor decks. The smaller one is a self-contained standard fission reactor which is used to generate our normal power requirements and the power necessary to trigger the fusion process. When we left Earth, we had a tank full of concentrated heavy water. Through an electrolytic process powered by the fission reactor, the deuterium is separated from the oxygen. It then goes into the feed for the fusion reactor where it is contained in a magnetic bottle. The macro lasers then heat it to an extremely high temperature while it is being squeezed by the magnetic bottle inside the fusion reactor, this also increases the temperature to the point where two deuterium atoms are fused to become one helium atom with a very large release of energy which we use to super heat the reaction mass into a plasma which is further compressed and released out the main engine nozzles at a significant percentage of the speed of light.

In effect, we have one very small thermonuclear bomb inside the fusion reactor. But without the deuterium, it will not operate correctly. I'm sorry, Tom, there is no way to make heavy water except through a very complex chemical and physical process in which it is concentrated by removing the normal water. There are only a few molecules of heavy water for every million or so molecules of normal water. I have no doubt there is plenty of heavy water in the Iceteroids, but we have no means of extracting it."

"How about the Sprites?" Rachael asked.

"Sprites?" Alexi asked, surprised. "How do you think they could help?"

"I don't know, Commander, but if they can make a shuttle disappear and transfer its crew to the mothership and then transfer the Martinovas from Mars's surface to the mothership, they might be able to transfer heavy water from an Iceteroid into our heavy water tank," Rachael said.

"How do you propose we ask them? So far we are on a pretty primitive communication basis with them," Alexi said. "Besides that, didn't you tell us that the Sprites want us to take the larger Iceteroid with us as well? I'm not sure we have enough power to even move it."

"Let me work on that, Commander," Rachael said. "Ichuro, I'm going to need your help in accessing all the relevant information from the digital encyclopedia and textbooks."

For three days Rachael, Ichuro, and Alexi pored over chemistry and physics texts to prepare themselves for communicating their need with the Sprites.

Finally, Alexi asked, "Do we have a complete set of blueprints or plans for the ship and everything in it?'

"Yes, we do," Ichuro answered. "What do you suggest we do, Commander?"

"Put them up on the big screen, so we can page through them and see if the Sprites can relate to them."

"Great idea, Commander, except a complete set is over 500 pages long," Rachael said.

"I figured as much, but I assume they are in increasing detail as you go deeper into them."

"True," Ichuro said as he brought up the file containing the blueprints and displayed the first page on the large display. "Now what?"

"Let's see what they might be able to do with them. Set up the tablet computer so it can be used to turn the pages. They seem to know how to use the tablet to communicate with us, so maybe once they see what we are doing, they will take over and go at their own pace," Alexi replied.

Ichuro did as asked and linked the tablet to the computer to control the display. The first page was an external view of the whole ship. Each succeeding page essentially zoomed in on some part of the ship in more and more detail beginning with the command module. Within minutes the Sprites called in more elements and soon the common area was filled with Sprites. Since neither Rachael nor Ichuro was familiar with the construction details, progress was very slow. Whenever the Sprite in Rachael's head needed more information, she had to ask Alexi.

After a few such incidents, a Sprite positioned itself in front of Alexi and danced up and down trying to catch his attention. He tried to ignore it, but, it got more and more animated.

Rachael watched this activity with wonder, then asked, "Commander, I think it wants to go inside your head to access what you know directly."

"I know it, but I am reluctant to permit it. I know things that are top secret and I am concerned about them being revealed."

"Commander," Rachael insisted, "they wiped out the enemy using God only knows what technology. What could you possibly know that would compete with that?"

"Alexi!" Ian interjected, "what have we got to lose? More importantly, what have we got to gain?"

"You know what I mean, Captain."

"I do. Would it help if I ordered you to do it?" Ian asked his friend.

"No. I don't seem to have much choice if we are ever to get home. What do I do, Rachael?" Alexi asked.

"Just usher it in with your hand. You will feel nothing. They seem to know how to integrate themselves into our brains without causing us any difficulties now, sir."

Alexi Petrovich Gargorin took a deep breath and brought his hand up and pushed the Sprite into his head. He paused for a moment and, like some of the others, revealed a series of emotional visages. Then, he settled back in his chair and exclaimed. "I'll be damned. You were right. I know it is there, but feel no intrusion."

With that, Ian waved a Sprite over and invited it in. "Amazing, it is a little like taking a perception enhancing drug, which I did as a kid. Okay, let's go."

In the next few minutes, everyone who had not melded with a Sprite did so.

Alexi began to turn the pages faster using the tablet. Ten pages flashed across the screen in rapid succession and then, one of the Sprites took over operating the tablet and the pages sped by, sometimes slower but more often faster. In slightly more than an hour, they were through the entire set of plans.

"That went so fast, I have no idea how they did it," Alexi said. "I know they accessed my visual faculties and saw the plans through my eyes. I also know that I did not know everything there is to know about the construction of the ship. When I was not sure they slowed down the images while I absorbed or interpreted what was on the screen. I seem to know a whole lot more now than I did when we started. Can you access the plans for the reactor system, are they in a separate file?"

"Yes, sir, Commander, but they are in a code word protected file," Ichuro answered.

"Sorry, I knew that." Alexi paused while he debated with himself whether revealing the code word was warranted. He looked at Ian who nodded assent. "I changed it from some random set of characters to 'tea-kettle' once we were on our way. Bring them up, please, Ichuro, wait, you need my thumbprint too," he said extending his hand over the tablet and pressing down with his thumb. "I actually don't know why they're so secret, any schoolboy could access the fundamental information from his computer."

As the reactor blueprints flashed across the screen in rapid succession, Alexi mumbled to himself. When they were finished, he sat back and looked up at the ceiling. "I never went through them before; they are not complete. I was right about the schoolboy; there is nothing revealing in those plans. They are mostly blocking diagrams. Admittedly, some of the construction details are probably proprietary, but what the hell, we have to use the damned thing." Alexi warmed to his diatribe as he went on. "Did they assume it would just keep working perfectly so we would never have to repair it?"

Ian stopped him with a wave of his hand. "What is the object of this activity people?"

"To show the Sprites how our propulsion system works so we can let the Sprites know why we cannot get home unless we obtain more reaction mass and more heavy water rich in deuterium, sir," Miriam said.

"Right. Make the screen white please, Ichuro," Ian commanded. "Now, Commander and AJay, look at the white screen and relax. I have seen something that may be of help. I have seen it mainly because I was looking at a blank wall and images were being shown to me as if they were printed on the wall."

Ichuro blanked the screen as suggested and everyone looked at it. "I don't see anything, Captain," Rachael said.

"Wait for it," Ian said.

"It's all there," Alexi asserted. "Not the way the engineers would have shown it, but how the Sprites see it. More in pictures than in blueprint detail and from the inside out as well. They are tracing the operation of the fission reactor now while it is working. I know nuclear physicists who would give their right arm to see what I am seeing. They know how a fission reactor works on paper and in theory and from their instruments, but I am actually inside it watching it work."

"Now, they want to know what the fusion reactor does. It is not running, so its operation is not obvious," Alexi finished.

"Miriam?" Ian said.

"Captain?" she replied.

"Would you start it up, please?"

"She cannot start it unless someone is in the reactor room, Captain. I'll go back to the reactor room to take care of things from that end," AJay said.

"Go to it, AJay," Alexi said to his back as AJay left the Common Room. Then to the rest, he said, "It will take him about fifteen minutes to bring everything up using the checklist."

They watched as ready lights began to turn green across the pilot's control board. "It's ready," AJay announced over the intercom.

Alexi nodded toward the captain who said, "just give it a short blast, Miriam. We don't want to give our position away in case the Cartel is watching."

"Don't worry, Captain, they're on the other side of Mars and cannot see us at the moment," Ichuro said.

"Yes, sir," Miriam said as she set the controls to momentary power and activated the engines.

The short rumble went through the ship indicating the engines were firing.

"Again," Alexi said and repeated several times. "Okay, they have seen it work and seem to be confused. I keep seeing an image of a star."

"Commander," AJay said from the intercom, "the reactor room is full of Sprites, sir."

"Thank you, I can see them through my Sprite," Alexi replied. "Miriam, again, please."

Miriam fired the engines half a dozen times at Alexi's request. Then she said, "That last one wasn't me, Commander, it was them."

"Okay, you can shut it down, Miriam," Alexi said, then over the intercom, "AJay, shut it down."

"Yes, sir," AJay said, then he shut down the fusion reactor.

It took several days before the Sprites fully understood the needs of the ship. They understood the operation of the fusion reactor but did not seem to understand the process of electrolyzing the heavy water to get the deuterium needed for fusion or even why heavy water was required at all. Then in a moment of brilliance, it all became clear. Without even overriding the controls, the Sprites initiated the fusion reaction inside the reaction chamber and maintained it for several seconds by apparently transferring either molecules of heavy water or the deuterium atoms into the reaction chamber. They were forming the magnetic bottle themselves and squeezing the atoms together without the use of the laser which was normally used to initiate the intense heat required to initialize the fusion process before the magnetic bottle compressed the elements into the minuscule volume required to complete the process and producing an order of magnitude more power.

"Now all we have to do is explain why we need more heavy water," Alexi observed.

"Let's go back to the diagram of the ship and show them the heavy water tank and the heavy water flowing from the tank into the fusion reactor," Miriam offered.

"Now picture how the fusion reactor works. They seem to already know what happens there considering they have activated the reaction several times."

Alexi seemed to go into a trance for several minutes as he concentrated on the process. He mumbled to himself in both English and Russian and finally looked around at the rest of the company. "That is quite an experience. They actually took me into the fusion reactor. Then they showed me the fusion process itself in what I would call slow motion or even stop motion. I could not see the atoms, but I could see the energy being released when they were forced to fuse. I think they were using just plain hydrogen, not deuterium and did fusion.

First, they take a pair of ordinary H2 hydrogen molecules and break them apart. Then they squeeze them back together in their magnetic bottle and in the process convert them into a helium 'He' molecule which converts two of the protons into neutrons releasing one hell of a lot of energy. At least that is the impression they gave me. Our fusion reactor has a lithium core chamber so there was no stray radiation. The power released was phenomenal."

"Are you satisfied it will work to get us home, Alexi?" Ian asked.

"Yes, sir, they are heating the plasma much hotter than we did in the rocket chambers. They did not do too much because we are still anchored, but I do believe it will be more than sufficient to get us home."

"Good enough, thank you. Now, Commander, can we move either of the Iceteroids with the power we have?"

"I can't see how, Captain. Assuming we bore a fifty-foot-diameter hole through either of them, the five hundred foot one masses at a net 1.75 million tons that is nearly one thousand times our mass when we left the moon. The 300-foot diameter Iceteroid masses at about 357 thousand tons that is about 150 times our original mass. Ichuro's suggestion the last time we discussed this was to bury the nose of the *Explorer* fifty feet into the 100 foot diameter Iceteroid giving us a net 11,000 tons, which is closer to being doable because it is close to our original mass. But if we bore all the way through the 100-foot Iceteroid, we would have slightly over 8,000 tons or four times our original mass and that is definitely doable. If we hype up the engines, we might be able to have some acceleration somewhere between one-tenth and one-quarter G."

"Right, Commander, as Jean-Luc Picard would say, 'make it so.' Now, how do we tell the Sprites the plan? And, didn't somebody say the Sprites wanted us to take the 500-foot Iceteroid? Will they accept the 100 foot instead once we explain the problems to them?" Ian asked.

"Hold on everybody, my Sprite still wants us to take the 500-foot Iceteroid," Rachael said and was closely followed by several others saying essentially the same thing.

After a brief pause, Alexi nodded and said, "They say, it will work, Captain. Damned if I know how, but they are insistent or perhaps emphatic would be a better term."

"Do they say how?" Then… "Wait, my Sprite is showing me how." After a few minutes Ian continued, "Well, that was quite an experience. I think I got it all straight. They left out some details but gave me the impression all would become clear soon. They seem to be completely transparent. It is amazing how they can cause images to appear in your vision. For some reason, the *Explorer* didn't look right and when I felt concern they assured me all was as it should be."

"You too, Captain? I have seen the same sorts of images for the past several days and some images of the reactors that do not agree with my understanding. How about you, AJay?" Alexi said.

AJay nodded in agreement. "It almost makes sense, Captain, but I cannot quite put my finger on what is different either."

"Rachael, will you and AJay please go out and release the mooring lines holding us to Phobos?" Ian asked.

"Yes, sir, Captain. We'll get right to it." She nodded to AJay and then nodded towards the rear of the ship where the shuttle was attached to the aft airlock. "I think we'd better disconnect the shuttle and move it out of the way. When we have released all the tethers we will stand off to the side as you back the *Explorer* away from Phobos."

Ten minutes later, Rachael and AJay detached from the *Explorer* and moved away. She did as she normally did and checked over the outside of the *Explorer* looking for anything that might be a problem. What she saw was a complete surprise when she viewed the engines at the aft end.

AJay released the closest mooring line from the *Explorer* and clipped it to the shuttle to keep it from drifting away. As soon as the shuttle was secure Rachael joined him as they went around the *Explorer* disconnecting the mooring lines. When they were finished Rachael reached up and gave the *Explorer* a push with her hand just to see if she could move it in freefall. AJay looked on amazed and looked quizzically at her as if to ask *what in the world are you doing?*

Rachael answered his unasked question, "I had to try! Almost no gravity to keep it on the surface, but one hell of a mass to move nonetheless. Now let's go back to the shuttle and get out of the way." Once they were in the shuttle Rachael used the steering jets to back away from Phobos and well out of the way of the *Explorer*. "Okay Captain, she's free to move." Then she added, "Miriam, take it very easy on the throttles when you go to move the ship because the main engine jets do not look anything like what they did before."

"Thank you, Major," Ian said with a smile. Then turning to Miriam he said, "Take us out if you please, helmswoman."

Miriam looked over at the Captain and in recognition of his naval formalism saluted and replied, "Aye, aye, Captain." This gave everyone a laugh, including Rachael who could be heard chuckling over the radio.

Miriam used the steering jets to back away from their anchorage on Phobos. When she advanced the throttles she was surprised at the power. The steering jets were producing much more thrust than they had before. As a result, the *Explorer* moved away from the surface of Phobos much more quickly than was expected.

"Rachael, did you see that?" Miriam asked.

"We certainly did. How much throttle did you use?"

"I just barely cracked it. I didn't think we would need much just to back out."

"You may have to recalibrate the steering thruster throttles, and the main engine throttles as well. From where we are, we can see some major changes that have been made to the steering thrusters in addition to the main engines," Rachael suggested.

"Ichuro is working on it now. Are we in any danger in the direction we're drifting?" Miriam asked.

"Not as far as I can see," Rachael replied.

A short while later Miriam said, "Okay, we are ready to try the steering thrusters to turn the ship in the direction of the Iceteroid. Let us know if anything unusual happens. We're going to try the new range of throttle settings that Ichuro is implementing."

"Roger, we're watching," Rachael said.

For the next several minutes, Miriam maneuvered the ship slowly and turned it in the direction of the Iceteroid. By the time it was turned, she had a good feel for how the operation of the improved thrusters worked.

"Great job," Rachael said after she had observed Miriam's maneuvering. "I think you're going to have to play with it a little bit more to get it fine-tuned but what you did worked fine."

"Thank you, stand by," Miriam said. Then speaking to the Captain she said, "Captain, I think it might be a good idea to use the steering thrusters to move the *Explorer* over to the Iceteroid. It will take longer, but I'm not too sure how the main engines might act and I don't think this is the place or the time to find out. Clearly, the Sprites have made some changes to the operation of the ship and I need to sort of feel my way along until I'm comfortable with them."

"Considering the amount of thrust available with the maneuvering thrusters, we should be able to make the move relatively quickly without the risk of surprises from how the main engines will work."

"Right, you're the pilot, Major," Ian said to Miriam. Then speaking to Rachael he said, "Rachael, redock the shuttle, the trip over to the Iceteroid is going to take longer than we originally thought."

"Yes, sir, Captain. We have been following the *Explorer* and we should be back aboard in a few minutes."

As they neared the 500-foot diameter Iceteroid, everyone was nervous. It was huge. They took turns looking through the forward view screen of the pilot deck. The thought in everyone's mind was, how were they going to connect to the Iceteroid so they could move it. The nearer they got to it, the bigger it seemed to be. Finally, when they were still several miles away and drifting very slowly, Ian asked, "Rachael, would you please scout ahead so we can see what to expect?"

The image from the shuttle nose camera was transmitted to the *Explorer* so everyone could watch on the big screen in the Common Room. The shuttle approached the Iceteroid dead slowly. The first things they noticed was it was not rotating and then that it was amazingly spherical and appeared to be slightly flat at the top and bottom. This was reported back to the ship as they continued their approach. Rachael brought the shuttle to a relative stop about 500 feet from the surface of the Iceteroid. Then began a slow equatorial transit without seeing anything except the surface of a sphere of ice. She wondered about the flat ends and decided to do what might be called a polar transit. As they neared the top they could see a hole and as they moved over the top and looked into the hole they were amazed to see it went all the way through the asteroid to the opposite end.

"You are not going to believe what we've found," Rachael said as she rotated the shuttle so the nose camera pointed down the hole and turned on the shuttle's front light. "There is a hole all the way through the Iceteroid. At what I am arbitrarily calling the top, I would bet next month's pay that is precisely the size of the forward end of the *Explorer* and looking down through the Iceteroid the hole appears to be larger at the other end. I will also bet that the hole in the far end will fit the main body of the *Explorer* as well. Assuming the hole in this end is exactly the same size as the nose of the *Explorer*, I cannot fly through because the wingspan of the shuttle is too wide, sorry."

Rachael continued the polar orbit towards the bottom of the Iceteroid. When they reached the bottom she reported as she flew the shuttle slowly into the opening, "This is unbelievable. The hole in this end will easily accommodate the main body of the *Explorer*. As you can see, I can fly the shuttle up inside. I guess we know now what the Sprites want us to do." Then she asked, "Miriam, are you ready for this?"

"As ready as I will ever be," Miriam replied. Then she moved the *Explorer* around to the "south" pole and tried to line up with the hole.

"I would be a whole lot happier if we had a mooring line we could toss to someone so they could anchor us to the dock and using a winch pull us in," Ian said. As he said he could not help visualizing how a ship would dock with a wharf.

The ship began to move towards the entry hole. Miriam immediately tried to compensate for the movement and found after a brief tug-of-war that the ship was being moved beyond her control. Frustrated, she said, "Captain?"

"Let it be, Major. The Sprites seem to be moving us," Ian replied.

It took thirty minutes for the *Explorer* to be rotated into the correct orientation, then it moved up into the Iceteroid and docked with a satisfactory thump.

"Rachael, can you dock the shuttle?" Ian asked.

"Oh, yes, sir," Rachael replied. "We are being docked now. There was a space just the right size and shape and at the right place for the shuttle to move up alongside the ship and dock at the aft airlock. We'll be with you in ten minutes or so."

Ian called a general meeting of the crew and the scientists after the evening meal. "I took a submarine down to Antarctica several years ago and we went under the ice and we went to McMurdo Bay where we picked up a couple of scientists who were due to go home. So having my ship surrounded by ice is not a new experience for me. But we didn't have to drag half of the Antarctic ice sheet back with us to Australia. I am open to suggestions. Miriam, have you begun to plot a course for home yet?"

"No, sir, because the only parameters I have are where we are now, more or less, and where home is now, more or less. I have no idea what our speed will be considering we will be dragging a million and a half tons of ice home with us," Miriam replied. "Actually, I really have no idea how much ice there is. The Sprites obviously made a good size hole in it to fit the ship. At the moment, because I can't see anything around the ship, the only part of the ship I am sure is securely attached to this ball of ice is the command module."

"I can help you with that, Miriam," Rachael said. "When we were docking at the aft airlock, I kept the shuttle's outside lights turned on. It looks like the front end of the reaction mass tanks is also firmly embedded in the ice, but the ice is not a solid mass, it is a structure of radials from the outer shell to the ship. From there back there was a lot of open area surrounding the ship. As we watched a collar was being formed around the front of the reactor module and radials were being created from the collar out to the inside of the ice shell to fix it in place. The area immediately in front of the shuttle was mostly open space except for where the radials were. Don't get me wrong, there is still going to be a tremendous amount of ice. However,

I don't think we are going to be dragging back the entire million and a half tons. Maybe only a million tons or so."

"Only a million tons, eh, that's a big relief," Miriam said. "Captain, the only way we're going to find out how we're going to get home is just to start."

"Okay, what would you suggest as a start?" Ian asked.

"We wait until the Sprites have finished embedding us and then we do an engine test to see if we can move it. Once we do that and we have some idea of how much acceleration we can expect, we can plot an orbit back to Earth."

"Not exactly back to Earth," Ian said. "I've been sending reports back regularly to Farside Base keeping them informed of the situation. It is been decided that we should position the Ice Moon at either the L4 or L5 point in Earth's orbit around the sun. The powers that be are nervous about having a million tons of ice heading straight for the Earth. They would rather that it be as far away as possible yet still be accessible in some manner. They have not indicated a preference for either L4 or L5. They are leaving that up to us."

"That's nice of them," Alexi said. "So which one do we pick?"

"Whichever one is easiest to get to, I assume," Ian said. "There you have it, Miriam.

When can we begin the tests?"

"Rachael, do you think you could go back into the shuttle in the morning and look through the viewscreen to see if the structure is complete?" Miriam asked. "Ichuro, let's err on the side of pessimism and determine when it will be the best time to leave Mars orbit. I wish I could give you more data than we have. Try feeding the computer a series of different acceleration rates assuming a mass of one million tons. I assume that we may need to spiral out and use the gravity slingshot to help build speed."

Ichuro worked through the night feeding the computer various scenarios in an attempt to determine when would be the optimum time to depart Mars orbit. In the morning, he reported. "Unless we can produce an enormous amount of thrust it is going to take forever to get home. I assumed the same amount of thrust as we had when we came as a starting point. Then I kept adding to it a little at a time until I got ten times the thrust we had on the trip out. None of the solutions look very promising considering our probable mass is nearly a thousand times what we had then. At ten times our original thrust and assuming we want to avoid colliding with either Phobos or Deimos or any of the other junk in orbit around Mars there isn't any one best time to depart."

"We have to assume that the Sprites know this and have some plan in mind for us," Ian said. "Alexi, why don't you and AJay go fire up your teakettle and let's see what happens. We were certainly surprised when we departed Phobos at the power of the steering thrusters. I am willing to assume that we'll be equally surprised at what will happen when we use the main engines."

An hour later Alexi reported that the reactors were online and ready to go. When the *Explorer* reached a position in its orbit where it was pointed in the general direction of the inner solar system, the tests began.

Miriam began with the lowest power setting for ten seconds. "Captain, the accelerometer shows that we actually accelerated at a measurable rate during that test. Ichuro, can you determine the new parameters of our orbit?"

"Yes," Ichuro replied as he read off the data. "We're okay for another test without causing any great problems."

Miriam went through a series of tests incrementally from the lowest thrust to ten times the lowest thrust. At each setting Ichuro recomputed the orbit and reported the results. "Captain, we are clearly getting farther away from Phobos and have entered a wider orbit. But, sir, if we are really going to get anywhere we are going to have to bite the bullet and try a higher thrust setting. If the settings that Miriam is using are linear, I think Miriam should try slowly advancing the throttles as much as she can next time around our orbit. From all that I've been able to see I seriously doubt it will do any harm as long as we keep a close eye on what's happening in the engines."

"Miriam, are you comfortable with that?" Ian asked.

"Yes, Captain."

"Alexi, are you comfortable with that?" Ian asked over the intercom.

"Yes, Captain, so far we don't seem to have put any strain on the reactors or the propulsion system. I will keep an eye on things back here and if it looks like there are any problems, I'll cut the power immediately if that meets with your approval."

"Let's do it!" Ian ordered.

When the *Explorer* reached the optimum point in its orbit, Miriam began slowly advancing the throttles, and before long, the acceleration was sufficient that items which were loose in the command module began drifting to the deck. When they reached the point where the acceleration was no longer driving them in the direction they needed to go, Miriam reduced the throttles.

"Miriam, we're almost at the point where we'll leave orbit and break free of the gravity of Mars," Ichuro said.

At the next optimum point, Miriam advanced the throttles quickly to the same point where she had cut them last time around. Then she steadily advanced them to what the instruments indicated was half throttle. The acceleration was immediately obvious and the ship began to visibly go farther away from the surface of Mars. Then when Ichuro and Alexi gave the word, she continued to advance the throttles up to full power. What was immediately obvious was they were accelerating at 0.5 G, an acceleration that would have been impossible on the trip to Mars and which certainly should have been impossible considering the mass of their system.

"Commander, how fast are we using our reaction mass?" Ian asked Alexi.

"We're not using as much as we were coming out. I have no idea what our exhaust velocity is, but it is very close to the speed of light so we are getting more thrust than before with less reaction mass. That plus the fact that we are surrounded by a million tons of potential reaction mass means we are not at risk of running out. I would also like to say that the engines are running cooler than before because the magnetic bottles in the nozzles are much smaller than they were. The Sprites have been showing me what they have done and, technically, it is impossible, but it works."

"Thank you, Commander," Ian said.

Ichuro fed the data continuously to the computer and suggested corrections to their course until he was confident that they were on a course and at a rate of acceleration that would return them to the orbit of Earth.

"Captain, I suggest that we aim for the L5 Lagrangian point and enter Earth orbit trailing the Earth. We should be able to do that in less time than it took for us to go from Earth to Mars, but we need to reduce our acceleration rate or we will go right past it, sir."

"When I was captain of a submarine that had a top speed of, um, that is still classified. I could almost keep up with the navigator, considering it was all done with accelerometers and satellites. I am not supposed to admit I cannot do anything my officers can do, but I confess this is beyond me. Just keep our position up on the large display and let me know if I need to make any decisions," Ian said as he sipped his tea out of a cup.

EPILOGUE

Soothing music was playing quietly through hidden speakers as senior hostess Nadine McCormick entered the Arrival and Departure Lounge. From long experience, she reached to the right and switched on the lights and artificial gravity. The lights for obvious reasons and the artificial gravity to prevent arriving passengers and visitors from being disoriented when they departed the shuttle bringing them to Icemoon One.

Nadine went about the duty of checking that everything was in place and properly organized should any arriving passenger be suffering from nausea or disorientation need assistance. A few minutes later, another hostess joined her.

"Hi, I'm Nadine," Nadine announced, extending her hand in greeting.

"Hi, I'm Julie Worthmore, pleased to meet you," the new arrival said.

"Worthmore?" Nadine asked before she realized she might be challenging Ms. Worthmore and making her uncomfortable.

"Yeah, it is an old family name given to a many greats grandfather who was a slave in America a couple of hundred years ago. When the slaves were freed, they typically took the surname of their owners, but my ancestor's owner was too proud of his name to allow it to be used by a freed black slave. My ancestor was very useful around the plantation, so he was given the surname

'Worthmore' and it has been passed down, which is probably more than you wanted to know," Julie replied.

"On the contrary, that's a fascinating story," Nadine said.

"I get asked about the name a lot," Julie said.

"I can imagine."

"I'm not assigned to greeting duty this week, so why am I here?" Julie asked.

"I'm going to tell you a story that I thought you might like to hear. Have you been here for arrivals before?" Nadine asked.

"Yes."

"Do you remember what it was like when the pilot docked with the airlock?"

"The two times I was here, there was a loud metallic clank followed by a grinding sound, then the latches were activated to hold the shuttle in place, why?"

"Today you are in for a rare treat. The shuttle will be here in a few minutes. You can watch the arrival through the viewport, in fact, I recommend it."

Julie eyed Nadine with an unspoken question and then did as suggested. She watched as the shuttle approached the dock. There were occasional puffs of exhaust from the steering jets, but the approach seemed to be slower than the last time. The shuttle grew bigger and bigger as it approached and the at the last minute there were a few more puffs, then it seemed to coast to a stop and the only sound heard was the click of the latches as the shuttle docked.

"That was incredible," she said as she moved over across from Nadine to her greeting station.

"Yup! You are not too likely to see the like of it again. Joe Mottoe is the pilot, but he didn't fly it over here or do the actual docking, a passenger did. Whenever she comes out for a visit, the pilots let her do the flying. Actually, they don't have much choice, because she has lots of pull with the organization," Nadine said. "Here they come. Follow my lead when she comes in."

"Seriously?"

"Seriously."

"How will I know?"

"Watch me. She will be the last one off except for the pilots," Nadine explained. When the light over the airlock hatch turned from red to green, she pressed the lever that opened the inside hatch of the airlock.

The arriving passengers entered the lounge in ones and twos, mostly men, a few couples, and one single woman. Nadine greeted each one as they came through the airlock with a standard greeting. "Welcome to our Ice Moon. If there is anything we can do for you, please let us know. Julie," Nadine said, indicating the hostess to the door, "will direct you to wherever you wish to go."

Two minutes later, two adults and three noisy children entered the lounge. Nadine looked at Julie and mouthed the word "money."

Julie nodded knowingly and, maintaining her greeter's smile, asked, "How may I help you?"

"I want to go to the freefall pavilion," the older son said in a manner indicating he expected immediate compliance.

"Look, Mommy, there's a Sprite," the daughter said in an excited voice as she pointed to a Sprite that hovered in a corner of the lounge.

"Yes, Jenny, I see it," Mommy replied in the universal voice of an exasperated parent who is on the verge of having a nervous breakdown from the necessity of herding her three children without much assistance from her husband.

"Can I have a Sprite?" Jenny asked. "Puleeeese, Mommy?"

"We'll see, dear," the harried mother replied.

"Aw, you always say that. You never let me have anything," Jenny, who was dressed in designer clothes, replied with a pout. "Excuse me, lady, how do I get a Sprite?" Jenny asked Julie.

Julie looked at the mother who rolled her eyes and dutifully replied, "You will have to ask your mother and then go to the area where you can find the Sprites in the central concourse." Then to the family she added, "Through the door and to the left to the registration area, please." The family did as Julie suggested with the father leading and the mother herding from behind.

The family was the last to depart from the shuttle. Julie began to gather up her handouts and other things in preparation to leave. "Was that what I was supposed to see?" she asked Nadine.

"No, just be patient," Nadine replied.

After a short wait, voices could be heard coming from inside the shuttle. A woman was thanking someone and a man was replying, "anytime." Then an older woman with graying hair entered the lounge.

Nadine struck a pose half bending or bowing and faced the woman and said. "Namaste, Madame Purlman-Kaniyar. Welcome back to our Ice Moon."

Madame Purlman-Kaniyar placed a box she was carrying on the counter and replied, "Namaste, Nadine. How are you? And, my name is still Rachael. Who is your friend?" Rachael Purlman-Kaniyar asked, indicating Julie.

"Rachael, this is Julie Worthmore one of our new crew members." Then said, "Julie, this is Rachael Purlman-Kaniyar. Rachael was the shuttle pilot on the first Barsoom Expedition," Nadine said as she provided the introductions. Then she said, "I am so sorry for your loss."

Julie bowed and, mimicking her friend, said, "Namaste, Rachael, I am pleased to meet you." Which was returned by Rachael, who then extended her hand in greeting.

"Nadine, would you please join me for dinner later in the Stellar Lounge? And, bring Julie as well," Rachael said. Then she picked up the box off the counter and exited the lounge into the Ice Moon.

"Her loss?" Julie asked.

"Her husband Kaniyar passed away about a month ago. She's here to place his ashes with those of all the departed from the original crew."

. . .

Nadine and Julie, who were dressed appropriately, entered The Stellar Lounge and began looking for Rachael. It didn't take long to find her seated at the corner table. She was surrounded by a group of admirers from both the crew and the public. The public including the family were requesting autographs while the crew just offered their respects.

"My name's Jenny, and I wanna be a pilot just like you when I grow up," Jenny announced in a voice loud enough to be heard all over the lounge.

Jenny's mother tried to shush her, but Rachael reached out and gave the young girl a hug and said, "Then I am sure you will be, but being a pilot isn't easy. You have to study hard."

"I will, I promise," Jenny said. Then the family returned to their table.

Nadine and Julie waited until the admiring crowd thinned out before they walked to the table. Rachael stood to greet them. They exchanged bows and then took their seats. They chatted as dinner progressed and when they finished eating they ordered coffee.

"Nadine, I asked you to join me not only out of friendship, but I have a request to make of you," Rachael said. "The next Barsoom Expedition is being assembled as we speak. I came over to Ice Moon from Farside Base not only to bury my husband but also to find people who would be good crew members. You see, I'm going to be the captain for this mission. We will be taking a large complement of what in other times might have been called settlers. Mars needs farmers and all of the other trades that are necessary to support a new settlement. Thanks to the Sprites, we now have a large dome within which we can maintain the atmosphere and provide water and other utilities to the settlers."

"Congratulations, Captain. I am truly pleased for you. But why do you need me as part of your crew?" Nadine asked.

"There are going to be over 200 settlers on the ship. I need an experienced person who can become the purser and manage the people appropriately. The rest of the crew are all essential to the operation of the ship and none of them are really appropriate for being the purser. The master-at-arms will be Tom Vernon who was a scientist on the first trip and who has since worked himself into the position of keeping order on the ship. He may be fifty-six years old, but he is an ex-Special Forces sergeant and should have no trouble keeping order. But he is hardly the person to keep them contented, peaceful, and occupied. That's where you come in if you will accept the offer."

"I am honored that you would think of me and I accept," Nadine said.

"You are also here at my request, Julie. I requested that you be transferred here from the International Space Station. I sent out a request for a trained medical professional with space travel experience several months ago. I have been informed by the Commander of the ISS that you are a licensed physician's assistant in addition to being a competent manager of people. With a complement as large as we are going to have for this trip, we will need a person who has medical training to act as the medical officer. Are you interested?" Rachael said.

Julie looked from Rachael to Nadine and back as she absorbed Rachael's offer. "Of course, Captain, I am interested. I have been in space for almost five years and I have dreamed of an opportunity like this. Thank you, Captain, I would be pleased to join your crew as your medical officer."

"Good. Then, it's settled. I have already told the Ice Moon commander that I was going to ask both of you. She has agreed to transfer you to me if you accepted. Please assemble your things and be ready to depart the day after tomorrow when the shuttle returns to the International Space Station where we will transfer to a shuttle for Farside Base."

- The End -